THE WAR BETWEEN

For Mom, my example in life.

And for Stuart, who believed in me with such conviction, it made me believe in myself.

THE WAR BETWEEN

Jennifer Withers

ISBN: 978-0-620-69447-6

Published by Jennifer Withers in 2016
Postnet Suite 1214
Private Bag X1007
Lyttleton
0140
Email: jenhwithers@gmail.com
Website: www.jenniferwithers.com

Cover design: Kokojelly Creative Media
Author Photo: Lisa Dewberry
Typesetting by Book Lingo
Set in 10,5 point on 14 point Georgia

ACKNOWLEDGEMENTS

The War Between is the first novel I've written that I felt was worthy to be sent out into the world. It's a better book because of all the people who helped and supported me along the way.

I'd like to thank, in no particular order, the following people:

Richard Beynon and Jo-Anne Richards, and all the writers at Allaboutwriting. Without your input, guidance, and sometimes brutal feedback, this book may never have been borne.

My husband – Stuart Withers. There is so much to thank you for: the endless cups of tea, your unfailing support, your unshakeable belief in me. Giving me flexible work hours so I can write. Mostly, for being my partner in chasing our dreams and never giving up. You are my rock.

My parents – Tina and Mark Fysh. There isn't enough space on this blank page to thank you for everything you've done for me. So all I can say is thank you for being my parents. I couldn't have asked for better.

My siblings – Michael and Tracy Fysh. For asking how the writing is going. For cheering me on. For debating the length of Sci-Fi novels and for being such avid readers. I hope you like this one.

My highschool English teacher, Lucinda Perreira, who, through her enthusiasm for teaching, instilled in me a passion for literature. Thank you. If not for you, I would never have gone on to study English at university. I hope you get to read this.

Lisa Dewberry, my only writer friend. Although we work in very different fields of writing, it's still good to have someone who gets it. Also, for my author photos – I love them. Thank you.

All my friends, whose ongoing love and support helped me through the rough patches. Special thanks go out to Jennifer dos Santos and Michelle Carstens. Thanks for never tiring of me prattling on about this book and my writing. Thank you for your support and friendship. I am a lucky woman indeed.

Lastly, to everyone who will read this book – thank you. Without the readers of this world, there would be no writers.

Chapter One

Dominico

The line of people snaked through the door of the shop and out into the street. Although the day was cold, the cloying smell of sweat filled the small room. I forced myself to breathe through my mouth and focused on the next person in the queue. A young soldier held out an impatient hand, his gaze fixed on a point above my head. His patched uniform was clean but badly fitted – the sleeves of his shirt rode up his arms, revealing thick, tanned wrists. I handed him his food package from the stock ear-marked for soldiers and added a container of water, taking care not to touch him. Without a word of thanks he took his rations and stepped to one side, making way for a young woman whose eyes looked huge in the frame of her gaunt face.

'Hi Mandy.' I held out her food and water parcel, but she reached across the counter and encircled my wrist, her gaze darting over my shoulder.

'Everton is in the back,' I murmured.

'Please, Dominico. I hate to keep putting you in this position, but my son -'

'It's okay. Here.'

I handed her the package marked with her family name. I glanced around, trying to look casual, and handed her an extra food parcel from the pile kept aside as rewards for those who pleased President Crane. I added a second canister of water, keeping my eyes trained on the next person in line, looking for a sign that we'd been discovered. Nothing. Mandy slipped the extra rations beneath her oversized coat, using her allotted package as a kind of shield against prying eyes. She squeezed my hand, and gave me a rare smile.

'Thank you,' she whispered.

As she moved from the front of the line, Everton appeared from the back room, heaving more parcels into place behind me. I looked at him, convinced that he'd seen us, but when his gaze fell on me, his face just twisted with his usual displeasure.

'What are you gawking at? Get on with it girl!'

I twisted around to face the person waiting at the counter. The tension flooded from my body, making my blood sing with sweet relief.

***

The last stragglers hurried in as Everton began closing up. The shop closed at 6pm sharp – latecomers who dared rap on the glass and plead their case after closing time were rewarded with Everton's beady glare and possibly a missing item or two from their next package. Reporting Everton was pointless - he was a skilled liar, and in the social hierarchy of Toria, no one took a field hand's word over a shopkeeper's.

'No deaths today,' Everton grumbled. 'Less food for all of us.' He glared at me with watery blue eyes, lips puckered into an ugly imitation of a kiss. 'By my count there should've been one more food package and canister of water.'

My heart threw itself against my ribs, making me wince. A bead of sweat formed at my hairline, tracing a single path down my neck.

'Well?'

I forced myself to meet his gaze. 'I think you miscounted, Everton.'

His eyebrows shot up and his eyes bulged. 'I don't miscount, girl! And that's *Mr* Everton to you!'

I dropped my gaze, pretending to be contrite. 'I'm sorry Mr Everton, but I think you miscounted.'

I dared not look at him directly, but out of the corner of my eye I could see his face turn scarlet, his grimy hands clenching into dirty fists.

I kept my eyes on the cloth I was using to clean the counter, feeling a grim satisfaction at his fury. He knew who my parents were. He knew the consequences of striking the daughter of government officials.

Turning, he stomped to the back room to organise his shelves. I let out my breath and painfully uncurled my fingers from their locked grip on the cloth. I continued wiping down the counter, willing my shaking hands to still. I dipped the cloth into a small bucket of grimy water, careful not to spill a drop.

Without bothering to let Everton know, I slipped from the shop into the gathering darkness, pulling the door shut behind me. Just being out of the stale air and away from Everton's stifling presence made breathing easier.

Out on the main street, I considered the narrow paths that stretched in different directions. It made no difference which one I took. They all led to the residential heart of Toria. I chose a path at random and started to make my way home. The houses on each side sat closely together, with barely a patch of dirt separating them. I thought of the stories we'd been told over the years – of cities so large it would take hours, or even days, to cross them. None of our homes were alike – houses were constructed with whatever materials were found or scavenged.

As I walked, the homes of neat brick and tiled roofs housing the guards and soldiers gave way to the scrawny, patched homes belonging to the cleaners, field hands and livestock handlers.

I rounded a corner, singing under my breath. A man I vaguely recognised stood surrounded by a small knot of soldiers. They had him pressed up against a wall. Two of the soldiers had raised the man's arms above his head, their hands clamped around his wrists. The third held what looked like a food package in front of the man's face. My first instinct was to duck my head down and keep moving. I didn't want trouble, and I'd already put myself at risk. But something stayed my feet. I glanced over at the scene, careful not to draw any attention to myself.

The soldier dangled the package in front of the man's nose, his other hand pressed against his throat.

I crept closer, keeping my back flat against the wall, slipping into the narrow passage between the houses until I was close enough to hear them. I crouched in the lengthening shadows.

'This belong to you?'

The man shook his head. The soldier's mouth crept up in an unpleasant smile. 'That's right, old man. It's not yours. Where did you steal it from?'

Fear etched deep furrows in the man's face. He raised shaking hands in a helpless gesture. 'Please... my family... they're starving. I only took... I only wanted to help feed them.'

'You know the penalty for stealing. Lucky for you this is your first offense. Do it again and you'll be lucky if your punishment is exile. Your rations for the next week will be halved. Now get out of here before my good mood wears off.'

The soldiers stepped back and released the man. One of them stuck out a foot as he passed. They roared with laughter as he fell headlong into the dirt. He attempted to get up, but stumbled again.

I couldn't take anymore. I rushed in and grabbed his hands to pull him up. The man's eyes were round with fear, his face flushed with humiliation.

'Girl, leave him be! This is none of your business. Move on or you'll be spending the night in confinement.'

I ignored the soldier. 'Are you all right?' I realised how I knew him. He was one of the field hands I often passed on my way to Everton's store.

'You better do as he says. They don't make idle threats.' The man gave me a gentle push. 'Get on home.'

I started to turn away but the man gripped my arm for a moment, drawing me near so his words fell close to my ear. 'Thank you. But don't make a habit of this – these soldiers run the city, despite what the government might think.'

'Hey! Did you hear what I said? Move on!' Before I could even think of obeying, the largest of the three soldiers grabbed my arm, his fingers digging into my skin. He wrenched me away from the old man, aiming a kick that sent him staggering away. The soldier yanked me towards him, my nose nearly touching his.

'Get lost, girl! I'm not saying it again.' He shoved me away and took off after the others, their laughter making my stomach clench with fury, my throat tighten with fear. The old man had disappeared. The streets were deserted. I rubbed the throbbing mark on my arm and glared after the departing backs of the soldiers, my fury dissolving into defeat.

***

I sidled through the front door, trying to get to my room without being seen. But as I stepped from the lounge area into the passage my mother's voice snared me.

'Dominico? Is that you?'

I sighed. 'Yes it's me.'

'Come into the kitchen honey. I need help with dinner. Why are you so late?'

I swallowed a groan and dragged myself into the kitchen.

The room was full of shadows, the only light coming from the few lit candles dotting the room. 'Power out again?'

Without looking up from the counter, she nodded. She was slicing an enormous blood-red tomato. A huge head of lettuce sat on the counter, its acid green colour making my eyes water. Their unnatural colours and size always made me wonder if genetic modification was really such a great idea. That, and their weird taste. They weren't anything like the produce I'd had in the lab.

'Hi love. How was work?' She looked up, and her eyes fixed immediately on the red welt rising on my arm. She dropped her knife and rushed to me, cool hands encircling my wrist. She led me to a rickety kitchen chair and gently pushed me into it. 'What happened?'

I tried to shoo her away. 'Mom it's nothing. I'm fine. Just a misunderstanding.'

'Dom – '

'Hello, household! How are my favourite girls?'

Dad stood in the doorway, his smile a warm and welcoming beacon.

The distraction shifted Mom's attention and I slipped out of the chair, making a second attempt at reaching the sanctuary of my room.

The wide smile directed at my father left my mother's face and the whip of her voice stopped me in my tracks. 'Not so fast, young lady. Sit back down. Now that your father's here you can tell us both where that mark came from.'

Dad crossed the room and looked at me enquiringly. I held out my arm without another word. He gently probed the welt, concern creasing his face.

'Three soldiers were harassing an old man in the street. I tried to help him.' Maybe if I said as little as possible I would be spared a lecture. I risked a glance at Mom. Her folded arms told me otherwise.

'Domo, what have we told you about antagonising soldiers? You could've been hurt. Or punished. Or worse.'

'What was I supposed to do, Mom? Turn a blind eye? You and Dad are always telling me the only way things will change is if we take responsibility –'

'Yes, but without putting yourself in harm's –'

'That's what you said. Your words.'

Mom sighed.

'We should report this,' Dad said.

'What for?'

'The soldiers were being abusive,' Mom said. 'We shouldn't just let this go.'

'They don't care, Mom.' I motioned to the mark on my arm.

Dad's expression darkened. 'New recruit, I assume?'

'I don't think so, Dad. He seemed pretty sure of himself.'

Mom wrung her hands. 'What were you thinking? They could've dragged you off to the stocks.'

'I almost wish they had. Would've taught them a lesson.'

My parents exchanged a look. 'You're not above the rules, Domo.' The command in Dad's tone, although quiet, was undeniable.

I sighed. 'Don't report it. There's no point – the soldiers won't be punished and the old man might get into more trouble.'

'What did he do?' Mom asked.

'He stole a food package. Poor guy was just trying to feed his family.'

'The food stores will have to be investigated. Someone is either giving out extra rations, or the owners aren't monitoring their store properly.' Mom's comment was directed at Dad. She spoke as if I were no longer in the room.

I tried to move from my chair, hoping I could slip away unnoticed. Mom's eagle gaze fell on me, rooting me back into place.

'The rules are there for a reason, kiddo. If we all did whatever we liked there would be no order, and plenty of starving families,' Dad said, ignoring my attempt at escape.

'There already are plenty of starving families,' I said.

Mom shot me a sharp look. 'Did Mandy come in today?'

I avoided her gaze, honing in on a minute piece of lint on the knee of my jeans. I nodded.

'And?'

'And I did my job and gave her the ration.'

'Nothing more?'

'Could you please stop interrogating me? You've drilled it into me – nothing illegal, no calling attention to myself –'

Mom folded her arms, a sure sign I was about to get it.

'Putting yourself in harm's way, after everything your father and I have done to keep you –'

'I know you risked everything taking me in. I don't need to hear it every day of my life.'

Dad stood, anger flaring in his expression for the first time. 'You're our daughter. It doesn't matter whether you were born to us or not. That's just biology.'

I avoided looking at Dad. 'I know, okay? They could kill us. You've told me a million times. Can I please go to my room now?'

Mom looked pained and I felt an unwelcome stab of guilt. It seemed like every conversation with my mother ended with her looking at me like a wounded dog and me feeling like the cow that kicked her.

Dad glanced at me, his reproach like a thousand tiny needles pricking my skin. I stomped to my room, slamming the door behind me. I threw myself on my bed, narrowly missing knocking myself unconscious against the opposite wall.

I rolled onto my back and stared at the ceiling, gathering all my concentration until it formed a pinpoint in my mind. The walls of my room dissolved. I stood on a bed of soft green leaves, a canopy of shade above my head, a whisper of wind trailing through the trees. I pushed harder and imagined I heard birdsong. I sank into the softness of the leaves littering the ground. They were blissfully cool, protected from the harsh rays of the sun by the leafy stretch of branches above.

A hand fell on my shoulder and I yelped. The vision disappeared and I was back in my bedroom, its closeness stifling.

Dad sank onto the edge of the bed, his expression apologetic. 'Nice forest you had going there.'

'Please don't lecture me about that as well. I've had enough for one day.'

He held up his hand. 'I wasn't going to. As long as you don't project outside, or practise your controlling skills on anyone, we'll be just fine.' He gave me a stern look. 'Your mother's upset.'

That wave of guilt again. 'I know. I always seem to know exactly what to say.'

'She worries – you know that. She's concerned that you're not being careful enough.'

'This place is a cage, Dad. There are rules for everything – right down to whom I can be friends with and the person I'm allowed to marry. Sometimes I don't feel like being careful. I want to be free. Don't you ever feel that way?'

'There are good people here, Domo. The government's only trying to do what they can with very limited resources.'

'If there are such good people here then why do I have to hide? Why do I have to pretend I'm like everyone else?'

Dad reached out and smoothed my hair away from my eyes, his expression tender.

'You know why, honey. The one thing people can't handle is someone who's different.'

He leaned over and kissed my forehead. 'Now stop sulking and come eat dinner. And apologise to your mother.'

Chapter Two

Syra

Istood on the observation deck of the highest watchtower overlooking The Waste. Beyond the entrance gate, I could see the crumbling walls of uninhabited houses and the cracking tongues of unused streets of the old human city – a grim reminder of what lay beyond our walls. The old city had been vast, whereas Jozenburg was small enough to cross by foot in just over an hour.

Far below me, watched over by the guards in their watchtowers, people queued to fill their buckets with the precious water in our well. It was the morning pick-up. So far, there had been no incidents of citizens taking more than their daily share. The guards had enough to do without having to deal with that as well. The last thing I wanted today was to have to drag a transgressor in front of the Elders.

'Syra!' I glanced behind me and smiled. Even waving up at me from the ground metres below, Ray was still one of the biggest men I'd ever known. I'd seen him turn sideways to move through a doorway. He was built more like a boulder than a man.

'Drake wants to see you.'

I moved to the edge of the tower and stepped off. The wind whistled past me as the ground rushed up to meet me. I landed lightly, a small puff of dust rising beneath my feet.

'Show off.' Ray grinned. 'There is a ladder, you know.'

I shrugged. 'Where's the fun in that? Anyway, it's only there for the Minders.'

'Gee, thanks. May I remind you that you are part Minder too?'

Ray was one of the few people I let get away with ragging me this way. Few others dared.

He nudged me forward. 'He's in there. I think he wants to show off one or two of the more promising trainees.' I started in the direction of the training hall, then glanced over my shoulder at Ray. 'Well? Aren't you coming?' He caught up with me in one seamless bound, landing a light punch on my shoulder.

'Some of us have other things to do besides flit around the city and oversee training, Fearless Leader.' He pressed his palms together and bent from the waist in a mocking bow.

'Really? Well say what you like but I know you're dying to see how the trainees are coming along. Be grateful I even invited you.'

'As if the lack of an invitation would've kept me away.'

We headed towards the middle of the city. The training hall was actually an old house two storeys high, the largest by far in the city. It was the centre of Jozenburg, both physically and socially. All of Jozenburg's youth gathered there, a place where they could safely practise and hone their skills under the guidance of their trainers.

We wove our way through the streets, turning familiar corners and sidestepping cracked pavements and disintegrating tar roads. A faded street sign announced we were in Oxford Street, a relic from the old pre-war days. I glanced up at what must once have been an office block. Its windows were now mostly cracked or broken, the remaining shards glinting like a predator's teeth in the sun. The building across the street sported a sign with several missing letters, spelling out Rsebk. They said it used to be a shopping centre before the war. Every shop inside had long since been picked clean of food, clothes and other supplies. It was an echoing space of empty stores, a long-dead dinosaur. In time, it would be broken down and the recycled material used to repair our existing houses.

I paused, my gaze roaming the destitute building. I shaded my eyes against the glare of the sun, heat falling over me like an invisible cloak.

Ray stopped beside me, glancing in the same direction. 'Why do you always stop here?'

I shrugged. 'I suppose it gives me hope to see unused resources.'

'Why?'

'Because it means we haven't yet run out of ways to house

everyone. And because there may be a little left over for more houses.'

'For new residents.'

'Exactly.'

He shot me a questioning look but said nothing. Despite growing up together in the laboratory, and through the long years of our friendship, Ray always observed the bounds that separated citizen and leader.

We approached the training hall, my ears picking up on the sounds from five hundred metres away – a new personal record. I studied the details of the building: the slow decay of its exterior, the way the door sagged against its hinges. The windows, once large and wide, had been removed and the resulting gaps filled in with brick. Only the south-facing windows remained, a necessary adjustment to keep the sun from turning the building into a furnace.

As I stepped into the hallway, shouts and cheers from the adjoining rooms rang painfully in my ears. The smell of dozens of bodies filled my nose, mingling with the aromas of the old building in a potent mix that felt like a physical assault. I could taste the emotion of the place – an infusion of anxiety, excitement and adrenaline.

'Syra. There you are.' Draiken motioned to me from the second floor, where the youngest of our trainees worked on controlling their abilities.

I took the stairs two at a time and arrived at Draiken's side.

He cast a sidelong glance at Ray, a smile creeping across his features.

'Brought him along, I see?'

I shook my head. 'Couldn't keep him away.'

They clapped each other on the back, grinning like fools. Despite their glaring differences in appearance, something about their obvious closeness made them seem like brothers.

I turned my attention to the training ring. Emery stood in the centre with her mentor, Raven, and I paused for a moment to watch her.

Raven glanced towards us, her gaze flitting over Drake and me, settling on Ray. She smiled broadly, causing him to shift uncomfortably. Drake and I followed her gaze, and I raised my eyebrows suggestively, causing Ray to shuffle his feet so energetically he looked like he was running in place. His eyes moved around the room, settling anywhere but on Raven. Unperturbed, she turned back to Emery.

Raven raised her hands. The marking on the back of her left hand glowed and waned in a rhythmic wave. Light pulsed from both her palms. I felt the heat of it from where I stood. Raven pushed the light away from her, striking Emery in the chest, knocking her to the dirt floor of the ring. Emery sprang to her feet immediately, her expression twisting into a mask of fury. She threw herself at Raven, who stepped aside. Emery flew right out of the ring, barely saving herself from landing on her face. She let out a scream of frustration, her face scarlet as titters of barely suppressed laughter filled the room.

Raven crossed to Emery and helped her up. 'If you let your rage get the better of you, if you lose your focus, you'll never win. You can beat me, but only if you keep it together.'

She pulled Emery back into the centre. 'Let's do it again. Concentrate this time. Don't lose your cool.'

Raven raised her hands again. Before she could do anything else, a spark shot from Emery's right hand, slamming into Raven's shoulder and unbalancing her. She fell to the floor in an ungraceful heap, laughing. 'Good! That's what I'm talking about.' Emery's face shone with pride, her grin so wide it threatened to spill off her face.

I turned to Draiken. 'She's improving.'

He slung an arm across my shoulders and pushed me to the smaller ring where several teenagers stood waiting.

'Yes she is. But Emery's not who I wanted you to see.'

He motioned to Trey, a lanky boy who was the one and only Converted of our kind. His presence still unnerved me, even though there had been no signs of instability in his behaviour. The conversion seemed to suit him, but I worried all the same.

'Trey. Demonstrate for Syra.'

Trey stepped forward silently. His brow furrowed, and his gaze centred on a line of tin cans propped on a table several metres away. One of the tins wobbled, threatening to tip off the edge. Then it rose, as if pulled up by an invisible string. It jerked towards Trey in fitful starts, occasionally pausing and hovering, then resuming its journey through thin air until finally, it landed neatly in Trey's palm. His smile of triumph was directed at me. I smiled in return. It felt strained.

'Isn't it remarkable?' Draiken asked. Without waiting for a reply he turned back to Trey. 'Watch again. He's a Physical too.'

I felt my alarm levels spike. 'He's a Dual?'

Draiken nodded, his excitement palpable. 'Trey. Show Syra.'

Trey took off towards the opposite wall, moving so fast my eyes could barely track him. Halfway across the room he leaped, his feet leaving the floor in a blur of speed. He landed gracefully against the wall and seemed to hover there, his hands and feet flat against the brick. Despite myself, I was entranced. He remained facing the wall, his hands and feet braced against it, for another moment or two before sliding to the floor again.

Draiken grinned at me. 'I think he's nearly as fast as you.'

'Amazing,' Ray murmured. 'And he's a Convert. Imagine the possibilities.'

Draiken shot me a triumphant look. 'Exactly.'

Trey sauntered back to us, arrogance creasing his face, his eyes burning with excitement. He looked at me expectantly, and suddenly all I wanted was to wipe that overconfidence from his face.

'Very impressive,' I said flatly. Disappointment flashed briefly over his face before he managed to arrange his features into a neutral expression.

I could feel the heat of Draiken's questioning stare searing into my temple.

I avoided his gaze. 'We need to talk.'

I turned around and made my way down the stairs, heading to the small room off to the right side of the front door. Draiken followed me and shut the door behind him, but not before I caught a glimpse of Ray talking animatedly with Trey, his face lit with excitement.

'What was that all about?'

I shrugged. 'You know the boy gives me the creeps. I told you from the beginning I wasn't comfortable with a conversion. And you went and trained him anyway. We're supposed to be making these kind of decisions together.'

Draiken snorted. 'I knew you wouldn't agree. I was hoping to win you over with his demonstrations. We're Converts, Sy. And look at us. We're perfectly normal. We're not hacking anyone to death with a dinner knife. Besides, the boy came to us. He risked his life to cross The Waste, on the off-chance we'd allow him to become one of us. We need more like him.'

The smile in his voice irritated me. 'The Creator converted us. He had more of a clue than we do. Do you think President Crane will be pleased if he hears we're doing conversions on humans?' I paced the tight corners of the room. 'You shouldn't be so flippant about this. You normally take my feelings seriously. Especially when they involve people.'

'This isn't one of your sixth sense feelings, Sy. This is you not taking to Trey, which isn't unusual for you. You're not exactly the warm and cuddly type. As for Crane – what does it matter? He'll never find out. At least not until it's too late.' He smirked. 'Anyway the boy could be from any of the human cities. No one knows for sure if Toria is the only one left.'

I shot him a look. 'This is absolutely not personal. He's a Convert, and a Dual. What if he becomes unstable?'

'Then we kill him. The only thing we'll have lost is time. I've had a look at the numbers and we need a drastic increase if we're going to manage the takeover. You already know this.'

I folded my arms. 'What does this have to do with Trey?'

'Converts are the way to get those numbers.'

'Draiken! You haven't discussed this with me.'

He held up a hand. 'I'm discussing it with you now.' He motioned to a nearby chair. 'Sit, will you? You're making me edgy.'

I glared at him but dropped into the chair anyway.

'We agreed that we would try something other than populating the natural way. There have been increasing reports of more and more couples having trouble conceiving. And when they do, some of the children have been born – '

'Deformed. I know.'

'Exactly. If more families have deformed kids then we may as well welcome humans into Jozenburg. Those kids are exactly like them. No skills. At least no useful ones.

'Those that are healthy grow quickly, yes, but it still isn't fast enough. Not if we're going to mobilise against the humans soon. I've already spoken to the Elders –'

I half rose out of my chair. 'Without consulting me? You had a gathering without me there? What the hell, Drake! You said we would lead together.' His face remained impassive, except for one raised eyebrow, admonishing me without a word. I sank back down, feeling his condescension in every pore of my skin.

'We agreed that I would oversee the training, didn't we? That's what I'm doing. We've got to play to our strengths. If you want to change the arrangement then say so, otherwise stop being a prophet of doom and let me get on with things.'

'Why did the Elders allow you to meet them without me?'

'They asked me the same thing. I told them I wanted to run it by them first, because you would need some convincing. They agree with me. We can't convince the humans we need another city, without the numbers to justify it.'

'I doubt we'll convince President Crane anyway... Wait. What numbers?'

'Don't act stupid, Sy. You know the humans have no knowledge of our problems with procreation.'

'So the Elders agreed to this ridiculous plan of yours? To convert humans? What about the loss of life?'

Draiken grimaced and shook his head. 'Honestly Sy. Why do you even think human life is worth preserving? Look what they did to this country – this world - with their greed.'

'Regardless, the Elders said a hostile take-over was out of the question. We do it peacefully, or not at all.'

Draiken rolled his eyes. 'Yes – the Elders are quite the idealists. I told them that converting would benefit us all. We won't take any humans forcibly. We'll offer them the choice.'

I rose, preparing to leave before my temper made a fool of me. Draiken's voice pulled me back. 'I need your blessing on this. The Elders don't want to force you into it. You know how they are – freedom of choice and all that sentimental crap.'

'Will they go ahead and do it if I refuse to be a part of this?'

Draiken gave me a look. 'Yes. But if the Elders decide we can no longer work together then both our positions are in danger.'

'I can't agree to this. I think it's a terrible mistake. We don't know the exact science of conversion. We don't know what will happen if one of the humans reacts badly to the change. You could be putting all of us in danger.'

Draiken reached for my hands and squeezed them. 'I need you on my team. Please. Trust me. I know I can make this work. And if I can't, if anything goes wrong, I'll stop. The Elders will never allow bloodshed among our own kind. I need your help with the conversions. Your gifts are too great not to pass on.'

My sixth sense screamed at me not to agree. The warning heat of going against my feeling flooded my cheeks, pulsed like a living thing behind my eyes, throbbed in the hastened beat of my blood. I couldn't refuse him. I had never been able to, even when we were kids. I owed him too much. Without him, I wouldn't be here at all. The memories of that night rushed through me, reeking of fear and blood. The screams echoing in the cavernous space of the laboratory. I clamped down hard on them. They went silent. Still I felt them, hovering in the darkest places of my mind, waiting to take flight again.

'Fine.' I ignored the drop of my stomach, the sudden film of sweat on my palms. 'But from now on I want to know everything that's going on, and I want to be present at all the conversions.'

Draiken hugged me tightly, his excitement enveloping me like an ominous cloud.

'Thanks Sy. I promise you won't regret it.'

I nodded and extricated myself from his grasp. I left the room, dread clotting my throat and filling my mouth with the bitter snap of regret.

Chapter Three

Syra

It took us less than two hours to cover the distance from Jozenburg to the front gates of Toria. We estimated it would take a human at least six hours to cover the same distance, a point of pride between us. I shared Draiken's impatience to get this over with. We had travelled alone, despite the protests of our soldiers that entering the human city unguarded posed too much of a risk. I wasn't thrilled about entering Toria with only Draiken at my side, but I knew the sight of dozens of superhumans walking into a human city would only create unnecessary tension and unwanted curiosity.

The gate was flanked by watchtowers on either side, much like Jozenburg. Four soldiers stood in each tower, guns glinting with malice in the morning sunlight. We were made to wait in the blistering sun until, finally, the gates opened just enough for a man to slip out from between its massive jaws. He carried no weapon, but the black eyes of eight guns trained on us were enough of a warning. His hands were impossibly clean, nails clipped with neat precision. His eyes moved over us with careful scrutiny.

'The superhumans, I presume.' He put an odd emphasis on "human", as if questioning our right to this claim.

'Yes,' I said in a clipped tone. Beside me Draiken tensed, and I picked up trails of his scattered thoughts as he spat silent insults at the man. I reached out a hand and squeezed Draiken's arm, willing him to remain calm. It was crucial to keep things civil.

The man nodded. 'I'm Rogan, the commander of Toria. President

Crane will see you now. I don't think I have to tell you that any offensive or threatening behaviour from either of you will not be tolerated.'

He motioned to one of the soldiers at the watchtower, and the gates began to open all the way, screaming in protest.

'Follow me. Keep close. Everyone here has been warned of your arrival, but no one is too thrilled about it. I don't need anyone dying on my watch.'

Draiken gritted his teeth. The grinding sound filled my ears and grated through me, flooding my mouth with a sharp metallic taste. The human continued forward, oblivious. I leaned into Draiken. 'Relax. They feel threatened. Did you see the soldiers? Aren't there normally guards stationed at the watchtowers?' He nodded, his shoulders dropping from their tense pose. Their fear pleased him.

Gradually, human activity ceased in our wake. Dozens of pairs of eyes trained on us and burned into our backs. Whispers rose behind us, curling like a poisonous fog. Their fear and hate filled me with visions of blood and bone, and made my skin heat until I felt like I might burst into flame. My tongue felt thick and useless in the desert of my mouth. I licked my lips and kept my eyes trained in front of me.

Only when the patchwork of cracks in the pavements disappeared, did I allow myself to look up. We stood in front of an impressively high brick wall, broken only by the imposing iron of a guarded gate.

Rogan motioned to the guards, who seemed to unfreeze in his presence, almost falling over each other in a bid to be the first to obey. The gate swung open. Colours seemed to rush at me and filled my vision with a brightness so intense I fell back a step or two, blinking frantically. The smells filling my nose blended into a scent so heady it scattered my thoughts. Textures sprang at me and ran over my skin like ghostly fingers, raising a scattering of gooseflesh on my arms. There were flowers and plants everywhere. Blooms in every colour – reds as rich as blood, yellows as warm as sunlight, oranges as bright as a sunrise. Trees creating canopies of shade, grass beneath my feet that grew a gloriously lush green. It wasn't until Draiken took my arm and propelled me forward that I realised I had stopped walking, gaping at the rich rarity of so many plants in one place.

I glanced at the commander and took in the odd expression on his face as he looked at me. My wonder unravelled into a pit of fury.

'This is where your water goes? To plants that don't even produce food?'

'Syra!' Draiken hissed.

Something flitted across the commander's face. 'As you can see, this isn't where *all* our water goes, otherwise we'd have a city full of corpses. And plenty of these plants do produce food. They're all genetically modified, so they need very little water to survive.'

He looked flustered by his own need to explain.

'President Crane doesn't answer to you. None of us do. And if you hope to leave here with what you came for, I suggest you swallow that smutty tone.'

No one had ever spoken to me that way. I opened my mouth, but the painful grind of Draiken's hand over mine snapped it shut again. His voice rang in my head, strident and furious. We argued silently, the commander moving ahead of us along the paved pathway.

Reaching the front door of the presidential home, he paused, and turned to us.

'My orders are to shoot should you pose a danger to President Crane, or any of my men, or myself. I have better things to do with my day than mop up your blood, so let's keep this amicable.'

Draiken and I glanced at each other, our argument forgotten. I could see him trying to suppress a smile without success.

Rogan glared at us. 'We know you're hard to kill. We have other methods.'

***

President Crane entered the office without warning, breezing in as if for a leisurely lunch with friends. Draiken and I both rose. President Crane waved us back into our seats, his smile steady. The commander followed closely behind him, shutting the door. The room suddenly felt dense and suffocating.

President Crane dropped into a chair across from us, with only the rich brown expanse of his desk between us. 'Well, I hope commander Rogan didn't come across as too intimidating. You must forgive him – he takes his position very seriously.' He offered Draiken his hand, which Draiken took coolly.

'Draiken,' he said shortly, and withdrew his hand with a haste bordering on rude.

President Crane's dark blue eyes settled on my face for a moment. I held my hand out for him before he could offer his own. The touch of his skin caused an involuntary shudder to skitter up my spine. I tried to reach beyond the depths of his gaze - to get a sample of his thoughts, but nothing came. His mind was like a canvas wiped clean. I released his hand, left with the distinct impression we were facing a formidable foe.

'Syra,' I croaked, and made a show of sliding back into my seat to hide my disquiet.

A light knock sounded. The commander opened it a crack and then pulled it open all the way, admitting a tiny young woman who held a tray of clinking cups and saucers. President Crane waved her in and she set the tea tray down carefully. She glanced at President Crane and he smiled reassuringly. 'Thank you, Sue. That'll be all.' She nodded and left the room.

The smell of coffee rose in tantalising tendrils, filling my nose and flooding my mouth.

'Can I pour for you, Syra?'

'Yes. Thank you.'

'Milk? Sugar?'

I nodded, not trusting myself to speak. He handed me a delicate cup and saucer painted in intricate detail with tiny interlinked flowers. I took a sip and the richness of the coffee burst on my tongue, momentarily shocking me into silence. The coffee we had at home was nothing like this, and what we did have was hoarded and drunk in frugal sips.

'Draiken?'

'No. Thank you.' Out of the corner of my eye I could see the agitated twitch of Draiken's jaw as he ground out the words.

'There are many privileges that come with leadership, wouldn't you say, Syra?' He smiled, his teeth an even spread of white enamel. 'Small luxuries like coffee and beautiful china.'

'If it's all the same to you, President, we would like to get things underway,' Draiken said.

'Of course.' Crane folded his hands in front of him and trained his attention on Draiken. 'My guess is you are here to negotiate land.'

'Yes. We've heard you're in the middle of converting some viable sections of The Waste into additional human cities. We are growing in numbers quite rapidly, and Jozenburg is already becoming overcrowded. We need another city.'

Crane's eyes moved to me. I hoped my face was as blank as it felt. Although not strictly a lie, Crane was not to know the methods we'd need to employ in order to grow these numbers.

'I'm sure you understand this is quite a request. Why should I grant it?'

Draiken's hands gripped the arms of his chair. A hairline crack appeared in each, marring the glossy perfection of the wood.

'We understand it's a lot to ask. But if we are to continue to live peacefully, we need resources, just as much as you do.' I forced my tone to remain neutral, resisting the urge to point out the glaring discrepancies between our resources and his.

'I wouldn't underestimate us humans. We were the ones generous enough to grant you a city in the first place. You have your resources because of us. That doesn't mean our generosity is boundless.'

'Your *generosity* guaranteed your safety,' I replied. 'Don't assume that continued peace is without conditions.'

Crane smiled. His eyes sparkled. 'I do enjoy sparring with someone as obviously intelligent and unforgiving as yourself. But I must confess that I knew my answer even before your arrival.

'The treaty with our neighbours is a tenuous one. Losing the human war forced us to concede more than we could afford. We too, have growing numbers.' Something in his tone made me look more closely at him. Trusting any human was folly. But trusting this human, in particular, was a dance I loathed to perform.

'We have major clean-up operations going on, yes. But between our limited man-power and the bothersome problem of the creatures of The Waste, we aren't making much headway. We can't afford to annoy the inhabitants of the neighbouring countries. Our trade agreements with them are not ones we can afford to jeopardise, despite their sporadic nature, and how long we wait for them. The supplies we receive are crucial to our survival.'

He rapped the table sharply with a closed fist, and I sensed our meeting was drawing to a close.

'I'm afraid I have to refuse your request. I just wanted to grant you the courtesy of telling you in person.'

He rose. 'Thank you for making the trip. I know it's a difficult and dangerous one. It was a pleasure meeting you both. Commander Rogan will see you out. I have other business to attend to. Excuse me.'

He turned to leave. I felt the heat of Draiken's leap a second before his feet left the floor. He seized Crane by the collar of his shirt, slamming him against the wall with enough force to wind him. The Commander ripped his gun from its holster and levelled it at Draiken. Time froze. Commander Rogan's finger moved around the trigger in a slow-motion curl. I could map every line and hair on his hand. His breath came and went in rapid gusts, the noise a howling gale in my ears. The smell of his sweat filled my head like a noxious gas, making my stomach clench. Words rose to my lips but seemed to lodge behind my teeth.

A moment later I was between the commander and Draiken, my palms raised.

'Please.' The word ripped from my throat as I struggled to breathe through my fear.

I glanced at Draiken. His hands were still wrapped in the folds of Crane's shirt. He pressed Crane against the wall with such force I was convinced it would collapse. 'Drake. Let him go.' He ignored me. 'Drake!'

The Commander moved the gun until it pointed over my shoulder. 'Now!' I yelled, my desperation and terror coiling in my gut, mocking black dots filling my vision.

Draiken dropped his hands and took one step back, his eyes fixed on Crane. The president smoothed his shirt and ran a leisurely hand through his hair.

'No need to see us out. I think we've both made our positions clear,' Draiken said.

The commander took a step towards Draiken but Crane held up a hand, stilling him in mid-stride.

'Leave them be. The guards will see them out.' He smiled, perfectly at ease. 'Have a safe journey home.'

***

The black markets sprang to life as dusk arrived. The vendors did nothing to hide their wares and made no secret of their illicit goods as they unpacked them outside their homes. Well-bribed soldiers kept the area clear of their unpaid comrades, waving them away with stories of unscheduled inspections of civilian homes. The atmosphere was frenetic and crackled with the precariousness of the agreement between citizens and soldiers. Our particular guard, who we'd bribed with two bottles of vodka so rare I'd been tempted to offer only the one, led us through the maze of twisting streets, arriving at a small knot of soldiers. One stepped away from the others, holding up a hand that halted our guide.

'Who are they?'

The guard's jaw twitched, betraying his nervousness.

'Well? We pay you to keep out unwanted visitors, not give them a tour.'

The soldier's companions snorted with laughter.

Draiken stepped forward, the movement deceptively casual.

The guard hurriedly pulled out a small package, unwrapping it with shaking hands, to reveal its contents. The soldier touched the tin of coffee, the bag of sugar. It pained me to see the luxuries beneath his hands, even though we'd kept them specifically for an event like this one. Still, I hated watching the soldier fawn over our hard-won items.

'Do we have an understanding?' Draiken asked.

The soldier took the package from the guard, then looked up at Draiken with a smile. I sensed what was coming before he opened his mouth.

'These are poor quality. You need to do better than this if you want access.'

I closed my eyes and sighed inwardly.

One breath, and Draiken's hand was around the soldier's throat.

'It would be unwise for you to try to cheat me. We've paid you more than enough for our entrance.' His hand flexed around the soldier's throat, tightening his grip. The soldier's eyes fixed on his comrades. None of them moved.

My nerves felt raw. The tension of the group seeped into me like the slow drip of poison.

'Come on Drake. That's enough.'

Draiken lowered his hand, then nodded to the guard. We walked past the soldiers and into the heart of the market. I kept one ear trained behind us, listening for any suspicious movement. We'd walked the length of one block before I was able to relax.

'I can't believe this,' I said to Draiken. 'Right under their noses. Do you think *Commander* Rogan knows about this?' Draiken snorted in reply. I watched the guard creep away into the gathering darkness, hobbling like an old man. 'Do you think he'll tell?'

Draiken shook his head. 'Between our threats and our bribes, I doubt it. My guess is he'll shut his mouth just to make sure he never sees us again.'

We passed along the street unnoticed, the poor lighting helping us fade into the seething mass of bodies and voices.

'How do we pick one?' I asked.

'Simple. We go for the one whose goods are the most illicit, with the highest price. We'll need to get closer. Walk slowly and keep your head down as much as you can.'

I sighed. 'Yes Boss Draiken.'

He shoved me playfully and we pushed through the crowd until we were right up against the line of tables spilling over with items ranging from food to bedding to technology goods from the world before the war.

The vendors followed our progress with beady eyes, always on the lookout for potentially thieving hands. We walked for a few minutes longer before Draiken pulled me up short in front of a stall stacked high with foods I had only seen many years before in the confines of the lab. Boxes of beautifully wrapped chocolates and bottles of aged red wine gleamed in the waning light, filling me with flavours and textures unknown or long forgotten, like mocking phantoms.

The vendor watched us as we paused at his table, our eyes roving over his wares. When we lingered, he hovered over his goods protectively, eyeing us with suspicion.

'If you want something then make me an offer, otherwise get away from my stall!'

His full face and soft body spoke of food few others had experienced. His greed hung around him like a foul scent.

Just to rile him, I ran a finger over a particularly expensive-looking box of chocolates, letting my touch linger until even the tips of his ears were scarlet with outrage.

Pulling away, I looked him in the eye. 'We want to make a deal.'

His eyes lit with interest, but his suspicion remained.

'What do you want?'

I motioned to the closed door of his home behind him. He shook his head. 'Deals are made on the streets, woman, or not at all.'

I shrugged. 'Fine.' I stretched out my left hand to him, palm down. I emptied my mind and focused, blocking everything else out. The marking on my skin glowed brightly for a second, then disappeared.

The vendor gasped and stumbled backwards. For a gut-wrenching moment I thought he would start to scream, but his gaze moved to my face and when he opened his mouth, his words were quiet.

'There were rumours that your kind would be visiting our city today. You're the first one I've ever seen up close. You look exactly like us.'

Draiken sighed impatiently. 'We're not live exhibits. Are you interested in a deal, or not?'

The vendor's eyes shifted to Draiken. 'That depends. What do I get?'

Draiken leaned close to the vendor. 'You get to live another day, and not die an agonisingly slow death.'

The vendor reared away from Draiken. I glared at him. 'Why don't you take a walk? I've got this.' He started to protest but then seemed to think better of it and stalked off.

I turned back to the vendor. 'You look like a man who knows his way around the rules. You're resourceful. That's what we need.' The vendor folded his arms across his chest, unimpressed.

'Listen lady. I'm sure you can appreciate we deal in trades and bartering. Your friend there would be unwise to threaten me. I know the soldiers here personally.'

'I do have a kind of barter for you. I need you to feed certain information to interested parties. Be warned - if the wrong people find out, my friend there will come back for you and rip out your tongue. And that'll only be the beginning. Understand?'

Beads of sweat formed at his hairline. His bravado was starting to slip.

'What do you want? I got sales to make here.'

I told him the plan. When I turned to leave, the vendor's excitement followed me through the throng of people, clinging to me like a wayward child.

Draiken was right – the vendor was the perfect pick.

Chapter Four

Rogan

I knocked briefly on President Crane's door before entering. He sat at his desk, a crystal tumbler filled with the amber warmth of whisky. He looked up at my entry and motioned to a chair. He pushed a second tumbler into my hand as I took my seat. I sighed inwardly and placed the glass on the desk, nudging it back in his direction.

'Ah yes. I forgot you're one of the few men who don't drink. Perhaps the only one.' He winked and knocked back his whisky, reaching for my glass and emptying it as well.

'Right. Down to business. Needless to say today didn't go very well. Not that I expected the superhumans to accept my decision, but Draiken is quite the temperamental one. His reputation precedes him.'

I folded my hands in my lap. This routine I did with the President was dull, but necessary.

'Your decision was the only one you could've made. I think they knew before they came that their request would be denied.'

'Why do you think they came then?'

I shook my head. 'I can only guess. Maybe they wanted to see the inside of Toria – see how it's grown, the layout – could be anything. Maybe they had another plan.' I paused. Diplomacy was key here. 'I think perhaps your tone, and not so much your refusal, is what set Draiken off.'

President Crane raised an eyebrow. 'My tone?'

'These are beings that are used to reverence and respect – they must be highly ranked in their city or they wouldn't have been sent. They have powers. They expect us humans to be cowed by them. And as you saw, Draiken is arrogant as hell.'

'Your point?'

'You treated him like an unreasonable child. You were polite, but condescending. I don't think he was expecting that.'

'Rogan, I'm the President of this region. I don't tippy-toe around anyone, least of all a *species* that tries to masquerade as human.' He stood, pushing his chair back. He walked to the window that overlooked the city, throwing it open. He motioned for me to join him. I crossed the room to stand beside him, following his gaze as he looked out over Toria. We could see beyond the gate bordering Crane's mansion, and watched as the city's citizens went about their daily business. Soldiers called out to guards, their laughter carrying in with the breeze. A small group of children ran perilously close to the mansion gates, eliciting a roar from the guards in the watchtowers. They scampered away, delighted by their own daring.

'All of this came at great cost. You weren't even old enough to tote a gun when the human war happened. We needed a way to finish the war that wouldn't cost us everything.' He turned back to me. 'Their assistance in that war was the only use we've ever had for superhumans. They are a scourge on this land, eating our resources and taking our water.' His eyes were lit with a feverish light. I waited. It would burn itself out, as it always did.

He returned to his chair. I followed, relieved that his rant was over for now.

'Sir, negotiations between us and them have to be done with a kind of –'

'A kind of what?' he snapped.

'A mutual respect. It's a ritual, a game. One that's expected to be followed.'

President Crane's expression turned stony.

'Diplomacy is the only weapon we really have to protect ourselves, to delay the inevitability of war. Sir.'

For a moment I wondered if I'd gone too far. Finally, President Crane shook his head. 'Sometimes Rogan, I regret choosing you as our commander. Someone without quite so many thoughts of his own would've been nice.' A hint of a smile crept to his face. 'It's getting late and you're giving me a headache. Go now and we'll meet with the Tribunal tomorrow and decide if a plan of action is necessary.'

***

The barracks was quiet except for the occasional snore. I felt my way through the darkness, avoiding the line of bunks to my left and keeping to the middle to avoid falling over anything.

The smell of the place was so palpable that it seemed to hang in the air like a persistent heavy mist. It made me think of dirty socks and ripe tempers.

I slipped into my lower bunk in the furthest right corner. A voice came out of the blackness. 'Fine time to come wake the rest of us,' Caiden said.

'Some of us have to protect the city while the rest of you get your beauty sleep.'

'Go wake up your household then. At least you've got one to call home. Would give anything to live in that part of town.'

'So you've told me. Several times.'

Caiden laughed. I heard him roll over. Minutes later his snores joined those of the others.

Caiden was welcome to the place, and all that went with it. The thought of Aunt Carrie brought my hand up involuntarily to trace the scar that ran from my hairline to my right eyebrow. I couldn't recall the pain – I remembered only my almost feverish gratitude that her belt buckle had miraculously missed my eye. But in many ways, I was grateful. Surviving Aunt Carrie had tempered my will. I no longer felt weak, desperate or alone.

I rolled onto my side and pushed the thought of Aunt Carrie away. Unbidden, an image from earlier in the day rose in my mind. I saw her as she'd stood between Draiken and me, her hand held out in supplication. She'd looked down the barrel of my gun with a fear not for herself, but for her companion. It was the first time I'd realised her height nearly matched mine, and wondered at the strangeness of noticing such a detail in a moment like that. The sharp clench of dread I'd felt at the possibility of having to shoot her gnawed at me, an enigma I was unwilling to examine too closely.

Dominico

The next morning I caught Mom before she left for work. My mumbled apology the night before had done nothing to ease the tension between us.

She was in our miniscule bathroom, a cup filled a quarter of the way balancing dangerously close to the edge of the basin. I still – years after the last drop of water had run from our taps - found it hilarious that we had a basin and bathtub. These days, all the taps produced were groans of protest.

She glanced at me briefly when I tapped on the bathroom door, nodding for me to come in. Her shoulders were in their usual rigid position, her unconscious response to my presence. She squeezed a tiny bead of toothpaste onto her ragged toothbrush. The tube was already flattened all the way to the top. Our next ration would only arrive at the end of the month – if, that is, the scouts managed to find any in The Waste.

'I'm sorry about last night,' I said.

She nodded and stuck the toothbrush into her mouth. Probably to avoid having to say anything in return.

'Mom, I'm trying here.'

She paused for a moment in her assault on her teeth, then spat and rinsed her mouth, her movements unhurried.

She finally looked at me. Her expression softened, and she reached out a hand, her fingers brushing my cheek and sweeping back my unruly curls.

'Your father always joked that you were a chip off the old block. Even when you were little, you two always somehow understood each other. He never wanted to punish you when you misbehaved. He said you were just spirited, that you had fire.'

Something flitted across her face. She dropped her hand and took a step back. The moment was gone.

'You better get to work, honey. Don't want to be late.'

Her voice had changed, shifting to the tone she normally used around me, the one that made me feel like nothing I did would ever make her really see me.

***

I wove my way along the paths, meandering from one section

of the city to the other, taking the longest possible route to work. I was going to be late, and without a doubt my tardiness would be noted. I didn't care. Free time wasn't something that was prioritised here. Some time ago, I'd come across a book of fiction in which I'd discovered the word 'weekend'. I assumed it was what it sounded like – the end of the week. Only the characters got to spend it as they liked. We, on the other hand, had our time filled for us. Like we couldn't be trusted with too much freedom.

I paused at a crossroad. The path leading straight ahead would take me to work. The one branching to the right led to the lower class section. I turned right.

The houses here could hardly be called houses at all. In school we'd been shown pictures of the world before the war. Toria was made up of a section of the previous city of Pretoria that had once been beautiful and prosperous. The part of Toria that I lived in retained some of that beauty.

The lower class section was now nothing but an ugly pit of human desperation. It was disintegrating, houses falling apart as materials within our walls became scarce, then non-existent. The scouts that were sent out regularly into the depths of The Waste often came back empty-handed, if they came back at all. There were plenty of crumbling buildings out there, if only we had the means to break them down and transport the material. For now, there was no way to patch the holes in the walls or the gaps in the ceilings that allowed in the cold and the rain - when rain actually fell.

I wandered between the houses, taking in the details of the miserable existence these people led. They lived on the edge of starvation every day. No matter what President Crane and his government officials spouted, there was no equality in this city. Those who could give more, got more. Becoming a soldier or an official was a top priority for most of my classmates. Their parents were predictably one or the other. The lower class had no options. They worked the inner fields where the crops were grown. They tended the livestock. I often thought it was unfair that such hungry people had to work with food all day.

Several people waved as they passed me, all on their way to work or school.

'Dominico!'

I returned Mandy's wave, expecting her to keep going, but she strode up to me, catching my arm and pulling me to a stop.

'Hey,' I said, a little surprised at this public interaction. Different classes weren't encouraged to mix. When I'd asked Dad about it, he'd said President Crane worried about the 'exchange of information' between the classes. His sarcastic tone had surprised me. In our home, we never said anything critical about how things were run.

'I just wanted to thank you for the extra rations.' She kept her voice low. Her eyes darted behind me, her body tense with suspicion.

'No need to thank me.'

I fidgeted. I wanted out of this conversation. Soldiers patrolled day and night, especially in this section. Part of their job was to root out 'disloyal' citizens. Standing here in broad daylight, on a path I shouldn't have been on in the first place, made me feel hot with discomfort.

I tried to edge away from her. 'Gotta get going. I'll be late for work.'

She blocked my escape, refusing to let go of my arm.

'I may have told a few people.'

I stopped. 'What?'

'I'm so sorry. I didn't mean to say anything. But one of the neighbours stopped by unexpectedly and saw the extra ration. I was afraid she was going to report me.'

'You said a few people.'

'I only told her. But...I know she repeated it.'

My throat felt like a hollow filled with ice. The sudden rush of adrenaline made my head throb. My hands were shaking.

'No one will repeat it to the soldiers. You know that, right?'

I nodded, not trusting myself to speak.

She squeezed my hand. 'You've helped me so much. You're the only one who seems to care about how we live, how little we have. We'll protect you. Keep your secret safe.'

I nodded again, not wanting to point out that it was already too late for that.

I finally looked up at her. Her eyes so large they seemed to fill her whole face. Cheekbones jutted sharply from her face, creating hollows beneath her cheeks. The shadows beneath her eyes were so dark they looked like bruises. Once, she had brought her daughter with her to pick up her ration. The little girl had looked so much like

Mandy. The constant hunger was stamped on her face too. Her eyes made me think of the bottomless dark of the city well, her need as endless as our quest for water.

'I know.' I returned the squeeze, giving her a reassuring smile. 'I'll try to help as many as I can.'

'Bless you.' She released my hand and hurried away, blending into the rush of the crowd.

***

Monday started out well enough. I made my way to school, if not exactly looking forward to, then at least preferring, the school halls to the musty cave Everton called a shop.

Kat called out a greeting, waving madly over the heads of the growing crowd. Just the sight of her lifted my spirits.

She looped her arm through mine, weaving between the bobbing bodies of our schoolmates. 'Fun "weekend"?' I smiled. It was our inside joke. 'Tons. Spending hours with Everton is the highlight of my Saturdays.'

I felt a shove from behind. At first, I didn't bother turning around. The first bell would ring soon, and in the rush to get to class, there was bound to be some jostling. I opened my mouth to ask Kat something, but then felt the unmistakeable heat of a palm against my back. I whipped around, my arm still threaded through Kat's. She yelped as she was dragged along with the force of my movement.

A sea of faces churned behind me. I turned back around, walking faster, pulling Kat along with me. I wasn't in the mood for this again. I went to so much trouble to blend in. To keep my abilities hidden. It didn't seem to matter. They knew I was different, even if they couldn't say why. It felt like a sign on my back in bright, blinking colours, no matter how hard I tried to hide it.

Kat craned her head around. 'Piss off!' she yelled at no one in particular. There was a titter behind us, but that was the last of it for the day.

***

Every day more desperate citizens arrived at the store with hollowed, pleading eyes. I couldn't help all of them and so I started a system – I would make sure that everyone who asked got an extra ration, but this could take weeks as I tried to keep Everton ignorant and myself safe from the stocks.

Something had gone wrong though. I arrived at work to find two soldiers waiting for me. Without a word they moved me inside and sat me down. They loomed over me silently, circling like hunters, eyes sweeping over me as if waiting for me to start wailing my confession. I kept my mouth shut, folding my arms tightly across my body like armour. The silence in the room stretched on and on, the only sound our mingled breaths and the crunching of the soldier's boots across the shop floor.

Finally Everton broke. 'Is this your idea of an interrogation?'

One of the soldiers shot Everton a look of pure contempt. 'Why don't you go move packages around in your storeroom or whatever it is you do? And let us get on with our jobs.'

Everton sniffed and shuffled away without argument. Once the door to the storeroom had closed behind him, the youngest solider turned to me. 'Right. We have better things to do than spend all day questioning you, so I'm going to ask you the obvious one – are you stealing from Everton?' He asked this while pretending to adjust his jacket, moving it in such a way that I got a clear view of the gun holstered at his hip. The other soldier casually pulled up a chair next to mine, leaning close, the blatant threat in his eyes sending a rush of dread through me.

'No...' Damn it. My voice was too high. I cleared my throat and looked him in the eye. 'No, I'm not stealing from him. Why would I? My parents are government officials. We have enough.'

The seated one leaned even closer, his stale breath sweeping over my face. 'There's never enough in this city, girl. You could be stealing on behalf of someone. You sure you don't want to change your answer?' A knife appeared from the depths of his jacket, the light catching its blade.

Panic beat violently in my chest, battering against my heart. My control was slipping. Heat flashed through me like a moving flame. My fingers tingled with the force of the blood rushing through them. I tried to catch it before it happened, but it pushed out of me with a force that left me dazed and breathless. The knife clattered to the floor. The gun strapped around the other soldier's waist seemed to unclasp itself from its holster and fell almost in unison with the knife, both skittering out of reach. Before either of them could react, I gave a hard push and, from the way their eyes remained fastened on the chair I'd been sitting in, I could tell they thought I was still there. They were seeing what I wanted them to see – a slip in reality, an image I had put up like a smoke screen. I rose, my fear threatening to spill over. I was shaking with the effort of keeping the illusion in place. I yanked the door open, knowing the moment it closed behind me, the image would dissolve and they would realise I was no longer there.

***

I didn't stop running until I reached home. I stumbled through the front door, trying to catch my breath and ignoring the black spots dancing in front of my eyes. I leaned on my knees and stared at the floor, forcing myself to breathe deeply until finally I felt I could lift my head without passing out.

A moment later I realised I wasn't alone. Mom laid a hand on my arm and pulled me into a chair, her brow furrowing into an expression I had come to dread.

'What are you doing home? Is everything okay?'

She folded her arms. 'Shouldn't you be at work?'

Might as well tell the truth. She always knew when I was lying. Either way a lecture was coming my way. 'Soldiers came to question me at work about missing food parcels and water canisters. Everton must've reported me.'

I realised my error a second later. Mom's eyes narrowed. 'Please tell me that Mr Everton was mistaken.'

I tried to rise but Mom clamped a hand on my shoulder and pushed me back in my seat with surprising force.

'I'm sorry, Mom. But I can't just sit by and watch people starve. I have the means to help them.'

'By stealing extra parcels? The ones that are used as incentives and rewards for government officials and soldiers?' Her voice had climbed several pitches.

'Yes, Mom, by stealing. The lower classes barely get enough food – 'She grabbed my arm with a force that made me wince. 'Why do you always have to find a way to disobey that puts all three of us in mortal danger? If they discover what you are –'

'*What* I am? Don't you mean *who* I am? My abilities don't make me another species, Mom. I'm still a person, a human being.'

'Don't even try that with me. You know very well what I meant.

We're trying to protect you. Do you want them to catch you? To catch us?'

I yanked my arm out of her grip. Tears threatened, closing my throat with fists of fear and frustration. 'I'm trying to help others. This isn't about you or Dad or even me – those people have no one to help them and I can't just do nothing.'

Mom drew a deep breath and lowered her voice. 'There are ways to help others without putting yourself, and us, in this kind of position.'

'You mean by talking?' I spat. 'Your endless negotiations with our useless president and the tribunal who care only about themselves?'

'Lower your voice. Someone could hear you.'

'Wouldn't want that, now would we? Wouldn't want the neighbours to know that I have any opinions of my own.'

I slammed out of the house and ran blindly, until I reached the wall encircling Toria on the far side. I sank against it, my sides heaving, grateful the streets were mostly empty. I couldn't go home. If Mom was this angry about my stealing food, she would be beyond enraged if she knew I'd used my abilities to escape. I buried my face in my hands, my eyes burning with unshed tears.

***

A hand fell on my shoulder, startling me from my coma.

'Dom? Are you ok?'

Kat peered down at me, her brow furrowed. I nodded slowly, the motion making my head spin. I rose stiffly, legs cramping in protest.

'I've been looking for you for over an hour. I stopped at your house and your mom isn't happy.'

'Tell me something I don't know.'

'What happened?'

'The usual – her giving me crap for being me.'

'She said you've been stealing food supplies.'

'I wasn't doing it for myself. I'm getting so sick of her acting surprised when I do stuff like this – this is how they bloody raised me – to think for myself, to be concerned for others and not be a self-centred bitch. I don't get it.

'Worst thing is she doesn't even know the whole truth. The soldiers threatened me and I freaked.' I ran my hand through my hair, tugging at the curls. 'Kat... I used my abilities.'

'Far out! Seriously? You bad-ass, you!'

I sighed, suppressing a smile that tried to push through my foul mood.

'They didn't know I was gone until I was already out the door and sprinting for home.'

Kat grinned and offered her hand for a high five. We slapped palms. She closed her fingers around mine and hauled me to my feet. We started walking through town. The streets had become a lot busier – people had finished work and were milling around, making their way to stores to pick up their food rations or meandering home.

'I can't believe you did that. You'll be in big doody if your mom finds out. Anyway you know it's just out of concern for you. Parents are paranoid. I'm surprised your parentals and mine are even okay with us being friends.' She raised her head and stuck her nose in the air, sniffing importantly. I laughed and gave her a squeeze, already feeling lighter. 'You know I don't give a shit about that class thing.'

'I've got just the cure for you. Remember I told you Seth and Nate were working on a way to do night raids?'

My ears perked up. 'Have they found a way out the city?'

Kat's face glowed with excitement. 'Yup – there's a hole in the city wall in between two of the guard posts. Seth and Nate are planning a trip out tonight. Want to join us?'

'Why not? While I'm already neck-deep in shit I might as well go all the way.'

'Awesome! Don't be late – timing is everything. Meet me at my place ten minutes before midnight.'

She walked me to my door and gave me a hard hug. 'See you tonight,' she murmured, then melted into the gathering darkness as the last light of the day seeped away.

***

I crept into the house, hoping to bypass Mom and Dad and get to my room without any further drama. I was already halfway down the passage when I heard them, their voices low and urgent. I hesitated. I didn't want to be caught, but why were they whispering?

I took two steps back, bringing them into my line of sight. Careful not to make a sound, I backed up another two steps, putting the wall separating the kitchen and the lounge between us.

'....do this?' Mom.

'Honey, there's nothing...' Dad's voice faded, as if he were leaning closer to Mom. Frustrated, I took another step.

'What if he finds out?'

'He's conducting these experiments...'

I still couldn't hear them properly. I knew another step would take me dangerously close to them. I sidled closer anyway.

'...doesn't mean she's in any more danger than before.'

I peered around the wall and through the doorway leading into the kitchen. Mom was in tears. I stared, unable to think of even one occasion I'd seen her cry.

'Why did he show us?' Her voice was thick with emotion. Dad ran a hand from the crown of her head to the small of her back.

'I don't know. But we'll be fine, we've been careful...'

His head snapped around, pinning me with his gaze. Caught, and not knowing what to do, I spun around and ran for my room. Their words ran through my head, spinning and bumping into each other, unable to coalesce into anything that made sense.

Chapter Five

Dominico

Kat blended so well into the night that it wasn't until I nearly tripped over her that I realised she was there. She was dressed in black from head to toe, her dark hair caught up in a ratty cap.

She grinned, her teeth stark against the olive of her skin.

'Right on time. Good thing you covered your hair or you'd be like a walking beacon.' I punched her arm, my other hand tugging at the black scarf I'd used to cover my head.

'Gee thanks. Cos it isn't a sore point or anything. Where are the guys?'

She tugged on my arm. 'They said they'd meet us at the boundary wall.'

I looked at her sharply. 'Isn't the boundary wall the worst place to meet? So close to the guard change?'

She rolled her eyes. 'Honestly Dom. You're starting to sound like your mother.' She gave my shoulders a squeeze. 'The guys have it figured out. They don't want to be caught any more than we do.'

We shuffled through the dark, making the turns and avoiding obstacles from memory. I held my breath without meaning to, releasing it again in noisy gusts that made Kat pinch me. Every tiny sound made us stop for moments that scared me so much I could feel my pulse jumping like a living thing under my skin. Excitement rushed through me until I felt drunk on it.

Finally we reached the boundary wall. Seth and Nate were leaning against it a few metres from the watchtower, trying to act casual. I couldn't see either of their faces clearly, but the air around them felt electric.

'About time, girls,' Nate drawled.

I tucked my hands into my armpits, despite the warmth of the night air. 'So where's the hole?'

'Eager, I see,' Nate said. 'I like it. But we won't be going through the hole – they discovered it this afternoon and closed it up.'

'What?' I snapped.

'Shhh!!' Seth hissed.

'Calm down, girlie.' Nate said. 'There's another way out. Let's go. Timing is everything.'

He led us along the wall, away from the watchtower. A feeling of dread started to eat at me. I had a decent sense of direction and I was pretty sure he was taking us towards the barracks.

'Are you crazy?' I hissed. 'We're going straight towards the soldiers.'

A hand landed on my shoulder. I jumped. Seth leaned close to me.

'Sorry. Listen, Nate knows what he's doing. He's been this way before. When the soldiers change over, there's about two minutes when the quarters are empty. The soldiers coming off duty give instructions to the new shift. We just have to have perfect timing, that's all.'

For some reason his words, meant to reassure me, freaked me out more. But I couldn't back out now. I had to go through with this. I'd been looking for a way to escape Toria, even for just a few hours. This was it. Swallowing hard, I pushed the feeling away. Kat's hand found mine in the dark. I latched on to it and allowed her to lead me.

The soldiers' quarters were deserted. It was so dark we had to move one in front of the other, our feet scuffing the old wood floor. Voices carried into the space through the open windows as soldiers moved closely around us. Nothing but walls kept us from being seen.

We stopped at a bunk identical to all the others. Nate squatted, motioning for us to do the same. At first I couldn't see anything. Tension made my body feel like lead. It blocked everything out except the dread of being caught. Then I saw it – a round latch.

'It swings inward, so we don't have to move the bunk. You'll need to feel your way down the ladder. We've got two minutes now. Quick!'

Before any of us could protest, Nate crawled under the bunk and pulled at the latch. A dull click sounded before the door swung inward. He lowered himself through the gap, disappearing into the dark.

Seth followed. Kat grinned at me before disappearing too. As I started to shimmy under the bunk, the voices outside became louder. They were at the door, heading inside. Taking a breath and holding it, I managed to slide beneath the bed. I slipped my feet through the hole and, without thinking about it, felt my way to the first rung.

'Close it,' Kat whispered from somewhere below me. I reached up and felt around until my hand closed around a handle. I pulled at it, closing us off from the light and sound of the quarters.

I made my way down the ladder, trying not to think how far down I needed to go, just concentrating on the placement of my feet and finding every rung. A circle of light appeared at my feet.

'Come on, nearly there.' Nate waved the cylindrical object in his hand, a beam of light bouncing crazily off the walls.

My feet connected with the ground. I wiped my hands on my jeans, trying not to show how shaky I felt. 'Is that a torch?'

Nate nodded, looking smug. 'One of the things I picked up from a raid. Batteries still work. It's one of the things I want to look for tonight. Need spares.'

Nate pointed the torch and the wavering beam lit a long passage.

'Where are we?' I asked.

'You'll see.'

We followed the passage for a short distance until we came to an open space. Nate shouted into the blackness, making me jump. His voice echoed, and then faded.

'Cool, huh?'

He trained the beam on the floor, revealing white lines on the ground, painted equal distances from each other. The paint was dull and flaking. He raised the torch and a huge thick pillar appeared in the dark. As we moved further in, several dark shapes revealed themselves. I gasped. I broke into a sprint until I reached one of the hulking forms. It was cold to the touch, hard and metallic. I ran my hand along its sleek lines. I wiped the front of it free of a thick layer of dust, revealing a panel of glass. It had metal protrusions, almost like ears. Moving around them, I realised they were mirrors.

'It's a car,' Nate said.

Kat glanced at me and we both rolled our eyes. 'We know,' she said.

Nate shrugged. 'Well, from the way you were staring... I figured this was your first time.'

'Of course I've seen one.' I tried to hold his gaze.

He raised an eyebrow at Seth and snickered.

My face felt hot. 'Okay fine. Only in books, from before.'

'Ah, don't feel bad.' Seth gave my shoulder a friendly slap. 'We've only seen one because we've been out of Toria a couple of times.'

'How many times have you done this?' Kat asked.

Nate shrugged. 'Maybe five or six. Need to get out of Toria sometimes. Too many stupid rules.'

I ran a hand along the car, until dirt caked my fingers and palm. Underneath, a dull red showed through, its colour coming off in tiny flecks.

Nate joined me, rubbing the window clean and dusting dirt off on his jeans. He pointed inside with the torch. 'See there? The key's inside. No point taking it out when no one can drive it.'

'Nate, we better keep going. We've still got a long way to go.' Something weird passed between Seth and Nate – a strange look, a moment loaded with something I didn't understand. Seth caught my expression and smiled, holding my gaze. I looked away, feeling oddly unsettled.

The boys led us down a slope that spiralled around twice before we finally came to the exit. We stepped out into the night air, bumping shoulders in our effort to stay close and use the light of the torch.

The only noise was the sound of our feet against the ground, and our breathing. The quiet was like a cloud that surrounded and kept pace with us. We trudged along for a few minutes, occasional gusts of warm night air touching our faces and trailing along our bare arms.

The buildings around us started to take shape. Gradually, without the help of the torch, I could make out several forms – untouched buildings surrounded by others with collapsing walls, kicked-in doors, smashed windows. The buildings gave way to homes – some still surrounded by brick walls and high fences, others with gates that sagged or gaps where gates must once have been. I noticed that we were leaving behind the office buildings and the crumbling structures that had once housed shops. I stopped, confused.

'Guys! Where are we going? All the good places are behind us, aren't they?'

Nate's voice floated through the darkness. He sounded irritated. 'Those shops were looted long ago. Obviously. They're closest to the city.'

I felt the colour rush to my face. Again. I glared at Nate's back, wondering why he had to be such a shit. Seth patted my shoulder sympathetically in passing. My cheeks burned hotter.

Kat threaded her arm through mine. 'Ignore him.'

'He's such a dick.'

'I know. You're really tense though. Why? We're too far from Toria to be caught.'

'It's not that. It's just –'

Nate interrupted us. 'Check it out. This is what we were looking for.' He motioned to a huge building. A door leaned drunkenly to the left. Inside, the blackness was so complete it looked almost solid.

Instead of moving inside, Seth sat on the edge of the pavement. Nate sank down beside him.

'Aren't we going in?' I asked.

Nate leaned back on his elbows. 'Just need a little rest. So...' He raised the torch to his chin, the beam of light travelling up his face and creating creepy shadows beneath his eyes. 'We've heard stories about you.'

I froze. My heart hitched and then heaved itself into a beat that pounded through me, like fists hitting me from the inside.

I tried to force my face into a bored expression. 'So?'

'Don't you want to know what we've heard?'

'No.' I pretended to stretch. 'Let's go inside.' I started to head for the lopsided door, too freaked out to look at Kat.

'We've heard you can do things. You know – *super*human things.'

My blood seemed to slow, clotting in my veins. My head felt unattached, like it had separated from my body and was floating above us.

Kat laughed, the sound high and fake. 'Where did you hear that? Honestly, Nate – do you really believe everything you hear?'

One look at Nate's face told me that, if he hadn't believed it before, Kat's reaction had changed his mind. His grin widened and his eyes sparked.

'Come on – show us. What can you do?'

I felt three pairs of eyes on me, catching and trapping me. Nate trained the torch beam on me. I didn't know if I should look at them or away – what was more likely to confirm their suspicions? I couldn't see Kat but her fear filled the space between us, her panic starting to catch.

I tried to laugh but it came out a strangled gargle. Someone moved and the beam bounced away to settle on Kat's face.

'You look pale, Kat. What's the matter?' Nate's voice was quiet. Threatening. I desperately wished I could see Seth; wished I could convince him to get Nate to back off.

Kat took my arm, about to march me away, but Nate was too quick. He stepped in front of us, his face so close his breath swept over me.

'Just show us, Dom. What's the big deal?'

Fury filled me. I planted both hands on his chest and pushed as hard as I could. He stumbled back a few steps, grunting.

'You little bitch!'

Before I could move he dropped his torch and grabbed my shoulder, using his other hand to yank the scarf from my head. He wrapped his fingers in my hair and pulled so hard tears came to my eyes. I shrieked and tried to break free, but his hand was entangled, close to my scalp. I tried to block out the pain, the fear. I tried to get myself to that place where I could free myself and protect Kat. But no matter how hard I tried, I couldn't get there.

Nate stumbled back, dragging me with him. I heard the dull thud of flesh on flesh and realised Kat had launched herself at him. Nate groaned. His grip loosened and Kat screamed, the sound ripping through me like a knife.

'Get your hands off me, Seth! Get off get off!'

Nate's grip tightened again and Seth's voice called out to us.

'Got her, Nate.' The torch beam rose as Seth handed it to Nate. He released me and trained the beam on Kat. Seth had one arm around her throat and the other around her waist.

Nate returned the light to my face. 'Try and run, and Seth will snap her pretty little neck. I'm bored with this now. Show us what you can do, or we'll kill her.'

Kat shook her head, frantic. 'No, Dom. Don't do it!'

I took a deep breath. It was just the four of us out here. If they tried to tell anyone else, it would be their word against ours. I had to get us out of this. It was my stupidity that got us here.

'Okay, okay, I'll do it. But just know that if you hurt her, I can kill you both, and I won't even have to get my hands dirty.'

Nate snorted. 'Let's see it.'

I paused to breathe. Slow, long breaths. My heartbeat settled and my pulse calmed to its normal rate. My mind began to clear. I would only have one shot at this. My mind blanked and I could feel the pull at my gut as I pushed outward, concentrating everything on Seth. I didn't notice the torch beam leave me until it was trained on Kat and him.

His arms dropped away. He flew backwards and fell flat on his back. Kat didn't hesitate. She sprinted away from him, grabbing my hand as she passed Nate. He seemed too stunned to stop us.

As I turned to follow her, I ran straight into a solid chest. Arms wrapped around me and lifted me off the ground. Kat's screams were abruptly cut off. I struggled to break the hold on me but my panic was too strong, too overpowering. I couldn't think straight, couldn't see through the fear that Kat was dead. Male voices surrounded us. I could hear the shuffle of what sounded like dozens of boots.

'Kat. Kat, are you ok? KAT!'

'Shut up girl, or I'll give you something to squeal about.' The voice was close to my ear. I recoiled in disgust, squirming to get free. The light from a torch swung around, its beam encircling Kat. Blood dripped from her temple, but her eyes, when they caught mine, were wide and fearful, and I felt relief flood me. She was alive. A moment ago, all I could see in my mind was her broken and lifeless body, an unloved doll used and tossed away.

Nate and Seth appeared out of the blackness, lit by the many burning torches held by the soldiers surrounding me. Nate strolled up to a nearby soldier. The man clapped him on the back, his lips peeling back in a grin.

'Well done, boy.' Seth stood beside Nate, eyes fixed on the ground. The soldier glanced at him.

'What's the matter with you? You did it. And looky here – we got her.'

Seth mumbled something I couldn't catch. The guard snorted, shaking his head in bewilderment.

'Nothing to feel bad about, son. She's a crime against nature. Too many of her kind running around and we can kiss the future goodbye.'

Seth finally looked at me. The apology in his eyes made me want to rip away from the soldier and tear at his face. I could get away from this, if I really tried. The walk back would take a while and give me the opportunity to centre myself. But a new fear had crept in – what had they done with Mom and Dad?

Chapter Six

Rogan

The girl was tiny. Her skin was so pale I expected to see the muscle and bone beneath. She was curled into a corner of her cell, her knees drawn up and her head resting on them. The clang of the cell door was loud, but she remained as she was, stiff and silent, refusing to acknowledge my presence. Looking at her, it was ridiculous to think of her as a threat. But four of my best men had described the same scene. Separated from him by several metres, she'd shoved the boy away from her friend, all without even raising her hand.

'Dominico, right?'

She said nothing. Didn't even look up.

I examined her for a moment, considering my options. 'Your friend is unharmed.'

At this, her head jerked up and she stared at me with eyes so full of relief I wondered for a paralysing moment if she was going to cry.

'What about my parents?' Her voice became strangled around the word 'parents'.

'That is something we can talk about later. Right now, I need to ask you some questions.'

Her chin rose a centimetre or two and her eyes hardened. Defiance. I felt an unexpected admiration for this girl. She couldn't be a day older than sixteen.

'If you want anything from me, you'll answer my question first.'

'I don't think you're in any position to negotiate.'

'What have I got to lose?'

'Your friend, for one thing. Kat, is it?'

Her bravado slipped. 'How do I know you won't kill her anyway?'

'You don't.'

She returned her head to her knees. I waited her out. Long minutes passed. I sat down on the wooden bench that ran the length of her cell. I leaned back against the wall and closed my eyes, making myself comfortable.

'Fine!' The word leaped out at me. I opened one eye and looked at her without bothering to lift my head.

She stared back at me.

I pushed away from the wall and stood.

'Good. I have six eyewitnesses that say you did something no human could do.'

'That's a statement, not a question.'

'Is it true?'

She held my gaze. 'Yes.'

'What did you do?'

'I pushed Seth away from Kat. Why are you asking me this? If you had six witnesses then you must know what happened.'

'I wanted you to tell me. You pushed him without touching him.'

She got up and leaned against the wall, folding her arms. 'So? Isn't that the difference between me and you, between me and everyone in this city? I can do things, *inexplicable* things.' I ignored her patronising tone.

'How did you become like this?'

'I didn't *become* like anything. I was born this way. I was a part of the group in that lab that was raided years ago.'

'But everyone in that lab was killed.'

She gave me a withering look. 'Clearly not.'

'How did you escape?'

She immediately clammed up. Her body seemed to fold into itself as she turned away and slumped back into her corner.

'Where are my parents?'

'Are they your parents?'

I expected more sarcasm. The answer to my question was obvious. No human could produce superhuman offspring.

She looked me in the eye. 'Of course they are.' I started at her reply. When a monster is described, you expect large gnashing teeth and claws sharp enough to slit you open from throat to gut. It was the picture Crane had painstakingly drawn. An enemy to fear and loathe. Looking at the girl before me, with her milk-white skin and flaming hair, it was impossible to reconcile that image with her.

'They're safe. They're being held in another cell.'

Until that moment, hope had clung to her, keeping her together. I watched as that hope slipped off her now, as though she had shrugged off a coat.

'I thought you'd be glad they were safe.'

'It's temporary.' I started to form a reply but she cut me off. The tears I had dreaded now filled her eyes and ran down her cheeks. Her chest heaved.

'Don't even try to lie to me. I know what will happen – they'll be executed! My mom told me so many times –'

She couldn't go on. She buried her face in her hands and let her grief take over. Her sobs filled the room. I waited her out, trying to keep my inward struggle off my face. Would I do the very thing to her that had shaped my life so irrevocably? Make her an orphan, if only for the short time between their deaths and her own? An unfamiliar feeling crept over me - a connection to her grief. I shook it off, silently berating myself.

She looked at me, her face wet with tears, nose running, eyes red. 'What about me?'

I didn't have to answer.

***

I stood outside President Crane's office. All I had to do was ask him, and confirm what I already knew. Maybe once I had heard his refusal, I'd be able to banish her face from my mind.

I raised a hand and knocked once. Nothing. I knocked again. Silence. I pushed the door open, expecting to see Crane's head bent over some document, too immersed to respond.

The room was empty. I started to back out. A thought niggled at me. If President Crane wasn't here, why wasn't his office locked?

Feeling uneasy at this uncharacteristic lack of security, I moved into the room. 'Sir?'

A neat stack of papers sat on his desk. I was so preoccupied by the sight of the pages – paper was so rare these days - that at first I didn't notice his office key sitting on top. I reached for it, my concern growing, and accidentally brushed the pile beneath it. The top sheet drifted to the floor. I sighed and bent to retrieve it. Straightening, I glanced down and my eye fell on its contents. It was a sketch of a body on a standard stretcher, identical to the ones we had in our hospitals for injured soldiers. It appeared to have been drawn in a laboratory, although I didn't recognise many of the instruments captured in the picture. It was precise, drawn in painstaking detail. I couldn't tell if the body was a corpse or a patient.

My eyes moved to the description written in a precise hand. *Specimen 1, Serum 3.*

Strange.

Without thinking, I lifted the sketch to see the page beneath.

The same handwriting, but this time an entire page was filled with it. I skimmed it, phrases springing out at me. I read the document once, twice. The third page contained four sketches, all close-ups. Deformities so severe it took me a moment to realise the subject had once been human. Sunken eyes in a grotesque, misshapen head. Twisted hands too large for its body. At the bottom of the page, one word was printed in neat block letters: TERMINATE.

I scrabbled for the other pages, revealing more sketches and extensive notes. I couldn't read them quickly enough. As I tried to get through them all, the pile seemed to grow instead of diminish. Finally I got to the bottom. A sketch of a corpse. Only this one wore a face I recognised. My heart paused in my chest and my breath billowed until it felt caught in my throat. I couldn't release it. Footsteps approached. I gathered the pages, my shaking hands making the paper crackle. In the silence, it sounded as loud as a gunshot. I managed to stack the pages, though the pile remained slightly askew. I dropped the key on top and reached the other side of the desk just as President Crane strode into the room.

'Rogan! What are you doing here?'

Did his eyes flicker past me to his desk? I couldn't tell.

I saluted. 'My apologies, Sir. I was concerned that your office was unlocked, and came in to investigate.'

He moved past me and slipped into his chair. 'Quite alright. There was a...disturbance. Did you need something?' He placed his hands on the pile of papers, closing a fist around his key. For a moment his eyes settled on the documents, and I felt beads of sweat form at my hairline. My hands itched to swipe at them.

The words I'd planned had deserted me.

'I just wanted to let you know that all the preparations for tomorrow's executions have been carried out.'

He paused. 'There's been a change in plan.'

'A change?'

He stood abruptly, hands disappearing behind his back. I knew they were folding into their habitual position of contemplation. 'The girl is pardoned from her execution. I want her to remain here in the city, and learn our way of life. She'll have limited freedom, of course.'

I blinked and shook my head, convinced I'd misunderstood. 'She won't be executed?' I resisted the urge to state the obvious. A superhuman, living here, went against every law he himself had passed.

Ignoring my stupidity, he went on. 'The officials she's been living with will receive no such reprieve. They are to be executed, as planned.' He looked at me. 'They must be an example of the consequences of disobedience. And a warning. The girl will be present at the executions.'

I remained where I stood, unable to form a coherent word.

'Is that understood?'

I forced my tongue to cooperate, my lips to form some kind of response.

'Yes, Sir.'

I saluted a second time and turned to leave.

'Rogan.'

I swallowed and forced my face into what I hoped was a neutral expression.

'Sir?'

He looked at me for a long moment, his eyes searching my face. I stared back, forcing my gaze to remain on his.

'Make sure everything goes smoothly tomorrow. No mistakes, you hear me?'

I dipped my head in acquiescence. 'Of course, Sir.'

***

The smartest thing to do would be to pretend I'd never seen those documents or sketches. If I could just blot them out of my mind and carry on with my ordered life, I'd be safe. But the rules I'd trusted and enforced now seemed to be nothing more than a farce. They were set up to blind us and keep us ignorant. The image of the soldier I had known and trained, dead on that stretcher, was seared into my memory. For the first time, I questioned the integrity of what I was doing. And who I was serving.

Even as I told myself to leave it alone, my feet took me to the prison block. I stood outside their adjoining cells. They looked beaten. I waved at the guards on duty.

'Take a break.' They snapped me a smart salute and moved off, no doubt relieved to be out of the dank misery of the cells.

The man rose from his bunk, eyes guarded. The woman stared at me with large dark eyes, grief stamped all over her face. Hope had deserted her.

Wordlessly I reached for the keys on my belt, selected one, and slotted it into the door of the woman's cell. I motioned her out. From the corner of my eye I saw the man tense.

The woman slipped past me into the hallway, making no move to run. I unlocked her husband's cell and waved her in. They exchanged a look of uncertainty.

'I understand you were both government officials?'

They seemed to jump at the sound of my voice, as if fearing I carried something contagious. Their distrust felt physical, like a punch to the gut. The force of it left me breathless.

Finally the woman spoke. 'Yes.' The word hung between us, a tremulous bridge of communication.

'Did you have access to classified files?'

They glanced at each other. An entire conversation seemed to pass between them.

Neither replied. I waited until the silence threatened to break me. 'Well?'

The man looked at me. Contempt was plainly written in his expression. He made no effort to hide it, nor his sarcasm when he finally opened his mouth.

'Gee – what a great opportunity to help you. Guess what? You're not getting a thing from either of us. Where is our daughter?'

That word. It passed so easily from his lips, as if he'd truly fathered her.

He moved to his wife as if to pull her to him, but before he could take a step, I closed the distance between us, grabbing the front of his grubby shirt and slamming him against the wall. The woman shrieked, her terror strident in the confines of the cell. Blackness was edging in, singing sweetly, wanting to pull me beneath the point where reason and logic disappeared. I leaned close, until we shared the same breath.

'Aren't you self-righteous? Especially for someone who's been harbouring one of those *creatures* right here in our city.' I hated myself in that moment. I was baiting him. More than that, I lacked the courage to admit, even to myself, that I was starting to see beyond what our president had instilled in us. That this enemy seemed very far from the monster he'd defined for us.

'Creature? Creature?' He threw himself against me, nearly knocking me over. I closed both hands around his throat, the blackness close to engulfing me completely.

He struggled against me, feet kicking wildly, trying to connect with my shins. His hands swiped at my face, but my thumbs against his windpipe weakened him. His face turned scarlet and then purple. He gurgled.

The woman clutched at my arm, trying to pull me away. 'Please! Please!'

I relaxed my grip. Her husband dropped to the floor, drawing huge, gasping breaths. She sank down beside him, her hands fluttering around him as if unsure where to land. I stood over them. My rage was still building. Flashes of the documents and pictures I'd seen churned through my mind, running on an endless reel.

'You will tell me every fucking detail you know, until I say we're done. You think you've got nothing more to lose? Try me. Tomorrow you can die quickly, or I can make sure your execution is one to remember.'

I hauled the man to his feet and shoved him onto his bunk. The woman followed without being asked, her arm slipping around her husband.

Reason was trying to force its way in. I pushed it back, burying it in the ugly folds of my temper.

'Did you have access to classified files?'

The woman gave her husband a squeeze. She looked directly at me. 'Yes.'

'Did you ever see any files that contained documents mentioning human experiments, or sketches of people with suspicious wounds?'

'Yes.'

One word. It was all it took to dismantle the world I had believed in, the one I had helped build.

'Soldiers, too?'

'Yes.'

'Why would he use soldiers?'

'They weren't suitable for conversions, but they proved useful material to work with.' Her words were heartless, but her face was full of the same conflicting emotions that churned within me. 'They were considered "unusable". They were too strong –'

'Too strong?'

'Yes, physically. Mentally too. Their refusal to obey orders without question, as humans, made them a threat. President Crane couldn't risk converting them and then being unable to control them.' She said this in a monotone, but her tears gave her away.

My throat felt painfully dry. I couldn't speak.

She searched my face. 'You don't get it, do you?'

Her husband interrupted. 'Crane wants to create an army. One that can defeat the superhuman race.'

I swallowed hard. 'That doesn't make sense. The only army that could defeat them would be –' I stopped, the picture forming. I finally got it. The one Crane had kept so well hidden.

'A superhuman one,' he finished.

I paced the cell. 'Crane hates superhumans. He thinks they're uncontrollable, beyond the laws of nature.'

'You saw the documents? The sketches?'

'Yes, but –'

'You don't trust your own eyes?'

Gone was the sarcasm. They looked at me with pity, seeing my inability to accept. The earth had shifted beneath me, turning everything inside out.

I clawed for my keys, returning the woman to her cell. She touched my arm, the contact shocking me. 'Our daughter?'

'She'll be there to watch your executions.' I glanced at the man, giving him the only thanks I could. 'She's been spared.'

I hurried out of the cells, glancing behind me in time to catch a glimpse of husband and wife, their hands clasped through the bars, weeping.

***

The girl looked up at my entrance. Her expression remained neutral. Her eyes followed my movements as I moved the bench outside her cell. Only once I'd sat did she look away, as if she felt safer with me off my feet.

'Come closer.'

She ignored me. She sat on the edge of her bunk, her torso turned towards the wall.

'I said, come closer.'

I hadn't meant to shout, but I was strained to the point of losing control.

She got to her feet, her face folded in an expression of insolence. She came to the cell door, her fingers closing around the bars in a gesture of defiance. She'd come closer than necessary, a pantomime of fearlessness.

I sprang to my feet and enclosed the fingers of her left hand in my fist. I held them loosely, an unspoken threat. She tried to jerk out of my grasp. I tightened my grip, grinding her knuckles together. She raised her gaze to mine. She remained silent, the only clue to her pain the line of sweat appearing on her forehead.

'Release yourself.'

'What?'

I spoke slowly, mockingly. 'Escape.'

I gradually tightened my fist. A few seconds more, and her fingers would break. I loathed myself for my tactics, but I had to see it for myself.

She glared at me, unmoved. The pain must've been excruciating but she didn't flinch, even for one moment. Her anger was so potent it overrode her pain and fear.

'Do it, or I'll break them.'

I could see her struggling to contain herself. I watched her face as several conflicting emotions pushed to the surface.

My hand was on fire. The skin burned as surely as if I'd thrust it into a raging inferno. My fist sprang open of its own accord and I stumbled back, my feet pin- wheeling beneath me. I landed on my rear, cursing.

I looked up at her. She was laughing soundlessly, tears running down her cheeks, her arms wrapped around her abdomen in a self-embrace. Not even the cradled hand against her chest dampened her hilarity.

There it was. The something I'd been waiting to see that would justify my actions. Even if only to myself.

Chapter Seven

Syra

Half a dozen possible recruits had arrived. All men. They were dusty and limp with exhaustion. Our soldiers looked as fresh as when they'd left. I shook my head, half amused and half dismayed at the soldiers' lack of empathy for the newcomers' limitations. I focused on each of them in turn. I circled them, examining them from every angle. One man waited out my scrutiny in silence, his quiet confidence impressing me. He carried that curious smell of his city – a mix of deeply ingrained dirt and suppressed desperation. He was tall and rangy and needed filling out. My eyes passed over the next man in line. The harsh drumbeat of his heart and the fine line of sweat above his lip contradicted his cocky smile. I looked over the other four, finding little that impressed me.

Draiken waited impatiently for me to finish. His tension was often close to the surface lately, and the slightest provocation caused him to explode. I knew he was nervous about the outcome of these transitions, but he tried to pass it off as general irritability. I wasn't fooled.

I nodded to him and he stepped forward, hands clasped behind his back. His presence made all six men take a mental step back, their sudden uncertainty springing up like a wall. It never failed to amuse me how humans reacted to Draiken. An instinctive fear.

He smiled broadly. It did nothing to set the men at ease. Opening his arms, he encompassed them as a group.

'Welcome! The fact that you are here and have made this decision to join us will be mutually beneficial. We want to do your transitions as soon as possible, so after a night of rest, we will begin tomorrow. You will all be assessed both physically and mentally, so we can classify you as a Minder, Physical or Dual.'

'What about what we were offered?' The man who'd withstood my scrutiny stepped forward.

Draiken's gaze swung to him, silently assessing him before answering. 'We offered food, boarding and safety. You are criminals, are you not? I would think avoiding execution would be enough of a reward.'

A second man stepped forward, his aggression impressive in the face of his opposition. 'We were promised things. Luxuries, rare items. Additional food and water.'

Draiken smiled. 'All of which you will receive.' Waving away any further questions, he motioned Ray forward. 'This is Ray. He'll take you to your sleeping places for the night.'

Before any of the men could protest further, Ray stepped forward and began to round up the men, leading them away to a residence that had been vacated to accommodate the newcomers. I watched them go with the same feeling of tension and dread I'd been carrying around since the start of this madness.

Draiken draped an arm around my shoulders and gave me a squeeze. 'Feeling any more confident about all this?'

'No. Not even a little bit.' I forced a breezy smile onto my face, trying to soften the force of my statement.

His smile remained intact, but something shifted in his demeanour. His body temperature seemed to cool, a projection of the true emotions he was trying to keep buried. 'When this all works out perfectly, you know I'm going to take a lot of pleasure in saying "I told you so"'.

'I will happily eat my words. With relish.' He laughed, the sound hard and hollow. It struck me then just how worried he was. It wasn't like him to be so unsure.

***

We had selected the convertors carefully. We tried to match them as closely as possible to their recipient – taking their natural human abilities strongly into account. There was the possibility of only one Dual – the quietly confident one. He was my convert. Another thing

Draiken had managed to coerce me into, despite my strong misgivings. I had tried protesting that I was a convert myself, that surely it was better for a born superhuman to do it. He waved my concerns aside. It annoyed me immensely that I couldn't say no to him.

The following day, we gathered the humans together. Only my convert looked refreshed. The others looked as I felt. As though they'd been up most of the night, sleep evading them.

Raven and the other convertors had taken their recipients to their homes, preferring to do the conversion in a familiar place. I led Evan into what passed for our lounge. I didn't feel comfortable closeting myself in a smaller space with him. Draiken was just outside our front door, claiming he was stationing himself close by should anything happen. His lack of confidence in me only fed my own feelings of inadequacy.

I stopped Evan in the middle of the room, and reached for his left hand. He had not said one word since arriving earlier this morning. I sensed no nervousness or fear in his silence. Instead, there was an eager readiness, as if he looked forward to shedding his previous life as a human.

'We've done one conversion before you, although I didn't do it myself. I'm sure results will vary from one person to another. You should expect some pain, and extreme exhaustion after it's done.'

He nodded, meeting my eyes. I clasped his hand in both of mine. I wasn't entirely clear on how to do the transfer. I breathed deeply, forcing all thoughts from my mind. I focused until I could feel the tell-tale throb in the pit of my stomach. It moved through my body rapidly, spiking my temperature and making my heart pound painfully quickly. Heat shot through my arms and into my hands. Evan yelped and tried to pull back. I tightened my grip on him. Something was happening. The heat seemed to slip from my body to his, leaving my skin icy. My heart seemed to pause mid-beat, as if time had ground to a halt.

Evan squirmed, then started to struggle violently. Pain shot through me – starting at our joined hands and pushing through me with such intensity I felt I was being cleaved in half. Black dots danced in front of my eyes, and a high buzzing filled my ears. My mind felt as though it were filling with clouds, dark and threatening. My grip on Evan felt abstract, as if my sense of touch had dimmed, as if I were slipping from my skin.

The buzzing faded, only to be replaced by a piercing whistle which sounded as if it was coming through a tunnel directly into my ears. My hand slipped from Evan's and I fell into the darkness, its velvet embrace welcoming.

***

Draiken's face swam into focus. His eyes bored into mine and then darted over my face. I tried to lift my hand to touch his cheek, but my arm wasn't responding. It felt heavy and clumsy.

'Don't try to move Sy. You're fine, but you need to rest.' He brushed a sweaty strand of hair from my face.

'What happened?'

'You blacked out.'

I tried to bring my elbows beneath me so I could sit up. They wouldn't hold me. I collapsed back against my pillow.

'What did I just say?'

'Sorry, sorry. What happened to Evan?'

'He's fine. Weak and exhausted, but he seems stable for now.'

I ran my tongue along the inside of my mouth. It felt furry and parched, like it was filled with sand.

'Thirsty.' He held a glass of water to my lips, tipping it only far enough for me to swallow tiny sips at a time.

After I had emptied half the glass, I waved his hand away. Nausea lodged in my throat. I breathed deeply, concentrating only on the rise and fall of my chest.

I looked up at Draiken. 'What happened with the other conversions?'

Something shifted in his expression. He moved away slightly, his grip on my hand loosening.

'Drake? What's wrong? Did something happen?'

He sighed. 'Four of the conversions were successful. Both the givers and the receivers are fine. They're all weak and shaky, but a day or two of rest should help with that. The other two... I don't know what to make of their symptoms. They're wild, and inexplicably strong. It took nearly six of us to contain each of them. We've confined them.'

The dread I had been struggling to fend off suddenly rose in me. Its heat seared through me, setting my skin on fire and pulsing through me, burning a path of seething embers along every nerve.

I licked my lips and tried to beat the panic back.

'What are we going to do with them?'

Drake shook his head. 'If they can't be controlled, they're useless to us. We don't have the time to find a way to calm them.'

I closed my eyes against the implication.

'This was what I was worried about. We can't predict the results, the reactions of the humans. We have to stop this Drake – too much can go wrong.'

'No. You promised you would see this through. Six conversions are hardly enough to draw any final conclusions. We need to see how the other two pan out.' He squeezed my hand. 'Please Sy.'

I pulled my hand from his, the effort making me lightheaded. 'I'm one of our strongest. Look at what happened to me. Do you honestly think everyone can survive a conversion? This isn't just about the humans. This is about our own kind too. You know what'll happen if there are any fatalities.'

Draiken stood, his expression taut. 'I'm seeing this through. And I know that at the end of this, you'll owe me an apology. This *will* work.'

He turned and stalked out.

***

I slipped in and out of consciousness. I couldn't tell if I was blacking out or simply falling asleep. A black veil seemed to cover me - leaden and suffocating. Shrugging it off felt impossible. I couldn't seem to wake, to get my eyes to open or my body to move. Occasionally I could hear voices, but I couldn't tell if they were real or imagined. They came from some distant place, echoing and distorted. Time meant nothing. My black and watery world was a tomb.

When I woke I was home, in my own bed. I managed to turn my head to look at the sleeping figure at my bedside. Ray stirred, then slowly opened his eyes, focusing on me.

His face split into a wide smile. 'You're awake. Thank heavens. We've all been worried about you.' He placed a huge hand on my forehead. 'Your fever's finally broken. You've been out for three days.'

I bolted upright. The room rocked and swayed.

'What?' I tried to shove the covers away. Ray pushed me back with gentle hands, looking exasperated. 'I've got strict instructions not to let you get up until you've rested for at least a day, and gotten some food down.'

'I've been resting for three days already, Ray.'

He shook his head. 'Just following orders. I do have other things to do besides play nursemaid to you. So don't make it any harder than it needs to be.' He waggled a finger at me.

I refused to lie down again. Ray sighed and helped prop me up with pillows. 'I want to talk to Draiken. I need to find out about the converts, if they're okay, if –'

The look on Ray's face stopped me cold. He busied himself arranging my blankets, avoiding my gaze. His usual cheer was gone.

'Ray. What's happened?'

'Draiken told me to call him when you came to. I'll go get him. He needs to tell you himself.'

As Ray rose to leave, Draiken appeared in the doorway. He looked terrible – his skin was so pale it looked translucent, the dark rings beneath his eyes stark in contrast. Ray placed a hand briefly on Draiken's shoulder in passing. Then he was gone. Draiken sank down next to me, his eyes cold, his posture one of defeat.

'Two of the human converts are dead. Kara's dead too. As soon as her human convert died...' He shook his head. 'Jade may soon follow.' He looked at me then, defiant. 'The men were too weak to survive the transition. We need healthier specimens.'

A coldness crept over me. I had known this would happen. Somewhere, deep in the recesses of my mind, this possibility had lurked. If I'd paid more attention, I would've known that it wasn't merely a possibility, but a certainty. My sense for the future had tried to warn me, but I had stifled it, too afraid to acknowledge it. Now we had three fatalities. A possible fourth. Blood on our hands.

Anger coursed through me, beating through my blood like a rabid animal.

'What about Kara? Was she too weak? She was one of us. She –'

His hand sliced through the air, cutting me off. 'Kara was an unforeseen loss. Unfortunate, but now we know to be more careful.'

'And Jade?'

He shrugged, his gaze fixed on his twitching hands.

I wanted to shake him. To rattle him until his teeth fell out of his mouth, until his bones loosened and collapsed and he longer looked like my brother. Maybe then I could look at him and not feel this raging resentment that had opened in me like a crater.

'We have to report this. The Elders need to know what happened.'

'I've already told them.'

'And?'

'And they have the same view I do – that it's too soon to tell, that we need to be more careful who we select.'

I watched him. Normally I could feel the bite of a lie before it came, but Draiken's face remained stony, his body showing none of the typical signs.

'But our ultimate law...it's against everything –'

'That's exactly what I'm trying to do, Sy. Why the hell would we be doing this if not for the preservation of our species?' I'm looking at this long term. As you would, if only you weren't -'

He looked me in the eye, without shifting or shuffling. Unrelenting.

'Why did she die, and not the others?'

'If I knew that, we wouldn't be having this conversation.'

'What's the link?'

'What?'

'There must be some kind of link, something we're missing.'

'All I know is, four of the transitions went smoothly – no upsets, no odd side effects or reactions. The other two, as you know, went haywire from the start. The only difference I can see is that Kara and her human died after a day.'

I stared at him. If Jade soon followed in the wake of her human convert, what did it mean? Had Kara died because her human had? Would they have survived if they'd made it past a day?

One day. Twenty-four hours. Was that the link?

Chapter Eight

Rogan

I didn't believe in higher forces. But when the orders came for me to escort the girl's caretakers from their cells to the public execution area, it felt like a higher being had played his hand. Now I had to play mine.

The girl had not been told the reason for her temporary liberation, as per President Crane's instructions. He didn't want her trying to escape when they took her from her cell. He seemed to think the less she knew beforehand, the better. It was precisely the kind of reasoning I'd been relying on.

A dozen soldiers had been assigned to escort the girl out. Timing was crucial – her parents were to be lined up for the firing squad by the time she was brought out.

I went to their cells alone. Several soldiers had offered to accompany me, in case the prisoners tried to escape, but I knew the man and woman would do anything to get one last glimpse of their daughter, even if it was only for a moment.

I accompanied the woman out first, securing her hands behind her back. I linked her ankles so they were pulled closely together, reducing her chance of escape. I did the same with her husband. Neither of them attempted resistance. They came quietly, as I knew they would.

I moved them out of the darkness of their cells into the bright morning sunshine. My hands encircled each of their arms. My eyes kept fixing on the knots that secured their wrists and ankles, pretending to check they were secure.

We reached the line of shooters too soon. I walked the man and woman down the ramp, lining them up against the wall, facing their executioners. My head felt heavy, my thoughts slow and nonsensical. I felt disconnected from myself. From what I was about to do.

Kat was tied to a chair set up on a higher platform. She was to be handed her sentence after the executions of the man and woman, but before the announcement that Dominico was pardoned. Dominico would be forced to watch her parents die, then her friend sentenced to a life of hard labour, with no hope of a reprieve. President Crane was seated behind Kat. I avoided his eyes, even as I felt them on me.

At first, I couldn't see her past the wall of soldiers. I heard the ominous clicks as the shooters cocked their guns, readying themselves. The soldiers escorting her parted, finally allowing her to see past them. At first, she didn't seem to understand what was happening. She looked around, her head flicking from side to side, taking everything in. Finally, her gaze landed on her parents. She stopped, causing the soldiers behind her to freeze. She remained rooted to the ground, unmoving. She looked as if she wanted to make a break from the soldiers, but then she caught sight of the firing squad. I wished I could see into her mind, know what she was thinking. A moment passed. She screamed. The sound seemed to carry in the open air, filling my ears until I could hear only her agony. The soldiers around her scattered. Their feet left the ground and they fell away from her in a wave, a mass of flailing limbs. Pandemonium broke out. The firing squad turned away, distracted by the noise.

All thought left me. I leaned down and yanked at the ropes binding the prisoners, first their hands, then their feet. My slipknot came undone with ease, the rope pooling on the ground. They both turned to me, their mouths open in shock. I leaned close.

'Run. Go to the soldier barracks. Under the bunk in the back right corner there's a hatch leading to an old lot. It's your only way out. I'll make sure your daughter gets out too. Go!'

They ran, disappearing into the heaving mass of bodies. I turned. I couldn't tell if anyone had seen me, but it hardly mattered. I would be held responsible for this either way. I looked towards the platform – as expected, President Crane had been rushed from the scene.

I couldn't see what was happening. Soldiers shouted over the noise, trying to restore calm. I pushed through the crowd, heedless of who I was shoving out of the way. I caught a glimpse of Dominico's hair. She was moving rapidly, in and out of my line of sight. To my horror, I realised she was heading toward Kat. Soldiers were surrounding the platform, closing in on her. Her parents appeared out of the crush of bodies. Her father swung at a nearby soldier, knocking him to the ground, reaching for his weapon. Her mother tried to get past, but another soldier grabbed her, pulling her against him and training his gun on her.

I changed direction and pushed my way to the platform. From where I stood, I had a brief view of Dominico. She loosened Kat's bindings, and heaved her out of the chair. It was only then that she looked up, and realised they were caught in a circle of soldiers and weapons. Her gaze swept over the crowd. She let out a cry of fear, and I knew she had spotted her parents. Weapons cocked, preparing to fire. There was no way I could reach her in time. I waited for the inevitable gunfire, but it never came. The soldiers stood, rooted to the spot. None of them moved, even as Dominico and Kat made their escape, even as her father shoved the soldier off him, taking his gun, even as her mother slipped away from the other soldier's grip. Only when they all disappeared through the doorway of the quarters were the soldiers able to break loose and careen after them. I watched them go. I felt numb with the enormity of what I had done. My choices came down to two – remain here and die, or escape.

Dominico

Everything passed in a blur. The shouts of the soldiers mixed with our screams. Their pounding footsteps blended into ours, until I couldn't tell if we had outrun them, or if they were close enough to reach out and grab us. I didn't turn around to look – I just kept running. Somehow we made it underneath the bunk and through the latched door, into the dark of the car storage space. We'd only gone a few steps when the door banged open. I turned and saw a soldier dropping down the ladder. Others were sure to follow.

I could barely see my hand in front of my face – Mom, Dad and Kat were vague moving shapes in the blackness. The only light came from the open trapdoor above. It threw one weak beam of sunlight into the darkness, leaving us running blindly into a freedom we couldn't yet see.

I placed my hands on the first human shape in front of me and pushed. 'Keep running. I'll try buy us some time.' I screamed the words, hoping they would hear me above the yelling of the soldiers and the pounding footsteps. Beams of light landed at my feet. In seconds they would find Mom, Dad and Kat in the darkness. I reached down deep, forcing all my focus inward. I concentrated on my breath. In, out. It surged out of me, but I was too late.

Guns fired, the sound deafening. A bullet whistled past me, so close that for a minute I wasn't sure if I'd been shot. I whipped around. In the crazy bouncing of the torch beams I couldn't make out what had happened, until my mother started to scream. *Dad?* I raced toward the sound of her voice. Footsteps closed in behind me. I tripped. I put my hands out just in time to break my fall. White-hot panic surged through me. Still on my hands and knees I turned, crawling back to what I had fallen over. My fingers found something hot and sticky. The smell filled my nose, heavy and metallic. I groped in the dark. Finally a beam of light fell on me. It wavered and then moved down – and my eyes fell to the liquid that covered my hands.

Kat lay on her front. Her body was punched through with bullet holes. Blood spread out in a steady stream around her. Mom kneeled beside me, Kat's blood painting her skin red as she gently rolled her over. Kat's eyes were blank.

Hands clamped around me, yanking me to my feet. More soldiers grabbed my mother. Vaguely, I heard Dad shouting, his rapid footsteps coming toward us.

A black cloud of fury filled me. A voice told me to catch it before it broke away, but it burst from me like a crazed animal. The soldiers holding me fell back. The hands on my mother dropped away as soldiers flew and landed several metres away, their feet clear off the ground. Dad appeared next to me, grabbing at my arm, trying to pull me away. But all I could see was Kat's lifeless body. All I could feel was the cooling of her blood on my hands. I tunnelled all my fury at the closest group of soldiers.

In my mind's eye, torch beams rose until every soldier was blinded by their brightness. Guns moved to shoulders. I pictured fingers tightening around triggers. It was only when I opened my eyes that I realised the soldiers were doing exactly what I'd pictured. Their guns were trained on each other.

'Domo – no.' Dad's voice was quiet, close to my ear. He took my hand, gently closing his fingers over mine, bringing me back from the edge. 'You've done enough now. We're safe. Let them go.'

He tugged at my hand, drawing me away. The group of soldiers stayed as they were, weapons still raised. I looked at Kat one last time, the vague outline of her body barely visible, and imagined her alive, trying to paint over the image of her broken body.

Syra

I stepped into the cool familiarity of our house, finally feeling myself again. I had been out of bed for three days, and it was only now that I felt ready to confront Draiken.

'Drake?'

'In here.'

I followed his voice to the kitchen, where he stood at the counter, slicing tomatoes.

He smiled stiffly. The tension between us since Kara's death was a new and uncomfortable feeling. Even as kids we had rarely fought. It pained me to see the wariness in his eyes, the taut set of his shoulders.

'We need to talk.'

He sighed irritably. 'What now, Sy? Haven't we already covered this?'

'You said you told the Elders.'

'Yes. And?'

'There's been no reaction from them? No consequences?'

I didn't want him to lie to me. I caught his eye and willed him to tell me the truth.

A beat of silence. 'No.'

I leaned against the wall, needing the support but also wanting to disguise my body language. I folded my arms.

'What?'

I waited. I had always been better at it than him.

He sighed and threw his hands up. 'Fine. I didn't tell the Elders.'

'No kidding.' My calm veneer was like the brittle shell of an egg. One tap, and it would splinter, pouring out my rage like the spill of the yolk.

'We've been over this. Kara's death was a freak accident. It's not going to happen again. I'll make sure of it.'

'What about Jade?'

He looked away, dropping his head.

'She's dead, isn't she?'

'Yes.'

I felt winded. My throat closed around my grief. I couldn't breathe.

'Their deaths are a tragedy. But two deaths can't mean the end of this.'

I finally caught my breath, fighting to keep my rage in check. 'Four deaths.'

'What?'

'There were four deaths, Drake. Not two. Human deaths count too.'

He waved a hand irritably. 'Don't give me your bleeding-heart crap again. You know what I meant.'

'You're letting your arrogance get the better of you. How can you make sure there are no more fatalities? It's impossible. And I just *love* how you've skipped over the part where you lied to me.'

Draiken banged his fist against the counter, the sound echoing painfully in my ears.

'Why do you think I lied to you? You fight me every step of the way. Why can't you just trust my judgement? This is going to work.'

I stared at him. 'You can't be serious. We can't take this risk. You know the Elders won't stand for it.'

'That's why I'm not telling them about Kara and Jade. Not until I have more recruits, and I can prove to them, and you, that their deaths are not a taste of what's to come.'

'You think they're going to take it lightly that you hid the truth from them?'

He dropped the knife and paced. His fury became a tangible thing between us, a wall thrown up that would keep me from getting through to him.

'Drake, please. I'm begging you. You promised me you would stop this if it proved to be too dangerous.'

He whipped around, his eyes bulging. 'Promised? You promised you would stick by me. That you would support me through this. And you've done nothing but get in my way. I don't give a fuck what the

Elders think. I'm going to do this, with or without your help. So just decide – in or out? Either way, I'm sticking to the plan.'

'Drake.' I knew it was hopeless, but I needed him to look at me. I needed to reach him.

When he finally did, his eyes were nearly black with rage. 'Don't do this. Please.' I reached for his hand.

His face went blank as he pulled away, cutting me off. 'One of us needs to be concerned about growing our numbers. Clearly, that's not you.'

I watched helplessly as he walked out. I couldn't reach him. It was done.

Chapter Nine

Rogan

For a long moment, I couldn't move. Soldiers disappeared through the doorway of the barracks, pursuing the escaped prisoners. So far, no one had thought to detain me. Even the soldiers from the firing squad had rushed into the thick of the crowd in an attempt to intercept the escapees. I knew it wouldn't last. The soldiers would reappear, and questions would be raised as to how my prisoners had gotten free of me. I forced my feet forward, moving against the hysteria of the crowd, heading toward the gates of the city. There was a slim chance the guards in the watchtower had been summoned to assist with the pursuit of the prisoners. Either that, or I hoped against hope they were just far enough away not to know anything about the incident yet.

It usually took me ten minutes. Today it felt like hours, trying not to run, trying to keep my footsteps steady. The watchtowers came into view. Two guards were stationed in each. Business as usual. Trying to calm the adrenalin pumping through me, I waved casually at the closest guard. He disappeared briefly and then reappeared at my side, snapping me a salute.

'Commander.'

'Open the gates.'

'Sir?'

'Open them.'

He hesitated. It was an unusual request. They had no prior orders or warning. The gates were generally only opened to admit visitors, and exile those being punished with banishment.

'Are you hard of hearing? Open the damn gates. Now!'

'Sir, yes Sir.' He whipped around and nearly fell over himself in his haste to obey.

The gates cranked open, the rusty squeal almost more than I could bear.

I walked out of Toria and into the dust and debris of The Waste. I turned back for a moment, my eyes moving over the home I would never return to. I looked at the guard. 'Close them.'

Without waiting for a reply, I strode out of the city, breaking into a sprint when I heard the final clang of the gates as they closed behind me.

Dominico

We ran until we couldn't move another inch. We took shelter in an abandoned building, making sure to climb some of the crumbling stairs, trying to put as much distance between us and the soldiers as we could. I slid down against a dusty wall, trying to slow my breathing, trying to push away my anger and grief. The moment played in my mind over and over – the gunshots, Kat's lifeless body, and her blank eyes. I gasped back a sob, knowing that now wasn't the time to fall apart. I had to keep it together. We had to get away.

Mom knelt beside me, her warm hands touching my face. I met her gaze. Her tears were gone. In their place was a steely expression, one I knew so well. She was putting away what had happened until we were out of range of the soldiers and every citizen of the home we had run from. Only then would it be time to let go.

'Honey? I know you're tired, but we need to keep moving.'

Dad joined us on the floor, one arm going around each of us. He hung his head for a moment, as if praying. When he looked up, his eyes were full of love and fear.

'They won't stop looking for us. Not until they think we're either dead or too far gone that we aren't worth tracking.'

'What about food? Water?'

I could tell from their expressions that they had been thinking the same thing.

Dad stood up. 'We'll find along the way, I'm sure. We'll manage.'

I always knew when Dad was lying. His left eye would twitch. He was lying for our sake, trying to keep us from thinking of dying of thirst or starvation. Deciding to humour him, I rose too, and looked out of the closest missing window. There were several buildings around us – most had rows of windows and were several storeys high. Dad had told me his father had worked in a building like them, a place where hundreds of people worked all at the same time. Not too far in the distance I could see what I was sure must once have been a shopping centre. I'd seen a picture of something similar in a book from school. It towered four stories high. I figured if we had any chance of finding supplies that would be our best bet.

I motioned to Mom and Dad to join me. 'Look. See that building? Maybe we should go there and see what we can find.'

They both nodded. 'Worth a shot,' Dad said. 'Let's get going. It won't be light for much longer.'

The shadows were starting to shift and grow. I glanced up at the sky and judged it to be late afternoon. Until now I'd been too focused on escaping to consider the other dangers of The Waste. Starvation and dehydration were just the start. There were other hungry things out here, creatures we'd been warned about in school. I'd always thought my teachers were lying or exaggerating– how could anything survive out here? But as the sun started its dip towards the horizon, I could imagine all too well the animals they had described in great detail.

We trudged back down the stairs and started the walk towards the centre. My feet felt too heavy to lift. Each step took such effort that, after only a few metres, I already felt exhausted. I kept my eyes fixed on Dad's back, telling myself that every step meant one less to go. I tried not to think about becoming a meal.

It wasn't until they were nearly at our backs that I realised they had found us.

I opened my mouth to scream, but a hand clamped over my mouth, pulling me backwards. I hit the dirt hard. The force of my fall vibrated up my spine and exploded in my head. The hand over my mouth shifted. I sunk my teeth into the fingers, biting down until I tasted blood. The soldier yelped and let go. I pushed myself to my feet, turning to see where Mom was. They already had her surrounded, their hands all over her, yanking her away. I turned again, looking for Dad. Three soldiers were crowding him. He was struggling violently, his hands flying at them, feet kicking. I had started in his direction when someone grabbed me from behind again, strong arms closing around me in an iron grip.

'Stop struggling,' a voice hissed close to my ear. 'Look.' A rough hand forced my chin up. One of the soldiers had a gun pressed against Dad's head. The other two grinned at me in the gathering darkness, teeth glinting in the fading light. My body went cold. 'Don't even think of using your voodoo shit to escape. If you do, your daddy's dead.'

Dad stared at me, his gaze locked on my face. He seemed to be memorising every detail, burning my features into his memory for safekeeping.

Then he drove his elbow into the stomach of the soldier holding him. The gun wavered, moving a few centimetres from his head. The soldier staggered. 'Domo, go! Do it!'

The stress was too much for me. I couldn't clear my mind, couldn't dig down deep enough. A moment passed. Then another. The time for escape was narrowing to a pinpoint, and still I couldn't move.

I looked at Dad. The other two soldiers had grabbed him again. The soldier he had elbowed was straightening, coughing roughly and raising his gun once more.

Somewhere behind me Mom was screaming, and the strange arms around me seemed to clamp tighter, squeezing the breath out of me.

I only had a second more, maybe two. I forced my focus inwards. Something flickered inside me – a tiny flame. I concentrated on it, willing it to grow. It burst out of me, but not far or strong enough. My focus was sloppy at best. I had only managed to free myself.

I wanted to throw myself at the soldiers' mercy. I wanted to give myself up. But one look at Dad and I knew he wouldn't allow it. If needed, he would provoke the soldier until they shot him, just to take the focus off me. I knew Mom would do the same. The only way I could hope to save them would be to abandon them. Indecision kept me glued in place. I couldn't tell if seconds or minutes had passed, but it wouldn't be much longer before someone grabbed me again. I couldn't understand why they didn't just shoot me, and get it over with.

'Domo! Move! He's coming!' Mom's scream drilled through me. My feet moved, breaking into a sprint. I raced past Dad, catching one last glimpse of his face. The soldier with the gun against Dad's head reached out to grab me, but his fingers only swept up my arm, snatching at air. Gunshots went off. The screams of both my parents followed me. I wanted to turn around. I wanted to look. Were they dead? Something passed by my face, nicking my cheek. It felt like someone had slashed me with a knife. Liquid flowed to my chin, sticky and warm. I kept running, crying so hard I could barely breathe.

Rogan

I was lost. Which was a ridiculous thought since I was in the thick of The Waste – of course I was lost. Buildings blurred together until they all looked just the same. I had walked out into this empty wasteland with nothing – no food, water or a change of clothes. I was still wearing my uniform, my old dress shoes. I knew very little of the layout of The Waste beyond the immediate borders of Toria. I should've known where the other human cities were – after all, I'd studied the maps with the routes often enough, in case of war. But I couldn't think clearly. My mind felt sluggish. The more I tried to picture the way to the closest city, to Reto, the less clear the route became. I was turned around, my bearings gone. Even if I found my way there, I worried it would be nothing more than an extension of The Waste. No one knew for sure if any other human cities remained. The ones marked on the maps were last sighted years ago.

I licked my lips. It was like scrubbing them with sand. My tongue was swollen and parched. My lips stung and burned. The sky was darkening, throwing off long shadows that confused my already clouded mind. The warmth of the day was disappearing rapidly, leaving a coolness that would soon turn icy. I needed to formulate a plan, but my brain refused to cooperate. It took all I had just to keep planting one foot in front of the other. I forced my head up, looking for a place to lie down and rest. Going on in the dark would be suicide.

I spied a building a few metres ahead. I hoped to find an area that was at least partially closed off, a barrier to protect me from the wind.

I wandered through the remnants of the crumbling structure. It was segregated into rooms with long inter-leading passages. In some of the rooms, desks and chairs dominated the space, covered in dust and grime. Most were missing pieces – legs or arms from the chairs, or whole sections of desks somehow broken off and taken by long-gone thieves.

Finally I found a room with a door still attached to its frame. All four walls were intact. It was a relief to be out of the open, hidden in the heart of the derelict building.

I scouted around a bit more, hoping to find bits of forgotten food, or a misplaced bottle of water. The place had been picked clean. I returned to my room and lay down on the filthy floor. I couldn't think about what would happen if I didn't find sustenance tomorrow, or the day after. I pushed the thought aside.

Chapter Ten

Syra

Kara and Jade's deaths were a lead weight that I trailed behind me everywhere I went. I felt torn between following the rules of our society and doing what I knew was right, or keeping what I knew a secret to protect Draiken. So far, no new recruits had arrived, but it wouldn't be long before more humans showed up and, when they did, they would be unknowingly offering themselves up as human sacrifices. Keeping these deaths to myself made me Draiken's accomplice, but no matter how much my conscience bothered me, reporting him to the Elders would be the ultimate betrayal. I had to keep pushing back the thought that he'd already betrayed me through his dishonesty. I rocked back and forth between hoping, and dreading, the moment when someone else would bring this tragedy to the notice of the Elders.

The atmosphere between Draiken and me was unbearable. I had tried everything– begging, reasoning, apologising. Nothing got through to him. Grovelling he simply ignored. Each time he brushed me off, my resentment grew. His refusal to even acknowledge my opinion had finally cooled my efforts to keep trying to reach him. Since then we had fallen into a mutual silence, the air between us clogged with unspoken anger. I was careful to steer clear of dipping into his mind. His aura of self-confinement was so thick it hung over him like a veil. I could read his thoughts without using my gift – he wore his feelings like a suit of armour.

I had avoided going into the training hall. Without saying so, I knew Draiken was relieved. I went about my other duties instead – checking on residents' health and wellbeing, running through security procedures with soldiers and addressing any issues that arose from communal living.

One afternoon, just as I was returning from visiting a sickly resident, I found Ray waiting at our door. He looked tense. His hands were tucked behind his back. As I passed him I saw that his fingers were twitching with nerves. The sharp tang of apprehension rose off him, filling my nose. When he finally met my gaze, his eyes were clouded with regret.

'The Elders want to see you.' He hesitated. 'They've called for Draiken too.'

Dread filled me. I knew what was coming. I nodded at Ray and smiled my thanks, trying to appear nonchalant.

Ray caught my arm as I tried to pass him. 'Sy. What's happened?'

I shook my head, trying to still the terror building inside me.

He turned me towards him, his free hand clasping my other arm. 'Talk to me. Maybe I can help.'

'There's nothing you can do. I don't want to implicate you in this. The less you know, the better.'

I gave his hand a squeeze before turning away.

I walked to the Elders' quarters, trying to keep my breath even and my mind calm. This was it. There was no way I could lie – even if I had wanted to.

Draiken was already there. I was surprised they wanted to question us together.

Azaiah rose from his place at the centre of the Elders' table.

'Let's begin.' He turned to Draiken, his gaze sharp and assessing. I could feel his sudden mistrust, his expectation that Draiken would try to worm his way out of this.

'Draiken – can you please relate to us the events of the day the conversions took place?'

For a long moment, he was silent. I could sense him organising his thoughts, trying to decide what to say. When he spoke, his voice was calm, his tone heavily laced with resentment.

'There's no need. You all know what happened. That's why we're here.' He looked at Azaiah, defiant. 'You all know Kara and Jade are dead.'

'Am I to assume then that you are putting aside your right to state your side of the story?'

'We did the conversions. Two of them went well. There were complications with the other two. A total of four fatalities: two of theirs, and two of ours. I stand by my conviction that it was an isolated incident and won't happen again.'

'The key issue is not that there was a fatality, although their deaths are a tragedy. The fact that concerns us greatly is that you hid the truth from us. Their deaths went unreported until it was mentioned to us in passing. It was assumed we already knew. You hid the truth from us deliberately, in order to continue with the conversions.'

Draiken didn't reply. His stony silence was enough.

Azaiah's gaze moved to me. 'Neither of you reported this death. As you both know, we take our position of authority very seriously. Our most important function is choosing the right leaders – leaders who have our society's best interests at heart, who are truthful and trustworthy. This hasn't proven to be the case with either of you. Because of this –'

Draiken stepped forward, steel in his gaze. 'I take full responsibility for this. I was the one who asked Syra to keep their deaths a secret. She did it for me. She isn't to be blamed.'

Every pair of eyes turned on me. 'Is this true?' Azaiah asked. I looked at Draiken pleadingly, but he refused to turn his head, his gaze fixed forward.

'It's true,' Draiken answered, without waiting for my reply. Azaiah was silent, deliberating. Then he waved us out of the room. 'Please give us a minute.'

We moved into the adjoining room. I forced myself to tune out. There was no point in listening in. I knew what their decision would be, and they would sense my intrusion.

Draiken moved to the other side of the room, as far away from me as the four walls would allow.

'Drake. You need to let me accept my part in this. Your punishment will be less severe. I did agree to it. That was my decision.'

For the first time in days, he looked directly at me. 'I coerced you into it. There's no point in both of us going down for this.'

I opened my mouth to protest but before I could say a word, we were called back in.

'We've reached a unanimous decision,' Azaiah said. 'Draiken, you are, as of today, relieved of all your leadership duties. You may remain in Jozenburg. But as a citizen.' I felt Draiken's shock as if it were my own. I closed my eyes, sorrow washing over me in waves.

'Syra, due to your smaller role in this deception, and because we feel you were put in a difficult position, your place of leadership remains. You are, however, on probation.' The Elders rose together. 'That is all.'

I touched Draiken's arm in an attempt to comfort him. His anger coursed close to the surface. Its heat pulsed beneath his skin. My palm burned. I cried out and yanked my hand back. His thoughts crowded into my mind, distorted and entangled. Images bled into one another, dark and indistinct. Draiken pushed me aside and strode from the room, leaving me with a feeling of dread so deep I was rooted in place by its intensity.

***

The drama of the day had left me drained. I couldn't think straight, and a migraine had begun its stealthy descent, starting at my forehead and creeping its way along until my head felt twice its normal size.

I expected to find Draiken home. Instead I was greeted by an ominous silence. I checked all the rooms, just in case. He wasn't there. The only sign that he'd been home at all was the mass of clothes heaped on the floor and spilling off the bed. I waded through the mess, my heart in my throat. I didn't know what I was looking for but something was urging me on. Draiken's room never looked like this. Had someone ransacked it? I shook my head. That didn't make any sense.

I turned in a full circle, my eyes travelling over the room. I couldn't tell if anything was missing. Draiken was up to something. The certainty lodged in my throat, cutting my breath short. I sprinted for the door, heading to the one place I was sure to find him – the scene of his humiliation.

Rogan

I had spent the entire morning following the cracked remains of what used to be a track for cars. Every now and then a sun-beaten sign would appear, keeping me on track. A night of sleep had cleared my head, and I had found my bearings again. My sense of direction had returned, and as I walked I passed the landmarks I had seen only as crosses on the map back home – the hulking skeleton of an abandoned fuel station, its name (*Engen*) bleached of all colour. Broken street lights lined the wide street, their glass casings and light bulbs long gone. I squinted at the faded signs on a street corner. The one I was on read Atterbury. The other was blank. Every letter had been obliterated by the sun.

A monstrous building rose a few blocks ahead of me. Its garish blues and yellows were washed out, the paint peeling in long strips. Balconies jutted out like teeth. A stained canopy-like structure shaded them, while slightly to the right, a globe-shaped object topped the structure, its previous white now a dirty shade of cream. I walked rapidly towards it, knowing from its odd structure that I was heading towards another landmark listed on the map – an old shopping centre.

I turned left at the next intersection, and found what I was looking for. Lois Street. According to what I remembered from the map, I should only be a kilometre or two from the gates of Reto. Assuming, of course, that there was a city in the first place.

Despite the throbbing pain in my legs and the dryness of my mouth and throat, I picked up my pace, imagining buckets of water and heaped plates of food. I shoved away the possibility that I would find nothing more than piles of rubble. I was so caught up in thoughts of my stomach that it took me a minute before I realised that not only had the gates of Reto appeared in front of me, but so had a man. He was just ahead of me, on the brink of reaching the city. I called out, all thought of survival overriding common sense. I sprinted towards him and the city gates, my relief and joy overwhelming my fatigue.

The man turned. When I opened my mouth to explain myself, I found him staring at me in shock. The guard at the gate was beckoning him forward, shouting something I couldn't quite catch. He ignored me completely. The man searched my face, and with a burgeoning sense of dread I began to back away.

The guard was still yelling, motioning frantically.

I finally got the picture. The man was a messenger. My uniform gave me away. Who else would be wandering The Waste this far from Toria, dressed the way I was?

I raised my hands in front of me, trying to appease the man. I couldn't believe this. I had been marked as a traitor. Hope of finding shelter and supplies vanished. If I walked into Reto, I would soon be walking out again, bound like a criminal and escorted back to Toria to face my execution.

The guard had left his post, cranking the city gates wide enough to slip through.

'Listen. No one will know if you just let me go. I'll just leave quietly, and you can pretend you never found me.'

'Enough!' The guard glanced behind him and said something to someone I couldn't see. I was sure he was sending for reinforcements. A belated thought occurred to me – I might actually have been better off staying and facing the firing squad. At least it would've been quick and not this slow, inevitable march towards death by starvation.

Shouts came from the watchtower. The man was focused on me now. He was inching his way around me, his arms spread wide, trying to block my escape. I lunged towards him, deliberately throwing my weight forward. We collapsed together, his feet kicking beneath me. He bucked wildly, nearly throwing me off. I shifted my weight until I sat on his thighs. I pinned his flailing wrists above his head with one hand, and landed a blow with the other. My knuckles merely grazed his cheek. He wriggled one wrist free and slammed the heel of his hand into my nose. Liquid warmth poured over my lips and chin. The pain bloomed behind my eyes, intense and distracting. I raised my hands instinctively, releasing his other hand. This time he punched me, the blow snapping my head back. He shoved me off him, springing to his feet.

I attempted to rise, but the man pushed me back, planting his foot on my chest and anchoring me to the ground.

I heard a familiar clang. I twisted around as much as my inert posture would allow. The gates of Reto were widening, spitting out a dozen soldiers.

I had only seconds to free myself and run. The man removed his foot warily. 'Get up. And don't try anything.'

I rose slowly, careful not to make any sudden movements. The soldiers encircled me, guns raised. The man stepped back, folding his arms with satisfaction. I felt like an animal caught in a trap. The more I struggled, the more my situation would worsen.

'I don't know who you think I am, but there's been a mistake.' I directed my words at the soldier standing closest to my right shoulder. He had an air of authority.

His gaze shifted to me briefly. 'That's about as likely as a flood. People don't wander The Waste for fun.'

'You.' He pointed at the man. 'Your job here is done. Return to your city and tell your president we'll be delivering this rat shortly.'

The man opened his mouth, his features deepening into a scowl.

'Get!' the soldier yelled.

The man turned and stomped away.

The soldier motioned at me with his gun. 'Move. We're taking you in until we can get some men together to return you. There's a generous price on your head.' He looked me up and down. 'What did you do, anyway?'

'This is mistaken identity.' Perhaps if I stuck to my story, he'd begin to doubt himself.

'If you tell President Crane you're bringing...' I trailed off, realising my error too late. The soldier's teeth gleamed as he grinned at me. 'Not too bright, this one.' His men laughed. I couldn't believe my stupidity.

He prodded me with his weapon. 'Let's go.'

I refused to move, stalling for time. I tried to quell the panic rising in me. Once they got me within the confines of Reto, escape would be impossible. Out in the open, I had a chance.

I pretended to submit and turned back toward the gates of the city. The soldiers moved around me, but not as closely as before. They seemed confident of my compliance. The head soldier turned his back to me, taking the lead. I calculated carefully. I was at least a head taller, and several kilograms heavier than him. I stepped forward and pretended to stumble. I fell against the head soldier and slipped my arms around his throat, using his body as a shield as I turned to face his men. He tried to raise his gun but the angle was wrong. He wouldn't be able to take a shot without the risk of injuring himself as well. His men reacted instantly. They raised their guns and loaded them. I found myself staring down the barrels of half a dozen weapons.

'There's no way you can get a clean shot. If you try, I'll kill him.'

I tightened my hold on the head soldier's throat. He gargled a little. It had the desired effect. Every soldier reluctantly lowered his gun.

I put my mouth close to my victim's ear. 'Give me your weapon. Now.' I unwound my left arm from around his throat. 'Do it slowly.'

He did as I asked. I kept my eyes on the soldiers around us, searching for any sign of possible insurgence. I took the gun and pressed it against his temple. 'Now I want all of you to walk back into your city. If none of you tries anything, I'll release him. Move!'

They shuffled into a tight group and marched towards the mouth of Reto. I watched them go, my pulse throbbing in my ears like a wound. Nearly there. They disappeared through the gates. I knew it wouldn't be long before they sent for reinforcements, and this time they wouldn't be so obvious as to charge me directly.

I stepped back from the soldier, both hands wrapped around his gun. 'Now you. Get going. If anyone follows me, I won't come easily. I'll kill as many of your men as I can. You understand?'

He nodded. I gave him a push, and he strode away from me. He'd only gone a few paces before he broke into a sprint. Within seconds he was gone.

I turned away from Reto and ran in the opposite direction. The next human city was at least a four-hour walk away, if I could find the old highway. It could take longer if I took a less direct route. But whatever route I took, I knew I was sure to be followed.

I ran until I was out of sight of the watchtowers. I stopped and bent over, my hands on my thighs, my breath coming in sharp bursts. Being a commander was more about planning than being a part of the action. I wasn't as fit as my own foot-soldiers. I was paying for it now. I straightened, recalising I'd dropped the soldier's weapon somewhere along the way. I cursed under my breath. No recovering it now.

I closed my eyes and tried to picture the map again. Tried to find the path that would lead me to the highway. There was no reason to assume that the other human cities weren't alive and functioning much as Reto was. Other messengers may have been sent. But I was out of options. Even if I could only get in and out long enough to stock up on supplies, that would be good enough for now. I couldn't think too far ahead. I had to take one moment at a time.

I straightened and continued in my chosen direction. Relief was flooding through me, making my knees feel like rubber. I hadn't gone more than a few steps when the sensation of being watched came over me. I turned. A figure stood some distance away, a hand shading his eyes. He let out a yell and started in my direction, feet kicking up dirt behind him. The messenger.

I ran. I headed towards a nearby multi-level building. I came to a skidding halt in the doorway, searching for a way deeper into the building. I needed to get higher – surely there was something, some kind of stepped structure which would make this possible? I sprinted to the left, but rounded the corner to find nothing but a heap of shattered timber that may have once been a desk. I raced back the way I'd come, knowing I had mere seconds before the messenger appeared ahead of me. I doubted he was alone.

Finally, I stumbled across what I was looking for. Stairs. Reaching the top, I darted towards the first door I saw. I yanked on the handle, but incredibly, it was locked. I could hear footsteps coming up behind me. I raced to the next door, my hands slippery with sweat and blood still dribbling from my face. I fumbled with the circular knob, but it slipped against my palm. The footsteps grew louder. I gave the knob a savage twist and threw myself against the door. It sprang open. I stumbled into the room, waving my arms in a frantic effort to keep from sprawling to the floor. Spotting a desk, I dropped behind it, peering through a gap in the rotting wood. A pair of feet appeared at the doorway, paused, and then moved on. Where were the soldiers? I stayed where I was, my head cocked, listening for the arrival of a possible entourage. Nothing.

Just as I was about to rise, I heard a soft crunch. I stayed crouched down and took a careful step back, hoping I wouldn't step on any rubble. I moved until I was on the other side of the desk, inching away from where I had heard the footstep. I peered around the corner of the desk. The messenger stood less than five metres away, his gaze circling the room. He was alone.

I darted out of my hiding place and threw myself at him. We crashed to the floor, his body beneath mine. I straddled his chest, his arms caught beneath my knees. Only then did I notice the pistol in his right hand. He bucked beneath me, trying to throw me off. He screamed for help. I clamped a hand over his mouth and reached for the gun at the same time. As my fingers brushed the butt of the pistol, his lips opened beneath my hand and his teeth sank into the soft flesh of my palm. I yanked my hand away, and, taking advantage of the diversion, he raised the gun and landed a glancing blow on my temple. I rolled off him, my hand throbbing and a trickle of warmth running from my head. He sprang to his feet, the muzzle of the pistol trained on me. He let out a laugh, near-hysteria evident in its pitch.

'Got you now, don't I commander Rogan?'

I studied his face for a moment, trying to place him. I was confident he wouldn't shoot me. President Crane would have his head. Besides, I was a fine prize to bring back.

He motioned with the gun, never taking his eyes off me. 'On your feet. We've got some trekking to do.'

I glanced over his shoulder, certain that at any moment soldiers would pour in behind him. He followed my gaze.

'After how that soldier treated me, he can forget it. I'm taking you in myself. Now I get all the glory.' He grinned, displaying yellowed teeth. 'Get up. Gotta get going.'

I didn't move. I wanted to enrage him, provoke him into doing something foolish.

'Hey buddy, you deaf? Get up.'

I deliberately raised my middle finger, looking him right in the eye.

He bellowed and clawed at my arm, trying to heave me to my feet. The gun wavered off target. I closed my hand around his forearm and yanked. I head-butted him hard enough to see stars. He went down, yelling the whole way. I went for his gun a second time, trying to pry it from his fist. It jerked dangerously between us. His finger found the trigger and a shot fired just past my head, the bullet leaving a hole in the ceiling as it tore through.

He shook my hand off and brought the gun between us in a slow, lethal arc. I closed both my fists around his grip, halting its progress toward me. We struggled, each of us trying to overpower the other. Gradually I started to overcome him, and the gun started to travel down toward him. He struggled beneath me, trying to raise a leg high enough to throw me off. His finger curled around the trigger just as I managed to lever the gun beneath his chin. I wanted to shout a warning, but before the words could leave my throat the gun went off, and he went slack beneath me.

Chapter Eleven

Syra

My sixth sense was screaming at me. Something had happened. I ran to the Elders' quarters, ignoring the stares and occasional questions of those I passed. I threw open the door and stumbled inside, yelling Draiken's name. The silence scared me even more. I moved through the rooms, pushing back the voice inside me that told me what I already knew – Drake was gone.

I found the Elders in the meeting room. Azaiah was propped up in his chair, head lolling forward, chin resting on his chest. I lifted his head carefully. His eyes stared through me. His neck was broken. I jerked my hand away and stumbled back, horror gurgling in my throat. It grew like a tumour, filling me until I was choking on it. I sank to the floor, trying to force air into my lungs. Threatening clouds gathered at the edge of my vision. Breathe! I sucked air through my mouth, gasping. Gradually the clouds retreated, leaving me weak and shaking.

I breathed slowly, in through my nose, out through my mouth. I forced myself to concentrate only on this task – in, out. Only when I felt steady enough did I rise.

The other six Elders lay scattered about the room, as if they'd been hunted down, one at a time, as they'd tried to escape their doom. I circled the room. Zeke lay face up, his eyes wide and vacant. Bruises bloomed on his throat, a perfect imprint of fingers. I kissed the index and middle finger of my left hand, and pressed it to his forehead. Our final farewell. The others had suffered similar fates. I sank down beside each in turn, my fingers trembling as I pressed them to each forehead. I knew they were dead. Still, I checked their pulses, hoping for a murmur of life. I circled back to Azaiah and sank beside him. I touched his cheek, his skin already cooling. My body convulsed with dry sobs. I couldn't produce a single tear.

I wanted to scream Drake's name but I could only manage a croak. He hadn't done this alone. There would be others missing. He would've tried to convince the best of them to follow him. I didn't know where he was planning to go, or how he was planning to survive, but I knew that we were now on opposing sides. He had deliberately put us against each other, leaving me to deal with his crimes. My own brother. My only family. Finally the tears came. I allowed myself to come apart, one molecule at a time, until I had completely unravelled.

I stayed on my knees until the cold of the floor and the pain of staying hunched finally drove me to my feet. I wiped my face and ran my fingers through my hair, my mind clearing. I left the quarters and made my way to the closest watchtower. Karl was on duty. I motioned for him to come down. His smile of greeting left his face as soon as he got close.

'Syra, what's wrong?'

'I need you and all the other soldiers currently on watch duty to gather everyone in the training hall. Every single citizen.'

'But what about our posts?'

'Trust me, the worst that can happen, already has. Please do as I say. I want everyone assembled within the hour.'

I walked to the training hall, rounding up citizens as I did. I could feel their unspoken questions burning into my back as I hurried them along.

Gradually, the training hall filled. It would be a tight fit, but I needed everyone contained in one space when I broke the news.

Finally Karl appeared at the door, and nodded to me.

I was standing in the central training ring. I raised my hands for quiet.

'I know you're all wondering what's going on. Before I tell you, I need you to know something – I will get us through this. But you're going to have to trust me.'

A ripple of whispers travelled the room. Their fear and anxiety clung to me, filling my lungs and entering my bloodstream, becoming my own.

'The Elders are dead.'

The room erupted. I raised my hands again, but no one paid any attention. I tried to yell over the chaos, but I couldn't get my voice to rise above the din. My ears rang with the feverish panic of the room. Their voices filled me up until I couldn't distinguish between spoken conversations and private thoughts. Every syllable was like a knife between my ears. The reek of fear filled my nose and throat until I couldn't breathe without drawing the noxious scent further into my lungs.

Ray appeared out of the crush and joined me in the training ring. His face was twisted with unspoken grief. He gave my arm a brief squeeze and then drew an enormous breath.

'QUIET!'

Immediately all conversation stopped. Every pair of eyes fastened on the two of us. Ray glanced at me. I nodded my appreciation.

'I know this is very upsetting news. But I need quiet and cooperation if we're going to get through this together.'

I started to pace the length of the ring. 'At this point, it seems Draiken is missing.' A low hum of shock travelled the room. 'I don't know if he's the only one, or if others are gone too. I need your help. We need to account for everyone. I need every household to gather together, and report to me or Ray if any member is missing.'

A hand waved at me from the middle of the group. 'Yes?'

One of the Minders, Tarell, stepped forward. 'Who killed the Elders?'

Dishonesty wasn't something that came naturally to me. I could read minds. I didn't live in a world where lying really existed. At least not for me. But in that moment, even though I knew the truth, I couldn't offer it.

'I don't know. Right now, I just want to make sure that no one else is missing. Can every household –'

'Was it Draiken?'

I forced myself to breathe. 'I don't want to jump to any conclusions just yet. Not until we account for everyone.'

Tarell opened her mouth to say more, but the look on my face made her shut it again. I was the only official leader left. Even if I were replaced, right now I was the only link left to our old order, to what we had known. She stepped back and started to gather the members of her household. The others followed suit.

Dominico

I had no sense of where I was going. The buildings meshed together into a mass of stone and brick. The broken streets had no signs – and when they did, the names made no sense. I felt as if I'd been going uphill for kilometres, with no descent in sight. The dust and dirt of The Waste closed in on me, a capsule of heat and desert. I thought of the stories. The ones about the existence of other human cities. But even if I had known how to find them, going to any of them wasn't an option. It would be easy to die out here – all I had to do was give up. I felt my guilt like a weight on my back, and it got heavier with every step, every metre I put between myself and Mom and Dad. Were they dead? Had those shots been aimed at them? I had been too much of a coward to turn around and look. I couldn't take the risk that I would have to add the images of their dead bodies to the one I already had of Kat's.

I wasn't sleeping. Closing my eyes and drifting off meant nightmares, and they were so vivid that, even when I woke up, I could feel the spatter of their blood, see the neat hole of the bullet, the blank glaze of their eyes.

I had no choice but to try and find the superhuman city. I had made a deal with myself. I would try to reach it, and that was all. I was one of them. Surely they would take me in? If they didn't, if they shot me on sight, then that was that. I would either die by the bullet, or I would die out here. If I somehow managed to live through this, I would try to go on. But my chances of survival were so minimal I hardly gave living beyond this day, this hour, any thought at all.

It was my second day out here. The towering buildings and fractured tracks made little impression on me. I just kept plodding, one foot in front of the other. My mind was too full of what had happened to pay much attention to where I was going, or the throbbing pain in my feet. The relentless burn of my throat and the cramps in my stomach got worse until I had to stop and rest.

I curled into a ball beneath the shade of a huge blue and yellow building, a small puff of dust rising and tickling my nose as I curled my knees to my chest. I closed my eyes, willing myself back in time, picturing the cramped warmth of our kitchen, seeing the curve of Dad's smile and hearing the pretty lilt of Mom's laugh. I held onto them, hoping the memories would leave no room for nightmares.

***

I opened my eyes. Someone was shaking me awake, and in that moment between sleeping and waking I forgot the shootings. I expected to find Mom standing over me, her smile wrapping me in warmth. Instead, a vaguely familiar face came into focus. I cried out and jumped to my feet, my hands raised in defence.

'Hey, take it easy. It's Rogan. Remember me?'

Gradually the fug of sleep lifted until I could place him. The commander.

I dropped my hands warily. I didn't know what to expect. Mom and Dad had told me he had helped them escape, but maybe his moment of empathy had worn off. He could very well be here to frogmarch me back to Toria.

'I'm not going to hurt you.' He offered me a sad smile. 'We're in the same boat, you and I.' I wasn't really listening. I was too busy watching his hand dip into a backpack and pull out what looked very much like a package of bread. When his hand came out a second time holding a bottle of water, I had to stop myself from tackling him to the ground.

He opened the package and broke the bread in half, offering it to me. I hadn't eaten for more than a day. Still, I held back, eyeing him suspiciously.

'It's unlikely we'll find food again while we're out here. Eat. I might not be so generous in another day or two.'

I snatched the bread from his fingers and stuffed a huge piece into my mouth. I had barely swallowed before I crammed in the second chunk. In seconds my share was gone. I wanted to cry at how little it was. All it had really done was get my stomach juices flowing. Rogan made no comment at my greediness. He ate his portion slowly and deliberately, then handed me the precious bottle of water.

'Go easy, okay? If you drink too quickly you'll only throw it up again. We can't afford to waste any.'

I took the bottle and forced myself to take small sips, even though all I wanted to do was pour its entire contents down my throat. I handed it back to him.

'Where did you get this?'

For a moment he looked weirdly guilty. He waved a hand.

'Never you mind. Got some dried fruit too, but I think we'll save that for later. Don't know how long we'll be out here.'

'Why do you keep saying "we"?'

'Because I'm including you.'

I folded my arms. 'Why?'

'It would be a waste of my efforts to let you die out here when I risked my neck to save you, don't you think?'

I looked away. 'I didn't ask you to do that. I still don't know why you helped us.'

'Speaking of which: where are your parents?'

The sudden boulder of grief in my throat made it hard to talk. 'The soldiers caught us. My dad started fighting back. The only way I could save them was to run.'

'Are they dead?' His question was gentle, sympathetic. I couldn't bear the look of pity on his face.

'Probably. No reason to keep them alive, right?'

He reached out a hand to touch my shoulder but I jerked away from him. Before I could think about it I threw myself at him, beating his chest with my fists, hot tears running down my face, screaming nonsense. He didn't fight back. He didn't push me away. He stood silently and took it, absorbing my rage without flinching.

I slowed and then stopped, like a battery run flat. I felt hollow, my grief poured out into the dirt. I sank to my knees, my back pressed against the wall of the building. I pressed my palms against my closed lids, hard enough to produce patterns in the dark. I opened my eyes, tilting my head back to follow the line of the wall. From where I sat, I could see the globe that sat at the very top. A gentle breeze sprang up, drying my tears and stirring a small dust storm.

'I'm sorry. Really. For my part in this, and so much more.'

I swiped a hand across my face. 'So you ran. Just like us.'

'It was that or execution. How's that for irony?'

A small smile found its way through my tears.

'What's your plan, exactly?'

'Funny, I was going to ask you the same thing.'

I shrugged. 'It doesn't matter. I thought of finding Jozenburg, but I'll probably be dead before then.'

'Jozenburg is the best option. I was heading there myself, in the hopes that I would find you along the way.'

'What for?'

'You're my ticket in.'

I scowled. 'So you're not feeding me out of the kindness of your heart?'

He smiled. 'What difference does it make what my motives are? This way we both get to survive.'

'What makes you so sure they'll even want me, never mind you?'

'They need numbers. You're one of them. Pretty logical they would take you in.'

'And if they refuse you?'

'Then there's always plan B. Let's go. The old highway isn't far from here and that's our most direct route to Jozenburg.'

'Who said I want to actually get there? And that I want to go with you? Once again I didn't ask for your help.'

His face darkened. 'You know, some gratitude would be nice.'

'My parents are dead. Kat's dead. I have no one left! What exactly should I be grateful for?'

He grabbed my arm and yanked me towards him. 'I don't need this. You're alive. Your parents were dead anyway. Kat might not have been in front of the execution squad, but her life wouldn't have been worth living. Labour camp would've broken her in a matter of months. They all died protecting you. That's something to live for, whether you see it now or not.'

He loosened his grip. 'See that there?' He pointed left, indicating a disintegrating track that looped out of sight. 'That'll take us to the highway. You see those?' He waved at the buildings around us. 'Every one of those means shelter for us. But we're not the only ones out here. Other things live here, and every building you see is a place for them to hide.

'Now you can either walk on your own, or I can help you along. Either way, you're going.'

Syra

Draiken hadn't gone alone. So far, we'd discovered that nine others were missing. Among them were Minders, which explained how they'd got past the watchtowers without being seen. I didn't know how Draiken had persuaded them to go with him, or if he'd even needed to, but he had managed to lure away half a dozen of our best. The two newly converted humans were gone too, along with Trey.

It took two hours for all the households to tally their numbers and report back. The number of missing had remained at nine – ten including Draiken. I had to keep a tight hold on the panic that flitted just beneath the surface. Once it got out, it wouldn't be long before everyone caught it, like an outbreak of the plague.

I stood in the training ring once more. This time there were no conversations, no shifting of feet. Every individual was focused on me, waiting for direction, instructions and comfort.

'Thank you for all your feedback. By my count, we are missing a total of ten. I would like all of you to think about our action going forward, whether you want to retrieve your loved ones, or if we should give them a little time. See if they return to us on their own. I would like all your thoughts and suggestions.'

A low murmur travelled the hall. I caught Tarell's expression. Her face was white and pinched. One of the missing was her partner. I glanced at Ray, seeking comfort in the familiarity of his face. But his grief at Drake's betrayal was a mirror image of my own. I looked away and cleared my throat.

'In the meantime, I need us to do a formal vote for leadership. I would like to suggest that Ray be promoted to second in command. If you are happy with this, and with me as first, you can cast your vote accordingly. If not, please make your suggestions for new leaders.'

I motioned Raven forward. 'Raven has already set up a voting station of sorts just outside the training hall. We've managed to scrounge up one notebook and a pen. Just write the name of who you are voting for. Please include two names.'

Raven waved her hands for the crowd to follow her, and immediately a disorderly queue formed.

Ray was waiting as I climbed out of the training ring.

'Let's talk while the others vote. We have a few minutes.'

Ray nodded and followed me out of the hall. We walked until we were some distance from the others, then Ray turned to me, his face troubled.

'Look, I'm honoured that you've shown such confidence in me, really, but I don't think I'm ready for this.'

Despite my weariness and the deep, bone-aching sadness I felt at Draiken's betrayal, I smiled. 'Don't get ahead of yourself now. The votes haven't been cast yet. They may decide we'll make useless leaders.'

Ray didn't return my smile. 'Are we really going to do this? Leave it up to the masses to decide on their leadership? Especially in light of what's happened?'

'It's democracy, Ray. We've always chosen our own leaders.'

'Yes, but under the guidance of the Elders. Never like this.'

'I know. But things have changed. Our choices are more... limited now. You're the only one I trust as much as I trusted Drake.' I swallowed against the grief clotting my throat. 'The Elders were formed over time and with careful consideration. We can't replace them in a matter of days. If we replace them at all.'

'Still - why me?'

'Fishing for compliments?'

A shadow of a smile crossed his face. He touched my arm. 'You weren't to know. None of us could've seen this coming. Not even you.'

'Not much of a gift if it doesn't help me see this kind of thing before it happens.'

'If we're voted in together, then I'll accept the position. But I'm not taking up leadership if it's not with you.'

'Fair enough.'

I glanced back towards the training hall. The line was dwindling. 'Time for us to do our bit for democracy.'

I couldn't say with absolute certainty if I wanted to be chosen. Without Draiken, I felt crippled and inept. We had been like two sides of a scale that balanced perfectly. Now all the weight was on my arm of the scale, dangerously unbalanced.

'Are we allowed to vote for ourselves?'

'Of course.'

'In that case I think I'll vote for you. You're definitely the better choice out of the two of us.'

'You still have to cast a second vote.'

'Then you'll be getting two from me.'

Chapter Twelve

Dominico

He walked ahead of me, leading the way. He was the one with the map in his head, but even if he hadn't known the way I would still have insisted he walk where I could see him. Despite sharing his food and water I was still suspicious. Helping us escape had been a crazy thing to do. He was now as much of an outcast as I was, except, unlike me, he had no hope of ever finding a home. His motives for helping me to Jozenburg made more sense – he was looking out for himself. And yet, I still wasn't entirely convinced. I trained my eyes on the swaying hulk of his back, reluctant to look away even for a second. His ease at having his back to me bothered me too. Shouldn't he be more on his guard? Either way, I was his ticket to survival, and yet he kept walking without looking back, somehow confident that I would follow. I was free to walk off on my own, I supposed, but who was I kidding? I had no other option.

We had been trudging for hours. The sun was starting to dip, the temperature dropping with it. My feet ached. My legs screamed with every step. We were following the wide emptiness of the old highway. Every now and then we would pass a car, left in the middle of the road by whoever had been driving it. In most of them, the keys had been left behind too, as if the occupant had simply driven the car until it ran empty. Pointless exercise if you asked me. There was no escape. Even if they had made it beyond the reaches of Jozenburg, there was nothing for hundreds of kilometres. All the land beyond, in every direction, was rumoured to be as much of a wasteland as this.

'Are we going to stop? We're not going to keep going in the dark, are we?'

He glanced over his shoulder. 'Not much further. We've covered a lot of ground today. Just looking for a spot that's not out in the open. Need to be protected from this wind, and we don't want anyone, or anything, finding us in the middle of the night.'

I thought of the possibilities of 'anything', and shuddered.

We veered onto a path that split off from the highway. A huge building came into view, its sign proclaiming 'Siemens', whatever that meant. It wasn't a word I knew. Rogan led me to it, and we moved through a gaping door into a cool interior, dark falling quickly. I couldn't see much beyond a hulking shape just ahead of us. Probably some kind of counter. We shuffled further in until we were out of the cold wind and away from any missing windows or doors.

I sank down gratefully, ignoring the grit beneath me. I was covered in two days' worth of dust and sweat. A little more wouldn't make any difference. I felt Rogan sit down nearby. He nudged me, somehow finding me in the blackness.

'Here. Eat. It's been a long day.'

I closed my fingers around a bag of something.

'Dried fruit. It's all I've got left. Some water too. Not much, though. So only a small sip or two.'

'Where did you get this?'

I couldn't see his face, but I felt him tense. 'I encountered a messenger. Let's just say he no longer needed it.'

Wishing I hadn't asked, I obediently sipped before passing the bottle back to him. Drinking the whole thing would be stupid, even though my throat burned with the need for more. We had walked almost the entire day without speaking. I couldn't judge his moods, or how he would react. I was normally good at reading people, but he was too unpredictable. Despite what he'd said, he might decide to kill me if I became too much of a burden, and find another way into Jozenburg. Or just another way to survive. The one thing I was clear about was that I shouldn't piss him off again. I would never let him know it, but what he'd said had stayed with me. If I died now, what would be the point of Mom and Dad having sacrificed themselves for me? Kat's death, too, would be for nothing. And even though I tried not to admit it, I still held out hope that maybe Mom and Dad were still alive, although it was a such a remote possibility that I tried not to think too much about it.

'Get some rest. We're only just over halfway to Jozenburg. Tomorrow will be an early one. I want to get there before nightfall.'

'How do you know I won't run away while you're asleep?'

He laughed softly. 'If you were going to run, you'd have done it already. You've figured out that sticking with me is your best shot. And I know, no matter how much you deny it, that you still have something to live for.'

He was right. I did have something to live for. Hope.

Syra

I needed to go after Draiken. He would never be allowed back into Jozenburg but I still needed to see him. I had to find out what his plan was. Nightmares had plagued me the night before. Visions of Draiken invading the human cities with an army of converts had stayed with me the entire morning. I couldn't shake the feeling that my visions were predictions of what was to come.

Murdering the Elders was only his first move, and I was sure it had been planned to clear the path for his next one. Unlike many of the others, I knew Draiken hadn't done this out of revenge or rage. He had done what he thought was necessary to get on with growing our numbers, even if it created a rift that could never be bridged. His certainty infuriated me. He believed I would stand back and do nothing while he lured in more humans and conducted more transitions. But why would he think anything else? I had always let him have his way.

The problem was explaining my absence. I didn't want to lie to the others but if they knew my plans, my loyalty and motives would come under scrutiny. Everyone knew how close Draiken and I were, and they had still elected me. I had tried to get around the issue by asking the other families how they felt about going to retrieve their loved ones. They hadn't reacted favourably. Searching for them was forcing the issue. They needed to return out of their own free will.

I didn't have that luxury. None of them had lost the only family member they had.

I spent close to half an hour looking for Ray before one of the soldiers pointed me to the watchtower flanking the front gate. I climbed the narrow stairs and found him overlooking The Waste. He was alone.

'Ray.'

He started, then boomed his contagious laugh. 'Didn't see you there. Scared me a little.' He put a beefy hand over his heart, grinning.

'Sorry. Deep in thought, I see.'

'Just thinking about the coming months. We've got a lot ahead of us.'

I moved to his side and followed his gaze over The Waste. 'Ever wonder what it was like before the war?'

'Sometimes. Must've been nice to have running water and food so conveniently available. All you had to do was pick it off a shelf or open a tap.'

'As long as you had money.'

'Right. Would've been nice not to have to walk everywhere. But it was still a world without us, so how great could it have been?'

'Good point. Still. Things were simpler. Cities that were open. Security that didn't involve shutting yourself behind these insanely high walls. And being able to travel the roads without dying of exposure.'

I glanced at him. I was stalling, which I'm sure he knew, but I wanted to keep talking like this, just for a little while longer.

'So... Raven seems quite taken with you.'

Blood filled Ray's face, flooding his features with colour all the way to the tips of his ears.

'It's nothing.'

'Really? Doesn't seem like nothing.' I waited for him to volunteer a few details, but he stared out at The Waste as if he'd never seen it before, his avoidance of me glaringly deliberate.

'She knows you're like all the rest, right?'

'What?'

'That you don't do monogamy? Should be a given, considering how I seem to be one of the few who still believes in a one-person commitment.'

He finally looked at me, exasperated. 'Can we drop this please?'

I held up my hands, laughing. 'Fine, fine.'

'So what's up?'

'What do you mean?'

'Come on Syra. You don't do small talk. You don't shoot the breeze. What did you want to talk to me about?'

I sighed. Ray was the only person besides Draiken who could read me like I had a flashing sign above my head.

'I need to find Draiken.'

Ray nodded. He placed both hands on the low wall of the watchtower. He leaned forward, closing his eyes against the hot breath of wind that gusted over us. 'I thought that was it. Wish I could come with you. Although I doubt he would survive the encounter.'

I laid a hand on his shoulder. 'What he did... you shouldn't take it personally.'

He snorted. 'Of course it's personal. What he did affects me. And that would've been something I could live with. But it's affected all of us.' He glanced at me. 'Including you.' He leaned back from the tower and folded his arms. 'He was my brother. Maybe not by blood, like you, but... I just can't believe he did this.'

'I know. I need to see him Ray. Despite all this, he's still family.

'I can't just go, though. Especially so soon after everything that's happened. But I can't just leave this as it is. I need to find out -'

'What his plan is?'

My gaze fell on the figures below us. Even from this height I recognised each individual. They were under our protection now. I glanced back at Ray.

'Yes. You know him as well as I do. He won't just go into hiding and keep a low profile. He'll find a way to survive out there.'

'I get it. You need to see that he's okay. But I would be careful. You know he'll try to suck you in and keep you with him.'

'I know. All the same, I have to go. I need you to cover for me.'

'As much as I understand your reasons, I don't agree with you going. Can't you take some of the soldiers with you?'

'For protection against my own brother? Come on Ray. This is Drake we're talking about.'

'Is it?'

I wanted to hug him. I knew he was more hurt by Draiken's actions than he was letting on. But Ray was proud. And my acknowledgement of his true emotions would only humiliate him. Instead, I laid a hand on his shoulder, pretending the contact was for my own comfort.

'Anyway it's not just him, Sy. What about the others? They might think you're there to bring them back to face the music.'

'By myself? It'll be fine, really. Besides, I need some time with him, alone.'

'To talk him out of whatever he's planning?'

I barked a laugh. 'Unlikely.'

'Okay, okay. What do I tell the others?'

'The truth. Or a version of it, anyway. Tell them I've gone into The Waste, for supplies. And that I went alone because I needed some time.'

I gazed out at the wasteland beyond our borders. Shouldn't be difficult to lose myself. I needed the solitude to try to make sense of things. *Ungirllike.* That's what Ray and Drake used to call me. While other woman talked through their difficulties, I worked through mine without outside interference. I preferred it that way.

'Think they'll buy it?'

'That's where you come in. Be convincing.'

Ray sighed. 'No short order, but I'll do my best. How long will you be gone?'

'Depends on how long it takes me to find them.'

'Which leads me to my next question – how are you planning to do that?'

I tapped my forehead. 'Gifted, remember? I'm hoping I'll be able to pick up Draiken's thoughts, or maybe get a clue from a vision.'

'Read his thoughts over that kind of distance? Is that even possible?'

'One way to find out.' I patted his shoulder. 'Relax. You're getting very unflattering worry lines.'

He gave my shoulder a playful shove. 'Such a charmer. Why did I ever agree to lead with you?'

I smiled. 'Because you can't say no to me.'

'Irritating, but true.'

I turned to go, my mind already preoccupied with what needed to be done before I left. I had only taken a few steps down when Ray called me back.

Annoyed, I half-turned. 'Ray –'

'Syra, there are two people approaching the gate.'

For a moment I thought he meant from the inside of Jozenburg, which was unusual but not unheard of.

'They're coming from The Waste.'

I leaped back up the stairs to his side.

I leaned over the edge of the tower, and sure enough, saw two figures were approaching the entrance of our city. The man I recognised immediately. 'What the hell is he doing here?'

Ray turned to me, startled. 'You know him?'

'In a manner of speaking.'

I made my way back down the stairs and yelled at the soldiers in the other watchtower. 'Open the gates!'

The gates swung open. Commander Rogan stood on the other side, a young girl coming up behind him. They were both filthy and dragging their feet, limp with exhaustion. Before either of them could set foot in Jozenburg, I was leaping off the low wall of the watchtower. I landed just behind them. It wasn't until I spoke that they realised I was there.

'Commander? What are you doing here?'

The girl stepped forward. 'He's here to try to get into your city. I'm his ticket in.'

She glared at him, her eyes defiant.

'Who are you?' I snapped.

'I'm a superhuman, same as you.'

I looked from her to the commander. He said nothing and avoided my gaze. 'I think you better both come through.' Ray, who had just arrived, started to protest. I laid a hand on his shoulder and leaned close. 'Just go with this for now, okay? If what she says is true, we have to give her shelter. She's one of us.'

He hesitated, then nodded. I waved the commander and the girl through, leading them straight to my home. I wanted to get them out of the open and away from prying eyes. Two soldiers had seen them come in, which meant that, by the time they returned tomorrow afternoon for their next shift, the whole city would know. I had very little time to ask the questions I needed to, and for Ray and me to make a decision. My trip into The Waste to track Draiken weighed on me – I had hoped to be gone by morning. Now it would have to wait.

I motioned them through the front door and gestured toward the living room. Ray followed behind them, his expression tight. Barely a day of leading together and already there was something we didn't agree on. I wasn't sure if his disapproval was aimed at the commander, or the girl or me.

'Please make yourselves at home. I'm sure you could both do with some food and water.' I glanced at Ray. 'Would you mind? You know where everything is.'

He moved into the kitchen without a word. The look on his face made me grateful for his silence. I sighed inwardly. It couldn't be helped.

I joined the commander and the girl in the living room. He had taken the one-seater while she opted for the couch that could comfortably seat two. Not wanting to be too close to either of them, I decided to stand.

Ray strode into the room, stiffly carrying a battered tray. All pretence of propriety gone, they reached for the food and water. Everything was gone in less than two minutes. I glanced at the girl. Her colour was slowly returning, and she sat a little straighter, lifting her chin and meeting my eyes. The commander still hadn't said one word. His silence made me uneasy. His posture of defeat worried me even more. I didn't know if he was putting on a show, or if he really felt the way he looked. Humans were much harder for me to read. I had lived among superhumans for so many years that I had become familiar with their gestures and tics. They were less likely to be dishonest because there were other Minders besides me who could hear their thoughts. Superhumans were naturally more straightforward – we felt we had nothing to hide from each other. But humans were practised in the art of deceit.

'Commander. Why have you come here?'

The girl started to speak but I held up a hand. 'I want to hear it from him.' She closed her mouth and folded her arms. I ignored the heat of her glare.

The commander finally looked at me. His expression wary, he shrugged. 'I had nowhere else to go.'

'What do you mean?'

'I escaped from Toria. If I hadn't, I would've been executed.'

'For what?'

He gestured to the girl. 'For helping her escape.'

'You mean she was living in Toria? In a human city?'

'Yes. None of us knew what she was –'

'Hello? I'm sitting right here you know.' The girl waved a hand around in an exaggerated motion.

I looked at her. She withered slightly beneath my gaze. She was tiny. Standing next to me she would probably fit beneath my arm. I reminded myself that she was just a girl. Barely beyond the years of her childhood.

'What's your name?'

'Why should I tell you anything?'

'You did just interrupt the commander to have your say. Now have it or shut it.'

Her eyes widened. Her mouth flattened in a mute line of fury. I heard her heart accelerate. I felt her indecision. She was struggling with a response.

'I don't have time for your smart-mouth comments. We're under no obligation to help you. So I suggest you ditch the attitude. You're only ensuring that I throw you out. And I won't feel any remorse either.'

'Dominico.' She spat the word out, her small hands clenched.

'Thank you.' I turned back to the commander. 'You were saying?'

'She was staying with two of our government officials. They were hiding her, raising her as their own daughter.'

'Where are they?'

'They were caught in The Waste. Dead, most likely.'

'How did you escape?' I asked Dominico.

'Told you. I have powers. Gifts. Skills. Whatever the hell you call them.'

Despite myself, I was fascinated. She must've come from the Creator's laboratory. It was the only explanation. But I couldn't recall ever seeing her before.

She gave me a flat smile. 'You don't recognise me, do you?'

I hesitated. There was something odd in her tone, something that warned me off saying too much.

'Should I?'

'You never saw me. But I knew all of you. By sight, at least.' She looked away, her hands tightly laced together. 'He never wanted me to mix with any of you. Told me I was his alone, and the only one of my kind. That I belonged only with him.' She seemed about to say more, but changed her mind and went quiet again.

My mind was spinning. The only one of her kind? What made her different from the rest of us? Why keep her separate? The Creator had always fostered a kind of communal living among us. He had said it was important for us to know each other. After all, we didn't belong anywhere else but with each other. I couldn't stand still. I paced the tight confines of the room, my feet as busy as my thoughts.

'Is that why you didn't escape with the rest of us?'

'It took them a while to get to us. The Creator's private lab was right in the middle of the building. When they did...' She trailed off. Her eyes were bright with tears. She blinked them back, methodically and silently.

'I managed to get away, but got caught in the main lab. The soldier sent the others away -'

'He didn't kill you.'

'No. He sneaked me into Toria, claiming I was his dead sister's child.'

'You were living with government officials. Your father wasn't a soldier,' Rogan said.

'He started out as a commander, like you. He was in charge of the mission. Because of its success, he was promoted to government official.' The word 'promoted' dripped with a tone I couldn't quite place.

I sank down beside Dominico, barely registering the way she shrank from me. This was too much to take in. A human rescuing one of our kind? Disobeying direct orders? I couldn't get my mind around the concept. The room felt hot and stifling. I stood again to open a nearby window, relishing the breeze that washed over me.

Ray had remained silent through the entire exchange, his eyes trained on the commander. 'It seems fairly logical to keep the girl with us. But why should we take you in? You're human. You don't belong here.'

The commander was quiet for a moment. 'You're under no obligation to take me in. I understand your people are your first priority. If I could just stay the night, and perhaps be able to take some food and water with me tomorrow morning. You have my word I'll leave at first light. Just keep the girl, will you?'

The girl half rose from her seat. A look passed between her and the commander. She seemed on the verge of an outburst, but a shake of his head kept her silent.

Ray glanced at me. I knew he didn't like it, but he nodded anyway. 'Fine,' I said. 'You can stay here where I can keep an eye on you.' I hesitated. 'As for the girl, we'll need to consult with all the residents. You can both remain here for the night. We'll talk again tomorrow.'

I started to leave, but the commander's voice caught me at the door. 'Syra?' I turned back to him, wondering what else he was going to ask for. 'Where is your brother?'

'Out scouting,' Ray replied. He took my arm and propelled me through the door.

Chapter Thirteen

Rogan

I stared up into the blackness, listening to the gentle rhythm of Dominico's breathing. I shifted my weight on the threadbare mattress, craving the sweet oblivion of sleep. A sense of panic lurked. It clawed at my chest like a crazed animal and the effort of holding it at bay kept me awake. I had nowhere to go. It was at least a day's walk to the closest human city, judging from its position on the map. Even if I managed to get there in my weakened state, I knew that either I would be handed back to President Crane, or it would only be a matter of time before a messenger arrived, requesting assistance with my capture. This had been a last resort. I hadn't really planned on this. Finding Dominico alone and asleep had hatched the idea. Hearing that her parents had been killed had tipped the scales. Despite what I had told her, I hadn't really thought I could use her as my way in. I had simply decided to finish what I had started.

For the first time in a long time, I had no plan. No idea how to get myself out of the mess I'd created. I'd made a choice that had forced me from everything ordered and familiar, and into a foreign place where my fate rested in the hands of those I had always thought of as the enemy. I couldn't have remained in Toria, not with what I now knew. I had managed to keep the images of those experiments buried, but in idle moments they surfaced, their details so vivid I felt I could reach out and touch them. The world I had belonged to and felt so safe in had turned out to be nothing but an illusion, a picture manipulated by Crane. It infuriated me how easily I had bought into the fantasy, how he had managed to dupe not only me, but also the entire city. His deception felt like a personal affront, however illogical that was. I had taken it badly, and I wouldn't be able to let it go. It had burrowed deep into me, finding a home of resentment and anger within me.

Syra woke me at first light. She looked the way I felt – weary beyond the help of sleep. She served me black coffee, sweetened with a spoon of sugar. Both were luxuries in Toria. In fact, Crane was the only one in the city who could ever hope to get his hands on either. She sensed my unspoken question. I wondered if she had simply read my mind. She laughed softly. I glared at her. She smiled, unapologetic. I breathed deeply, catching hold of the anger that tried to surface.

She sat down across from me, her chair creaking beneath her weight. She was one of the few women who only had to tip her head slightly to look me in the eye.

She blew on her coffee, sending a drift of steam my way.

I knew this was my opportunity to convince her. Ray was nowhere to be found, and I sensed I would have a better chance at pleading my case without his presence.

'Planning to send me on my way?'

Her gaze was direct, but neutral. She was skilled at keeping her thoughts hidden. 'That would be the logical course of action.'

'Unless you could find a use for me.'

She smiled. 'I doubt that very much.'

Her patronising tone set my teeth on edge. I clenched and unclenched my fists beneath the table, willing away my tension and trying not to betray my anxiety at her possible refusal.

'There's no denying the advantage you have. But I know you need numbers.'

'Thinking of adding yourself to our population? No offense meant, Commander, but I don't see what you can offer us.'

'Can't you transfer your powers? Make a human superhuman?'

She blinked, failing to hide her surprise. 'Let's just say that isn't an avenue I'm willing to pursue. Besides, aren't you supposed to hate us and everything we stand for? Aren't we considered unnatural by your kind?'

'Becoming something else, even what you are, is better than dying.'

She folded her hands atop the table. 'You're going to have to do better than that.'

Something occurred to me. Why was she debating with me? Why didn't she simply throw me out? I decided it was a good sign. I felt my body soften as I relaxed a little. Her face folded ever so slightly, tight lines appearing between her eyebrows. It was disconcerting how well she read body language.

'I have other things to offer. Insider knowledge.'

'How can I trust what you tell me? For all I know you're fabricating stories to save your hide.'

'Fair enough. How about a trial period? I'll give you a piece of information, and when it proves to be true, you'll know you can trust me.'

She paused. Despite the early hour, the sounds of people waking and readying themselves for the day drifted through the open window. Already the sun was warming the room. A half hour more, and the inside temperature would be unbearable.

She followed my gaze. Crossing the room, she drew a curtain across the window, shutting out the light, before joining me back at the table. She lifted her mug to her mouth, taking a slow, deliberate sip, setting it down with exaggerated care. Finally she met my pointed stare.

'You'll need to serve an ongoing purpose, or I'm going to have trouble justifying your presence here. If I decide to keep you, I'm going to come up against plenty of opposition.' She tipped her head, studying me. 'Besides, I haven't made up my own mind about you yet. It's going to be hard work defending my stance on something even I'm unsure of. More than that, helping you directly violates the treaty agreement with Crane.'

Keep me. As if I was some stray animal in need of a home.

'The knowledge I have will be beneficial in the long term. I can assist you with war tactics, give you information that President Crane entrusted only to me. The peace treaty will be null and void once war is declared.'

'War tactics? What makes you think we intend on going to war?'

'Give me some credit here. I'm not an idiot. Draiken's absence means something. If he has broken off from the rest of you, as I suspect, then even I, who knows very little about your brother, can figure out that he's up to something. And whatever it is, I'm certain it has something to do with Toria.' I folded my arms. 'I assume President Crane will be hearing from him very soon.'

She stiffened. Her natural elegance became distorted with the emotion she was trying to contain. I wondered if I had gone too far and played my winning card too soon.

She rose. Despite her fatigue, and her bottled emotion, it was difficult to focus on anything else with her in the room. She stretched, the casual movement displaying the slim line of her arms and the incredible length of her legs. She seemed to shrug off her grief, discarding it as easily as an item of clothing. She caught my eyes on her. Colour warmed her cheeks. She abruptly dropped her arms, sitting down again with a thump, all her previous grace gone. I had, however briefly, gained the upper hand. She was temporarily thrown, and her discomfiture pleased me.

She cleared her throat. 'You're free to make whatever assumptions you like. Even if I feel you can serve a purpose here and assist us, it's not my decision alone.'

I waved a hand. 'So talk it over with Ray.'

'Everyone has to agree, Commander. Every citizen. One vote against your presence here will mean you'll be going out the same way you came in.'

My warm glow of triumph went cold.

***

Syra had left me to my own devices. She hadn't posted any guards at my door, nor had she forbidden me from leaving her house. I took it as a sign to go wandering. Stepping out of her front door, my gaze swept over the layout of her neighbours' homes. They stood tightly packed together, with only a single wall between each house. It was a haphazard collection – some were built with brick, others plastered. Some were mostly plastered, with odd patches of brick here and there, as if a hole had been covered up. Most of the homes had corrugated iron roofs, which meant poor insulation. They would absorb and contain the heat of summer, while failing to keep out the icy drafts of winter.

I passed several citizens. They stared at me openly, turning to whisper to their companions without waiting for me to pass. I concentrated my gaze straight ahead of me, avoiding eye contact. The last thing I needed today was to unintentionally antagonise anyone. My chances of staying here were already slim. I didn't need to give Syra another reason to boot me out.

I walked the crumbling cement paths, following branches of smaller intersecting paths at random until I found myself advancing into a large open area. A reservoir stood in the middle, unguarded. There were no fences or barricades of any kind around the structure, giving anyone who happened to pass it free rein to take as much water as they wanted. Curious, I crept up to it, wondering if there was any water to take. On closer inspection, I noticed a child perched on the edge. The cover of the reservoir looked heavy enough to take at least four men to move it. And yet, it was only partially covered. There was water in it all right. So much that it lapped at the edges of its container, threatening to splash over the side. The child hadn't seen me yet. I watched him perch there, dangerously close to the edge. Three boys stood several metres away.

'Come on Elliot, do it.'

I backed up a few steps, not wanting to be seen. Crouching against the wall of a nearby house, I was riveted by the sight of superhuman children. Did they have the same kind of powers as the adults?

The child called Elliot crept forward, stretching a hand toward the surface of the water. His fingers skimmed across it, sending a small arc of water into the air. His eyes were huge as he teetered a little, and for a minute I was sure he was going to tip into the mouth of the reservoir. He flailed his arms, managing to recover his balance. He slid safely to the ground and ran to the waiting group of boys. They greeted him with jeers, their mockery loud and unforgiving.

'What a chicken,' one of the boys scoffed. 'We said go into the water, not just touch it! Call that a dare?'

Elliot mumbled something I couldn't hear. The exchange caused the other boys to howl with laughter.

'Just paddle and kick. Like in the book. Come on, it'll be easy.'

I wondered briefly if I should intervene. Elliot looked miserable. But I found myself holding back, reluctant to make myself visible. As it was, I was close enough for any movement to be noticeable.

The biggest of the three boys was now standing over Elliot, poking him in the chest. 'Don't be such a baby. If you don't want to paddle or kick, you can just get in and hold on to the edge, then get out again.

Otherwise you can't be part of our group.'

A voice carried from one of the nearby houses. 'You boys, what are you doing? You better not be playing near that reservoir.' A woman appeared, hands flapping at the boys in agitation. 'Go on. Go play somewhere else. You know you're not allowed near there.' When the boys failed to obey her instructions, she marched towards them, sending them scattering like a flock of pigeons. She glanced toward the reservoir and, seeing it partly uncovered, shook her head.

She stepped up to it, muttering to herself. She thrust her hands out in front of her. Her palms began to glow with a pulsing light, and the heavy cover scraped against the concrete opening, pushed by invisible hands. I stared in fascination as the lid kept moving until it slid into place with a final thud. The woman nodded to herself.

'Elliot, come inside.' The boy hesitated. The woman slipped an arm around him and guided him indoors, disappearing into its depths and shutting the door behind her.

As soon as her door closed the rest of the boys crept out, laughing behind their hands. They waited, as if confident Elliot would reappear. A minute or two later, he did. He shut the door with exaggerated care. The boys pushed Elliot forward, urging him on silently.

Elliot turned away from the boys and dragged himself back to the reservoir. He stood for a moment, staring mutely at the wall, then raised his palms the same way the woman had. The cover of the reservoir moved with a groan. He gave it a second small push, uncovering the water just enough to allow himself the space to climb in. He scrambled up the wall again, perching on the ledge. He sat there, staring at the water, the boys frantically urging him on with flapping hands. He seemed to gather himself, then holding onto the edge with both hands, he tentatively dipped a foot in the water. His gaze met mine. He started, his hands lifting from the ledge. The movement propelled him from the safety of his perch. He fell hard, banging his chin against the edge. He slipped beneath the surface of the water. It happened so quickly it took me a moment to realise he wasn't resurfacing.

I wish I could say I immediately broke into a run. Instead I hesitated, wishing I'd just stayed within the four walls of Syra's house. I didn't want to get too closely involved with anyone here. I wanted to stay not because I felt any sense of home, but because this was my only option. I glanced back at the place the boys had been standing, but they were no longer there. They had scattered. Of course.

Reluctantly, I rushed to the reservoir. Placing my hands on the edge, I slipped into the water. I kicked desperately but couldn't feel the bottom and for a brief moment, I felt a fist of panic in my throat. Taking a deep breath, I plunged beneath the water, groping blindly through the murk. I couldn't find him. I rose to the surface, groped for the edge and took another long breath before slipping under again. My hesitation had stripped away valuable seconds, and I was starting to wonder if I would find a corpse beneath the water – or whether I would be able to rise from its depths myself. Finally my hands grazed something that felt like an arm. I closed my hands around it and pulled. Finding the bottom, I kicked off hard. I flailed my legs wildly and somehow, through sheer desperation, managed to get us above water.

I surfaced with Elliot, trying not to notice the fish-like pallor of his skin, the odd purple-blue of his lips. His nose looked disjointed, as if it were broken. Clutching for the reservoir's edge, I climbed out, clumsy with the effort of keeping him from sinking back to the bottom. I pulled him from the water and laid him down in the dirt, putting my ear close to his mouth. He wasn't breathing. Pinching his nose shut with my fingers, I tipped his chin back. I breathed into his mouth, then paused to listen. Nothing. I did it again, praying to a god I didn't believe in that this boy would surface. As I was about to fill his lungs a third time he sat up, spluttering and coughing up water, his small chest heaving and his mouth wide with the urgency to draw breath.

He stared at me with huge eyes, water slipping down his body in small streams. He seemed about to say something when approaching footsteps made us both turn.

Two soldiers and the young woman I had seen earlier ran towards us, followed by one of the boys. The soldiers looked from me to Elliot and then grabbed me, hauling me to my feet. The woman was sobbing as she fell to her knees and gripped Elliot with frantic hands.

'He's fine,' I said.

One of the soldiers cuffed me behind the head. 'What did you do, huh? Did you push him?'

I opened my mouth to defend myself but Elliot spoke before I could get a word out.

'Yes he did. He pushed me.'

I struggled against the soldier's grip. 'I pulled him out. He slipped. I didn't – '

The woman looked up at me, her death grip on her son loosening. She rose deliberately, her hands clenched into fists. She leaned over me, her eyes never leaving my face. She opened her hand and drew back her arm. The blow against my cheek clinched my humiliation.

One of the soldiers laughed. 'Get up scum.' Together they started to haul me away. 'Humans. Nothing but trouble.'

Syra

Ray stared at me. 'You can't be serious.'

I sighed. I resisted the temptation to rock back in my chair. It would never hold my weight. Besides, it was only one of two chairs in Ray's house.

I leaned forward, willing Ray to hear me out.

'I know it seems crazy, but he could help us Ray. He knows Toria and all its inner workings. He knows President Crane. Trust me – having an insider's knowledge of that man will be a huge bonus. If we're going to have him as an enemy, then we need to know how he ticks.'

'And of course, his reward is to be allowed to make his home here.' Ray shook his head. 'I really don't like this. I don't trust him. How can you be sure he'll tell us the truth?'

'We put him to the test. He needs to offer us information on something that would happen soon. And if it does, then we know.'

'You know we'll have to put this up for a vote. I think the chances of everyone buying into this will be slim, at best.'

I shrugged. 'Then he goes.' I hesitated, not knowing if pointing this out would put Ray out even more. 'Don't you wonder why he saved her?'

'Of course. But I don't think he did it for her benefit. I think something pushed him to it. Why would you willingly make yourself an outcast and leave yourself with no options?'

'Whatever his motives, he still saved her.'

Ray looked at me, his expression hardening, his gaze intense. I suddenly felt like he could see right into me. I shifted, feeling a sharp prick of discomfort and unable to explain its source.

'You seem very intent on this. Why?'

He had touched on something I had been trying to pinpoint myself. Humans were our natural enemy. And yet, despite having been a superhuman far longer than I'd ever been merely human, I could never forget that fact. I had once been one of them.

***

For the second time this week, I called for a city meeting. Everyone crammed into the space, standing shoulder to shoulder. I scanned the sea of familiar faces. Raven stood near the front, arms crossed tightly across her chest. Tension lined her face. Emery was next to her. She wore an expression of such apprehension that I suddenly felt weighed down with guilt at asking them to make another decision so soon after their world had been upended. It felt like I was saddling them with more responsibility, and not taking on enough of the burden. Ray stood next to me. His solid presence gave me a small sense of comfort.

I raised my hands for quiet. The low murmurs of conversation faded.

'I know you're wondering why I've called you all together again so soon. But we need to make another decision. You may have noticed or heard that two strangers arrived in our city yesterday. They have asked permission to stay.'

My gaze fell on Raven. Her face had gone rigid, her body taut. I looked out over the crowd. Every one of those present reflected her fears. They held themselves so tightly I knew they were clasping at that fear, wearing it like a shield. No one spoke. They stood together, stiff and silent, their uncertainty rising up over them like a storm cloud.

'Before you make your decision, you need to know the facts. One of the strangers is a young girl. She's one of us.' The silence was shattered as the crowd all started talking at once. I raised a hand for quiet. 'She was in the lab with us, but kept apart by the Creator.' Several hands shot into the air, but I waved them away.

'I don't know much more than that. Any other questions, you'll need to direct at her. I ask you to remember our most revered law – to protect our own.' I paused. There was nothing to do but spit it out. Direct and to the point. There was no sugar to coat this news. 'The other stranger is a human.' The voices rose again, like the snapping growl of a canine. I waited, knowing their curiosity would soon overtake their need to talk.

'He's asking to remain here in exchange for information. He was Toria's president's most trusted soldier. It is because of him that the girl is alive.'

The door to the training hall banged open. Two soldiers came through the doorway. They moved through the crowd and beckoned for me to come out of the training ring.

'What is it? You're all supposed to be here.'

Rueben looked apologetic. 'Sorry Syra. But something has come up. The human...' he hesitated as several heads turned his way.

'You need to come to the cells,' he finished.

I sighed. 'Everyone return to your homes. We'll finish this later.'

The crowd dispersed and I followed Rueben and Travis, silently cursing the commander.

Reaching the cells, I waved the soldiers away. The commander was sitting on the crude bench inside, his head in his hands. He looked up at the sound of my footsteps. He shot to his feet and closed the distance between us in two strides, latching onto the bars of his cell. For the first time since he'd arrived here, he looked truly frightened.

I folded my arms. 'The soldiers say you pushed him.'

'He climbed in of his own free will! The other boys were goading him and he slipped and knocked himself unconscious. They saw. They were all there.'

He was babbling. He was coming undone, unravelling with the precariousness of his situation. 'Slow down.' I waited for him to compose himself. He took several slow breaths, the colour returning to his face. 'Good. Now explain yourself.'

'I took a walk through town.'

I threw up my hands. 'What were you thinking?'

'You didn't tell me not to leave the house.'

'Because I thought it was obvious!'

He glared at me. 'Do you want to hear my story or not?'

'Fine.' I crossed my arms again. I pushed them hard against my chest, until finally the discomfort forced me to relax my stance.

'I ended up at the reservoir. Elliot and some other boys were there. They were goading Elliot, trying to get him to climb in. When he did, he slipped and banged his chin on the edge. I pulled him out.'

'Why do the soldiers think you pushed him?'

He gave me a withering look. 'What else would you expect from a human, right?'

There was no feel of deception coming off him. I dipped into his mind, just to be sure. His thoughts were racing, but I found no reason not to believe him. He didn't seem to be hiding anything. Still, I couldn't be sure. He was human.

He shuddered as I withdrew. It was unusual for a human to feel my invasion.

'So now you know. I didn't do it. Can you let me out now please?'

I felt the force of his desperation. But this wasn't a decision I could make on my own. I needed to consult Ray.

'You'll need to sit tight a bit longer. I'll be back in a little while.'

'What? You heard what I said. You read my mind. You know I didn't do it!'

'Procedures need to be followed. I need to talk this over with Ray.'

He paled. 'If it's left up to him, I'll rot in this cell.'

I didn't say so, but he was right.

I had just stepped out of the claustrophobic dark of the cells when Ray appeared. 'I was just about to come looking for you.'

'Is he in there?'

Ray looked furious. His neck had turned a mottled red. His fingers were curled into fists so tight his knuckles were white. I put a hand on his chest, fearing that he would push past me and go straight for the commander.

'Yes. Look Ray, there's been a mistake. Did Rueben and Travis tell you their side of the story?'

'Their *side* of the story? Surely there's only one version. Of course the bastard would deny it.'

'Listen to me Ray. I probed his mind. He says he didn't do it. I believe him.'

'Just like that? Come on Sy. You've always said you can't read humans as well as us. You don't know this guy. You don't know what he's capable of.'

'I know Ray. But I just... have a feeling. Why can't you trust me on this? You know my abilities. He wouldn't do something like this. Stop letting your personal feelings about him get in the way of your judgement.'

The minute it was out of my mouth I regretted it. Ray didn't deserve that from me, however true it was. When he spoke, his words were measured, his tone carefully neutral. I could tell how much it was costing him to remain calm.

'We're at a stalemate. You believe him. I don't. I can guarantee that everyone else will feel the same way I do. We can't just let him out of the cells and allow him to roam free when we're not sure exactly what happened.'

'I know.' We were silent. I knew that this incident would only cement the certain outcome of the vote, and I would have to go along with the wishes of the majority. The city around us was strangely quiet. I had instructed everyone to return home, but the usual constant babble of conversation and laughter, the bangs and thuds and scrapes of people moving around in their homes, was absent or muted. It was as if the whole city was holding its breath, anticipating another blow to its morale.

'Were there any witnesses?' Ray finally asked.

I shook my head. 'The commander claims there were. I think we should question him together. See what sense you get from his version.' Ray gave me a look. 'It's the only thing I can think of to do. And between finding the Elders dead and Draiken leaving, too much has happened. I don't even know where else to start.' I felt dangerously close to weeping. I rarely cried. I was the collected one, the one who could be counted on to think rationally. But the collective weight of responsibility, and the deep, gnawing fear that I could make a decision with a terrible outcome pressed on me. I missed Drake. It was a feeling that clawed at my gut, an animal wanting to tear its way free.

Ray turned away, giving me a minute to collect myself. My gratitude at this small gesture of kindness nearly broke my last vestige of control. I swiped at my eyes and swallowed hard, pushing back at the tightness in my throat, berating myself for being so pathetic.

Ray moved through the doorway of the cells and I followed, finally getting a grip on my emotions. The commander looked up, his expression a mask of calm. In the few minutes that we had been outside, discussing his fate, it seemed he had become resigned to what would follow.

'We need to ask you a few questions,' Ray said.

The commander sighed. 'Fine.'

Ray ran through a long list of questions, all of which I had already asked myself. The commander answered each one the same way he had answered mine. Again I could sense his sincerity. There was no indication he was lying.

Finally Ray wrapped things up. He took my arm and turned, then hesitated. 'Were there any witnesses?'

The commander sighed impatiently. 'Yes. You already asked me this.'

'Can you describe any of them?'

I stared at Ray. Did he believe the commander's account?

The commander paused, mulling the question over. His thoughts were as clear as snapshots pasted to the wall.

'Well?'

'Give me a moment.' We waited. His face folded with concentration, his mouth flattening and then pursing.

Finally he shook his head. 'I can't recall any specific details. It happened...so quickly. I was mostly focused on the boy.' His face had settled into a carefully constructed mask. He kept his fear beneath, holding it down as fiercely as if it were a man who'd assaulted him.

Ray shook his head.

I waited, wondering if the pressure of the situation was contributing to his inability to remember specifics.

After a long moment, Ray motioned me out of the cells. I followed without a word, glancing back briefly at the commander. He had latched onto the bars again, as if afraid of being dragged away from them to a worse fate.

Emerging into the vivid brightness of the day, I shaded my eyes against the light. Ray sighed. 'I don't want to fight you on this, Sy. But I still don't believe him. He can't recall a single descriptive detail of anyone he claims was there.'

'Look Ray. I know you want a direct answer from me. But I can't give you one. I just know he's telling the truth.'

Ray folded his arms. 'I can't base my decision on your intuition.'

I stepped back, affronted. 'Of course not. It's only one of my strongest abilities.'

'I know. I'm sorry, but I just –'

I sighed. There was no point in us fighting among ourselves. He was sure of his stance. So was I.

I touched his arm. 'I'm sorry for what I said.'

Ray shrugged and offered me a small smile. 'Why? It was the truth.' He looked at me. Something shifted in his eyes. His pupils dilated, and his focus on me became intense. He seemed about to say something more, but I cut him off.

'What are we going to do with the commander? We need to go on with the vote, but I'm pretty sure no one here is going to vote yes after what happened. And we can't expect them to accept him just because I think he's telling the truth.'

Ray said nothing for a moment. His feet moved in the dirt, kicking up small clouds of dust. He finally looked up, an odd expression on his face. I had the feeling that he'd wanted to say something important, and my interruption had unsettled him. 'There isn't much you can do. You'll present his side of the story. You'll say you believe him. Then it's up to them to make up their own minds.' He looked at me for a long moment, as if considering his next words with care. 'You seem a lot less suspicious of him than other humans we've come across. You almost seem to trust him, even though you barely know him.' He touched my arm briefly. 'I've known you a long time. And I've never seen you...like this.'

I felt strangely defensive. The sun felt unbearably warm against my skin. I shifted uncomfortably, suddenly wanting nothing more but to get out of the heat. 'If you want to ask me something Ray, then ask it.'

'You know what I'm saying.'

'I really don't understand it myself. I just get this sense from him. A sense that he's trustworthy, or as trustworthy as humans can be. The fact that he's now saved two superhumans makes him unusual, you have to admit. Have you considered why he would push Elliot into the resevoir, only to pull him out again?'

'To create a situation that makes him a hero? To give us a reason to reconsider letting him stay?' Ray's face had closed up again. I wondered why he would initiate this conversation when he obviously hated hearing what I had to say.

'Ray. I don't have to tell you how much Elliot's death would've affected us. All of us. He's one of the few healthy ones conceived naturally. Losing him –'

Ray raised a hand, his expression weary.

A long silence stretched between us. 'We could call the boys in. Ask them what happened,' I said.

Ray looked horrified. 'We can't interrogate them. It'll only inflame the situation. No one will take kindly to you questioning the children in favour of a human.'

'It's not an interrogation, it's just a few questions.'

Ray shook his head, his agitation growing. 'We can't Sy. Not for him.'

I sighed. 'You're right.' I motioned towards the centre of town. 'Shall we?'

'Let's get this over with,' he muttered.

***

Everyone was gathered in the hall for the second time today. I had explained what had happened, and retold the commander's side of the story. The overall reaction was much the same as Ray's. They wanted him out of the city. Their collective fury was so intense it felt like a living thing taking up all the space in the room. The hall felt airless and heated. When I announced that I believed the commander's version of events, the hall filled with an angry buzz of disbelief.

I raised my hands for quiet. The noise died down into a hostile silence.

'My belief that the commander is telling the truth doesn't obligate any of you to feel the same. But you chose me, and as one of your leaders, I'm asking you to consider all the facts before you make your decision.' I looked over the crowd, the sea of faces turned up at me. I knew my words had left them cold.

Rogan

From the minute she appeared I knew it was done. She started to say something, but I held up a hand.

'There's no need. Let's just get it done.'

She nodded and unlocked my cell, stepping back to allow me through. As I passed her she placed a hesitant hand on my shoulder. The strangeness of her touch, and how unexpected it was, made me jerk a little in response, and she dropped her hand, her face puckering into a mask of tension.

'I'm sorry about this.' She said it so quietly I wasn't sure I'd heard her correctly.

We stepped out of the dark closeness of the cells and into the warmth of the afternoon. I blinked against the brilliance of the day, blinded by the abrupt change. When my vision cleared, I saw what looked like the entire city's population gathered around. The moment they noticed me, the buzz of conversation died, and every pair of eyes fixed on me. I couldn't tell if this assembly was planned or spontaneous. My gaze roamed over the unfamiliar faces. I found Dominico in the front, her tiny frame further dwarfed by the backdrop of people towering over her. I felt a spark of regret at having to leave her. Despite our tenuous arrangement, I was still the only familiar face to her in a city of strangers.

Syra came up behind me, accompanied by Ray. In silence, and without force, they motioned me forward, moving with me as I started to walk towards the city gates. Unnervingly, the crowd followed, the only noise the sound of their feet scuffing the ground.

I kept my gaze fixed ahead, taking in the ramshackle collection of houses and paved paths with their web of cracks spreading out in front of me like a bizarre map. The choking smell of dust filled my nose as a sharp breeze came up and whipped the dirt into frenzied whirlwinds.

The city gates loomed ahead. It was a bitter moment of déjà vu. I glanced back at the crowd. My eyes travelled over their faces, until I found the small boy I'd saved. He looked away, minutely shaking his head. My last hope for reprieve died a silent and unnoticed death.

Syra signalled the waiting guards, and the gates swung open, their creaking protest the only sound breaking the heavy hush of expectancy.

I kept walking without being told. My feet moved me closer to the threshold of The Waste, putting the relative safety of the city further behind me. I knew what awaited me. I slowed my steps, reluctant to hasten my march towards certain death.

'Wait!'

A boy darted in front of me, waving his arms. I looked at him and felt a jolt of recognition. He was the one from this morning, the instigator of the group.

'Adam, what are you doing?' Syra hissed at him. She tried to take his arm but he evaded her grip, darting behind me. He let out a squall of protest as Ray grabbed him.

'I need to tell you something,' he shrieked. Ray ignored him as he started to escort him back into the waiting arms of a woman I assumed was his mother. The boy was squirming, trying to slide out of Ray's grip. 'I was there! I was there! I saw what happened! Let me go!' Syra touched Ray's arm. 'Let him speak.'

Adam yanked his arm away, rubbing the spot Ray had been gripping, a pained expression on his face.

'Well?' Syra said.

'I was at the reservoir this morning. When Elliot... fell.' His gaze darted to me. 'He wasn't pushed.'

I felt hope flare in my chest, small but bright.

Syra's face was growing dark, her expression so filled with fury Adam took a step back. I wondered if he was considering running from her.

'I'm sorry,' he squeaked. 'But it wasn't just me. All of us were there. All the boys.'

'And?' Syra barked.

'We dared him. So he could be one of us.'

The crowd was stirring. They had been silent, straining to hear what was being said. Now what had started out as murmurs became shouts.

Syra raised her hands for quiet. She leaned into Ray and said something I couldn't catch. He nodded and took Adam by the arm. He yelled over the clamour of voices. 'Ever! Gregoir!' Silence fell again as the woman I had thought to be Adam's mother stepped forward. Following behind her was a man I assumed to be her partner. They closed around Adam, a parental shield. Ray stepped back and released their son's arm.

Syra motioned to them and then to me. 'Follow me,' she said through gritted teeth. 'We need to deal with this without an audience.' Our departure was met with a roar of questions and a wave of disapproval. I looked back, watching the guards trying to contain and calm the crowd. In their frenzied state they looked every bit like a human mob. The thought left a strange taste in my mouth.

Chapter Fourteen

Syra

I sat Ever and Gregoir down together, placing Adam opposite them. Rogan stood uneasily near the front door, as if needing to be near an exit. Ray hovered between Rogan and me, as if unsure where he was most needed.

Adam sat with his hands swinging limply between his knees, his head hanging. I felt a brief pang of sympathy.

'Adam.' He dragged his gaze from the floor to my face, flinching as his eyes met mine. His thoughts were like rabid animals, crashing into each other and screaming for his attention. He looked dazed.

'Tell us what happened.'

'It was my fault. The other boys were there, but I was the one who started it. I kept telling Elliot to do it.'

Gregoir glared at his son. 'You dared him, knowing that he doesn't know how to stay afloat?'

'He was supposed to hold onto the edge and slide in. But he slipped. He... he banged his chin.'

'And you ran?' Ever's hand twitched convulsively at her side. She looked ready to slap her son.

Adam hung his head. His shame was like an anvil around his neck. 'I went back. And that was when I saw...' he waved his hand in Rogan's direction without looking at him 'that human pull Elliot out.'

Ever stood and started to pace in front of her son, movements sharp with agitation. 'Why did you only tell us now? Were you there when the soldiers took him away?'

'Yes.' His voice was small. He looked every inch his 8-year-old self. Every trace of the bravado I imagined he'd displayed in front of the other boys was gone. Feeling my gaze on him he looked up, his eyes pleading. 'I was scared they'd blame me.' His whole body shook with the effort of keeping his tears at bay.

Ever looked at me, and then Ray. 'What will his punishment be?' She said it quietly, with resignation.

For the first time, Rogan spoke. 'The boy came forward. Elliot is fine. Is punishment necessary?'

'You know this doesn't guarantee your place here,' Ray snapped.

'That's not why I helped Elliot.' Rogan's voice was even. The sharpness of his tone belied his attempt at remaining neutral. I glanced at Ever and Gregoir. 'You're his parents. Do you think he should be punished?'

They glanced at each other, a look of understanding passing between them.

'Leave it to us,' Ever said.

I nodded. 'You're all free to go. Let's reconvene in the training hall so we can finish the vote.'

Ray looked as if he were about to protest. 'In light of what's happened, he deserves a second vote.' My tone left no room for argument.

Ray nodded tightly.

'Commander, stay here please. I'll let you know the outcome when we're done.'

***

The silence of the house made me wonder if Rogan had decided to leave after all. I stepped into the kitchen. He sat at the counter, turning at the sound of my footsteps. His face was calm, his exhaustion evident in every laborious movement of his body.

'The vote was unanimous.'

He nodded and rose, preparing to leave.

'They voted for you to stay.'

He blinked at me. 'What?'

'You saved one of ours. We're grateful.' I wanted to ask him why. He owed us nothing. He could've left Elliot to drown. What did one superhuman life mean to him? Even that of a child's?

I didn't tell him the outcome confused me as much as it did him. Many of us felt indebted to him. But Ray's refusal to believe the Commander left me stunned at his decision. What had changed his mind?

'Get some sleep.' I motioned to the couch. 'Not the most comfortable, but all I can manage for tonight. I'll sort out the other bedroom for you tomorrow.'

I started to walk toward my room when Rogan's voice stopped

me.

'Thank you.'

Dominico

I opened my eyes to an unfamiliar ceiling. For a minute I had no idea where I was. I sat up abruptly, then sank back as I remembered. My body ached from the days of travelling, and my stomach rumbled. I lay still, listening for noises. There was nothing at first. Then I heard the sound of a woman's voice, too low for me to make out what she was saying. I had slept without nightmares, a temporary relief. But being awake brought me back to the reality of what had happened. Hearing a woman's voice in the house made me think of Mom, and how she used to sit on my bed, her hand warm against my cheek, waking me with that teasing lilt in her voice. *'Time to shine, Domo.'* My throat closed. My eyes stung. I didn't know how to begin to grieve. I had lost the only three people in the world I had loved. I swallowed hard, blinking rapidly until my eyes were dry.

Syra appeared at my door, knocking softly before coming in.

'Hi. You ok?'

I nodded, refusing to sniff or wipe at my eyes and let her see I had been on the verge of bawling.

'How did you sleep?'

'Fine. Thanks.' My stomach rumbled again.

She smiled. 'How about some lunch? We need to discuss arrangements for you anyway. Might as well do it over a meal.'

'Lunch?'

'You slept through breakfast. I didn't want to wake you.'

I followed her out to the small table that filled the space between the kitchen and lounge, serving as a kind of dining room. The furniture in this house was pure luxury compared to what we'd had back home. The couch I had sat on the day before was a faded blue, its material soft to the touch. Its cushions were so comfortable that when I had sat down, I'd felt I could easily be swallowed into its folds. The table and chairs were sturdy, and the kitchen sported gadgets I had only ever seen once before, in the offices of a government official. I wondered idly if they worked, or if, like so many other things, they were relics left behind from the world before.

Syra motioned to a chair and I sank into it, watching her flit around her kitchen with a natural grace that made her movements seem choreographed.

Within minutes she had whipped up a meal. She laid a plate in front of me. A salad, so fresh and crisp it seemed the lettuce had been picked just minutes before. Strange looking orange globes, which reminded me vaguely of tomatoes. A hunk of bread, its crust golden and inviting. I dug in without waiting for her to join me. It tasted every bit as good as I imagined. The vegetables at home, while edible, had none of the flavour and texture of these. I wondered what the superhumans did differently. Maybe it was simply the soil, although I couldn't imagine any of the ground, even in this city, being any more fertile than our own.

At home we had always had enough, despite the rations. Since both my parents were government officials, we got more than other families. I had never truly experienced the bite of hunger before. It had left me greedy, with the need to cram down every last morsel as if it were my last.

Syra left me to eat, taking dainty bites of her own food in silence. Only when I had eaten the last crumb off my plate did I look up at her.

'What arrangements do we need to talk about?'

She brushed at her lap, then stood up and took both plates through to the kitchen. When she returned, she held two glasses brimming with water. She handed me one and waited for me to take a slurp or two before she sat down again.

'We've got limited space, so I've offered for you to stay with me. I thought since we've already become somewhat acquainted, you would be most comfortable here.'

I shook my head, confused. 'Wait a minute. You're telling me I'm going to stay here?'

'Of course. Did you think we'd be throwing you out?'

'Well. Yes, actually.'

'Why would we do that? You're one of us.'

'Except I'm not. Not really. I lived like a human for years. And even when I was in the lab, I was never one of you.'

'You're superhuman. You *are* one of us. Our most sacred law is to grow and protect superhuman life.'

I felt like all the air had been sucked from the room. I had been so sure this would be the end of the road for me. That I could put my head down and give in. Fade away. No more having to fight or brood about how alone I was. And how I was to blame.

I was being given another shot at life, one that I hadn't really thought about taking. It should've been a gift, but it felt like a burden, a weight I just wanted to drop and walk away from.

'You ok?' Syra was working hard on keeping her expression neutral, but a tic of annoyance flattened her mouth into a thin line.

I wasn't jumping at her suggestion, ungrateful wench that I was. Despite her little speech about protecting superhuman life, I could tell that she was doing this only out of some sense of duty, not because she wanted me to stay. But really, what more could I expect?

'Do I have a choice?'

'You would rather take your chances with dying? Not much of a choice, I would say.' She looked at me for a long moment, long enough to make me shift uncomfortably. I felt like a bug, trapped in a jar to be studied. She stood, brushing her hands together briskly. 'But you're free to do as you like. We won't keep you here if you'd rather leave.'

That thought came to me again. The chance that Mom and Dad could be alive. Maybe Crane had decided to spare them, hoping to lure me back. From what I had heard about him, he didn't like his plans to be upset. If I decided to give up now, I would never know if I could've had a second chance.

'What will I do?'

'You'll join the training.' She gave me a brief smile. 'Be with others your age.'

'Train?'

'Yes. They practise their abilities; learn how to use and control them. Raven is the instructor now.'

'Who was before?'

'What?'

'You said now. Who was the instructor before?'

'My brother.' She hesitated. 'You'll hear it around town so you might as well know. He's left here with several others. There's been a lot of speculation. Don't believe everything you hear.'

Something in her manner made her seem defensive. There was more to it, but right now I had other things to think about.

'So I train. What else?'

'You help out here at the house. Cooking and cleaning. We'll take turns. In time you'll also assist with other things – working in the fields, doing repairs around town. Everyone around here does their share.'

'What about rules?'

'There's only one. Keep the peace. No violence. Killing one of our kind means banishment.'

'You don't have rules for work? Or for supplies? But how -'

'How do we keep order? We don't live just for ourselves here. We help each other out. Everyone benefits from every individual's efforts. Our survival depends on it.'

She shot me an amused glance, her annoyance gone. 'I know you were probably told we were a bunch of savages who ate each other when supplies ran low. But in a lot of ways we're more civilised than humans. We've learned what most humans have never understood – the value of community.' She rose. 'Take today to look around the city, maybe meet a few people. Tomorrow your training starts.'

Her assumption irritated me. 'You seem pretty confident I'll be staying. Don't I get any time to decide?'

'You've already decided. You're here, aren't you?'

***

The training hall was an old house, the biggest I'd seen in Jozenburg. Two training rings took up most of the bottom floor. I craned my head to follow the curve of the staircase, wondering what was on the second floor. When I arrived, everyone else was already in the thick of training. It was a small act of rebellion, but it gave me no satisfaction. For a full ten minutes no one noticed me – or the fact that I was late. A woman in one of the training rings finally spotted me and made her way to me, yelling instructions over her shoulder.

'Why are you standing around?'

She was tall enough that I had to crane my neck. Her body had a muscular definition that made her intimidating. Her eyes were so blue they reminded me of an iceberg I'd once seen in a book. Her features were small and delicate, completely at odds with the masculine strength of her body.

'Well?'

I realised I'd been staring mutely at her. 'Um, sorry. I'm here for the training.'

'Stating the obvious. You're the new girl. I'm Raven. If you're late again, you'll be put on field duty every day until I say you're done. And before you ask, field duty is very unpleasant. Hard, back-breaking labour.'

The urge to fire off a smart comment rose in me with a strength that was hard to resist. She waited, a dark eyebrow raised.

'Sorry,' I mumbled, hating her already with an intensity that made my gut burn.

'The others usually get a mentor, someone who can guide and help them with their skills. But since you've got on my nerves already, I think we should get into a ring together.' She seemed pleased at my weak attempt to hide how much I hated the idea.

She motioned to the ring closest to us. 'Watch them for a few minutes until they finish up. I'll be back by then.' She moved back into the second ring, yelling at the two boys facing off.

I turned to watch as I'd been told. The trainee was petite like me, with long black hair tied back into a tight ponytail that whipped around with the force of her movements. Unlike the others, she was alone in the ring, her mentor standing aside, watching in silence. At first I couldn't tell what the trainee was doing. She kept throwing her arms out in front of her, as if warding off an attacker. Her face was furrowed with concentration and increasing frustration. After a few more attempts at whatever she was trying to do, she let out a little shriek and broke into an agitated dance of annoyance. Her mentor laughed gently and motioned the girl over, placing a hand on her shoulder. She murmured something, too quietly for me to hear. The girl sighed and nodded, moving back to her original place in the ring.

She stretched her arms out in front of her in a long, fluid motion, her eyes drifting closed. Her body relaxed, her face smoothing. I watched her chest expand and contract as she took deep breaths. For a full minute nothing happened. Growing restless, I started to look towards the second ring, when a flash of light drew my eyes back to the girl. Her palms were glowing. A cone of light moved out from her hands until it floated in front of her, condensing into a radiant wisp. It hung there, suspended in space. I couldn't tear my eyes from her. It was the first time I had ever observed another superhuman in action.

The wisp remained in place. I frowned, wondering what was supposed to be happening. The next moment the wisp exploded into a blaze so bright the whole room looked as if it were alight. My eyes watered from the intensity and the sudden wave of heat that threatened to singe every hair on my body. It lingered only for a second or two, abruptly cut off by a wall of ice that had appeared from nowhere. Through the translucent block, the heat burst into flames, which licked at the ice. Rivulets of water dripped from the wall, rapidly growing from tiny drips to a steady stream.

'Good, Lily. Now stop.'

The light and heat dissipated as quickly as it had appeared. The ice evaporated. Lily pumped her fists in the air, victory stretching her mouth into a grin. The room erupted into whistles and applause.

'Not bad, huh?' Raven had reappeared beside me. I nodded, unable to find my voice. I was blown away. 'She can control the elements. Whatever heat is in the air, she uses it to build into fire. From one drop of moisture she can create ice. Just a pity it all disappears when she stops casting... Ready?'

'Ready,' I squeaked. The idea of showcasing my abilities right out here in the open in front of everyone made my palms sweat and my stomach knot. It was hard to shake the feeling that I was doing something wrong. Years of hiding my abilities, of knowing my life depended on it, had made me feel ashamed of what I could do.

Raven led me into the ring Lily was just leaving. Her eyes moved over me with a scrutiny that left me feeling exposed. She met my gaze briefly, her expression filled with disdain. The need to turn and run flooded though me. Lily wasn't the only one staring. Dozens of eyes drilled into my back. They were studying me, and waiting to find me unworthy. My armpits felt damp.

I forced my feet forward until I was standing in the ring. Raven seemed to notice my discomfort. 'This isn't a performance people. Eyes off the new girl!' My face felt hot. Several people snickered before turning back to their own training.

Raven smiled, her expression kind. 'Don't mind them. It isn't often that we have new people in the city. They're just curious.' It was much more than curiosity, but I kept my mouth shut. Their hostility was natural. I was a stranger. I wouldn't trust me either.

'So what can you do?' Raven asked.

I made myself concentrate on her, trying to blot everything else out.

'I can project, and I can do mind control.'

She looked at me blankly.

'I imagine something – a scene, or an event – and I project that image out. Then others see what I'm projecting.'

A strange expression flickered across Raven's face. 'So you can alter reality?'

'I guess that's one way of looking at it. But I don't actually *change* anything. I just project what I'm imagining so that others see it. Kind of like layering over reality with my own image.'

'And the mind control?'

'Basically I can take over people's minds and bodies for short periods.'

'So you could make me do anything you like?' Her tone suggested otherwise.

I hesitated. I knew she didn't believe me, or thought I was exaggerating. But there was something else that I sensed she was struggling to keep from surfacing. Fear? Envy? Maybe a bit of both.

'I can show you,' I said, to avoid answering her question directly.

'This I have to see. Start with the projection first.'

I wasn't surprised at her disbelief. I knew I was the only one who possessed these abilities. The Creator had told me often enough.

'What must I make you see?'

'Something from the time before. You saw some of the books, I assume?'

'Yes.'

'Good. Let's do it.'

I took a deep breath, clearing my mind of every thought until it was still and empty. I started to build the scene. First, the trees. I concentrated on the image until it was so clear I felt like I could reach out and touch the length of the trunks, run my fingers along the reach of the branches. Then I imagined the look and feel of damp earth littered with the crunch of autumn leaves. I finished with a sky that was dark with clouds, the smell of coming rain riding a breeze that I felt on my cheek as surely as if it were really blowing. I brought it all together in my mind – the visuals, the smells, the sensations. When I could see every detail, contain every scent, and feel the sensations of the wind against my skin and the soil beneath my feet, I gave a hard mental push. I felt the image drive out of me, connected but moving outward.

Raven's gasp was gratifying. I held the image out a moment longer, then let go of it. The training hall came back into focus. Raven stood motionless, her eyes fixed on me. For a long moment she did nothing but stare. I shuffled my feet, finding a patch of dirt on the ring floor to fixate on.

'Well.' She cleared her throat. 'That was definitely a first.'

I said nothing. Her disbelief had been rocked. I couldn't tell if she was surprised, or threatened.

'Let's see this other ability of yours.'

I looked up. 'Are you sure?'

'Do as I say.'

I closed my eyes and collected myself again. The control ability was harder than projecting. It took every ounce of my concentration and willpower to overpower another person's mind and body. I hated doing it. The only time I had ever practised it was in the lab. The danger of breaking through the barrier of their individuality permanently was always at the back of my mind. It was unlikely, but still possible to erase their free will and ability to think independently, forever. Turning Raven into a zombie wouldn't exactly win me friends here.

I shoved the thought away and focused all of my attention. The concept was the same as the projecting ability – creating a picture in my mind of what I wanted to do, and then pushing it out of me. The difference was in attaching the imagery to Raven, without ever losing focus. The moment my attention strayed, I would lose the connection.

Heat surged through me, igniting me from the inside out. I pushed it towards Raven, and the air between us shimmered like heat rising off a hot pavement. When it connected with her and attached itself, it was as if I had stepped out of my own body and into hers. I felt the warmth of her skin, and the breath leaving her body. Her fear was my own. I raised her arm as I would mine, and felt her wave of shock as if it were my emotion. I made her take two steps forward, and then forced her to turn in a circle, pushing against her resistance.

Just as she began to give up absolute control to me, I withdrew. I hadn't yet learned when to let go once a subject stopped resisting. I couldn't take the risk of going too far. I released her, and the heat immediately evaporated, leaving me weak and shaking. I leaned over with my hands braced against my thighs, breathing hard. It took a minute before I could lift my head. Raven was sitting on the floor of the ring, her skin a deathly shade of white. Her chest lifted and fell in quick panicked breaths. I willed my legs to move and crossed the short distance between us to kneel beside her.

'Take slower breaths. And deeper ones. It'll pass.'

'I can't, can't... get...enough –' A hand landed on my shoulder and shoved me away. A boy knelt beside Raven and tried to calm her. A sea of angry faces engulfed me with everyone talking at once, firing questions that, even in the chaos, sounded accusing.

Lily shoved her way through the small crowd and glared at me. 'What did you do? What's wrong with her?'

Before I could reply, Syra appeared out of nowhere. She pulled me out of the crush and made her way to Raven's side. She leaned close and spoke into Raven's ear. Gradually Raven calmed, her breathing slowing. The colour returned to her face.

Syra stood up. 'See? She's fine. Everyone back to your training.' The crowd reluctantly broke apart and went back to what they'd been doing before. I kept my eyes on the floor. I didn't need to look up to register their hostility. I could feel the heat of it on my skin, their silent accusations like needles probing my back. I clenched my jaw against the threat of tears, forcing back the fist of loneliness clogging my throat. When I looked up at Syra, my eyes were dry.

Chapter Fifteen

Syra

The timing was terrible but I had to go. I had already been delayed for three days, and I couldn't afford a fourth. Ray's expression told me everything without his saying a word, but he helped me load up my backpack nonetheless, muttering instructions without meeting my eye. Things had been tense between us since Adam's admission. Although Ray had readily acknowledged his misjudgement of Rogan, he had withdrawn, his thoughts shuttered away from my reach. I felt this second loss like an old wound.

I slipped a final water bottle into the pack, then lifted it from the floor, testing its weight. I nodded, satisfied. I glanced around my kitchen, one hand skimming the cool surface of the counter. I wondered how long it would be before I saw it again.

'Right then. Be safe. Come back as soon as you can.' Rogan's words were directed at me even as his eyes remained fixed above my head.

'Ray.' I waited for him to meet my gaze. After a long moment, he did. His eyes were guarded.

'What is it?'

He shook his head. 'It's nothing. I don't want you worrying about anything else but getting home.'

'I'm already worried. You're distant. You seem... upset with me.'

The stillness of the morning, punctuated only by the occasional cry of a lone crow, emphasised the silence between us. It was close to dawn. Soon the others would be getting ready for the day ahead, and I would've lost my opportunity to leave quietly.

Ray sighed and ran a meaty hand over his bristled head. 'I'm worried, Syra. Our choices have not been in line lately. I voted for the commander to stay only because I couldn't have him thrown out after what he did. That doesn't mean I like it. You, on the other hand, seem strangely comfortable with his presence here. I don't understand it.'

'We're all unsettled, Ray. But hasn't the commander proved himself?'

He looked at me with evident disappointment. He knew I was avoiding a direct reply. But I was doing it only because I had no answer to give. None that would satisfy him, or me, at any rate.

I squeezed his shoulder briefly, the only peace-offering I could think of. My mind was already filling with plans for what I would do when I found Draiken. I had no room to think of much else.

'I'm sorry I'm leaving you with all the responsibility at a time like this. I have to go.'

Ray gave me a half-smile. 'I know. Good luck. Send word if you need help. Carolyn knows you're going. She'll keep the channels open for communication.'

***

I made my way north. For the most part, I was following my gut, and what I thought Draiken would do. My guess was he would remain close to the human cities to ensure as much distance as possible between him and us. Toria was as far away from Jozenburg as you could get without venturing too far into The Waste. No predictive visions had come to me as yet, but I was hoping that if I was on the right track, I might get flashes of him the closer I got.

I hadn't let on to Ray how much it worried me that I had no real plan. I was carrying supplies that would last me a week. Ten days, if I was careful. Food wasn't the real problem – I could hunt if I really needed to. I was carrying a knife for just that purpose.

I paced myself. Pushing too hard too soon would only fuel my need for water. If I went the wrong way and had to backtrack, I could easily run out. I reached out to Draiken tentatively as I walked, probing the distance between us for a gap into his mind, but either he was too far away, or he had deliberately cut our connection. At the same time, I kept an ear out for any warning sounds of an approach, or scents that might precede an attack. For the most part, The Waste was silent. The occasional caw of a lone crow was the only accompaniment to my footsteps.

The shortest and most obvious route to Toria would've been along the old highway that ran north to south. A few of the old signs remained, the blue background of the huge signboards looming over the remains of the tar, the white writing fading into oblivion. As soon as I could, I veered off on to the back routes. I sidestepped clumps of scrub, making my way along sanded paths. I passed warehouses rotting in the sun like forgotten carcasses. I stayed away from the tar roads, even the smaller ones. Although these areas were more frequented by the war-engineered animals of The Waste, it was rare to come upon any humans. When they ventured out, it was only to places where they might find supplies.

I hadn't worked out what I was going to say to Draiken. There was nothing to be done about his past actions. The murder of the Elders was something I'd kept shuttered away. I wasn't ready to deal with it yet, to sift through my grief and try to find a way to forgive him. I could never excuse or justify what he had done. But his abandonment of me, his twin and only family, dug deeper than anything else. His betrayal of everything we had been working towards was more prominent in my mind than the lives he had taken. The selfishness of this thought shamed me, but Drake had always been everything to me.

I came out of the shadow of a decrepit building, and startled a small flock of crows. I watched as they took flight, wings flapping in a synchrony of flight. The heat was so intense that the sky had been bleached white, all traces of blue leached by the sun. As I stepped forward, I realised they'd been picking over a carcass. I bent over it, taking in the long, slim tail and the stiff whiskers. It had been a long time since I'd seen a feline. They were the canines' primary prey. I hoped with their demise, the canines would die out too. I pinched my nose shut against the smell. The scent of death always rushed up my nostrils like tendrils of toxic gas, lodging there with the tenacity of a leach. I glanced around uneasily. The day had quietened, as if the desert mourned its loss. I wondered idly if the crows would return if I took cover. I thought of the knife in my pack, and how a well-timed throw would mean meat on the menu tonight. Not a great meal, mind you. Their flesh was stringy and left an unpleasant aftertaste.

I walked on. The heat enveloped me in a clammy embrace, slipping its moist arms around me until I was sodden with sweat. I stopped in the scant shade of a tree, its spindly branches displaying an array of pointed thorns. I reached into the side pocket of my pack for my water bottle. My hands were slippery and, as I opened it hurriedly, water spilled over the lip. It dissipated swiftly into the baked earth. I stared in disbelief at the damp patch of dirt, wishing I had Lily's powers of extraction. I'd managed to spill a quarter of the bottle's contents. Trying to reassure myself, I dug into my pack again, searching for the four other bottles I'd packed. I came up with only three. I closed my eyes, trying to picture myself packing the fourth water bottle. Nothing. I'd been too distracted by Ray and the prospect of seeing Drake again.

No need to panic. Ration it.

Hours later, as the disc of the sun slipped towards the horizon, I kept this thought in mind, repeating it like a mantra, trying to block out my thirst even as my throat ached and my tongue swelled.

By nightfall my feet were dragging. My body throbbed with such intensity I could barely move towards the building I'd earmarked as a rest stop. My throat burned with a fiery thirst that only grew with every minute.

Finally, I made it to the building. It was mostly intact. A part of the roof had caved in, but there was still plenty of sheltered space for me to choose from. I shuffled into a long corridor and peered around the battered open door. Picked clean and abandoned, but perfect for one night. I slid my pack off, grateful to be free of its weight.

I was stiff and tender in a way I'd never experienced before. My physical limits far exceeded those of a human, and yet one day of walking had reduced me to a half-cripple. I was exhausted, as if I'd used my abilities all day. The only thing I could put it down to was the unrelenting heat. I felt sapped of every gram of energy, every reserve of strength. I pulled out my tattered sleeping bag and slid into it, savouring the warmth now that the heat of the day had disappeared with the setting of the sun.

I had my second slow drink of the day. I had to force myself to lower the bottle again, pushing away the thought of drinking every last drop. I pictured myself beneath the merciless sun, shaking my water bottle in a pointless effort to slake my thirst. The image was enough to make me return the bottle to my pack. I unpacked the food I'd rationed for the day, eating slowly, savouring every bite. I slid further into my sleeping bag until only my head was uncovered. I closed my eyes, convinced my aching body would keep me awake. It felt like only minutes later when I woke to the rising heat of the morning.

I rose gingerly and flinched as I stretched. I massaged my calves gently, rolled my sleeping bag and shoved it into the pack, doing a quick search before lifting it to make sure I had everything.

I stepped out of the building, shading my eyes against the overwhelming brightness of the sun. It was later than I'd originally thought. I needed to get moving. My stomach growled. My tongue felt furry, as if it had morphed into a tiny creature overnight. I hesitated, then slid my pack to the ground, fishing out food I could eat on the go.

I took a minute to orientate myself. If I kept going north, I'd be heading towards Toria. I hoped that my suspicions were right and I'd find Draiken and the others close by.

I nibbled and sipped my water as I walked. When I was done, I shoved the bottle deep into my pack alongside the sleeping bag. I wanted to make it as difficult as possible to reach it. Maybe that would keep the temptation at bay.

To my left I could make out the winding black expanse of the old highway. Signs attached to long metal arms curved over it. Streetlights towered above, the poles still intact. I wondered if the glass and bulbs were untouched, the only things to survive The Waste.

I trudged along the dirt track, kicking up small clouds of dust. I kept an eye out for pigeons or crows. Any opportunity to hunt would ease my mind about food supplies. I wished it was just as easy to replenish my water.

I emptied my mind to search for Drake again. Reaching across the span of The Waste, I investigated every sound and movement, hoping to catch something that belonged to him. With all my attention focused on my search, I had none left for the world outside my mind. I couldn't blank everything out for too long without risking losing my way. But I couldn't stop. I'd already lost time this morning. My anxiety grew with every passing minute.

I searched for him a bit longer. There was nothing but a ghostly silence. I sighed and allowed myself to tune out, the details of The Waste returning. I took several more steps before I realised I was no longer on the dirt track. The air was cooler than before. By my count,

I'd only tuned out for a few minutes, but the sun was already dipping towards the horizon. I turned around twice, convinced the path must be nearby. The only thing close by was a building with collapsed walls and a missing roof. I couldn't believe it. I must've been searching for Drake for hours. I shook my head in denial, unable to accept the depth of my stupidity.

The low growl took a moment to pierce my thoughts. I stilled and backed up a few steps, returning to my previous spot alongside the derelict building. I sniffed the air, my eyes darting from the scatter of rocks to my right to another crumbling building half a kilometre away. Canines were big, but any one of the rocks would provide enough cover to hide the beast. Buildings were a favourite, sheltering the creatures from the sun during the day and from the cold at night. I strained to hear the shift of scattered dirt beneath moving feet, or the muted breath of a stalking animal. I tried to still the stutter of my heart, drawing a long breath and holding it, trying to diminish all the outside noises that could distract me from the sound of the creature's approach.

The snap of a twig sounded to my right. I spun towards the source of the sound. Nothing rushed at me. There was no animal in sight. A snort came from my left, but again, there was nothing there. A terrible thought came to me. A discussion I had once had with Draiken. We had been trying to address the water shortage in Jozenburg, when the idea came for a small party to brave The Waste to try to find an alternate water source. Draiken had told me that canines were pack animals. Their survival depended on a community of cooperation. They never hunted alone.

I waited, indecision and fear rendering me motionless. I could easily outrun them, if only I knew how many there were. They were smart. They wouldn't all run at me at once. They would be stationed at different points, hoping to close in on me and cut off my escape. I pictured being eaten alive, limbs and organs torn from my body. The agony of being ripped apart. My fear felt like a weight on my back, keeping my feet rooted to the earth and scattering my thoughts like dust picked up by the wind. My normally highly attuned senses were becoming unresponsive, growing sluggish as my panic mounted.

I willed the morbid thought away. I drew a breath, picturing the air filling my lungs. I exhaled, concentrating on the oxygen leaving my body. I could do this. I was faster, stronger, smarter. I slipped my pack off, keeping my eyes trained ahead. The knife was where I'd put it. Right on top, just beneath the teeth of the zipper. I clenched it in my hand, reminding myself that it could slit a canine from throat to tail.

Silence fell. I stared at the building ahead. There. The flick of a tail. Another growl, rapidly followed by a second. They were circling. Closing in. I could feel the intensity of the hunters' eyes burrowing into me, like parasites trying to get beneath my skin. The tension of waiting, of not knowing where it, or they, were, was starting to break my paralysis. The agony of indecision became too much and I bolted forward, nearly unseating my backpack from my shoulders as I broke into a sprint. A chorus of snarls punctuated the air. I glanced over my shoulder, the compulsion to see my pursuers too strong to resist, and counted four canines rushing at me. Two were trying to flank me, while the remaining two ran behind me, closing in with every stride.

My heart felt like it might burst from my chest as I pushed myself harder. My lungs caught fire as I struggled to breathe through my terror, my mind a maze of unconnected thoughts. I was pumping my limbs as hard as I could, but I knew I still wasn't running fast enough. The deep connection my mind had with my body, the driving force behind my speed and strength, had disconnected. I was too unfocused, too afraid.

The humid breath of a canine caressed the back of my neck. I heard the gnash of his teeth as they came together in a fruitless snap. I had only seconds before the beast would be on me, and once I was beneath its crushing weight I would have little hope of escaping. I poured everything into getting my body to perform, trying to re-establish the spark of connection to my mind that would rocket my body into overdrive. The canine barked, the sound piercing through my skull. A strange calm came over me, muting the raw fear and slowing my mind. This is it. This is how I'm going to –

I slammed to the ground, my face meeting the earth with a crack that freed a river of blood from my nose. The creature was on my back, its claws knifing into my pack. I tightened my grip on the knife, grateful I hadn't dropped it in my fall. The canine scrabbled furiously, trying to dislodge the pack. From my position in the dirt I saw the other canines, slathering and snapping around me. I squirmed beneath the weight of the animal but this only intensified its efforts, whipping its companions into a frenzy. I felt the pack slide from my shoulders. I tried to slip through the momentary gap but the canine slammed me back into place with one huge paw, its claws opening the skin on my back. Out of the corner of my eye, I caught a glimpse of the second canine circling behind me. Seconds later I felt the tear of fresh wounds opening along the length of my calves. I bit back a scream. I couldn't turn or move my torso. The pain felt distant and removed as my mind started to shut down. I lifted the knife over my head and made a weak stabbing motion, hoping to sink the blade into the canine's throat. I was slipping into a tunnel, the darkness beckoning me with the warmth of an old friend.

***

'Syra!'

I jerked a little, like someone called back from the edge of sleep. The weight of the canine was gone. In its place was a bright throbbing. Something was touching me.

'Sy! Can you hear me?'

Someone. The voice familiar, but not. As if I had not heard it for a while.

Hands on my face, gently stroking. I felt my body leave the ground, as if I were floating above it, as insubstantial as mist.

Images filled my head. Visions of Drake, his face lined with worry. Pictures of us together as children, his hand warm in mine, his laughter a sweet lullaby of home. His voice moved among the images, an invisible presence, fading in and out, at times so loud I was convinced he was right beside me.

Gradually, more noises pushed through the fog. My head started to clear. I opened my eyes, with what felt like an extraordinary effort.

His face swam into focus, his smile radiant with relief.

'Welcome back, Sy.'

***

It took two days before I could sit up, and an additional day before I could get out of bed. I was weak, the open wounds on my back needing constant care. I was lucky to be alive. If that canine had sunk his teeth into me, I would've been dead.

It was on my fourth day that I wandered out of the buildings that

Drake and the others called home, hobbling with a protective hand at my back. They had found a cluster of buildings, mostly intact, disturbingly close to Toria. A climb to the roof of the building they used as housing showed the human city in all its walled splendour, a distance I estimated to be less than ten kilometres away.

He came up behind me and put a hand on my shoulder. As much as his touch was warm and familiar, I resented the implication it carried – that he felt comfortable enough to do it, thinking that I was once again on his side.

'Nice view, don't you think?'

'A bit close for my taste.' I slid out from under his hand.

'Look Drake. I'm very grateful that you helped me out in The Waste. But as I'm sure you know, this isn't a social call.'

'Ah damn. Really? And here I was about to break out the fine china.'

'How can you be so flippant? You killed the Elders. You broke our most sacred law. And –'

'Left you behind without a backward glance? Not true Sy. You were part of my plan all along. I knew you would come looking for me. Now we can do what we always planned – lead. Together.'

Shock glued my tongue to the roof of my mouth. For a long moment, I couldn't think how to form a single word, never mind string a sentence together.

'You murdered our leaders. How can you stand there and act as if it was just a part of the plan?'

A shadow passed over him. His gaze shifted from my face to a point over my shoulder. For a brief second I could feel his guilt, his suppressed shame.

'I didn't want to kill them. I tried to make them see reason, and overturn Azaiah's decision. He wouldn't listen. None of them would. When I pushed it, Azaiah tried to have me thrown out. I... lost it.'

'And killed them all? Surely, Drake, after you killed Azaiah –'

'I should've been shocked into stopping? I tried to. But they went crazy. They all rushed me at once. I thought –'

'They would kill you?'

He nodded, his mouth pressed into a thin line of tension.

I turned away from him. His words hung in the air, reeking of deceit. A warm breeze blew up, carrying with it the scents and distant sounds of the human city. The building that Draiken called home was eerily quiet, as if its occupants were holding their breaths, their ears cocked to catch our conversation. The thought left me uneasy.

'And the others? Did they come willingly?'

'Yes Sy. I didn't force them. They share my vision. They want to live in peace, without the threat of humans hanging over them.'

I choked back a snort of laughter at the irony.

'There's been no threat, Drake. We've been living in peace for years.'

Draiken shook his head.

'How long do you think that will last? Don't tell me you haven't felt it. I'm not nearly as intuitive as you, but even I've had the sense that something is coming. You might not want to face it, but war is inevitable.' He took my hand in both of his and squeezed, willing me to look at him.

'Join me. Together we can win this, and then this country is ours. A stepping stone to the rest of Africa.'

My hand rose to my mouth. I took a step back, shaking my head. 'What will happen when there are no more humans to turn, Drake? What then?'

He dropped my hand in disgust. 'Do you honestly think I haven't thought of that? I've thought of everything. When we win this war, the humans will be under our control. We can turn as many as we like. Keep them breeding. We'll never run out of numbers.'

I stared at him in horror. A superhuman factory. 'You've lost your mind. You can't do this!'

'With your help, I can. Convince the others. Convince them that the only way is for us to be a united front. A temporary joining. For the sake of our survival.'

A knock at the door leading to the roof made me bite back a retort. Mohina's head appeared around the open doorway. Her arrival at that moment felt planned, as if she and Draiken had rehearsed it. A well-timed interruption to cool my growing temper.

'Syra!' she trilled, as if my presence were a pleasant surprise. I eyed her warily. Out of all the superhumans, I had always found her the most difficult to read. She kept her thoughts closely guarded at all times, her emotions on a tight rein. I still felt the coolness of her insincerity beneath the façade.

'Mohina.' I kept my tone deliberately flat. Her smile faltered.

'Sorry to interrupt. Can I offer you something, Syra?' Her forced politeness grated on me.

'No.' I stared at her pointedly until she retreated, the door banging shut behind her.

'Of course your most faithful follower would be here with you.'

'Don't be snide. You obviously came here to say something to me. So say it.'

I looked at him, seeing not the man in front of me, but the child he had once been. Those large dark eyes, lashes that were far too long to be suited to a boy. It gave him an odd vulnerability.

'However you're planning to provoke the humans, please don't do it. I don't share your confidence that winning is a given. I think you're underestimating them. We can't afford to lose more numbers.'

'We? There is no "we" anymore, Sy. We're now on opposing sides. I thought you would see the logic in this, the obvious choice. But you're hell-bent on protecting those humans.'

'It's not the humans I'm worried about. It's us. Our numbers.'

'You still don't see it, do you? Our numbers will continue to dwindle until there are no more of us left. Gaining control of the humans is the only way to ensure our survival. If it was left to you and the Elders, we would die out, simply because you say it's not morally sound to take lives.'

He turned away. 'This is it. We're not walking the same path anymore. I don't know if we ever were.' He moved to the edge of the roof, his shoulders hunched around his ears in his habitual gesture of pent-up anger. 'Mohina will stock up your supplies. I think it's time for you to leave.'

I stared at him in shock. Just this little climb to the roof had left me breathless. And that was without a pack. But more importantly, I couldn't leave like this. Not with things as they were.

'Drake –' He caught my hand before it could reach his shoulder. His grip was brutal. I gritted my teeth against the grind of bone on bone. I looked him in the eye, making sure he heard me. 'If you change your mind, I'm here. You'll always be my brother. I'll leave the others if that's what it takes. But not like this.'

He shoved me away from him, but not before I caught sight of his face collapsing into a mask of grief.

Chapter Sixteen

Rogan

Syra still hadn't returned. I remained mostly within the confines of her home, reluctant to face the stares of the others. Some didn't bother to hide their suspicion. Their accusations were silent, but clear nonetheless. Some had rushed up to me shortly after my release, falling over themselves to shake my hand and thank me. I almost preferred the hostility to the praise. It felt more honest.

I had seen Dominico briefly as she returned home each day from training. I had learned not to ask her for details regarding her activities. My first and only attempt had been met with a withering stare. Her eyes were red-rimmed and swollen. I thought it best not to comment.

The lack of a work routine and the boredom of having nothing to do were starting to wear me down. I could tell Ray didn't know what to do with me, and was grateful for my absence. I had taken to wandering the rooms of the house, listening to the sounds of a functioning city outside, and wondering what would happen when Syra returned. Despite the vote, I didn't trust them. I wasn't among my own kind. The familiar tensions between us and them wouldn't simply cease to matter, despite their gratitude. I was still the outsider. I missed the camaraderie of my soldiers, the comfort of an easy fit.

The door banged open with an unholy shriek. Syra stumbled in, her pack sliding from her shoulders. Ray was behind her, a supportive arm around her waist. The intimacy of the gesture surprised me.

I moved towards them to help, but she waved me away and

dropped into the tattered armchair nearest the door. She closed her eyes for a long moment, and Ray and I exchanged a look. The silence stretched, taut and loaded.

Ray put a hand on her back and her scream was so unexpected that Ray nearly fell off the arm of the chair. He snatched his hand away.

'What is it?'

She was panting. Her jaw twitched as she gritted her teeth, the sharp grind of enamel making me flinch. 'My back. Had a...incident.'

She looked up at me, her forehead covered in a fine sheen of sweat. 'Help me to my bedroom. I can't go any further.'

'I'll do it.' Ray said.

She shook her head. 'I need you to get the Healers. Tell them I was attacked –' she broke off as she dragged another breath into her lungs '...by canines.'

'What? Why didn't you let us know? Carolyn was focused on keeping the channels open –'

'Ray. Please. Now's not the time.'

Ray left the house running.

I slipped an arm around her waist, careful to avoid touching her back. The closeness of her made me feel itchy, as though something bit at my skin through my shirt.

A quick downward glance revealed that her calves were caked in dried blood. She leaned her full weight against me. Her skin felt overheated, as if she were running a fever.

We crossed the open area of the lounge at a slow shuffle, stopping every few steps so she could catch her breath. The fact that she had made it out of The Waste in this condition was a miracle. An unexpected wave of admiration washed over me.

It took us nearly five minutes to get to her bedroom. By the time we reached her bed, we were both drenched in her sweat. Her face was so pale the pillowcase appeared yellow by comparison.

I searched her bathroom, opening cupboards until I found a facecloth. Despite the situation, I still felt strange searching through her things. It was oddly intimate, seeing her possessions in their drawers and on their shelves.

I poured some of her allocated water into a shallow bowl, wishing it were colder, and dipped the facecloth into it until the fabric was damp. I laid it over her forehead and she sighed, her eyes closing.

'Better?'

She nodded, the movement slow and sluggish, a sharp contrast to her usual natural grace.

'Thank you.' She opened one eye. 'I'm in pretty bad shape, huh?'

I blinked at her, reluctant to answer.

She smiled. 'Your thoughts are pretty loud. Especially when you're trying to keep them to yourself.'

I heard the front door open and retreated to the doorway of Syra's bedroom. Three strangers strode past me, giving no indication they'd seen me. Ray came up behind them, taking up the last bit of space in the room. I teetered on the threshold, reluctant to leave before I could hear what the Healers thought of her condition.

One of them removed the cloth from her forehead, replacing it with his palm. He looked at the others and shook his head.

'She's running a fever. Help me move her. We need to examine her injuries.'

The other two came to stand with the first, and together, they gently rolled Syra onto her side. She was now facing me, but her gaze went right through me.

The Healers lifted her shirt and peeled back the strips of fabric from her legs. They examined her in silence, giving no indication of what they were thinking. Finally, they began to murmur to each other. I couldn't catch what they were saying. I glanced at Ray, who stood with his back to me, and could read from the set of his shoulders that he too, was confused.

The Healers rolled Syra again, this time onto her front. She let out a muffled moan, her hands clenching the sodden sheets. I got a glimpse of her exposed back and legs before the Healers' hands settled just above her skin. Several deep wounds slashed her back open along its length and down her calves. The gashes looked red and swollen – a sure indication of infection. The Healers stood over her, chanting quietly. Their hands began to glow, filling the room with a steady pulsing light. I watched in awe as the scarlet gashes on Syra's back started to knit themselves closed, the angry swelling disappearing. Less than a minute later, her injuries had disappeared, all signs of the attack gone.

My eyes moved to her face. It had returned to its normal colour, the flush of fever gone. Her eyes remained shut, moving beneath the delicate lids as if she were caught in a dream. I glanced back at the Healers. They pulled her shirt down, and gently rolled her onto her back. Their hands flitted over her, resting briefly on her face, shoulders and arms. They nodded to each other, and for the first time since their arrival, acknowledged my and Ray's presence.

'She'll be fine now. She needs to rest. Make sure she drinks plenty of water when she wakes, but small sips at a time. And she must eat. She can't be alone for the next few days.'

Ray and I looked warily at each other, the unspoken thought hanging between us.

Ray scrubbed his hands over his face, sighing deeply. 'I should be the one to do it.' He glared at me. 'You're a complete stranger. She should have someone beside her who she knows, and trusts.'

I shrugged. 'Then do it.'

'And leave everyone leaderless, at a time like this?'

'Then you have your answer, Ray. What do you want from me? I'll look after her. I'm staying here anyway. It's the most obvious arrangement.' I hoped my discomfort didn't show on my face.

'And you owe her your life.'

'Yes,' I said simply. 'I know you don't think much of me, and I don't blame you. You don't know me. I'm human. I tick all the boxes to earn your distrust. If you can't believe in my good intentions, then believe in this – this city is my shelter now. I have nowhere else to go. I wouldn't jeopardise that.'

Ray nodded. 'You're right. I've never met a human who didn't put himself and his survival first. Fine. You will keep an eye on her. And I will keep an eye on you.'

The Healers left the room in silence, leaving the three of us in the confines of the small bedroom.

'At least now we have an actual use for you,' Ray muttered as he squeezed past me into the living room. 'I'll be back to check on her every day. If anything happens to her, I can think of several very painful and unpleasant ways for you to die.'

He slammed out of the house without waiting for my reply. I looked back at Syra, her face relaxed and childlike as she slept. I had hoped to remain separate from the inhabitants of this city. To do what was needed to remain within the safety of its walls, but to remain separate. It seemed the more I tried to distance myself, the more involved I became. Looking at her face in the dwindling light, I knew I had failed at remaining a mere observer.

Dominico appeared just as I was starting dinner, her face set in its habitual blank stare.

'Hi.'

She nodded in return, her eyes moving to the steaming pot of soup on the stove.

I moved it off the heat. 'Help yourself.'

She snatched a bowl from the kitchen table and yanked a drawer open, rooting around for a moment before coming up with a spoon. She filled her bowl to the brim, slurping it before she had even reached the table. Some of it slopped over the bowl and onto the floor, leaving a red trail in her wake.

She hesitated before taking a seat, regarding the bowl dubiously. She turned to me and raised an eyebrow.

'I know. I had a little trouble figuring it all out. Never had to cook for myself. It's probably inedible, but unless you're volunteering to take over, this is what you're in for.' She nodded and dipped her spoon, her movements somewhat less enthusiastic than before.

I turned back to the pot. The soup had started out thin, watery and red, thanks to the tomatoes I'd discovered. Now it was thick and glutinous, and so intense a scarlet that it almost hurt to look at it. I stirred a little more, although there was no salvaging it now.

'Is Syra still not back?'

'You haven't heard.'

'Heard what?'

'She got back late this afternoon. She was injured. Attacked by a canine. Actually a pack of them.'

Dominico paused, her spoon halfway to her mouth. 'Is she ok?'

'She is now. The Healers were here.'

'The Healers?'

'The superhuman version of a doctor, I suppose. Except I've never seen a human doctor do what they did.' For once, Dominico's permanent scowl had given way to something else. It was so odd to see a different expression on her face that it took me a moment to recognise it. Fascination.

'What happened?' She had stopped eating, her spoon lying

forgotten in her cooling soup, her eyes fixed on me.

'They did this chanting thing and kind of waved their hands over her. Her wounds healed. Just like that. I've never seen anything like it.'

She smiled a little. It softened her face, smoothing away the lines of tension and bringing back a touch of her youth. 'We're not so bad, after all, huh?'

I busied myself with fixing a bowl of soup for Syra, even though she was still sound asleep. I didn't want to discuss my growing respect for these beings, especially not with this volatile child.

'I've got to take this to Syra.'

'Fine,' she muttered. I risked a glance at her over my shoulder. The scowl had settled again between her brows. Seeing her guard rear up, I suddenly regretted my withdrawal.

***

Using my foot to push Syra's door open, I set the tray of food beside her bed. Her eyelids flickered then opened, slowly, warily, as if she were waking from a pleasant dream she would rather not leave. Her gaze fell on me and she blinked several times, with slow deliberation.

'Rogan?' It was the first time she had ever called me by my name, instead of my station.

'Hi. How are you feeling?'

She tried to lift herself into a sitting position, but only got as far as propping herself up on her elbows. I leaned closer, reaching for the pillows behind her. She glanced up at me through heavy lids, our faces so close her features were blurred. With every breath her scent filled my nose. I fought the urge to rear back. Hastily stacking the pillows against the wall, I eased her into a sitting position.

'Tired. What happened?'

I reached for the tray, slipping it into my lap. 'The Healers were here. They said you'll be fine. You need to eat. And you need fluids.'

'And you're my nurse?' Her tone was teasing, but there was something else beneath the forced lightness, a loaded question.

'Ray wanted to be here. But –'

'He has a city to run. I get it.'

She reached for the bowl, making an effort to steady her hands. For a long moment she continued to reach for the food, then finally dropped her hands into her lap. A crescent of sweat lined her lip.

I sat on the edge of the bed and dipped the spoon into the soup. She scowled, then opened her mouth and accepted the soup grudgingly.

I kept feeding her until the bowl was half empty. A slice of bread remained on the tray. I was about to offer it to her when I thought about how close my fingers would be to her mouth. I reached for the glass of water instead, allowing her small sips, until she waved it away. The intimacy of feeding her, nursing her, made the room feel tight and airless. I sat back, needing to breathe my own air.

'I appreciate you doing this.' I got the impression she was saying this merely to fill the silence and ease our mutual discomfort. 'I know it's not what you signed up for.'

'It's fine. You want more of this?'

'No, thanks. Don't have much of an appetite.'

'Plus the soup is awful.'

She smiled. 'Yes it is.'

'Doc says you need to eat.' Ray's voice startled me, and I had to grab the tray to prevent it from sliding off my lap.

He filled the room with his presence. I slid off the armchair, handing him the tray. 'You can finish up then. I'm sure you have plenty to discuss.'

I slipped from the room, neither of them acknowledging my departure, their easy laughter seeing me out the door.

Syra

'Glad to see you're awake.' Ray's voice was gruff. He took the chair the Commander had left, placing the tray on the bed beside me. 'You need to try to finish this.' Cradled in his hand, the bowl looked like a teacup from a child's play-set.

'The human look after you alright?'

I laughed weakly. 'Yes, *the human* did fine. A bit uncomfortable, though.'

Ray looked repentant. 'I figured it would be. We just can't spare anyone. He's the only one in this city not doing something to contribute.'

'Don't worry, Ray, he'll be put to work soon enough.'

'What happened out there? We thought you were okay when we didn't hear from you. You know – no news is good news and all that.

Why didn't you let Carolyn know you were in trouble?'

'It happened too fast. When I first heard them stalking me, I thought maybe I was imagining things, and then when I realised they were really there, it didn't even cross my mind to message for help. No one would've reached me in time anyway.'

'How did you get away?'

'I didn't. It was... Draiken. He found me.'

'Found you?'

'Yes. He's been closed off to me ever since he left. But he must've heard me somehow. And he must've been close by. We didn't really discuss it.' I felt the familiar thickening of my throat. The feeling was becoming synonymous with thoughts of Draiken.

'It didn't go well.' His sympathy almost pushed me to the edge. I could've taken his lecturing, or even him saying I told you so. But this unexpected sympathy was almost too much for me.

I shook my head mutely, trying to gather myself.

'You could say that.' I looked down at my hands. They were clenched together, like two people in danger of drowning. With effort, I unclenched them and settled them back into my lap. 'He wouldn't listen to reason. I went to try to make him see, to change his course, but I also went because I *had* to see him. Living without him... it feels all wrong. I don't know what I thought would happen. It's not as if he could come back.' My hand had found its way into Ray's. He gave it a gentle squeeze.

'Do you know what he's planning?'

'War. He's going to provoke the humans, push the tensions between us and them to breaking point. I don't know how.'

'War is inevitable. Even without Draiken, it would happen eventually. The humans' fear of us only grows with time. Their solution is to get rid of the thing they fear.'

'Draiken won't be open to negotiations. He hates the humans too much. And his plan, for when we win the war, is to force humans to transition. That's how he'll keep our numbers growing.'

'You have to admit, it is a solid plan.'

I turned on him, about to give him a verbal lashing. He held up a hand. 'Before you kill me, hear me out. We haven't found any other way to increase our population. So far, the only way is the conventional one, and correct me if I'm wrong, but we only have ten children. Ten. In all the years of us living in Jozenburg. And even if we could populate at the same rate as humans, there aren't enough families for in-breeding not to become a problem eventually. Unless we all have ten children each. But that's a moot point. What, exactly, is our plan?'

The rest of my soup was growing cold in Ray's hands. I wasn't hungry. Still, I wished I could fill my mouth with the crimson liquid, just to avoid having to answer.

The anger seeped out of me, replaced by a feeling of clawing desperation, as familiar as an old friend.

'I don't know, Ray. The alternative isn't a choice. But can we live with enslaving another species just to ensure our own survival? Can you?'

'So we face certain death?'

There was a shuffling sound at the door. I hadn't realised until now that Ray had left it open. Dominico stood in the doorway, her expression of shock confirming my fears. She had overheard every word.

'So that's it?' her voice was low, every syllable trembling with her anger. 'You just wipe out an entire human city? She took another step into the room. 'Why stop there?'

I tried to sit up, wanting to go after her. My head swam, the room swaying and tilting until I was forced to lie back again.

'Dominico – '

'Don't talk to me,' she spat. 'I know most of the people that live in Toria. They're more my people than any of you are, or ever will be.'

Ray was on his feet. 'You mean the people who tried to sentence you to death, just for being different? Those people?' They stood toe to toe. 'We're your salvation. Your only hope. You think any of the other human cities will take you in? Assuming there are any left? Crane will have made sure you'll be delivered straight into his hands. Syra campaigned to let you stay. She reminded us all that we are compelled, by our law, to help one of our own. And that's what you are. *One of us.*'

'Ray. Give us a minute.'

Dominico tried to stomp away, but Ray reached for her, blocking her exit. His grip brooked no argument. She sank into the chair beside the bed.

The door closed behind Ray. I looked at her steadily. 'I understand your reaction.'

Dominico snorted.

'As you heard, I'm not for this plan either. I want you to understand something. Our most sacred law is to uphold life. Not just our own, but all life. This will go directly against everything we believe in. But if the humans declare war on us, we will fight back. That's all I can concentrate on right now. I don't know what will happen after.'

She refused to look at me. Her gaze remained fixed at her feet. 'I won't fight for you.'

'No one is forced to fight. When the time comes, it'll be your choice which side you defend.'

Her head snapped up. 'I have a choice?'

'Of course.'

'Even after... you took me in?'

'A sense of belonging can't be forced. If you decide to return to Toria, or any of the human cities, that's your decision. This isn't a prison.'

Hope lit her eyes, her whole face brightening. 'You think President Crane will take me back?'

'If there's something in it for him, you can bet your life on it.'

The light left her face. 'Because he's human, right?'

'No. Because he's Crane.' It was an odd certainty, given my limited contact with him. It was an intuition. One I felt compelled to listen to.

She thought about this for a moment, already learning to block me out of her mind. I could only catch snatches and broken fragments, none of which added up to much.

Not wanting to leave things as they were, I leaned forward, hoping to engage her for a minute.

'So I hear you've got quite the talents.'

She looked up despite herself, her expression wary.

'I don't know what Raven told you but –'

'She told me you were gifted with two exceptional abilities.'

Dominico's face relaxed, the stiffness of her shoulders melting away.

'Oh. I thought after what happened she'd be angry.'

'Raven has seen a lot in her years of being a mentor. It's not the first time she's been affected by someone else's power. She likes her role as a lab rat. Her words, not mine.'

This brought a brief smile to the girl's face. The gesture changed her whole countenance. She looked her age again, her habitual guarded expression slipping to reveal that last vestige of youthful innocence.

A moment later she seemed to catch herself and withdrew again, shoulders hunched as she fixed her eyes on the floor.

I sighed inwardly. 'I'm tired now. Bring Ray back in for a minute, will you?'

Chapter Seventeen

Dominico

The attention I was getting after every training session was starting to get on my nerves. I hated the way they stared at me, how whispered conversations halted when I got too close. I didn't care what they were saying about me. I might as well get used to it. I was going to spend my whole life being different. Here at least you'd think I could blend in with everyone else. Instead, I stood out like a flashing beacon. None of them tried to talk to me, something I was grateful for. It was only when I missed home, and Mom and Dad, that I ever really missed being talked *to*, not talked *about*.

One afternoon, after we were dismissed early, I walked home under a grey sky, heavy with clouds. I couldn't stop looking at it. The air felt damp and electric, as if in anticipation. People were scurrying around, kids yelling with excitement. Buckets of all shapes and sizes were brought out of the houses and put out in the open, and only after I passed yet another home with three buckets out front did I realise what they were doing. Catching rain water. It wasn't something we had ever done in Toria. I had never really thought about it, but now it seemed a totally obvious way of stretching water rations. I wondered why no one in Toria had thought of it. Maybe it was one of Crane's endless rules, another way to control us.

'Hey.' I was so used to no one besides Syra and Rogan talking to me that I carried on walking, assuming the greeting was meant for someone else.

'Hey!'

I stopped, confused. A dark-haired girl walked up to me, her sleek black ponytail trailing a dark ribbon down her back. Lily.

I eyed her warily.

'Geez, didn't you hear me?'

'Sorry,' I muttered. 'I was thinking about something.'

She laughed, the sound surprisingly girly. 'You seem to do a lot of thinking, Domo.'

The casual way she used the nickname, the one my father had used, made me prickle with resentment.

'Don't call me that!'

'Whoa, touchy.' She leaned close and lowered her voice, as if confiding something. 'People think you're a tad unfriendly, you know. They even have a nickname for you. Ice Queen. You might want to work on that.'

I whirled on her, feeling my hands close into fists. 'Why I should care what any of you think is beyond me.'

She looked at me, her eyes bright. She patted my shoulder. 'I knew I'd like you, Dominico.' She said my name with exaggerated emphasis, but there was no malice in her tone. Her smile was warm, and something about the openness of her face, the toughness I sensed underneath, reminded me of Kat.

'I thought you all hated me.'

Lily waved a hand. 'Nah. They don't hate you. They've just never seen anyone like you.'

I frowned. 'This is a city full of superhumans. *Everyone* is like me.'

She shook her head. 'You really have no idea, do you?'

'What?'

'Raven has never seen a power like yours. She's been a mentor for years. You gave us all a bit of a heart attack when you flattened her. Including me.' She grinned. 'Hence all the hostility.'

This was starting to feel like a chat. A conversation for no other reason than to shoot the breeze. Like we were friends or something.

'Was there something you wanted?'

'You really are hostile.' She said it without a hint of annoyance. This girl was impossible to offend. 'I just thought you could use some interaction, with someone who's a little closer to your age than those crones you're living with.'

I hesitated. The only thing that had kept me sane these past few days was the fullness of my days. Coming back to Syra's place every day, it was all I could do not to fall asleep in the doorway. But it kept me from thinking too much, from replaying that moment in The Waste before I had run, leaving my parents to their fate. It kept me from picturing Kat, placing the moments we'd had together next to the final image I had of her, like some macabre before and after.

'So you can control the elements. I watched you that first day of my training. That must be pretty cool.'

Lily made no comment at my change in attitude. Instead, she walked next to me the rest of the way home, talking the entire way, only pausing to hear my answers to her barrage of questions. She left me at my front door, waving goodbye. I watched her go, my loneliness fading for the first time since my arrival in the city.

*****

I went to bed feeling better than I had in weeks. I thought of Lily and the possibility of having a friend here. I could have someone to talk to, even if it was only about trivial things. I fell asleep without my usual struggle, a sweet breeze blowing in through my open window.

I woke up the next morning to sunlight pouring into my room. I blinked against the brightness. The curtains were open wider than I remembered. I was sure I had left them open just enough for the night air to make its way into my room. I rubbed the sleep from my eyes and pushed off the edge of the bed, stumbling across the room to close the curtains against the glare.

Something crunched beneath my foot, bare toes sinking into something soft and yielding. I yanked my foot away and looked down. What looked like a small pile of rags lay on the floor near the window. My heart accelerated, my mouth as dry as the dirt in The Waste. I picked up the pile and unwound the rags, keeping the bottom layer intact. It took my brain a minute to figure out what it was looking at. A dead pigeon, its wings matted against its bloody body, delicate bones broken. An empty eye socket stared up at me. Death's scent rose from its tiny body, filling my nose with the stench of decay. Something white squirmed in the open wound of the bird's chest. I gagged and dropped it. Tripping over my own feet, I fell backwards and narrowly missed hitting my head against the bedside table. I sat where I'd fallen, my chest heaving with the effort of not screaming, of keeping the tears at bay. I covered my face, muffling the dry sobs that wracked my body.

Stop it. Stop being a baby. It's just a bird.

I blubbered a while longer, until finally I was able to swallow without feeling like I had a fist stuck in my throat. Scrubbing at my face, I stared at the gore seeping into the old threadbare carpet. A stain was forming, one I knew I wouldn't get out, no matter how much I scrubbed it. A reminder of my place in this city. A cold rage filled me.

I got to my feet, throwing on clothes without noticing what I was putting on. I opened my door a sliver and peered out. The house was silent. I closed the door again, careful to do it quietly. Searching my measly closet, I finally settled on an old pair of socks I normally wore at night when the weather turned chilly. I slipped one of the socks over my hand. Breathing through my mouth, I pulled the sock over the bird and hid it beneath the bed, hoping the smell would stay contained. I would bury it later.

Just as I was straightening, a knock sounded at my door.

My eyes fell on the bloodstain. I moved to the door and, opening it just wide enough to see who was there, positioned my body in the way of prying eyes. I would rather die than bring this to Rogan's, or Syra's attention. I didn't want their pity.

Rogan smiled in greeting. 'Morning.' He started to say something else, but he must've seen something in my face. I tried to rearrange my features into a blank mask, hoping that whatever he'd seen had disappeared.

'Everything ok?'

'Sure.' I smiled, the gesture so forced it made my cheeks ache. 'Just fine.'

***

I found it hard to focus on training. A refrain had started in my head, playing over and over, demanding all my focus and attention: You don't belong here. The voice was my own, but there were others mixed up in it – my parents, President Crane, Syra and Rogan.

It didn't seem to matter that I had a growing friendship with Lily, or that not everyone in this city hated me. The voice whispered that, no matter where I went – human cities or otherwise – I would always be an outsider. As much as the Creator had loved me and treated me as his own, he'd had no business playing God.

***

The others were enjoying my lack of focus. Sophie managed to take me down twice. Her superior strength and speed brought me to the floor of the training ring over and over again, breathless beneath her solid weight. She strutted out of the ring to the cheers of our audience. Raven looked puzzled, but said nothing.

Two more defeats, courtesy of Angeline and Rafe, and the noise in the training hall became deafening. They loved the spectacle of me eating dirt. It was no contest. The more I tried to concentrate, the louder my inner voice became.

After Rafe had mopped the floor with me, Raven called for a break. I avoided making eye contact, hoping she wouldn't decide this was the time for a pep talk.

'What was that all about?' Lily plonked herself down next to me.

I shook my head. 'Just didn't sleep well last night.' As much as I liked Lily, I wasn't keen to relive the grisly details, even if just in the retelling.

Lily was eyeing me suspiciously. 'Why are you lying?'

I couldn't get used to how direct superhumans were. They said whatever they thought. It still took me by surprise.

'I just... I don't want to talk about it, okay?'

'Something's wrong. I can feel it coming off you.'

On any other day, I might've welcomed her concern. But today, the image of that dead bird was branded into my mind, alight with detail, and even though I knew it was unfair to assume the worst of her, I couldn't help but wonder if she'd had a hand in it. Be friendly to the new girl. Pretend to be her friend. Ha ha.

I shook my head again, knowing if I opened my mouth, my uncensored thoughts would spill out.

'Okay, break's over,' Raven called.

I made my way back to the ring, trying not to feel bad about snubbing Lily.

'Levin and Dominico. Let's see what you've got.' Raven placed a few random objects in the ring – an old deflated soccer ball, a busted chair.

Snickers circled us as we faced off in the ring. He grinned, cocky as ever. It was the first time we had trained together, which I was sure was no coincidence. I'd watched him against other opponents and he was useless. His attitude was completely at odds with his abilities.

We met in the ring and shook hands, my skin crawling at his touch. He leaned close. 'Like my little present?' His breath washed over my face, leaving me with the urge to rub my face.

I froze. He stepped away, bouncing on the balls of his feet like a boxer, his smile so wide I wished his teeth would fall out.

Suddenly the thought of the dead bird was no longer paralysing. I latched onto the image, using it to drive the anger and outrage that were mixing inside me like a lethal poison. I focused on Levin, ignoring the shouts of the others, blocking out everything but him. I wanted to teach him a lesson. I wanted him to feel the helplessness, the *aloneness* I'd felt this morning.

He went for the soccer ball. Typical. Easy stuff first. He got the ball suspended mid-air on his first try. He let it hover in place, taking his time, letting me get a good look at it. I waited. I wanted him to feel the impending victory. I hoped he could taste it, sweet and round on his tongue.

Finally, he made his move. I could almost hear him make the decision, and at that exact moment I reached out, stilling his mind and crowding it with my own instructions. The ball started to move towards me, then stopped. It hovered in the air, quivering between us. He was fighting me. I was surprised by the fierceness of his rebellion. For an instant, my confidence flagged. I watched the ball slip back towards me. If I lost control now, it would fly at my head and my humiliation would be complete. That thought, and the sharp image of the dead pigeon, tipped things in my favour. The ball flew across the ring and smacked Levin right in the forehead. He collapsed to the ground. Faker. I hadn't even hit him that hard.

Raven leaped into the ring and crouched beside Levin. She muttered something and then helped him to his feet. I searched the faces of the crowd and found Lily. I waited for the appreciation I knew would be there. But her eyes were wide, her mouth open, and even from where I stood I could read her expression. Disapproval. I shifted my gaze to Sophie. She looked at me with frank disgust.

Raven frowned at me. 'Take a break.' It was only then that I realised I was smiling.

Syra

The following day I felt well enough to prop up my own pillows, and to rest against them without any help from Rogan. I had started calling him that. Rogan. Not commander. I wasn't sure when that had happened.

He swept in with my tray. When I sat up unassisted, he raised an eyebrow. 'Feeling stronger today?'

I nodded. He placed the tray beside the bed, movements brisk and business-like, eyes trained away from my face.

I glanced at the contents of the tray. Two slices of what looked like pork. A stack of carrots and potatoes. My mouth flooded.

'You've been asleep most of the day. I didn't want to wake you.' Before I could reply, he hurried on. 'Ray agreed it was best to let you sleep.' He said this defensively, as if I had accused him of neglect.

'I guess wrestling a canine can be exhausting.' The joke fell flat. I wanted to snatch the tray from him and fill my mouth with food just so I would stop talking. Why was I trying so hard to put him at ease? Especially when my attempts seemed to have the opposite effect. He shifted and smiled weakly, his strained politeness unbearable.

He settled the tray in his lap, preparing to feed me. I shook my head and reached for it, discomfort making me clumsy. As he handed me the tray it started to slip from my grasp. He caught it, managing to keep all the food on my plate. I let out a nervous giggle. He looked at me and finally relaxed, his smile reaching his eyes. The painfully taut line of his shoulders loosened.

'Easy does it.' He put the tray on my lap, making sure it was stable. He sat back and watched me cut my meat and vegetables with painstaking slowness. Getting the food to my mouth was easier, my hands much steadier than the day before.

I expected him to leave, but instead he settled in his chair, getting comfortable. I glanced at him, wondering why he was lingering. Reading my expression, he shrugged.

'Ray has given me strict instructions to make sure you eat it all.'

I stuffed another forkful into my mouth, my cheeks rounding with the excess of food.

'Although I don't think that's going to be a problem.'

Realising he was teasing me, I tried to smile, but it was impossible with my mouth so full. I swallowed noisily.

A long silence followed, the only noise the clatter of cutlery against my plate.

'You know, if we're going to be working together, we may as well get to know each other.' As soon as the words had left my mouth, I wanted to take them back. Why was I such a loon around this human? It was if my skin no longer fit, as if I no longer knew how to inhabit my own body.

He looked at me, his expression wary. 'I suppose so. What do you want to know?'

That threw me even more. What did I need to know, beyond his professional skills, and the knowledge he claimed to have?

Sensing my discomfort, he spoke quickly into the vacuum of silence.

'I don't know much about you, other than you're the leader of this city. Come to think of it, I have very little clue about how this place runs, either.'

'Ray didn't put you to work while I was gone?'

'Quite the opposite. I got the feeling everyone would be more comfortable if I didn't show my face too often. So I was mostly here.'

'Really? That's unlike Ray.'

'People seem uneasy about having me here. Which makes it even more of a mystery that the vote went my way.'

'They're grateful. For what you did.'

'But no less suspicious of me.'

I tipped my head to the side, scrutinising him. 'Wouldn't you be? Suspicious? If one of us were in your city?'

The question seemed to irritate him. 'I've done nothing to warrant their suspicion.'

'Agreed. But you are human. Different to us. Isn't it our differences that makes humans distrust us?'

'You were human once.'

'Yes but –'. I trailed off as I realised what he'd said. 'Wait. How do you know that?'

'Crane makes it his business to know his enemies.'

'You might prove to be an invaluable font of information after all.' Crane's knowledge of this, of me, was unsettling. What else did he know about us? And where was he getting his information from?

'I was human a very long time ago.' I tried to drag my thoughts from maddening speculation. 'I don't remember most of it, only the last year or two. Before the lab.'

Something in my tone got his attention. He looked at me with open curiosity, but didn't pursue it.

'What about you? What was it like in Toria? Crane seems very... regimented in his methods.'

Rogan laughed. It occurred to me how seldom he let his guard down long enough to laugh. Then I realised it had been sharp, its echo leaving a bitter aftertaste.

'I had it better than most. More rations, better housing. The ear of the president.' He seemed to drift for a moment, lost in thought. 'But the best thing was the companionship between the men. I was never alone. We stayed in the barracks. We worked together, spent every waking moment together. The men looked out for each other.' He shook his head, smiling a little. His face looked flushed, the colour high in his cheeks. 'I miss that.'

I studied him. There was something poignant about his words. Something lay beneath, a need that had driven him into a career that guaranteed him company. With a start I realised I had stopped trying to read his mind, or pry into it and uncover the things I imagined he was hiding. I was trying to get to know him the conventional way. The way two humans would work their way, through polite conversation and gentle probing, from being strangers to becoming friends. I pushed the thought aside. I needed to know things about him. I knew every resident who currently lived in this city. And knowledge of him was even more important. To know your enemy as well as your friends.

'What about your family?'

He snapped out of his daze, his eyes clearing. His guard came back up so sharply it brought an audible chill to the room. 'I have no family.'

***

I was itching to get on with things. After three days, my bed felt like a coffin, my room like a burial chamber. It was stifling and hot, and I had nothing to occupy my mind but books I had read a dozen times already and my own relentless thoughts.

The monotony of doing little besides sleeping and eating was wearing on me. I needed to do something useful. Something that didn't involve being in bed.

Ray surprised me that morning by bringing me breakfast himself. Rogan was nowhere to be seen. He had left so abruptly last night that I wasn't able to call him back and apologise for my intrusive question. I should've known better. The human war had broken up so many families. There seemed to be few that remained intact.

Ray handed me the tray. Oats, with a scattering of sugar. I took a few mouthfuls. 'I need to get out of this bed. I feel much better. Strong enough to at least take up some of my duties. We need to talk seriously about Draiken, and the war. And we need to talk to Rogan, find out what he knows.'

'You're on a first-name basis now?'

'You're the one who left him to nurse me.'

'I thought you'd understand. I didn't have a choice. Someone –'

I waved a hand, already regretting my outburst. 'Forget it.'

A heavy silence filled the room, clouding it with a fog that reeked of resentment.

He rose. 'After breakfast we can call a meeting with Rogan. We need to talk to everyone, have a mass meeting, and prepare them for what's likely to come.'

Rogan appeared at the bedroom doorway, as if summoned. 'Raven is here to see you.' I tried to catch his eye to convey my apology, but he left as quickly as he'd appeared. Raven stepped into the room, a strange expression on her face.

'I'm glad I caught you both. I need to discuss something with you.'

Ray crossed to the other side of the room. He leaned back and crossed his arms, focusing his attention on Raven. He took up nearly half the length of the wall.

I waved her in, grateful for the interruption. 'What is it?'

'This new girl, Dominico.'

'What about her?'

'She's growing more powerful every day. She has unusual control over her abilities, especially for someone so young. But her abilities are growing at a rate I've never seen before. When she first got here she could only create false images that she layered over reality. Now, those scenes feel completely real, like she's dropped you into another world. You can touch the things in the scene, and they feel solid, real.

You can smell the scents too. It's unbelievable. And it seems to be effective, no matter who you are. I got her to try it on a few of the others-'

'Raven! You know you're not supposed to do that.' I sat abruptly, causing both Rogan and Ray to start towards me. An odd tension was emanating from Ray. I turned my attention back to the discussion, trying to ignore the atmosphere of the room.

She held up a hand. 'I know. But hear me out. Her abilities remain the same, no matter who she casts on. No matter how powerful her opponent, she can influence everyone I've put her in the ring with. Same goes for her mind control ability. No one can withstand her.'

'What's the issue?' Ray asked.

'Don't you see? She has no loyalty to us. What if she decides to go back to Toria? If she's not our ally, we're in trouble. Fighting against her, if it came to that, would be pointless. No one can overpower her.' Raven's face clouded. 'Her only weakness is her temper.'

I shook my head. 'What do you mean?'

Raven shook her head. 'I think there's something going on with her and the other trainees. I've been putting her against the others, to judge how they're all improving. There was... an incident yesterday with Levin. She used his own powers against him, and nearly concussed him in the process.'

I didn't like where this discussion was going. 'You shouldn't allow them to practise on each other. You know that's not how it's done.'

'Traditionally. Personally, I think it's time to look at a new approach.'

'But you just said Dominico could've really hurt Levin,' Ray interjected.

'All the trainees I have are able to control their abilities. Now they need to hone them. What's better practice – for them to keep repeating the same old exercises, or for them to learn to fight back on someone as powerful as this girl?'

There was silence. I could feel the tension in the room, an unwelcome visitor intruding on our discussion. 'Let's look at this logically. She doesn't have the option of returning to Toria. She escaped. There's no motivation for her to go back.'

'Unless her parents are alive,' Ray said.

I thought back to when Rogan and Dominico had first arrived.

'Rogan said they were caught in The Waste.'

'That doesn't mean they're dead.'

I felt an icy finger of dread run along my spine. 'Crane is smart. He could've kept them alive. But only if he knew how powerful she was, surely?'

'Not necessarily.' Rogan's voice made us all turn. 'We need to have that meeting. There's something you all need to know.'

Rogan

This was the moment to play my card. The one that had got me through the gates of Jozenburg, and out of Crane's reach. Once I did this, there would be no turning back. Once I exposed Crane and handed my knowledge of his plans to his enemies, I was aligning myself with them. The thought left me oddly bereft. The strangeness of this city felt like a knot around my neck, tightening one inch at a time. But if I withheld what I knew, I was putting myself in a precarious position. In the furthest part of my mind, I felt the prick of morality. I had promised Syra information. She had taken me in on good faith that I would keep my word.

We gathered at Ray's house. Syra, despite his protests, had insisted on having the meeting anywhere but within the confines of her own home. The short walk to his place seemed to both revive and tire her. She leaned on Ray for support, her steps careful and halting. Raven walked beside them, alternating between concern for Syra, and shooting me looks loaded with suspicion.

Arriving at Ray's home I stepped back, allowing the others to step inside ahead of me. I glanced around as I moved through the doorway. The lounge was furnished with a ragged two-seater, and an armchair which sank in the middle, giving the impression that someone had recently vacated it. There was only one small window which allowed snatches of sunlight, lending the room a vaguely morbid feel. From where I stood I glimpsed the kitchen, a tiny nook of a room which looked just as dark as the lounge.

Ray motioned for us to sit.

'Take her for a second, will you?' He carefully propped Syra against Raven and then disappeared into an adjoining room. Syra leaned away from Raven and shuffled to the chair, attempting to seat herself whilst ignoring Raven's protests. Ray returned with a faded throw pillow. He shot Raven a pointed look.

Raven threw up her hands. 'You know how she is.'

Syra sank into the armchair, a smile of triumph lighting her face, despite her obvious discomfort. He waved the pillow at her. 'May I?'

He positioned it behind Syra's back. She sighed. 'Enough with treating me like I'm an invalid. I'm weak, not dying.'

Ray ignored her and motioned for Raven and me to take the two-seater. Raven sat at the far end of the couch, eyeing me warily.

Ray remained standing, uneasy in his own home.

'Let's get started.'

I cleared my throat. The words I needed felt lodged in my mouth, a stack of blocks refusing to fall. I felt a cold wave of panic. There would be no returning from this moment. All allegiance to my previous life, to the people in it, was about to evaporate.

'Well?' Raven snapped, her feet tapping out an impatient beat.

I willed my tongue to unglue itself from the roof of my mouth.

'Crane has a plan for the war. He's been planning it for some time, from what I can gather. He's amassing an army –'

'Well this is hardly news.' Raven said.

'Let me finish. His army isn't human. They're like you.'

This silenced even Raven.

'I know it sounds impossible. I didn't believe it myself. But I saw the sketches. The notes. He's been experimenting, trying to find a way to create more superhumans.'

'You must be mistaken,' Ray said. His face distorted as he struggled to digest my words, but beneath his incredulity I sensed a glimmer of dread.

'I saw one of my own soldiers in those sketches. A soldier with a long history of disobedience and rebellion. He disappeared from the barracks one night and was never seen again. Until I found those sketches.'

Syra had not said a word. She had gone pale, her dark eyes darting around the room. Her fingers drummed out her agitation on the arm of the chair.

'I don't know if he's had any successes. There were too many pages of notes and I couldn't get through everything. But I know Crane. He won't stop until he's satisfied, until he's sure he can defeat you.'

'How would he know how to turn them? The Creator was the only one with all the knowledge, all the equipment. How...' Syra trailed off. I could see she was putting it together in her mind, fitting the pieces together to form the whole picture.

'The lab was burned to the ground, along with everything in it,' Ray said.

'They must've raided the lab before they set it alight. They must've taken all the equipment, his notes. It's the only explanation.' She turned to me, her expression tight. 'Were you there?'

All eyes fixed on me. It was a question I had expected earlier, but it was one that seemed only just to have occurred to them. 'No, I wasn't. I was still in training then. I was too young to be sent out on a mission of that... magnitude.'

Syra sat back, her fingers stilling from their relentless drumbeat. Her face lost its pinched look and some of the natural colour returned to her skin. Ray and Raven hadn't lost an ounce of their suspicion. Both of them stared at me openly, their eyes like searchlights, trying to find the fault in my story.

'How do we know you aren't trying to mislead us?' Raven asked.

'I can't force your trust. I've told you this because I gave my word I had valuable information.' I glanced at Syra. 'I know some of you consider the coming war an easy fight. Now you know better. Crane creating these superhumans could mean anything – beings like you, or beings faster, stronger, meaner. I'm betting on the latter.'

Raven stood and paced the room. 'Dominico could be our winning card, especially since Crane has no idea how powerful she is.'

Syra held up a hand. 'That child has no loyalty to us. I think if it comes to a war, she won't fight for us.'

'She'll fight for the humans?'

'If her parents are alive, Crane will use them to bring her back,' I said. He may not know the extent of her abilities, but it'll be one more superhuman fighting for his side.'

'I don't get it,' Ray said. 'I thought Crane hated all superhumans. Why would he then willingly create and house an army of them?'

'Crane will do whatever it takes. If he wins the war, he'll simply destroy what he's created. Nothing and no one is indispensable to him. He's willing to take the risk if it means the annihilation of every one of you.'

'If Dominico goes back to Toria, we don't have a prayer.' Raven sank back onto the couch. She looked stunned. She stared at her hands for a moment. 'We could imprison her. Make sure she can't escape.'

'No.' Ray glanced at Syra. She nodded. 'We can't lock her away like a criminal,' Ray continued. 'She's one of us. She should be treated as such. Besides, if Crane decides he wants her, standing in his way will only make things worse.'

'We could join forces with Draiken.' Syra's voice was quiet, her gaze fixed on the opposite wall.

'That's madness!' said Raven. 'After what he did? How can you even suggest that? We can't trust him.'

'I'm not saying he should be allowed back into Jozenburg. That door's closed forever. But if we fought together, we would have a better chance. Ten more superhumans, and one of Drake's talents, would even out the playing field.'

'No one would agree to that.'

'It's that, or certain death. Drake wants to be rid of the humans. He risked everything – his home, his life, and his only family – to get the Elders out of his way. So he could go ahead with creating more of us. To win the war.'

'Crane will be expecting all of you.' Every pair of eyes swung in my direction. 'He doesn't know about this division in your ranks. He'll have made sure he's more than made up your numbers. You'll need every fighter you have.'

'Will we put this to a vote?' Raven's question was directed at Syra, but even I could tell she already knew the answer.

Syra shook her head. 'After what he did, they'll vote against it. And then there's a good chance none of us will survive the war. If Draiken turns on us, I'll be the one to deal with him.'

Chapter Eighteen

Rogan

'I think a tour of the city is long overdue, don't you?'

Syra stood in my doorway, looking pale but much more herself. I felt a relief that I was unwilling to examine too closely.

I blinked stupidly, certain I'd misheard her.

'If you're going to be living here, you'll need to know how things run. I thought I'd show you around a bit. You'll need to start doing your share. Better if you at least have an introduction to everything beforehand.'

I nodded, still not saying a word.

'What?'

I shrugged. 'I thought you'd be itching to get back to your duties.'

She scowled. 'Ray has designated the easier stuff to me. I've already done it all.'

It was only midday. Whatever he'd given her to do, it clearly wasn't enough.

I shut the door behind me. 'Let's do it.'

We wound our way along the outskirts of the city, looping halfway around the length of it until we arrived at the fields. Old sheets had been attached to poles to protect the plants from the sweltering heat. Their position meant that, at the hottest time of the day, like now, the plants were well shaded. The fields were dotted with figures, some bending to pick at the crops growing close to the ground, others stretching to reach the fruit ripening on the trees. Everything was planted as closely together as the plants allowed. We took shelter from the heat beneath one of the shade nets.

Syra waved a hand, encompassing it all. 'We take turns harvesting, digging, planting and monitoring the watering. All the plants have been adapted to require very little water.'

I nodded. 'Our plants in Toria too.'

She smiled and shook her head. 'Our seeds are modified a little differently than yours.'

'What do you mean?'

'Ours are not done in a laboratory. Nor do we have any seed from before the war.'

I was stunned. 'You mean...some of you have the talent to modify plants?'

She nodded. 'Lily can influence the elements. Tarell can change the genetic makeup of plants. Animals too, although that's only been proven with a hadeda, never anything else.'

I stared, fascinated. 'What did she do?'

'She changed its appearance. Turned it from brown to blue. Lengthened its wingspan. Gave it bigger talons. She released it afterwards. We still see it around here every now and then. Her modifications turned it into a predator.'

I couldn't verbalise my thoughts. She seemed to take my silence as judgement. She stiffened and turned the opposite way, starting to walk back towards the heart of the city.

I followed, wanting to correct her assumption, and feeling perplexed by my need to do so.

We walked in silence for a while, the sounds of a busy city coming back to us a piece at a time as we drew nearer to its centre.

She motioned to a building on our left, a squat brick structure which was missing a window, and a section of its roof. 'That's the school. Kids from the age of five years start at the lowest grade, and finish when they're sixteen. From there they go into training, to learn to grow and control their powers.' She was avoiding my gaze, looking everywhere but at my face.

I nodded. 'Same with us. Except at sixteen, they're evaluated to determine what they're best suited for. As guards, teachers, field hands...' I trailed off when I caught the expression on her face. 'What?'

'You mean they can only pick one? And they're stuck with it, forever?'

'I wouldn't put it that way. But yes.'

She looked horrified. 'So one person can get tasked with doing field work their whole lives?'

I understood her horror. It did nothing to keep my defensiveness at bay though. 'You make it sound like a punishment.'

'Doing it my whole life, day in and day out? Yes, I would consider that punishment.'

'Not everyone is qualified to do anything else. Like Jozenburg, everyone has to pull their weight in my city too.'

She shook her head and walked ahead again, forcing me to trail behind her like a stray animal. 'Some more than others.' She said it over her shoulder, still moving, and a familiar rush of fury flooded me.

I lengthened my stride to catch up to her. Once I did, I made sure to match her pace. It was juvenile, but I hated following in her wake. It made me feel oddly inferior.

Scattered throughout the city, at regular intervals, the white grace of the wind turbines towered above. I pointed to them. 'Were they here when you first arrived?'

She paused to follow the direction of my finger, craning her head to follow the impressive height of the closest turbine. 'Yes. One of the few useful things from before. They must've been struggling with resources even back then.' She glanced at me, her face partly in shadow as we stepped out of the afternoon sun and into the shade of a nearby house. 'I saw you have them in Toria too. I noticed that a great number of them are around Crane's home.'

She took satisfaction in this fact, as if it alone proved everything that was wrong with Crane, with Toria and with humans. On its own, the number of turbines so close to Crane's home might seem innocuous, but viewed with other facts, like Crane's eternal stash of coffee, it presented a picture impossible to ignore.

Just weeks ago, before I'd seen those papers on Crane's desk, her words would've angered me. I would've jumped to his defence, self-righteous and sure in my belief in him.

'No one questions him. He does as he pleases.'

'Not even you?'

I couldn't look at her, even as I felt her eyes boring into me.

'Especially not me.'

She said nothing for a moment. Out of the corner of my eye I saw her turn her head away, as if sensing my discomfort.

The afternoon wore on. I fast grew weary of her determination to be my tour guide. I felt uneasy in her presence, my skin hot as much from the sun as her nearness.

Finally, we had circled the city and were starting to make our way back to her place.

We passed a building which looked very much like the outside of our jail cells.

'What's that?'

She followed my gaze, then quickly looked away. She seemed intent on passing it, but my pause brought her to a hesitant halt.

'In the past we've had some issues with superhumans who got out of hand.' She looked reluctant to say more, but my pointed stare seemed to convince her to continue. 'Children, who were born with either too many superhuman qualities, or too few.'

'There's such a thing as too many abilities?'

'When they are unable to control them, yes. We haven't had many cases, but it has happened that we've had to separate some of them from the rest of the city, for their safety and everyone else's.'

A breeze came up, briefly taking the edge off the baking heat. She paused, tilting her face towards it. 'Passing on our abilities isn't an exact science. Reproduction is the same for us as for you except, instead of kids inheriting the colour of your eyes, or your laugh, ours receive the ability to read minds, or the gift of superior strength. Sometimes they get every ability their parents have. Sometimes they get nothing at all.'

It took me a minute to fully understand the implication of her words. 'They're punished if they're born with no abilities? They're locked away, for being born different?'

She glared at me, defiant. Beneath her anger was something else, a glimmer of shame. 'I told you, it's for their own protection.'

'Protection from whom? Their own kind?'

'They're not our kind. That's the point.' She said it quietly, her anger gone.

'But they're still children, children produced by superhumans. They still belong to someone.'

She finally looked at me, weary and sad. 'They rarely live beyond their childhood years. We don't know why, but their lack of abilities seems to make them susceptible to disease. We keep them together this way because they need constant care, and, like everything else, we share this responsibility.'

I felt awful for my assumption. I wanted to apologise, but sensing my intention, she cut me off.

'The ones that have too many abilities are often uncontrollable, and usually end up dead too. By their own hand.'

I reached out without thinking, brushing her hand briefly with mine. The contact felt alien and yet familiar, her skin every bit as soft and yielding as any woman's.

'I'm sorry. I shouldn't have assumed.'

She nodded, and we walked on, leaving the building behind. I glanced back, watching as it receded with each step, a sense of pity for its occupants filling my feet with lead.

We walked several minutes in silence, nearing the city centre. The words were out of my mouth before I could rethink them.

'Have you ever tried converting them?'

She shuddered, despite the relentless heat. 'Never the children, no. But it's been done with a handful of humans, with varying results. We lost two of our own, not too long ago, when they tried to pass their abilities on. Their recipients died within a day. Their givers soon followed.'

'I'm sorry.'

She nodded. 'I often wonder about that – them dying within a day. It seems like a kind of link, you know? That maybe, if one survived, the other would too.' She shrugged. 'Just a guess. No way of knowing for sure now.'

I would look back on that afternoon as the moment my perspective really shifted. Seeing her that way, open even though it pained her, honest even though it cost her, I started to see her less as another species, and more as just a woman, someone I could relate to, someone I even had things in common with. She was more human than I'd ever considered. And if she was, then there was the possibility the other superhumans were too. It was a thought that stayed with me.

Dominico

I couldn't understand why I was back in Toria. I moved through our house, the comfort of being home wrapping around me like a cloud. I walked through each room, its silence weighing on me. Mom and Dad's absence left the house an empty shell, the memory of their voices and laughter like ghosts haunting their abandoned home.

I reached their bedroom, sinking onto the edge of their bed, running my hand over the familiar faded blue duvet, touching the pillows and imagining my parents sleeping here, their faces turned toward each other, their hands loosely linked.

Something lay in the middle of the bed. For some reason it lay in shadow, even though the room was brightly lit. I reached for it, and realised it was my father's gun, the one he had strapped to his chest every morning before he became a government official. I picked it up carefully, the way Dad had shown me. The smooth metal was warm to the touch, as if it had been recently fired.

Someone was shouting. It sounded as though it were coming from just outside the house. Before I could even rise from the bed, more voices joined the first one, mingling into a chorus of words that made no sense. I made my way blindly through the rooms, feeling my way along the walls, the light suddenly gone, the gun growing heavy in my hand.

Come outside. The voice spoke right at my ear. I felt the tickle of someone's breath against my cheek, making me jump and claw at the air. There was no one there. A feeling of dread crawled over me. It felt like a million insects on my skin, and even though I knew there was nothing there, I slapped frantically at my arms and shoulders, until the sting forced me to stop. I stood trembling in the darkness, feeling pulled towards the door but wanting to stay where I was.

I fumbled my way to the front door and closed my hand around the handle. Dazzling light appeared at my feet and climbed up my body as the door swung wide. I tried to cover my eyes, but my arm stayed at my side, limp and unresponsive.

Gradually, figures took shape. My eyes began to adjust to the light, and as they did, hundreds of people appeared in front of me. They were somehow featureless, a sea of faces without the lines and shapes of eyes, cheeks, mouths and noses.

One figure separated itself from the crowd and strolled forward. As he walked towards me his features filled in, as if an artist were sketching in the finer details of his subject. I blinked. President

Crane's cool green eyes filled my vision, growing larger as he drew closer, looming over me like an all-seeing being. I wanted to turn and run, to slam the door on him and his ever-growing group. He held out his hand to me, palm up. I tried to keep my hand at my side but it rose anyway, sliding into his, even as I shuddered and tried to shrink away from the brush of his skin against mine.

He smiled, a silent threat lurking beneath his forced geniality. He motioned to the crowd, his mouth moving, his free hand waving maniacally. I couldn't hear a word he was saying, despite the strange silence of the crowd. I was growing anxious, straining to catch his words or at least read his lips. Finally, I looked in the direction he was gesturing, following the line of his finger. My breath stalled in my throat. My heart slowed until I could no longer hear it, and I drifted from the anchor of my body, floating above the scene, watching my parents approach. Their faces were alive with a joy I felt removed from, even as I watched my mouth split into a smile a mile wide.

My body ran into their waiting arms. Dad's hands moved over my face in a frenzy of touch, while Mom stroked my hair over and over. I longed to hear their voices – the sweet lilt of Mom's tone, the unrestrained boom of Dad's laughter.

A hand grabbed my arm, pulling me away from them. I shrieked, feeling the vibration of my vocal cords but hearing no sound. President Crane yanked me towards him. My eyes fell on the faceless crowd. For the first time I noticed their weapons – guns of every description. Some carried nothing at all, the disproportionate bulk of their bodies swaying as they moved to the front of the crowd with a speed that belied their size. They reached out to me with meaty fists, their eyes blank with the stare of death. They advanced on Mom, their shadows falling over her and Dad. *Choose.*

I shot up out of bed, falling to the floor in a tangle of bedding. My scream vibrated through the room, bringing Syra to my door, her eyes wide with alarm, her mouth moving soundlessly. I let the tears run down my face unchecked, my heart a stone fist in my chest.

***

I arrived at training feeling exhausted and wrung-out, like an old dishcloth. I forced my eyes forward, having learned not to look around the hall. I hated the stares, the inevitable whispers. Their growing hostility was becoming commonplace, an accepted and acknowledged way to treat me. Of course we must freeze her out. She's the unknown. It's the only thing to do. The irony of their fear seemed to be lost on them. The last training session with Levin had only worsened things. They now saw me as a heartless bully.

Even Lily was keeping her distance. I wasn't sure if this was because I'd refused to confide in her, or because I'd gloated over defeating Levin. Probably a combination of the two. Still, she was the only one who met my gaze. Her expression was tight and unreadable, but the coolness in her eyes was unmistakable. Having ruined my only chance of friendship in this city, I felt more alone than ever.

Raven motioned me into the middle of the ring, singling me out again, while the others fanned out around us. Despite myself, I caught several people rolling their eyes. Fatigue and frayed nerves had brought me to the edge, and I clenched my hands, digging the nails into my palms, to stop myself from screaming at them.

'Right. Let's start with Levin.' What? I stared at Raven, convinced I'd misheard her. I risked a glance at Levin – he was also looking at Raven, his mouth open. She waved a hand. 'Time to get over your little spat. Dominico – I want to see more control from your side.' I knew she meant my temper, not my powers. 'Levin, you did well last time but you need to try to withstand her.' I cringed inwardly. This enlarged the sign on my back. Raven was calling even more attention to my abilities. Surely she could see how this wasn't a good idea? Especially since I'd beaten and humiliated him yesterday, despite being distracted. I could do much worse today. I felt torn between earning my reputation, and allowing him a piece of his pride.

Raven placed the same old rickety chair in the middle of the ring. 'Well?'

Levin struggled to maintain his usual air of overconfidence. We faced each other with the chair between us, neither of us making the move to shake hands. Raven didn't comment.

Levin zeroed his concentration in on the chair. Technically, I could stop him right there and prevent him even from lifting it, never mind throwing it at me. I waited him out, leaving him to make the first move.

It didn't take him long to take advantage of my hesitation. Within seconds the chair was airborne. Once he threw it, my only option would be to get out of its path. I wondered at Raven's weapon choice.

It wasn't a strong chair, but it was still a piece of furniture, and Levin was guaranteed to throw it as hard as he could. Was she that confident that I would overpower him?

Any moment now, it would be too late to stop him. Would it help me if I let him win? Let him think that I had peaked, and that, with practice he would be better than me? Would that satisfy him enough to stop tormenting me?

The image of the bird came to mind. The wound, which had looked purposely, and cruelly, inflicted. The missing eye. Its delicate wings matted to its body.

The chair jerked in my direction, but paused and hovered in mid-air. I glanced at him, taking in his wide eyes and the line of sweat on his forehead. A wave of something destructive was building in me, pushing me towards the edge. Suddenly everything that had happened to me focused on Levin. I knew this was irrational, but it didn't matter. All I needed was a target, an outlet for the poison churning inside me.

I reached for him, and instead of gently probing, I shoved my way in. He didn't have a chance to resist. I took complete control, without allowing him a single thought of his own. A voice was telling me to stop, but it was thin and reedy, nothing more than a distant whine.

The chair hovered uncertainly for a moment, and then flew at Levin at a speed I knew would knock him off his feet. I could feel his fear, his overwhelming urge to duck. At the last second I let him go. He fell to the floor. The chair sailed past, narrowly missing his head.

***

Raven took me aside after practice, waiting for the hall to clear before saying a word.

I expected her to yell, to tell me how irresponsible I was, how I could've killed Levin.

'You're growing stronger.'

I blinked. Her voice was quiet, her tone neutral.

I opened my mouth to reply, but she abruptly changed the subject. 'Do you like it here?'

I struggled against the enormous lump that had formed in my throat. I swallowed until it was gone, unable to look at her. I was too afraid of what I might see in her expression.

'I see you've become friendly with Lily.'

I didn't bother to correct her. Only yesterday that statement would've been true. But I was learning. Nothing was permanent. Change was the only constant.

'Yeah,' I mumbled. 'She's nice.'

Raven seemed to be waiting for me to say something else.

'It's fine.'

She shook her head. 'You hate it, don't you?'

I wanted to keep it all inside, buried from sight. I didn't want pity or sympathy. But it came out anyway, as reflexive as vomit.

'All the kids hate me. They talk about me behind my back, and they don't even bother to hide it. They threw a dead, stinking pigeon into my bedroom window, so that even when it's hot I sleep with my window closed.' I was close to tears. I clenched my fists, swallowing rapidly, trying to beat back the emotion.

'They fear you.'

'What?'

Raven put her foot on the rope of the training ring and leaned forward.

'You're an unknown. You're different. They don't know what to think of you. Lily is the only one who sees past that.'

'But I'm a superhuman. Like them.'

She straightened. 'Yes and no. They are all on an even playing field. They all have a chance of beating each other in the ring. But with you, they're beaten even before they begin. You can incapacitate them before they even make a move.'

She hesitated, then reached out a hand and awkwardly patted my shoulder. 'You know, if you ever need to talk, you can come to me. We want you to be happy here. You'll see that in time the other kids will forget your differences and be less wary of you. It'll be ok. Now go home. You look exhausted.'

She started to leave, then paused and turned back to me. 'I suspect that Levin is behind a lot of what is happening to you here. I'll talk to him. But what you did today was unacceptable. Don't do it again.'

I walked home slowly, kicking at the occasional stone, sending it skidding across the path. Ironically, this city was similar in some ways to ours. The houses were made from whatever materials could be found. Some were brick and had plastered roofs. In Toria, these were the houses everyone wanted. They were given only to government officials and their families and sometimes soldiers, along with better and larger food portions. I had often wondered why the other families didn't resent this. I asked Dad about it once, and he'd said that government officials offered an important service, and the others admired this. I had never said so, but I'd thought that Dad was only partly right. There were those who hated us for it, who saw the cracks and brutality in our society, and who blamed people like my parents.

Thinking about home made me feel hollow. At first I had wanted to burst into tears every time it came to mind, but now it was as if a plug had been pulled and all my feelings had drained away. Mom and Dad were constantly with me. I would hear them talking to me throughout my day – encouraging me when I felt awful, and praising me when I got through the bad moments. I knew they were just in my head. But that was ok. At least I had them with me.

Things were tense between Syra and me ever since I'd overheard her conversation with Ray. Her words hadn't left me since. The possibility that I could return home, even if President Crane had ulterior motives, was sometimes the only thing that kept me going. If Mom and Dad were there, were alive, it wouldn't matter that I was a social pariah. It was no different here. At least I would be with them. My usefulness to President Crane would guarantee their safety. And if they were dead, at least I would be in a place they had once lived in, a place we had once called home.

I wouldn't have to worry about hiding – everyone in Toria knew what I was, and I wouldn't be punished for it. I couldn't think about the alternative. My world without Mom and Dad was nothing but an empty landscape.

Syra

Draiken paced the length of an unfamiliar room. Mohina flickered in and out of the room, like a candle flame caught in a breeze. They talked, their words garbled and rapid, as if they were speaking a foreign language. At times it felt as though I were inhabiting his body, seeing through his eyes, speaking with his tongue. At other times I was myself, present in the scene and yet somehow disconnected from it.

The room disappeared and was replaced by a much larger one, reminding me of the training hall at home. It was filled with superhumans, their combined energy giving off a low, constant hum. I scanned the crowd, unable to grasp where they had all come from, why there were so many of them. A familiar face sprang out at me. I cried out, but no one seemed to hear me. I reached out for Riley, trying to touch his face, trying to check if he was real. My hands brushed nothing but air, my movements as unnoticed as my voice. The last time I had seen him was that night at the Creator's laboratory. I thought he was dead.

Someone was yelling. I forced my eyes from Riley. A familiar figure had appeared beside Drake. I recognised his stride. His scent reached my nose, triggering the image of a solitary crack along the otherwise flawless wood of an armchair. He shook hands in front of the crowd, a cheer rebounding around the room. Suddenly more familiar faces appeared in the group, their features standing out from the sea of strangers. Becca. Norton. Malcolm. My heart was a hammer in my chest, blotting out the noise of the crowd.

***

The visions had begun two weeks after seeing Draiken. At first, I couldn't tell if I was awake or dreaming. I would jerk out of them the same way I jolted from a nightmare, my breath trapped in my chest, a scream clawing at my throat. It always happened when I was alone, and always at night.

I could only retain scattered details of every vision. What I remembered most clearly was the fear and confusion, and the feeling that I was overlooking something glaringly obvious.

After the third vision, I finally figured out I wasn't dreaming. Every vision centred on Drake. He was present in all of them, somehow the key figure. I couldn't be sure where these visions were coming from – if my missing Drake was somehow conjuring them, or if our connection had been re-established. My frustration at not being able to recall the details gnawed at me. I only had disjointed, disconnected images that seemed unrelated and made no sense.

Sleep would often desert me after these visions. I would try to remember the details, try to piece the fragments together, my overactive mind chasing away any possibility of rest. I couldn't find any pattern or meaning in the images I could recall. When the frustration of it would overwhelm me, I would think of Drake. I would go over the memories of our childhood, taking them out one by one like precious jewels, examining them and then reluctantly putting them away. This was all I had of him now. With my senses I could invoke his scent, the distinctive sound of his laugh, pick out the unusual flecks of gold in his otherwise dark eyes. I watched us walk together, both only six years old, his hand in mine, our communication silent but constant. I saw us in the Creator's laboratory, the night he took us from our human parents, and felt the dampness of my brother's tears on my palm as I wiped them away.

I only allowed myself these moments with him at night, when I had nothing pressing to do, no leadership duties to carry out. I felt guilty allowing myself even this. I was often exhausted in the morning, and I know Ray had noticed my lack of focus. He had said nothing so far, but I knew it wouldn't be long before he asked me why I was so tired, and I wasn't sure if I could tell him the truth. He, and all the others, said they understood Drake was my brother and that it was natural for me to miss him, yet I could feel their concealed anger at him and his brutal actions. Deep down, I knew they all expected me to see him as they did. A monster. A murderer. The problem was, I could never reconcile the Drake I knew with the killer they saw.

Chapter Nineteen

Rogan

Something had shifted since our talk. Syra seemed more at ease in my presence, as if her doubts had been set aside. I sensed a grudging respect from Raven, although she maintained her distance and kept up the pretence of being aloof. Ray was more comfortable with me, although he still seemed over-protective of Syra in my presence.

I was learning the daily schedules of life in this city, and it felt good to be useful again. Without discussion I was given physical tasks to carry out, as if Syra knew this would suit me best. Whether she knew this from delving into my mind, or if it was simply a coincidence, I didn't care. I was happy to get my hands dirty, to feel the satisfaction of sweat on my skin, the stretching and contracting of my body as I worked.

Today I was assisting with patching some of the many crumbling houses. Resources were scarce and those we did have were mostly unsuitable for the job. I stood over a haphazard pile of rubble, trying to figure out how to patch a hole in the side of a house without anything to keep the material in place, or any tools to shape the brick or stone.

I glanced over at the man next door. Sensing my scrutiny, he looked up, his face unreadable.

'Think you can help me with this?'

His shoulders rose to his ears in a gesture of reluctance. He strode over, eyes filled with suspicion.

'How do you get it to stick?'

Without a word he selected a large rock, lifting it with ease and measuring it against the gap. Its considerable weight did nothing to hamper his efforts.

He turned to me, careful to keep his distance. 'The trick is to smooth out and size the rock, or brick, or whatever you're using, to a size that fits the gap. It's not an exact science, but we have to make do with what we have.' He set the rock down at my feet, as if I had any hope of actually lifting it.

Before I could thank him he marched off. I stared at the rock. What was I supposed to shape it with? I glanced around hopefully, wondering if I had somehow missed a stack of tools I could use for the job.

'Having trouble?'

Ray had appeared behind me without a sound. It was a habit of his, one that annoyed me immensely. He was as stealthy as a canine, approaching me in absolute silence. I couldn't understand how a man of his size could move like that.

'A little. What am I supposed to use?'

'Here, let me show you.' Ray picked up the rock as easily as if he were plucking a blade of grass. He fitted his hands around it until he could hold it out in front of him, centimetres from his chest. Streaks of pulsing light shone from between his splayed fingers, and the rock seemed to shrink in size, gradually, as if it were a block of ice melting from the heat of his palms.

The light disappeared abruptly, and Ray placed the rock against the hole, carefully rotating and pushing it until it slotted into the gap. It was a perfect fit.

It took me a minute to gather my thoughts. Every time I witnessed what these beings could do, I was newly amazed. My suspicion of their powers was fading, replaced by a wonder that felt oddly child-like.

I cleared my throat. 'Well. Not exactly something I can do.'

Ray smiled. It carried none of the warmth that he so generously bestowed on Syra and the others, but at least it reached his eyes. 'I don't think your role in this was made very clear. You can sort through the rubble, find suitable materials for the others. What you can't move, the superhumans will.'

I looked down at my hands. I had always considered them large and capable. Looking at Ray, who easily dwarfed me in both size and strength, I felt frustrated. There were things here I couldn't begin to do. Tasks for which my assistance was almost unnecessary, because of my human limitations. The thought startled me. I had never thought being human was a handicap.

Ray caught something in my expression. 'Hey, don't worry about it. Your greatest use is the knowledge you're giving us. Having an insider who knows Crane is much more valuable than anything you do here. This is just to keep you out of trouble.'

I tried to ignore the implication as he patted my shoulder awkwardly and strode away.

When the end of the day finally came I dragged myself back to Syra's, wondering if tomorrow would be another day where my contribution to this place would be so minimal as to almost go unnoticed.

I came through the front door, breathing in the rare aroma of cooking meat. Syra looked up from the stovetop, a spatula in her hand and an apron hugging her lithe figure. The domesticity of her stance and the way she was dressed made me pause in the doorway. The smile of greeting that had been on her lips had faded into an indecipherable expression.

'Hi,' I managed.

She nodded in return, turning back to the meat.

'Beef tonight. One of the calves died suddenly. We lucked out since it's our turn for meat.'

'Our turn?'

'Whenever meat is available, there's a rotation system. That's why it's obviously better if a fully-grown bull or cow dies. More to go around.'

She stooped to open the oven door, then straightened and finally met my eyes. 'There are potatoes too.'

She leaned over the table, apron stretching across her breasts. I forced my gaze away. I could cross the room in two strides. Breathe her in. See if she smelled the way I imagined.

The front door banged open and I turned away, startled out of my thoughts. Dominico stamped inside, leaving tracks of dirt in her wake, having once again ignored Syra's repeated requests to leave her shoes at the door.

'Hi,' she muttered in our general direction. She crossed the room, halfway to her bedroom, then stopped and turned back, seeming to sense the atmosphere. The corner of her mouth tilted upwards, the gesture somehow obscene.

'Well, isn't this cosy? So domestic.' Hearing my exact thoughts come out of her mouth made me shift uneasily.

'So dear, how was your day?' I asked her sweetly. She glared at me and stomped to her room, the slam of her door reverberating through the house.

Syra ducked her head, but not before I caught the smile she was trying to hide. She sighed. 'That girl. I don't know what to do with her. She's permanently in a foul mood.' She took the pan off the heat and, donning tatty oven gloves, pulled out the potatoes, their warm aroma filling the room.

'I think I need to find her another place to stay. The problem is I don't think anyone will take her. The only friend she seems to have made is Lily, and neither of them is old enough to live on their own.'

She glanced at me. 'Sorry for the delay in finding a place for you. Housing is a bit of a problem.'

'No one wants to take me either?'

'You're welcome to stay here as long as you like.' Her face was turned in my direction but her eyes were fixed on a point beyond my shoulder. 'I suppose the best arrangement would be for you to have your own place. We're planning on a trip to The Waste once all the houses are patched. We need to find the materials to build more houses. It might take a while though.' She opened her mouth to say more but I raised a hand.

'It's fine. Really. I appreciate you putting me up here. Living with a human and a moody superhuman teenager can't be easy.'

Dominico reappeared. 'Sorry,' she muttered. It wasn't clear who her apology was meant for.

'Let's eat,' Syra said lightly.

Dominico

I didn't like what this place was doing to me. I was becoming someone I didn't recognise, someone who was rude all the time, someone who always had something biting to say. I cringed to think what Mom and Dad would have to say about my new attitude, if they'd been here to see it. Irrationally, I was starting to blame my circumstances, my losses, on every superhuman in this city. Their very existence had created the fear and loathing that had landed me here. I needed someone to blame.

My training had been put on hold. Raven hadn't said why, or for how long, but it wasn't a hard one to figure out. No one was a match for me. The resentment of the other trainees had become so obvious that even Raven couldn't deny its presence. More than that, even I recognised that I had become a danger to the others. I was relieved, but also afraid. I needed to fill those hours with something. My mind needed a distraction from my thoughts of loss and revenge.

I was too lost in thought to notice the small crowd that had gathered, until I nearly bumped into them. I looked up and found myself eye to eye with Levin, his smirk turning my stomach. A band of trainees clustered close behind him, leaning toward Levin in a bid not to miss one word.

'Well lookey here. Just the famous superhuman we were waiting for. You know, me and the others here have been talking, and we wanted to know if you've been liking the presents we've been dropping though your window?'

The bird hadn't been the last of it. The past few mornings had brought me more unpleasant surprises. I thought of the cow dung that I had stepped in, barefoot, before the smell had hit me. The mud slung specifically at my bed, so that I had to strip it and wash both the duvet and the cover before Syra or Rogan noticed. How Levin was prising my window open, I had no clue. I kept it closed permanently now.

Whatever Raven had said to him, it hadn't worked. I was starting to suspect that she had only fuelled the fire.

I glared at Levin, keeping my chin up, my gaze level and fixed on his. 'I really think you could be more original, don't you, Levin? I have to admit the pigeon was a good one. How long did it take you to find it? I'm really flattered that you would go to so much trouble looking for something especially for me.' His followers tittered a little, giving me a small flash of satisfaction.

His face filled with colour. He took a step closer, his nose an inch away from mine. 'You think you're such a hotshot, yeah? Well you might be able to beat all of us, but you're this lonely little loser who we all hate. We don't want you here.' He reached out and flicked at my cheek, his smile growing as I flinched back from the unexpected sting.

The taunt started quietly, towards the back of the group, growing until the words reached me. '*Hot*shot, *hot*shot, *hot*shot!'

My tongue felt like a dead thing in my mouth, useless and limp. The faces behind Levin were blurring into one menacing face, one hideous creature. The urge to use my powers, to shut the crowd up, overwhelmed me. I was close to the edge. If I gave in, I'd be breaking the rules. The urge grew as the urgency of the crowd increased, their mob mentality reaching a fever pitch.

I left my body and hovered over the scene, no longer feeling the slap of their taunts, nor the feel of Levin's hands as he pushed me. The sound of the crowd was muffled. I couldn't make out any of their words. The fear and anger I had felt only seconds before felt distant. I was somehow removed from the scene, a mere observer. It felt like déjà vu. Levin threw a punch at my face and my alarm felt like someone else's emotion. I felt sympathy for my body the same way I would for a loved one's pain – involved but removed at the same time.

The need to fight left me. I waited them out, knowing they would soon tire of me. I watched as they circled my body, each of them taking a turn to strike out at me. The girls were tentative. They slapped instead of punching, their blows unconvincing. The boys were less restrained. A rock flew at my head. From a distance, I heard someone scream. At first I thought it was me, but then Lily appeared, tearing through the mob, shoving them aside until she was beside me. By some miracle, I was still standing. She looped an arm around my waist, and suddenly I was dropping like a stone back into my body.

Levin was sneering at us, spit coating his chin. The others had fallen back, their taunts fading, their hands limp at their sides, as if shocked by their actions.

Lily glared at Levin as he blocked our exit. 'Get out of my way.' He wavered for a moment, then finally stepped back and allowed us through. 'This isn't over. If you stay here, we'll keep reminding you that you don't belong.'

His words had little effect on me. I could barely hear him over the roar in my ears. The fear he was hoping to instil melted away in the face of the physical pain of my injuries. Something wet was running into my eyes. I reached up and wiped my forehead. My hand came away scarlet.

Lily urged me forward, patiently taking a few stuttering steps with me, then pausing as I stopped, my chest heaving with the effort to breathe. It felt like forever, but finally we reached my front door. Lily pushed it open. 'Syra? Syra!'

When Syra's voice called back I nearly collapsed with relief.

'Lily? Aren't you supposed to be at...' Her eyes found me and her mouth dropped open. She rushed towards us and slipped an arm around me from my other side. Together, they got me to my bedroom and laid me down on my bed. Lying down was so good I felt almost ecstatic. I tried to curl up, but Syra's hands were moving over my body, her fingers fluttering over my skin. She touched my forehead and I flinched at the stabbing pain which followed. She said something to Lily but I couldn't hear her, or anything else. I was wrapped in the haze of my pain.

Syra

Dominico's chest rose and fell in the first peaceful sleep she'd had since Lily had brought her home. I knew without being told that the long, nasty gash across her forehead, and her other bruises and cuts, had been inflicted by the other trainees. My gaze moved to her face. She looked much younger without her habitual scowl. Her closed lids hid the haunted look that had settled in her eyes. I felt responsible for what had happened to her. Raven had warned me of the tension between Dominico and Levin. I had thought it would blow over, like so many other teenage issues.

She stirred. I was almost sorry to see her leave the peace of sleep.

When she saw me she sat up abruptly, then sank back down, a hand moving to her forehead, her fingers exploring the length of the cut.

'How are you feeling?'

'My head... hurts. My whole body hurts.'

'Do you feel well enough to talk?'

Her eyes dropped to her lap. 'Do I have to?'

'I need to know who did this to you.'

She finally met my gaze. 'Surely you already know.' There was no accusation in her tone, just a sad resignation.

'What happened?'

'They attacked her.'

We both turned at the sound of Lily's voice. She stood in the doorway, her arms folded across her chest. I must've looked unimpressed by the interruption.

'The door was open,' she said, by way of explanation.

'How much did you see?'

'Enough. It was unprovoked. Dominico was just walking home.'

'That's not true.' Dominico struggled to sit up a bit more. I reached out to help her but she waved me away. 'It wasn't unprovoked. You were at training, Lily.' She turned to me. 'I baited Levin. I made a fool of him. I should've known what would happen, considering the dead bird, the cow dung and the mud.'

I shook my head. 'What are you talking about?'

'Levin was throwing things through my window. I wanted... to teach him a lesson.' She blinked rapidly. 'They caught me on my way home.' She looked at me pleadingly. 'They won't stop, Syra. They'll keep coming for me. Raven already spoke to them and they don't care about being punished. They want me out. Maybe the others will stop after this, but Levin won't. He won't.' Tears ran down her cheeks unchecked. Her fear and loneliness left a sharp tang on my tongue, filling my nose with a scent that made me think of burnt hair.

'I will deal with Levin, and all the others involved in this. They won't touch you again.'

She turned away from me, and even though I couldn't see her face, I felt the sting of her disappointment. 'Please go away.'

'The Healers –'

'Go away!'

I motioned for Lily to move out of the room ahead of me. I closed the door behind us, but not before Dominico burst into loud, racking sobs. I shut the door on the sound, but I could still hear every pain-filled syllable as clearly as if I were still sitting beside her.

Dominico

I couldn't count on any of them. Not for protection, or anything else. Levin would keep coming at me and, despite what I'd said to Syra, I wasn't convinced he'd do it alone. He struck me as too much of a coward for that.

I lay flat on my back, staring up at the ceiling. I followed the odd dark patterns that dotted its surface. Years before any of this, before superhumans, before even my own birth, I imagined this house had formed part of a typical suburb in former Johannesburg. I wondered what the previous owners had done to lend the ceiling its odd grey colour.

I thought about this, trying to distract myself from the real reason I was lying here in the first place. Without realising it, I was picturing Levin's face in the swirl of stains above my head, in the same way I used to lie on my back and watch the shift of the clouds, imagining animals and people in its formations. I pictured his face and then what I could do to it, without ever laying one finger on him. I wanted him beaten down the way I was. If only for a second, I wanted him to be filled with the dread and fear of knowing he would never belong. That he would forever float like a mote of dust caught in the wind, destined never to land or settle.

Chapter Twenty

Syra

It took me two days to convince Dominico to allow the Healers to close the wound on her head and to heal her various scratches and bruises. She sat through it without flinching, even though it must've hurt. Her eyes were vacant. She said nothing unless spoken to, and even then she responded only some of the time.

On the third day, when I was sure she was asleep, I met with Ray. We sat in the kitchen, keeping our voices low, listening for any movement from her bedroom.

'She won't get out of bed.'

'Maybe she just needs time to regroup. That head wound looked pretty nasty.'

I shook my head. 'I haven't spoken to Levin and the others yet. I don't know if I should. Raven already had a talk with him before the incident and I think it only made things worse, only spurred him and the other kids on. If we can't keep her safe, we can't expect her to stay. And there's only one place she'll go.'

'Toria.'

'Exactly. And if she does, Crane will have her.'

I stood and paced the room. 'The war is coming, Ray. I know it isn't how things are traditionally done, but we need to make a final decision about Drake and the others. We can't put it to a vote. It's up to us.'

'You've already made up your mind, Sy. If I decide I don't want to do it, then we're at a stalemate.'

'Is that what you've decided?'

He held up a hand. 'I didn't say that. But I do think we need to discuss it in depth. I know he's the only family you have, and I can't help thinking that's clouding your judgement. How are we going to control him?'

My stomach clenched. 'You make him sound like an animal.'

He gave me a look, his expression tightening. 'He was like family to me too. But I can't overlook this because... of our ties. He killed our Elders. And even after that, the others went with him. He has an influence on people. Most of them don't see him for who he is.'

'And you're such an expert on who Draiken is? You may have been close to him, but no one knows him like I do.' I hated this. I hated my accusatory tone, and the rift I knew this would cause between us. But I was afraid. With Drake, I had never worried about what would become of us. He made me feel safe and somehow protected, as if his very presence meant things would work out. Together we would find a way, as we always had in the past.

'Sy.' Ray reached for my hands. I let him take them, watching his fingers fold over mine.

'This isn't going to be a power struggle between us. But I need some answers. We can work this out together.'

My hands were still in his. The warmth of his skin was comforting, like coming home. I looked up at him. Something moved across his face and he pulled me closer, my head tipping back to hold his gaze. A strange pulsing heat was passing from his palms to mine. The scent of his skin had changed.

Dominico coughed. I whipped around, dreading the thought that she had witnessed the exchange. We were still alone in the room.

I pulled away from Ray, the moment broken. What was that?

Ray cleared his throat. Even without looking at him, I could feel the tension radiating off his body. His thoughts blared for a moment, like the old radio I kept in the kitchen. He caught them, reeled them back, until the only sound in the room was our breathing.

I sank into the nearest chair, creating a pocket of space between us. He remained standing, his gaze roaming my face. I used the height difference as an opportunity to avoid his eyes, focusing past him to the open window instead.

'I think Draiken poses a danger.' He said this as if there had been no interruption in our conversation.

I gathered myself, making sure my voice was controlled. 'I know Ray. I don't know how to reassure you on this, except to say that you should know Drake would never do anything to endanger me.' Except that wasn't really true. He'd endangered me the moment he decided on this path. I pushed the thought away. 'He wants the same thing we do – autonomy from the humans, for this city to be truly ours. I don't think bloodshed is the answer, but Crane clearly isn't open to negotiation. This is about our survival.'

'No one is going to support our decision. You may be safe from him, but what about the rest of us?' I could sense his irritation at having to look down at me. He raised his hand, his fingers moving to the back of his neck and working at the muscles.

'We're their leaders. They will see reason. I don't believe Draiken will harm any of us. He's free to do as he pleases now. And we're going to help him get what he wants – freedom. That's what we all want.'

Uncertainty flickered across Ray's face. His resolve was weakening.

'What about Rogan?' I blinked at the abrupt change of subject.

'What about him?'

'How's this going to work, with him being human and all?'

'He's already proven himself. He's given us vital information.'

'And when the war comes? Do you think he's going to face his former soldiers, the men he used to lead, look them in the eye, and shoot them down?'

I didn't want to admit that I'd thought about this too, and I had no idea what role, if any, Rogan would play in the war.

'His loyalty to you will only stretch so far.' I wondered at his choice of words, at his tone around the word 'loyalty'.

'Maybe he needs to stay out of the war altogether. He doesn't have to fight for us. He's serving his purpose with the information he's giving us. He can help us with tactics. It was never a part of the deal that he would fight beside us.'

'He doesn't strike me as an idle man. Do you honestly think he'll stay out of it?'

'What are you saying Ray? That he'll go back to the humans? Don't you realise that's not an option for him?'

'Crane seems like a practical guy. If he thinks he can use Rogan, in any way, he'll let him return. Rogan has seen everything here. He could take back information to Crane.'

'This is Crane's city. He knows it inside out.' Ray sighed. He took the seat beside mine.

'He doesn't know we now have knowledge of his experimental army. What's he going to think if he finds out we've been harbouring Rogan? All our agreements -'

'I know. I've considered all of this. But I think you're wrong about him. Why do you persist in thinking the worst? He's proven himself to be trustworthy.'

Ray threw his hands up and sprang to his feet, his movements clumsy with agitation. 'He can do no wrong as far as you're concerned. It's as if you've forgotten he's human.'

I felt my cheeks grow warm. I raised my hands to my face, wishing for just a hint of a breeze through the open window. 'What are you implying?'

He folded his arms, his anger just below the surface, the struggle to keep it contained distorting his features. 'I think it's pretty clear.'

I clamped down on my growing fury. It was building within me, creating an unbearable pressure, seeking a release.

'Don't presume to know what I'm thinking.' I fought to keep my voice level, my tone neutral. 'We can't fight among ourselves. Our city needs united leadership. Especially at a time like this.

'I'll have a discussion with Rogan about this. Get a feel for what his plan is.'

'*You'll* discuss it with him?'

'You make no secret of your distrust of him. Your presence will just cause unnecessary tension.'

'So much for *united leadership*.'

He stormed out of the house. I stared at his retreating back until the door slammed shut behind him.

I dipped my head until it met my open palms. I sat that way for a long time, wondering how things had become so complicated so quickly. Ray's outburst was so unexpected that even though I wanted to go after him, I couldn't make my feet move.

The creak of a floorboard made me look up. Dominico had wandered out of her room and stood just outside the lounge, staring at me with huge eyes.

'How long have you been standing there?'

She shrugged. 'Long enough. Lover's quarrel?'

Despite myself, I laughed. I sensed her surprise at my reaction. 'Not quite.'

She was wearing an oversized t-shirt. It used to be white, but now looked like a faded shade of yellow in the late morning light slanting through the lounge window. Baggy tracksuit pants hung from her narrow hips. The clothes made her look like a child, her tiny frame barely wide enough to keep them in place. There were dark rings beneath her eyes and her usually pale skin looked translucent.

She folded her arms self-consciously. 'What are you staring at?'

I wanted to reach her. To make her feel safe in a city that had made her feel vulnerable and loathed.

'Hungry?'

'No.'

'You need to eat.'

'Raven took me out of training.'

'I know.'

'What am I supposed to do all day?'

I motioned to the couch. 'We can find you other things to do, when you're well enough. Don't worry. You won't be bored.'

She remained standing. 'What about Levin?'

'I still need to talk to him. I need the names of the others, Dominico. He wasn't alone in this.'

'No.'

'How can I protect you if –'

She shook her head, as if amazed at my stupidity. 'Don't you get it? They don't want me here. I'm not one of you. I'm a freak.' She shoved her curls back. Sweat glistened at her hairline.

'Levin will be punished. If you give me the names of the others, they'll be punished too.' I paused. 'Lily was there. If you won't tell me, I can ask her.'

'Go ahead. You think that's going to solve the problem? That being punished because of something they did to me is going to make them suddenly like me?'

'You didn't help your cause. You aggravated their fear of you. We have to show them that, although you're stronger than they are, you are still a superhuman. Still a part of us. Not a threat, but a friend.'

She snorted. Ignoring her, I ploughed on, my desperation growing.

'Once their fear is removed, they will no longer feel the need to drive you away.'

She pondered this for a moment. I waited, tentatively reaching for her thoughts. Miraculously, she allowed me in.

You're just like them.

She turned on her heel and returned to her room, slamming the door behind her.

Dominico

I needed to get out. I couldn't stand being here anymore. Staring at these four walls was starting to drive me nuts. Lily had come by a couple of times over the past few days, but I'd told Syra to send her away. I'd done enough already without making her a pariah for being friends with me.

On the fourth day after the incident, I finally left my room. I waited for Syra and Rogan to leave the house, then slipped out the front door, keeping my eyes on the ground, hoping to go unnoticed. The heat of the day beat down on me, making the back of my neck burn. It was exactly the kind of day that would have got Mom going about staying out of the sun. Too hot for anything to be out, she'd say. How I'd hated her nagging. Now I could do whatever I liked.

I walked, glancing up furtively to check my surroundings. I clenched my hands, the sweat on my palms coating my fingers. I forced myself to keep going, refusing to let Levin's possible appearance stop me.

Gradually my heart slowed. The sweat on my hands dried, and I could finally breathe easier. Sitting in my room these last three days, I would've given anything to have Mom and Dad with me. Thinking about them made me feel winded, like I'd taken a punch to the gut, but I couldn't pack the memories away, couldn't stop picturing them.

A voice broke through my thoughts, someone yelling something I couldn't make out. I ducked against the bricks of a nearby home, slipping into its shadow. I held my breath, waiting to be called out, imagining Levin and his cronies gathering just around the corner, ready to finish the job. Beneath my fear something else was growing. I wanted to make Levin pay. I wanted to humiliate him. I wanted to hurt him. I peered around the corner of the house, half-hoping and half-dreading to see him. Nothing. Whoever had called out was gone. I slid down the rough brick, ignoring the burn of my skin as my back chafed against the surface. I buried my face in my hands. Home. Home.

I pictured our lounge, and the way the morning sun would pour through the windows, until the temperature of the room became unbearable and Mom would attempt to lower the blinds, muttering about how they always got stuck. I thought of her standing in the kitchen, wearing those awful threadbare purple slippers she loved so much. I imagined Dad sailing through our front door, his voice booming out a greeting, his arms closing around me even as I tried to bat him away, shrieking in mock protest.

That weird feeling of leaving my body washed over me. I could feel the disconnection happening, my inner self leaving my physical form. And then, I was home. The lounge was no longer a picture. I was standing in it. I couldn't feel the tiles beneath my feet, or the movement of the breeze that lifted the floral curtains, but I was still surrounded by the walls of my former home.

I moved forward through sheer force of will. How I was moving without being in my body was bizarre, but somehow I moved from the lounge to the kitchen. Pieces of my dream came back to me. I was sure that at any moment I would hear a voice call out to me, urging me to go outside.

There was only silence. The house looked the same, but not. The mixed feeling I'd always had in this space, of being safe and trapped at the same time, was gone. The door to my parents' bedroom was open. I ran my hand over the bedspread. Something was wrong. There were things here that weren't theirs. I picked up the bedside lamp. For as long as I could remember, it had been blue, with several cracks running along its base. The lamp I had in my hand was cream, and intact.

Feeling a pulse of fear, I walked into the bathroom. The things littering the sink weren't Mom's. The shampoos had different labels. The hairbrush was blue and plastic, instead of the old-school silver antique Mom had inherited from her mother.

The last hope I'd had of finding them alive shattered. Someone else was living here. My home was no longer mine.

Air rushed by me as I dropped back into my body. I slumped against the house. I had nothing left to live for. They were dead.

Just like Kat, they were dead because of me.

Chapter Twenty-One

Rogan

I found her crumpled against a brick home, her shoulders shuddering. Thinking she was hurt, I rushed to her side. I searched her face for injuries but there were none.

'Dominico. What's wrong?'

She jumped at my touch, snatching her arm away and curling further into herself. She wailed something I couldn't make out, the words muffled by her knees, which were drawn up tightly against her chest. I rocked back on my haunches for a moment, at a loss. I couldn't just leave her here. I lifted her out of the dirt, trying to avoid her flailing limbs, ignoring her howls of protest. Her weight was no more than that of a child. Looking down at her tear-streaked face, at the paleness of her skin and the fatigue that ringed her eyes, she looked more human than ever. It was easy to forget what she really was.

The streets were filling with people on their way home from their various duties. A man streaked with dirt appeared from the direction of the fields, hoisting a food package and water ration under each arm. He eyed me suspiciously, but moved past without a word. A woman with her child had started to cross my path, but changed her direction mid-stride, drawing her son closer and hurrying him along. I half walked and half jogged in my haste to get to Syra's house. No one asked any questions, or offered any help. We were the outsiders, and in that fact, we were united.

Dominico had gone limp. Her arms swayed with the movement of my stride, her head lolling back. I hitched her higher against my chest, cradling her head like a new born. The intimacy of her closeness made me feel like I'd broken out in a rash. I felt a deep sympathy for her, for the tragedy of her isolation. But that same sympathy left me uneasy. I wasn't used to feeling anything but suspicion for this species. The change in me, first with Syra and now with this girl, made me feel like a stranger to myself.

I carried Dominico through the front door and crossed to her bedroom, settling her on the bed. Her eyes were blank. She didn't move, except to blink. Her stillness was frightening. I moved my fingers to her wrist. Her pulse was steady.

'Dominico?'

Nothing. She continued to breathe and blink, the only signs of life she displayed.

'Rogan?'

I turned at the sound of Syra's voice, relieved I wouldn't have to deal with this alone. 'In here.' She came through the doorway. Seeing Dominico, she rushed to my side. 'What's the matter with her?'

'I found her like this.' I waved a hand in front of her face. Blink. Breathe. No reaction to the movement, despite her wide-open gaze. 'She's in some kind of stupor.'

Syra's hands moved over Dominico.

'She isn't hurt.'

'Was she alone?'

'Yes. Why?'

'There wasn't anyone else close by?'

I shook my head, perplexed. 'No. What is this about?'

'The other kids...they've been picking on her. There was an incident a few days ago.'

She sighed and ran her hands through her hair, head dropping to her chest. 'This is my fault. I should've listened to her. She kept trying to tell me she didn't feel safe here, and I kept reassuring her that talking to the perpetrators would solve things.'

'The other kids were violent towards her?'

Syra rubbed her eyes, looking exhausted. 'Yes.'

Typical. The thought was a reflex, an old habit. It slipped into my mind before I could stop it.

Her head snapped up, her eyes fixing on me. Her exhaustion had slipped beneath the surface, replaced by a look of fury.

'Typical? We're not a violent species by nature. This was unforeseen, one agitator inciting the others and causing trouble.'

I rose, suddenly wanting to get out of this room, away from her stifling closeness. 'You can call it whatever you like. They attacked one of their own.'

She got to her feet, straightening to her full height, eyes level with my chin. She stepped into my space, crowding me against the doorway. I sidestepped her, a toxic mix of revulsion and attraction churning in the pit of my stomach.

'You still haven't shaken this thing, have you? That instinct to think of us as an anomaly, a freak of nature?'

'Nature didn't create any of you. Man did.'

Her face seemed to fold in on itself as her expression tightened. 'Right. Of course. Which makes us nothing more than a science experiment.'

A hitch in Dominico's breathing made us both turn. Her eyelids fluttered several times. Her eyes focused on me, the former blankness melting away. She sat up slowly, propping herself up on her elbows.

Syra stepped towards the bed. 'Are you okay? Do you need something?'

Dominico shifted her gaze to Syra, blinking blearily. 'What happened?'

'Rogan found you. You must've fainted... We couldn't revive you. How do you feel?'

'Weird. Shaky.' She raised a trembling hand, illustrating her point.

'Do you remember anything?'

Her eyes shifted away from Syra for a moment. 'No. Just that I went for a walk.' Her face closed up. 'I'm fine. Tired.' She lay down again, rolling onto her side and facing the wall.

Syra rose, looking stung and weary enough to drop where she stood. She moved out of the room ahead of me, her body rigid with tension. In the lounge, she turned to face me. 'I thought we had reached a kind of understanding. I thought you were starting to see us as more than just a fabled enemy.'

Her words were like a physical blow. Since my arrival, I had allowed myself to fall into the routines of this city, to forget the reasons I had always feared and hated its inhabitants. I had allowed myself to be lulled by its growing familiarity. But I would never belong here.

I regretted her catching my thought, but how was I supposed to be on my guard every moment I was with her?

'I didn't say it. I thought it. And thoughts are supposed to be private.'

'Then why did you let me hear it?' All anger had left her voice. Her tone was neutral, flat.

'I'm not used to having to watch what I think. If you don't want to know, then stop probing.' I crossed the room and closed the space between us. The urge to maintain my distance evaporated. I stood over her, my body inches from hers. The heat of her skin filled the space between us, her scent filling my nose. She looked up at me, an unspoken challenge. She could drop me right now if she chose to, but instead she closed the gap between us, pressing her body into mine. I could feel the give of her breasts against my chest, the taut line of her leg against mine. It felt like a taunt; a dare one child might set for another. I stepped back, reason chipping at my desire. She was maddening. I was torn. I wanted her, even as the old repulsion rose in me. The ancient fear and loathing.

She backed off, crossing the room until she was as far from me as she could get without leaving the house. 'You don't have to remain here out of some mistaken sense of duty. You've told us what we need to know.'

A rush of anger made my fingertips tingle. A blaze licked at me from the inside. I locked my jaw against it, pushing back until it calmed to a flame. 'I've outworn my usefulness.'

She raised her chin, meeting my gaze head-on. 'You can see it that way if you like.' My jaw tightened at her tone.

'Will you have any place in this war, Commander? Surely, with how you clearly still see us, you don't plan to fight with us?'

It took me a minute to absorb the abrupt switch in her tactics. 'There is only one other side.'

'My point exactly.'

'Are you demanding an answer? Does your continued hospitality depend on my reply?'

'I think it hardly matters to us which side you choose to fight for. I think it matters more where your true loyalty lies, which side you think has the most right to survival. Both groups won't come out of this alive. And if they do, one will be in the minority. Easy to stamp out.'

The late afternoon sun had heated the room to a slow bake. I felt like a pigeon who has been dropped in temperate water, which is gradually heated until it's boiled alive.

'I want peace.'

She gave me a look that made me feel like a wilfully stupid and stubborn child.

'You know that's impossible.'

'I'm not saying there won't be a war, although it would be ideal to avoid that altogether. I think there's a way for humans and superhumans to live in the same world, without bloodshed.'

'By holding onto the assumptions and ingrained fears that you have?' She didn't wait for my reply. 'There will still be a war, whatever comes afterwards. And you'll have to choose a side.'

Syra

I retreated to my room. My home was no longer a haven. Rogan and Dominico's alliance to us was hanging by the barest thread, like a fractured web torn down to a single strand. Draiken's absence in my waking moments and his presence in my visions was blurring the line between reality and fantasy. I felt disconnected from my life, watching from a distance as everything came apart.

I stared at the four walls of my room for hours, trying to puzzle out what was to be done. Waiting for Crane to make his move was excruciating, like pushing a blade beneath a nail. We couldn't declare war first. There was still the smallest possibility, despite what I'd told Rogan, that Crane would continue to leave us in peace. For now.

The pounding on my bedroom door jerked me from a deep sleep.

'Syra? Syra! Come quickly!'

I pushed myself to my feet, throat clotting with dread. Things were about to get worse. I could smell it. I forced myself to breathe through it, to shift my paralysed limbs long enough to wrench the door open.

Ray stood on the other side, his face flushed, his breath coming in rapid bursts.

'What is it?'

'Crane... is... here.'

Static filled my ears. Ray's mouth was still moving but I couldn't hear him over the sound of my terror. I wanted to ask Ray if Crane was alone, or accompanied by his army, but I couldn't get my mouth to form the words. If his arrival meant war, we'd been caught completely unprepared. I closed my eyes against the tide of panic sweeping over me.

He grabbed my shoulders, fingers digging into my shoulder blades, shaking me. I blinked rapidly, trying to earth myself. I beat at my fear, picturing it as a real, solid thing, something I could fight and fend off.

'Take me to him.'

***

A crowd had gathered by the time Ray led me to the gate. To my horror, Crane had been left waiting at the threshold of the city, both feet still planted in The Waste. The guards stood aside, the entrance to the city wide open. They were silent and still, their gaze trained beyond the visitors, but I wasn't fooled. From Crane's wary stance, neither was he.

Our usually noisy city was silent. Glancing briefly at the crowd, I noticed Elliot pressed into his mother's side, his mouth a perfect circle of fear.

I hurried to Crane, both hands extended. The eyes of those gathered drove into me, like dozens of tiny blades cutting at my skin.

'President Crane. What an unexpected surprise. Please, come in.' I forced my tongue around the words, modulating my tone until even I was convinced of my sincerity.

He nodded curtly, displeasure curling his mouth. His clothes shed tiny clouds of dust as he brushed at them, coating his hands in dirt. He stared at his palms in disgust.

He put one foot beyond the gates of the city, hesitating before he allowed the other to follow. His guards shadowed him, their eyes sweeping their surroundings, weapons clutched in hands so sweaty I caught the stinging scent of it as they passed.

I felt Ray's objection before the words could form on his tongue. I placed a hand on his arm. We couldn't add further insult by asking Crane to enter Jozenburg unarmed. We had to maintain the illusion of mutual trust.

I led him away from the others. Ray created a protective barrier by walking between us. I could smell the acid scent of Crane's hostility, even though his face remained passive.

I guided him into my home. Remembering the pristine opulence of his own home, I winced at his derisive sniff. He ran a finger along the back of the armchair, his finger catching on the small ridges of the fading material, as if checking for dust. His face puckered into a scowl, his scorn like a cube of ice down my back. He hovered beside the chair instead of sitting in it, gazing around the room as if hoping for an alternative. Finally he sank into the offending seat without an invitation. He sat on its very edge like a crow perched at the end of a branch.

He hadn't spoken a single syllable since I'd led him from the gate. Even now, as Ray and I waited for him to speak, he continued his scrutiny of my living room, taking his time. I was sure this was a deliberate tactic, his way of keeping control of the situation. Maybe he was hoping the longer he paused, the more likely it was that either Ray or I would break down and confess to harbouring a human. I pressed my lips together painfully, forcing my hands to lie relaxed in my lap. Out of the corner of my eye I could see Ray struggling to keep his composure. I sensed the tension within him, strained to the point of breaking. I pleaded silently with him to remain quiet.

Crane finally turned his gaze to me, his expression genial. I felt myself stiffen. Although I couldn't reach his thoughts, I sensed his plan. He was going to try to coerce me into handing Dominico over.

'I would like to speak to you alone.' He kept his eyes on me, speaking as if Ray wasn't in the room.

'Ray is the co-leader of this city. Whatever decisions are made for its people, are made together.'

'Ah.' He stroked a hand along the line of his jaw, in an oddly intimate way that made me ease away from him, despite the comfortable distance between us. 'Draiken's replacement, I presume?'

A jolt ran through me, as if I'd touched an electrical wire. 'What?'

He laughed gently, mockingly. 'Nothing that goes on here escapes me, my dear. After all, it's a city on loan to you, is it not? It still belongs to me.'

An image from one of my visions filled my mind. The faceless man that had shaken Draiken's hand.

'Have you seen him?' The words fell from my tongue before I could catch them. Ray's head swivelled sharply. I felt his silent warning, but a desperate hunger filled me, a hunger that had nothing to do with food. I wanted news of Draiken so badly I was willing to take it from wherever I could get it.

He gave me a strange look. His hands jumped a little, like an unsettled feline, then stilled in his lap again. 'Where would I have seen him?'

A question in place of a denial. Hope flared in me again. Ray, as if sensing it, shot me a warning look.

'What can I do for you, President Crane?'

'I believe you have something that belongs to me. Two things, in fact.'

Heat rushed to my face. Silence filled the room, taking up every inch of space, until it felt as if all the air had been sucked from the house.

I forced my chin up, and my gaze to meet his. Gradually, my body temperature dropped.

'Really? And which things are you referring to?'

A slow smile crawled across his face. His eyes remained cold.

'No games, if you please, Syra. If you hand them over to me now, without trying to conceal them or deceive me, then I will take them without recrimination. But if you try to keep them from me, I'll be forced to use the terms of the treaty. Let's avoid that unpleasantness, shall we?'

Panic beat in my chest, like a trapped bird banging against a window. My first, shameful instinct, was to point the way to both the commander and the girl and do my duty to my people. Then, finally, I would be rid of the source of so much of my aggravation.

'The girl is one of us.'

'So she's here?'

I cocked my head, opening my eyes wide in mock surprise. 'I thought you knew everything that happened in *your* city?'

His fixed smile slipped a notch. Ray's silent fury battered at me, but I refused to look at him, afraid that his fear would latch on to mine, and shatter the little composure I was clinging to.

I settled back in my chair, attempting a casual pose. 'You hate us. You have laws forbidding our presence in Toria. She's one of us. So why the change of heart?'

He pressed the tips of his fingers together, his expression calculating. 'I don't like loose ends.' He smiled behind the steeple of his fingers. I felt my self-control slip. As if sensing this, Ray jumped in.

'And the human?'

I gaped at him. After all his concern about Crane finding out about Rogan, he'd given us away in the space of three careless words.

Crane showed no surprise at this outburst. 'The commander will be sufficiently punished, until I'm satisfied. After that, I may keep him, if he proves himself of some use to me.'

Crane rose with infinite care, trying not to touch anything unnecessarily. 'Bring them to the gate. I need to return to Toria before dark.'

He swept out of the room, his guards saluting him at the door. They fell in behind him in a flap of grey clothing and blinking steel.

I turned on Ray. 'You say only three words, and those are the ones you choose? What the hell is the matter with you? Don't you know what the consequences will be?'

He stared at me. 'Yes. They'll take him back to where he belongs. And we'll no longer have to worry if we can trust him.' He cocked his head, his expression cold. 'Isn't it the girl you should be worried about?'

My rage pulsed, pushing my self-control to the edge. A red haze hung around Ray, like a negative aura. I wanted to fly at him and pour out my fear and confusion until I was empty. Maybe then I would stop feeling as if I'd lost something.

I forced the air into my lungs with long, controlled breaths. Closing my eyes, I concentrated only on the sensation of oxygen filling and leaving my body. Gradually, every sound receded and I was alone in a vacuum of peace and silence. Don't lose control. You are a superhuman. You are not weak. My rage faded. The loss I felt grew smaller, until it became insignificant enough to bury at the back of my mind.

I allowed the sounds of the city to filter back into my consciousness. Voices. The cry of a faraway hadeda. They trickled in as if from a great distance. I opened my eyes.

Ray stood next to the armchair Crane had just vacated, his hand gripping the back of it. He kept his gaze fixed in the direction Crane had gone. His whole body radiated with controlled anger.

'Ray.' He seemed not to hear me. He remained where he was, his body turned away. His face, in profile now, was as familiar as my own. My childhood in the laboratory was stamped with as many memories of him as of Drake. He was like my second brother. I'd always thought he'd felt the same. But now, as I studied him, I wondered at the reason for his rage.

'Ray.' He turned, his face stony. I wanted to reach out to him. I wanted to say something that would fix everything, something that would bandage the wound and staunch the bleeding. But I knew he would pull away and my words would fall at his feet, ignored and unappreciated.

'Let's go.' We walked towards the gate together, with just enough distance between us to guard against an accidental brush of arms or shoulders. From a distance, I imagined we looked the way we should – a united front. But the new chilliness between us felt boundless.

Chapter Twenty-Two

Rogan

Something had happened. The city was unnaturally silent, as if everyone in it had disappeared. I walked the perimeter of Jozenburg, keeping my head down. At this moment I'd never wanted to escape a place as badly as this one. I had nowhere to go, but still the desire to get away from here, from her, was overwhelming. As I neared the city gates, a crowd of what seemed like every citizen of Jozenburg had gathered, their mutual silence unnerving. They stood facing the same direction, their attention held by something just ahead.

Syra appeared, detaching herself from the crowd. She raced towards me, arms flapping at her sides in agitation. I stepped out of her path, but she blocked my retreat by stepping directly in front of me.

Her words spilled out in a torrent of confusion, melding together in a mass of syllables.

She kept talking, despite my obvious incomprehension.

'Syra. Syra. Syra!' She finally went quiet, her words running dry.

'I can't understand a word you're saying. Speak slower.'

'He's here. For you and Dominico.' Her voice trembled on the syllable 'he'.

For a moment I had no idea what she was talking about, as if she'd switched to a foreign language. Her agitated state alarmed me more than anything else. It was unlike her to be so close to losing control.

'I can't hide you. I can't violate the treaty. He'll take the city, he'll –'

I didn't hear the rest of her sentence. Crane was walking towards me, arms open and hands extended, as if welcoming an old friend. Two men flanked him. One wore the grey and red colours of Toria's Guard. The other bore the black uniform of a soldier.

Syra clutched my sleeve. 'I'm sorry. I want to help you. I don't want Crane to take you – '. I put a hand on each of her shoulders. Crane was closing in. With each step, one more moment was lost.

'Listen to me. You couldn't have prevented this. I shouldn't have come here. I've put you all in danger.' I leaned closer, making sure she heard me. 'Thank you for taking me in. I'll never forget it.' I moved her aside.

Crane stopped in front of me, smiling, his hands still extended. I stared at the insignia stitched in blue on the breast pocket of the soldier's uniform. Clasped hands. What a mockery of unity. My gaze moved upwards. Caiden. I jerked in shock. He met my eyes. His were so full of loathing that my greeting died before it could pass my lips. I glanced at the guard. Bradley. Why had I expected them to be strangers? I was the enemy who'd betrayed them all. They were no longer my friends, my comrades. They would be my punishers and my executioners.

'Commander Rogan.' Crane's hands remained suspended between us. I kept mine at my side, a pointless snub.

Crane's smile grew. He dropped his hand casually, unmoved by my rudeness. 'Well. It's been quite some time, hasn't it?'

'I'll go with you without a fight, on one condition.'

'Negotiating, are we? Very well. What is it?'

'There is no retaliation on your part –'

'And the treaty remains intact,' Crane finished.

He waved a hand. 'Fine fine. I have what I came for. No harm done.'

His agreeable attitude put me on guard immediately. Surely this gave him the perfect motive for declaring war? I glanced at Syra. She met my gaze, her expression tight. Her eyes flicked between Crane and me. I could sense her urgency. She was trying to tell me something, but I couldn't see past her anxiety.

'Where is the girl?' Crane was shifting, his feet kicking up small clouds of dust. The sun was merciless, its heat like a relentless enemy. A trickle of sweat ran unchecked down his temple. He seemed determined not to let his discomfort show.

Syra tore her gaze from mine. 'Ray has gone to get her. She should be here shortly.'

Crane motioned to Caiden and Bradley. They moved around me, each taking an arm. Caiden pressed his handgun into my side with enough force to leave a bruise.

'One wrong move, and you're dead.' He refused to look at me. He spoke without turning his head. I thought about the easy camaraderie we'd had. He'd brought constant laughter into the barracks and was the kind of man who got on with everyone. He'd never abused his position as a soldier. He abhorred cruelty. The loss of his friendship felt as painful as a shattered limb. He would merely be the first in a long line of others.

'Bring her to the gate.' Crane swept past us and moved ahead. I followed the two men glued to my side. I didn't dare turn my head to catch a final glimpse of Syra. Any unexpected movement on my part could mean my last breath. Crane wasn't known for his mercy, and I doubted he would prevent Caiden from firing a bullet into my side. I couldn't suppress the thought that perhaps it would be a better fate than the one which awaited me in Toria.

They marched me to the city gate. My gaze ran up the length of the city walls, the only walls in this place that were smooth and intact, with no visible fissures or gaps. As the gate loomed closer, I recalled how I'd felt when I'd first stepped through them. I'd hated walking into a place I would never belong in. Now I'd gladly trade the certain animosity of my former friends for the suspicion of these strangers.

I felt the crowd's eyes on me. They followed my progress in silence, the air thick with anticipation. As I drew closer, I caught a woman's gaze. Elliot's mother, Ever. She stood slightly apart, her son clinging to her side. Irrationally, I hoped she would step forward. As if reading my thoughts, she looked away, but not before I saw her face contort with guilt. This time there would be no last minute reprieve.

Dominico

The city was quiet. Too quiet. A quick glance out of my bedroom window confirmed my suspicions. There wasn't a single soul out on the street. The path that passed my window was a popular one, as it led directly from one end of town to the other. People used it on their way to work, school, and back again. Not today. I crossed my room and stepped out into the doorway. 'Syra? Rogan?' I didn't really expect an answer. They'd left earlier this morning, but the silence was starting to feel eerie, and the sound of my own voice, even unanswered, gave me a small measure of comfort.

I leaned out of my window, craning my head to see as far along the path as I could without leaving my room. My unease grew. Something was happening. Dread squirmed its way through my thoughts like a worm, until I couldn't take it anymore. I turned from the window and crossed to the front door. Before I could close my hand around the handle a knock sounded from the other side. A small scream escaped me. I clapped a hand over my mouth, annoyed at myself.

'Dominico?'

I opened the door to find Ray on the other side.

'Crane is here.'

The floor swayed under my feet. The walls swooped towards me, tilting everything upside down. I made myself breathe, and the room slowed. My head swarmed with so many thoughts it was hard to pick one to say aloud.

'Did you hear me?'

I managed a nod.

'We can hide you. Crane can't prove that you're here at all – he's acting on a hunch.' He motioned urgently. 'Come. We don't have much time.'

Although he seemed genuinely concerned, I didn't think it was for my safety. Even as he said the words, I could feel his fear. I sensed he was doing this because he thought of it as his duty. My worth lay in my abilities, and having that taken from them was a huge blow.

'I'll go with him.'

What more could I say? No one else was going to die protecting me. Mom, Dad and Kat were already three too many. I knew I would be punished, possibly even put to death. I couldn't predict Crane's plans for me. It didn't matter. I had nothing keeping me here.

Ray paused, shaking his head half-heartedly. I knew the terms of the treaty. If they hid me and I was found, it would fall away. Crane could take their city. I didn't want to stay here. I wanted to go home, even if it meant I would die there. I belonged nowhere, so why not be a misfit in a city I knew?

'Ray. You don't have to hide me. I want to go.' I thought of being free of Levin and his cronies' taunts. A silver lining, at the very least.

'What if he executes you?'

'I'm valuable, remember? Besides, I'm willing to take my chances.'

Ray stood helplessly as I brushed past him, heading for the front door. I paused with my hand on the handle, looking back at him. 'Well?'

He shook his head, stubbornly refusing to follow.

'Ray.' He stayed where he was. He folded his arms across his chest, looking ready to settle where he was for as long as it took to convince me.

'He'll take the city.' His expression lost some of its determination. 'I can't be responsible for that. This way, you all have a chance. Let me go. I know you don't want to fight. I know the numbers you have now are precious, and one lost life is too many. Crane knows it too.' I touched his arm. 'You don't have to protect me. I know my parents are probably dead. But I don't belong here. I want to go home.'

'Dominico, wait. Without you... if you fight for Crane... we'll lose.' He stared at me, imploring me to stay, but my mind was already mapping the way home. He hesitated a moment longer, then finally motioned for me to walk ahead. He looked miserable. Standing in the doorway, I glanced back at the house one last time, my gaze moving over the now-familiar furniture, the faded blue curtains that lifted in the passing breeze. I stepped outside, my stomach churning with so many conflicting emotions I felt sick. I knew I was going home to a city that was now devoid of the people I loved. But I couldn't stay here. Every day I'd be reminded of how different I was in their eyes. They would always see me as an outsider. My heart felt too big for my chest, like it would explode out of me if it beat any harder. I had no other choice. It was time to go home.

Syra

I watched her approach. The sun was riding high as early afternoon set in. The heat enveloped me like a scratchy blanket. Ray and Dominico were backlit, their shadows leading them. I raised a hand to shield my eyes, unable to read either of their expressions. As they drew closer her thoughts came at me in a barrage of confusion. They were wild and tangled, like animals tearing at each other.

There was nothing I could do. I hated standing here, knowing we were losing her, knowing what it meant. But how could I risk everyone else's lives to keep her here? Our law was to preserve life, and if it meant one for dozens of others, it was a sacrifice I'd have to learn to live with. I didn't think Crane would execute her. She was too valuable. But I was also certain that her future in Toria would be a bleak one.

I glanced at Rogan, willing him to look at me. He stood between the two men, back rigid. His hands were clenched into fists so tight his veins stood out against his skin. The path his blood beat through them sounded in my ears.

I regretted our argument. I'd been too quick to anger. I always felt defensive around him, as if letting down my guard would make me seem weak. His leaving felt different to Dominico's. I was supposed to mourn her loss. I should've been celebrating his departure, but instead I felt a mix of relief and regret so powerful it felt like I'd swallowed a sweet but lethal poison.

Despite what Crane had said about the treaty, I'd felt the blow of his lie in every nerve of my body. I feared that Crane was taking Rogan not only to execute him, but to extract every piece of information that he could before he let Rogan die. Our knowledge of Crane's secret army would no longer be a secret, and any element of surprise we'd hoped to extract from Crane's ignorance would be gone. I feared for Rogan's fate, but I dreaded the knowledge he could pass on. We were in mortal danger, and all of it rested on how much Rogan was forced to reveal. We were, once again, at the mercy of a human. I closed my eyes for a moment. Giving them up would change nothing. Perhaps it would delay the war, but only by days. But we needed those days. To plan, to prepare, to come together. Crane's power lay in his knowledge of our numbers. Now, to keep our freedom, and our city, those numbers would be threatened. There was nothing I could do but plan for the inevitable.

Ray and Dominico reached us. She gave my arm a fleeting squeeze as she passed, her mind thrown open like a door caught in the wind. No words were necessary. I felt her gratitude through the warmth of her fingers. Her eyes caught mine. In that moment my burden of guilt shifted, leaving me lighter. She was returning home not because Crane had come for her, but because she wanted to. I couldn't tell if she understood the chances of her survival once she walked through Toria's gates, but it didn't seem to matter. She arrived at Crane's side, her feet buoyed by hope. The man in the black uniform left Rogan's side and took Dominico's arm. From where I stood I could sense his revulsion at the feel of her skin against his own.

Crane turned to me and bowed slightly. I sensed the mockery in his gesture. I clenched my teeth against the overpowering urge to disarm his bodyguards and flatten him into the dirt, just to see his reaction.

'Syra. Always a pleasure. As much as I enjoy these meetings of ours, I hope this will deter you from doing anything else that might require my presence here.' He waggled a finger at me, as if rebuking a persistently disobedient child. Ray moved to my side and brushed my arm. Despite his anger, he still stood beside me, anchoring me with his air of calm.

Crane turned and swept out of the gates, trailed by his entourage and their captives. I watched Rogan and Dominico until the city gates closed behind them, my goodbye frozen on my lips.

Chapter Twenty-Three

Rogan

The walk home was long and arduous. Crane hobbled, struggling to negotiate the terrain when it became slightly rocky. I wondered why he'd elected to come himself, when he could simply have sent a handful of his best men. Perhaps he'd counted on the fear his appearance would generate. After all, Crane hadn't left the security of Toria since his election to president.

Kilometres of dirt and dust in every direction, hulking buildings and craning street poles the only objects to break the flatness of the skyline. The road unfurled ahead of us, the tar so raised and fractured, it was impossible to traverse. Instead we walked alongside it, Caiden and Bradley flanking me, Dominico sandwiched between us and Crane.

I found myself hoping that Crane and his cronies would lose their way, and we'd wander these dusty plains until our bodies gave in. We would rot under the relentless sun, our bodies turning to dust. It seemed a far better fate than the one I imagined awaited me in Toria.

Several times I thought about attempting an escape. I had trained Caiden and Bradley. I knew that Caiden was slow to draw a gun without both hands. He would have to release me for the few seconds it would take him to reach his weapon. Once he had both hands on the gun though, he was an excellent shot. My only hope would be to disarm him before he could get his hands on the gun. Bradley was lethal in hand-to-hand combat. The knife he was carrying was superb for just this use, but more importantly, it doubled as a throwing knife. His aim was faultless. The problem was, I couldn't disarm both men at once. Several times I tried to catch Dominico's eye when we stopped to rest. She studiously avoided looking at me, as if sensing my intention. Studying her, I wondered why she hadn't attempted an escape herself. I'd seen her abilities at work. All she would have to do was project an image of a false landscape, one in which we appeared, while we walked away. She could flatten them all with one gesture, and yet she kept her head down, not saying a word or showing any resistance.

Her fate would be worse than execution – she'd be Crane's puppet. I thought about how her punishment had been commuted from death to imprisonment. Maybe that had been Crane's intention all along – to stow her away with the others he was creating, until he had a use for her. The thought made my stomach grow leaden. But she had her one hope to cling to. If Crane kept me alive, it would merely be a prelude to my execution.

We stopped for the night not far from the old highway, spotting a ruined hotel. The door was ajar but still firmly attached to the doorway, making it possible for us to close and secure it behind us. There was just enough light coming through the windows flanking the door to navigate by. The fading sun cast eerie shadows, keeping us keenly attuned to any movement or sound. Crane and his guards assessed the crumbling staircase before settling us all on the ground floor. Taking a left from the front door, we came upon a broken machine. Its glass case revealed rows of empty slots, the contents of which I could only guess at. Neat black buttons with fading letters and numbers framed the right side of the glass. A metal slot caught the dying rays of the sun, glinting mutely. I stared at it for a moment, trying to puzzle out its use.

I felt the prod of a gun muzzle in my back. 'Keep moving,' Caiden snapped.

At the end of a long corridor, a lone vase sat on an intact table. Stalks still protruded from its mouth. I touched them as we passed. They crumbled to dust between my fingers.

Bradley gripped the handle of the first door we came upon. The door swung inward. The light from the stripped window revealed a torn and filthy mattress. The frame of the bed was missing. But the window was intact, as were all four walls. Bradley and Caiden glanced at Crane. He nodded. 'Good enough as any.'

We moved into the room, dropping gratefully to the floor. Deep in The Waste, something howled. Canines. We all sat silently, knowing that noise would draw them to us.

Caiden grudgingly handed me a small package of food and a canister of water. He still hadn't looked me in the eye. Dominico had settled on the opposite side of the room. Caiden and Bradley didn't object. She'd lulled them into a false sense of security with her docility. Now would be the perfect time to attempt an escape. Now when they least expected it. The coming darkness would make it easier for us to disappear, provided we found a place to hide before the sun set altogether. But she sat silently, not having said one word since our departure, and ate her measly portion. She drained the canister, and then curled up in her corner and promptly fell asleep.

Caiden took up the first watch. As exhausted as I was, I couldn't sleep. Every time I closed my eyes I saw myself staring into the black eyes of several guns, my former friends gathered to watch my execution. Instead, I stared into the darkness and listened to the others. I could tell from Caiden's occasional snorts that he was drifting off and jerking awake again. Finally he gave into his fatigue. His breathing became deep and even, his snores punctuating the silence.

Nothing was stopping me from escaping. It wouldn't take much for me to lift Dominico and carry her out of here. But we'd be running blind.

'I know what you're thinking, Commander.'

Crane's voice came at me from the darkness, startling me.

'There's nowhere for you to run. And if you try, the girl dies. I know you can't have something like that on your conscience, now can you?'

'You're bluffing.'

'Am I?'

'What do you want with her, anyway?'

'Don't take me for a fool, Rogan. I know what you saw in my office.'

A fist of fear had clamped around my throat. The blackness of the night was suffocating.

'You walked right into it.'

I'd heard him clearly. And I grasped his meaning immediately.

But unable to accept my stupidity, I shook my head, as if my denial would make it untrue. 'Excuse me?'

He laughed. The sound was muffled, as if he'd raised a hand to his mouth. I wondered if he was afraid of waking Caiden and Bradley.

'When have you ever known me to be so careless, Commander? Leaving those papers there, out in the open? With my office door unlocked? Such a coincidence. I was sure you'd see through it.'

My mouth was parched. I longed to flood it with water – anything to get rid of the metallic fur that coated my tongue.

'Why would you test me? I was always loyal to you. You had no reason to doubt me.'

I couldn't understand why I was so furious. What did I care if he'd questioned my loyalty? He wasn't a man who deserved it, from me or anyone. Still, he'd seen it coming, whereas I'd been taken completely by surprise by my own actions.

'Are you angry that I was able to predict your reaction? Or because you were so easily swayed by a few sketches and notes? I have to know, at all times, who is loyal to me. I can't have my commander taking things into his own hands and upsetting my plans.'

My hands clenched. I wanted to get up and find him in the dark, and finish this conversation with my fists. My recent lack of control was starting to worry me. Aunt Carrie had always predicted that my temper would ruin me. As a child, she'd beaten me every time I'd thrown a tantrum, or spoken a decibel louder than she liked. I let her voice fill my mind and drown out everything else, reminding myself that the last thing I wanted was to fulfil her prophecy.

'You're experimenting on people. Your own kind.'

'Yes, but not just them, as you well know. Do you think their lives are less significant than ours?'

I snorted. 'You don't see your hypocrisy, do you?'

'On the contrary my dear Rogan, I'm not singling out one species.' I heard him shift in the darkness, and sensed he'd moved closer. 'Don't you see its merits? We'll be able to do everything they can. They'll no longer pose a threat. Through them, we'll be able to run faster, possess unimaginable strength, read minds... Why wouldn't you want that opportunity?'

'Don't you take me for a fool, President Crane. You won't keep them. You'll destroy them all, once they've fulfilled their purpose.'

'Perhaps. But then again, they would be powerful allies to have, wouldn't they?'

'Provided you can control them.'

He fell silent. I wondered if I'd hit a nerve.

'What do you think everyone in Toria is going to think when you reveal what you've been doing? Do you think they'll approve of you harbouring so many of them in a city where citizens die for doing the same?'

'You mistake me, Commander. I have no interest in what they think. I'm their president, and have we not schooled them in the art of unquestioning obedience?'

Yes, we had. And I'd been an integral part of that, enforcing laws without question, even those that I'd privately considered brutal and unnecessary. I'd thought that, because I had never participated in, nor allowed the cruelty that other soldiers found so amusing, I was a commendable leader. How very ironic.

Dominico

The gates of Toria shimmered in the distance, like a mirage in the heat. I'd wanted to ask President Crane about my parents ever since we'd left Jozenburg. But his bodyguards scared me. I recognised both of them. Caiden and I had been on friendly terms. He used to wave whenever he saw me, and if we passed in the street, he would always ask about Mom and Dad. Now he acted like we were strangers. Bradley had been one of the guards with a bad reputation. There'd been a lot of talk of the kind of soldier he'd make once promoted.

I thought it was weird how they guarded Rogan, but didn't once put a hand on me. I got the feeling that neither of them wanted to touch me, as if they thought my abilities could be passed on like a contagious disease. Crane seemed confident that I wouldn't cause any trouble, which made my hope balloon.

My underarms felt damp. So did my palms. It was a sweat that had nothing to do with the heat. My throat felt closed, like it was swelling shut. I kept coughing, trying to clear it, until Crane shot me a dirty look that made my insides curl together so tightly I thought I'd throw up. For a panicked minute, I wondered if I should've tried to escape after all.

The city gates swung open on noisy hinges. Absolute silence

greeted our arrival. From where I stood I could see hundreds of figures standing motionless. One man had stopped in the act of reaching for a package on the ground. His arms were still outstretched and his back bent. It would've been funny, if I hadn't felt their hatred drilling into me like knives at my back. I straightened, forcing my chin up and my gaze through them. All I had now was the last scrap of my dignity.

Crane was staring at me. I resisted the urge to look for my parents in the crowd, afraid that I wouldn't find them, and what it meant if they weren't here. The mix of anticipation, fear and excitement filled me until I felt giddy enough to float away.

Crane motioned to Caiden and Bradley. 'Disperse them.' He waved in the direction of the crowd. The men hesitated. 'Leave him. He has nowhere to run now.' They released Rogan for the first time since we'd left Jozenburg. I glanced at his arms. Angry red circles marked his forearms. He rubbed them, his eyes dark and flat.

'This way,' Crane said. The gates closed behind us. A grating shriek, and The Waste disappeared from view. I swallowed hard and turned away, following Crane and Rogan back into the depths of my former home.

***

I thought Crane would take us to the stocks. Somewhere to stow us until he'd decided what to do with us. Instead, he led us to the fields. The white canopies of the shade cloths flapped in the breeze, throwing dancing shadows over the bent figures of the workers. As we moved closer, two people straightened, shielding their eyes against the glare. A moment later they were rushing towards us, arms flapping like wings, their shouts ringing out in the afternoon air. I blinked as they ran straight towards me, my mind too full of questions to realise what I was seeing. Only when I was picked up like a kid and twirled in circles did the pieces fall into place.

I knew I was shouting, but I couldn't hear my voice over theirs. Dad put me down only long enough for Mom to grab me in her arms, her hair falling between us. My cheeks felt damp from her tears. She held me against her for so long I was sure I was caught in one of my dreams again, and soon I'd awake to find the tears on my face were my own.

She finally held me at arm's length. Dad stood behind her, his hands on her shoulders. They were both grinning. I looked more carefully at Mom, and my throat tightened.

Her cheekbones stood out sharply against her skin. Under her eyes there were circles so dark they looked black. A red welt ran from her earlobe to her chin. It looked fresh.

I whipped around to face Crane. 'What did you do to them?'

'Domo...' Mom reached for me but I shook her off.

'You kept them alive. What for? So you could teach them a lesson?'

Crane watched me, his face blank. 'Death is a release, child. Why would I allow them that escape when I have something far worse planned for them?'

I thought about him reaching for the gun at his belt and putting it against his temple. I pictured him pulling the trigger, and his body dropping to the ground like a sack of stones. I could pull a veil over the soldiers' eyes and create a false backdrop while we escaped. But I kept seeing Kat's broken body, the horrible twist of her limbs as she'd fallen. All it would take was one bullet, and one moment, and I could lose Mom or Dad. Or both of them.

I turned away. It took everything I had to bury my anger and fear. I could use it. But now wasn't the time.

I looked back at Mom. There were lines around her mouth that hadn't been there before, so deep they looked like they'd been carved with a knife. Her hair was still long, but now it hung in a tangled clump, greasy and unwashed. Its golden blonde colour had turned a muddy brown. Was he so depraved that he couldn't even allow them basic necessities like soap?

Mom touched my cheek as my own tears spilled over, her mouth smiling but her eyes filled with pain.

I didn't want to look at Dad. I was too afraid of what I'd see. I forced my gaze to his, and couldn't stop my gasp of shock. He'd stepped out from behind Mom. He was so skinny his clothes waved in the breeze like clothes off a washing line. His normally clean-shaven face was studded with stubble, eyes like hollow sockets in his skull. My eyes darted between them. Their clothes were filthy and tattered. I knew field hands were mistreated, but I feared their punishment would be even more so. Just for being my parents. Dad put his hands on my shoulders. His palms felt rough and cracked. This moment wasn't how I'd pictured it. Crane had stolen it from me, like everything else.

Rogan

Crane couldn't have wounded Dominico more if she'd found her parents dead. I knew she would punish herself for every bruise and mark on their bodies, and she would gather every injustice against them until she was so full of their pain there would only be one possible outlet for it.

Crane dragged Dominico away and sent her parents back into the fields. The woman paused long enough to lay a hand on my arm. 'I didn't get a chance to thank you for what you did.'

I stared at her. Thank me? For this? She smiled. I could tell it took effort, but it transformed her. That spark that I'd seen so often in Dominico was there in her. Buried, but quietly burning. 'You can't blame yourself. You did more than anyone else would've done for her.' She looked at me with sympathy. 'You'll pay dearly for it, but you did it anyway.' A soldier yanked her by the arm, shoving her so hard she stumbled and fell to her knees. I turned away, bile clawing up my throat and filling my mouth.

'Come, Commander.' I wondered why he kept referring to me by a rank I obviously no longer possessed. He waved one of the soldiers over. His face was only vaguely familiar. A new recruit.

'Take the girl to my office. Stay with her until I return.'

He smiled. 'The commander has many people to get reacquainted with.'

***

The barracks looked the same. I stared at the open doorway, wishing the building would collapse and I wouldn't have to face the men inside.

Crane motioned me ahead of him. I blinked as my eyes adjusted to the semi-darkness. I'd always hated how few windows there were.

The men stood in several lines like pious school children. My appearance broke the silence, and the shouted insults rang out until they ran together in a stream of animosity. I forced myself to look at them squarely. I refused to hang my head like a beaten animal, as if I had something to be ashamed of.

Crane stood beside me and raised his hands for quiet. 'Your commander has returned.' Laughter. He turned to me. 'Well? Get your things.'

I had to push past the men to reach my bunk. Hands on my back shoved me forward until my feet gave way and I stumbled into my old bunk. More laughter. I drifted for a moment, feeling suspended in a life that couldn't possibly be mine. I'd belonged here. I'd fitted in with these very men. I'd been their leader.

A glob of something wet hit my cheek. I swiped at it. Phlegm. I gathered my measly belongings and straightened, meeting the gaze of the nearest man. Most likely the one who'd spat at me. Riley. Young and arrogant, I'd considered him a dangerous choice for a soldier. A position of power should never be given to those who'd wield it like a weapon. He smirked, enjoying my humiliation. My control slipped a notch. I turned away. If I looked at him a second longer I would give in to the need to slam my fist into his face.

'Nothing to say commander? You above us now that you've spent time with those superhumans?'

I gritted my teeth against my response. What was there to say? Before I'd left this city, I'd felt the same way. Part of their training was to educate them on the dangers of the other species. *Educate.* That was the word Crane had used.

I shoved my way back to Crane. A punch grazed my shoulder. I didn't bother to see who had thrown it. The edges of my vision were pulsing with a kaleidoscope of fury. They were prodding me the same way children poked at an animal in a cage. They wanted to see me snap.

Without waiting for Crane's permission, I made for the door.

A patter of insults followed me, the words joining together until they formed one word. The men chanted it like an incantation. Traitor.

***

Without Crane having to say a word, I knew where we were going next. There was only one person who could add to my humiliation now. Crane knocked on the door and it swung wide with a familiar long-suffering groan. Aunt Carrie stood in the doorway, her mouth set in its habitual grim line.

'The hero has returned, I see.'

Crane bowed. Aunt Carrie beamed. She was blind to the mockery of the gesture.

'To your care, Miss Whitemore. I know you'll keep him in line.'

I met her gaze head on. I had nothing to fear. I was no longer the child indebted to her. But staying here, left under her supervision, was a different kind of punishment.

Her beady eyes swept over me. 'So they let you stay. And fed you, by the looks of it. Like a well-kept pet.' She smiled, displaying her missing front tooth.

Crane turned to me. The agony of not knowing my fate was haunting me. His expression gave nothing away. 'Tomorrow you'll report to my office. Your aunt and I have discussed the terms of your staying here. As long as you remain in her good graces, you'll have a roof over your head.'

He bowed a second time to Aunt Carrie, and she grinned widely in return, her adoration of him both pitiful and sickening. He turned and left, walking slower than before. The trip through The Waste had tired him. He was growing older. The thought cheered me somewhat, knowing that someday, we'd all be free of him.

'Don't hover.' She waved me in. Despite her impatience, I hesitated in the doorway. The intervening years fell away, and I was again the child whose parents had left him without so much as a word or a note.

In the corner, I glimpsed her cane. She only used it around the house, despite her pronounced limp. The sight of it took me back to the many nights I'd run from her while she brandished it like a sword. It didn't take me long to realise that running only delayed the inevitable. Always four strokes, and always along the length of my back. I learned to submit as soon as she picked it up. I'd take my beating quietly, refusing to flinch even as she used more force in an effort to break my silence.

The beatings had stopped as soon as I'd grown old enough to overpower her. The last time she'd come after me with the cane I'd simply taken it from her, amazed at how easy it was. She'd surrendered it without a word, but she was anything but cowed. The score was still the same – only now she'd use her tongue instead of her hands.

'How nice to have you home.' She hobbled through the doorway and disappeared into the kitchen. 'Something to drink?'

I forced my feet forward. I stepped into the dank dark of my childhood home. It still smelled the way I'd always imagined a prison would – the close, humid stench of things growing beneath the floors.

I walked into the kitchen. She held a jug aloft, the one that boasted faded blue daisies. A relic from my childhood. The water only reached a quarter of the way up, barely enough to fill one glass. She poured it into a tumbler and held it out to me, a game from my childhood which I'd detested. I stared at the liquid, already imagining its sublime coolness. I met her eyes. 'No thank you.'

Her ill-concealed glee slipped. She shrugged and slurped the water down. A stream escaped her mouth and ran down her chin, spotting her faded blouse. She returned the glass to the counter with a resounding thunk, swiping a hand across her mouth. The gesture did nothing to hide her smile.

Chapter Twenty-Four

Syra

Raven heard me enter and glanced across irritably. She thought I was checking up on her, although for the past two days, all I'd done is watch.

Since Dominico and Rogan had been taken, I'd thought about nothing but the terribly obvious detail I'd overlooked. The gift of this city had merely been a way to placate us after the human war. Crane had seen his chance to lead and taken up the role with such confidence that no one thought to question his motives. He'd bided his time, waiting for the human numbers to grow, for enough time to allow the training of many more soldiers and guards. He'd built up the cities and allowed us to call Jozenburg home. I was starting to think it was a deliberate move. He'd kept us apart, supposedly to maintain the peace. He'd given us time to build up the resources. Thanks to us, the city would be habitable and functional, with every process implemented and running smoothly. Which now made it the perfect time to take it back.

Raven continued her training as before. The trainees practised on each other and, despite my reservations about injuries, I knew it was necessary. Without Dominico, we were facing a war with too many disadvantages already. The last thing I wanted was for them to set foot on a battlefield ill-prepared.

At my insistence, Ray was at every training session. I needed three pairs of eyes to look for inconsistencies and weaknesses. It was difficult for me to admit I needed the help, but now wasn't the time for pride. He kept his distance, my attempts at conversation met with grunts or monosyllabic replies. He only spoke in full sentences if the subject was something I needed his opinion on. He kept his arms crossed and planted against his chest, his gaze turned resolutely away from mine.

Despite Raven's irritation, she still reported to me without my having to ask. 'Emery's improved dramatically. See her response time?'

She motioned to the girl, who'd stopped Levin's attempt to fling a chair at her. It had simply dropped in the middle of the ring, as ineffectual as a tossed pebble.

I nodded. Raven's gaze shifted to Levin, and her expression of pride turned to a scowl. 'He, on the other hand, shows zero improvement. I've put him against all the other trainees and he doesn't seem to learn a damn thing from any of them.'

I said nothing, but Levin worried me too. Our lectures over his conduct towards Dominico had done nothing to dampen his arrogance. Despite his obvious lack of skill, he strutted around like a king among his subjects.

Now more than ever, I felt Draiken's absence. The only person I could've turned to was Ray, and now even that was impossible. I felt like an idiot for failing to see it sooner. Looking back, I realised all the signs had been there but, at the time, I'd taken them for indications of an old friendship and the zealous over-protectiveness of a brother.

I waited until every trainee had practised in the ring. Usually the trainees went several rounds, but today I had other plans.

I tapped Raven on the shoulder. 'Finish up. I've got something important to discuss with you and Ray.'

I expected her to protest, but instead she did as she was told. Ray grunted an acknowledgement and walked ahead, his long stride eating up the distance until he disappeared from view. 'Meet you at the Elders' quarters,' I called after him, hating the artificial brightness of my tone.

The trainees streamed out after him, their conversation swelling around us and then fading as the training hall emptied. Raven and I stood alone in the quiet, a slant of sunlight streaming through a small gap in the blacked-out window. Dust danced in the beam, swirling to a silent rhythm.

Raven gave me a sidelong glance. 'What's going on with him?'

'I think he's interested in me.' The words fell from my mouth, surprising us both. Raven blinked. She hadn't expected an answer. At least not the one I'd given.

'I figured as much.'

'What?'

She hesitated. 'He came to me last night.'

This was why I'd never pursued female friendships. The intimate trade of knowledge left me feeling naked and vulnerable. Ray and I were close in the same way that Drake and Ray had been – companionable but strictly vague on details like these. I believed in monogamy, despite this not being a widespread custom among superhumans. Ray was part of the majority.

'Oh,' I said. The training hall felt stifling. I started walking, giving Raven no option but to follow. She caught up to me, matching her stride to mine.

She shook her head. 'He must be hurting. He's been trying to find a way to tell you.'

I felt as though I were trying to find my way through a maze, blindfolded. 'What are you talking about?'

'You honestly never suspected?'

'That things had changed? No, of course not. He's my friend, my second brother.' *Was.*

'He stopped seeing you that way a long time ago. Even before Draiken left. He was planning to tell you. Then Rogan arrived.'

The sound of his name sparked a sharp pain in my temple. Out of the hall we turned left, moving towards the less populated part of the city. I wished fervently that someone would interrupt us, if only for a minute. 'What does he have to do with this?'

Raven shifted uncomfortably. 'Well... you know.'

'Clearly I don't.' I knew what she was going to say. I could feel it coming off her, the tension and uncertainty before someone tells you something they would rather not. I didn't probe her mind. I didn't have to. Her body language was unmistakable. But I needed her to say it, if only to hear it spoken out loud.

'You seemed...close.' Her voice rose on the last word, as if she'd meant it as a question. Nonetheless, it came out sounding like a statement.

We'd reached the doors of the former sanctuary of the Elders. Ray thought meeting here was masochistic, but I found it soothing to be in a place where they had once been, despite what had happened. It reminded me of a time before this, when Drake and I had still wanted the same thing, when everything in my world still made sense.

I pushed through them, hoping Raven would take my silence as a hint. I regretted saying anything at all, and made a mental note that it would be the last time I confided in her, or anyone, for that matter.

Ray stood in the middle of the foyer, the dusty windows allowing only muted light through. He stood bathed in a pool of blue, as though I were seeing him underwater. The floor to ceiling stained-glass brought to mind the religious places people used to go to before the war. I searched my mind for the word. Churches.

The picture I'd seen in a book belonging to Azaiah looked so much like this place. The same windows that threw shards of colour so bright it hurt to look at them. Azaiah had told me that, soon after the war, many of those places had been set alight and burned to the ground. People had stopped believing in a higher power. Drake had often joked that maybe that was why they hated us so much. We represented what had been lost.

Ray turned at the sound of our arrival, our footsteps echoing back across the stone floor. His eyes moved to Raven. Had he gone to her because he knew it would be simple? That she'd take him in without question, allow him to lose himself in her? I shoved the thought away.

I walked past him through the foyer and into the Elders' meeting room. I motioned to the heavy table that dominated the space, its surface covered in a light film of dust.

'There are two things we need to discuss. Firstly, we need more trainees.' Ray sat across from me.

Raven looked puzzled. 'All those that are able to train, are.'

'I know. But with this war coming, we need everyone. I'm thinking of taking some of the kids out of school and putting them into training. Only those who are nearly sixteen.'

Ray shot from his chair. 'What? You know we can't do that. It's not procedure. Besides, there are only five who are nearly sixteen.'

'I'm well aware of all that. But this war was supposed to be ours. Stupidly, we hoped Crane would pull out when he realised how much he'd stand to lose. But the war is his now. We need everyone on board. We can start an intensive training programme, which I'd like to oversee with Ray.'

'The parents won't agree to it. Those are their children. They're too young to fight.'

'Come on Ray. They're nearly of age. What do you think will happen if Crane wins the war? Do you think he'll spare the children? We have to do what's needed to preserve the life –'

Ray banged his fist against the table, sending a swirl of dust into the air. 'Sending kids to the battlefield is no way to preserve life. Have you lost your mind? No one will vote for this!'

'I'm not putting it to a vote.'

Silence followed, growing heavier with every second.

'You can't do that.' Ray's voice dropped, his tone dangerously controlled.

'We're supposed to lead together. This is turning into a dictatorship.'

Raven half-stood, reaching out to Ray. He snatched his arm away from her touch, like a sulky child refusing to be comforted. She sat back, her offending hand returning to her lap. Her face remained calm, but her body stiffened until I feared her spine would snap.

I pretended to ignore Ray's outrage and Raven's barely suppressed anger. 'The second thing is, I want to contact Drake to discuss fighting together for the duration of the war.' Before either of them could reply, I pushed on, running the words together before they could interrupt me.

'I know most people won't be happy with this either, but Drake took some of our most powerful fighters with him. He's one of our best, too. This arrangement will only be for as long as the war goes on. None of them will be allowed to return to Jozenburg, but while we plan strategy and train, they'll need to stay here.'

I wanted to go on, but Ray's expression froze the words on my tongue. He advanced towards me slowly, approaching me as if he fully expected me to bolt like an alarmed animal. He laid his hands on my shoulders, touching me for the first time since things had gone so wrong. He looked me straight in the eye, his intensity making me want to look away.

'This isn't you. I know you're afraid, and you feel you have to do something radical to protect us. But that doesn't mean going against everything we believe. You always stood by our belief system. You need to do that now. We can figure this out together. You don't need to do it alone. You said it yourself. Our numbers are too precious.'

He spoke carefully, enunciating every syllable, his tone soothing and calm. For the first time since I'd known him, I felt a fury so deep I wanted to punch him. I wanted to see him reel with the pain of it. His condescension, the complete lack of faith he showed in my abilities, made me feel that he had never truly known me. It felt like a betrayal.

I stood, forcing his hands to drop. 'I'm not afraid. I'm thinking more clearly than I have in months. Drake will be so happy to be killing humans that he'll listen to me. I'll be in control of this. It'll be on my terms. And this will save us.'

I stepped up to him again, pointing at his chest in an unspoken accusation. 'I've followed the rules my entire life. But the Elders are no longer here. It's time to buck the system. It's right, I can feel it.'

'How do you expect to get the others -'

'None of them have ever questioned me, because they believe in my ability to make the right decisions. Maybe you should follow suit.'

I turned to Raven. She took a step back, hands raised. 'I'm not getting into the middle of this.' She glared at me. 'Why did you involve me? This is between you. You're the leaders.'

The truth was, I'd hoped to garner her support. She was more cut-throat than Ray, willing to do what needed to be done, even if it wasn't the traditional way. But I should've known from the moment she told me about her and Ray that I'd be alone in this. Raven had made no secret of her attraction to Ray. She'd always played it non-committal, but I had long suspected she wanted more from him than he was able to give.

'You're the trainer. I'm asking for your opinion.'

'What for? You've made up your mind.'

'You agree with Ray?'

'I think you're being too hasty. You need time and deliberation for a decision like this. You're rushing into it.'

I rose, hoping my face was as blank as it felt, like blinds pulled closed over a window. 'Thank you for your honesty.' I included them both in this, although I couldn't manage to look at Ray directly. 'I'll make the announcements tomorrow. That's all.'

I was agonisingly aware of their movements as they left the room, their thoughts meticulously shuttered away from my reach. Their animosity felt like a fourth person in the room, exhaling its foul breath over me and enveloping me in a cloud of solitude of my own making.

Chapter Twenty-Five

Dominico

The skin of my inner elbow was dotted with blue and yellow bruises. The doctor hovered over me, his gloved hand holding an empty syringe. His face wavered in front of my eyes, features drifting out of focus and then snapping back again. I tried to centre my mind several times. It was impossible. My attention wandered, thoughts scattered and disconnected.

I sucked in my breath as the needle broke through my skin and settled in my vein. Blood rushed into the plastic container. It took only a couple of seconds to fill, and I counted each one silently. The doctor removed the needle, and his hand left my arm. I stared up at the cool white ceiling. I couldn't turn my head. The band securing it to the stretcher would no doubt leave a vicious red stripe across my forehead. And when he was finally done with me, I knew my skull would feel ready to crack open and spill my brains across the spotless floor. I could feel the pain building already.

They kept taking blood. I'd lost count of how many times I'd been stuck with a needle, and how many vials had been filled. He wore a mask that covered the bottom half of his face, but I knew it was the same doctor every time. His eyes were a weird green, so bright they glowed like neon signs in the harsh light of the room. There seemed to be endless electricity, undisturbed by the constant blackouts I remembered growing up. When I'd been brought here, I'd noticed that Crane's surrounding property was dotted with twice the number of turbines we had in the entire city.

I knew what was coming next. From the corner of my eye, I saw the doctor walk in from another room, a nurse at his side. She bent over me. She wore the same mask, hair pulled back so tightly her forehead looked stretched. I could tell she was smiling because of the tiny wrinkles that appeared at the corner of her eyes. She was trying to get me to relax, but it had exactly the opposite effect. She seemed to enjoy seeing me strapped down and defenceless.

'Roll her over.'

The nurse reached over me and unsnapped the headband. She moved to my arms and feet, until I was free of all the straps. I willed my arm to move. I wanted to slap that smile right off her face, but my hand flopped a centimetre or two off the stretcher, then puddled limply at my side.

The nurse tutted. 'No no. Don't struggle.'

Her smile remained fixed in place, like the brick of a house. She lifted my head and took my pillow, rolling me over so my face slotted into a hole in the stretcher and I was staring down at the tiled white floor. I felt faint. The tiles shifted and wavered, blurring together. I was strapped back down. They jabbed something into me right at the base of my spine. I blinked back the tears, trying to catch the shriek that filled my mouth. It escaped anyway. The nurse giggled. 'They're more human than we think, aren't they, doctor?' Her words were muffled by the mask, but I heard her loud and clear. I wanted to scream at them. I wanted just one clear moment. Just long enough to lift my hand and claw at her. I wanted to draw blood. To mar her perfect skin.

They rolled me over again. My back ached. The puncture throbbed at the base of my spine. I closed my eyes and tried to picture Mom and Dad. Not as they'd been when I'd last seen them, but as they'd looked before. Crane had promised I could see them. But I was sure that was weeks ago already. The last thing I heard before giving in to the blackness was the nurse tutting her fake sympathy as she mopped the tears from my cheeks.

Rogan

Crane was at my door every morning as the sun appeared over the horizon. I blinked in the wan light, feeling the grit of fatigue crunch behind my eyelids. Early mornings, and late nights. I often fell into bed after midnight, seeking sleep with every molecule in my body. It evaded me for an hour or two until finally my body would give in to exhaustion. Scenes from the day would play in my mind, flickering along the ceiling. The smells of that laboratory followed me home, stuffing my nose with the acrid stench of pain and fear.

'Good morning.' His greeting was the same every morning – as if this were our routine before work, just a couple of men shooting the breeze before getting down to business.

The sky was rapidly lightening as we walked towards Crane's mansion. The darkness gave way to scarlet, orange, and finally a faded blue. I thought of her, and wondered if she was awake. Wondered if her life was any different now that the girl and I were gone. This too, was now a ritual of the morning.

Dominico. I'd glimpsed her several times through the glass doors of the laboratory before she disappeared into one of the windowless rooms that led off it. Once or twice I thought she'd seen me too, but each time she'd shuffled off with no sign of recognition.

Crane walked beside me, rattling on companionably. It didn't seem to matter to him whether I listened or not. We reached the doors of the mansion. The guards ignored my presence, snapping off smart salutes in Crane's direction. I felt their eyes on my back, although they never looked at me directly. They would follow my every movement, as if taking stock of my whereabouts.

I followed the familiar route through Crane's home, turning towards the winding staircase on the left. It looped up two flights to the third floor, where the laboratory was housed.

A nurse unlocked the doors and stepped back to allow us through. She bowed her head. 'Good morning, President Crane.' Her tone was bright and grating, her smile a permanent feature, like a tattoo etched into her face. There seemed to be only a handful of staff working here. Not a government official in sight. How had Dominico's parents known about this place?

In the weeks I'd been coming here, I'd done everything from mopping up blood to helping sedate hysterical patients. *Patients*. Not a word I'd use for the unfortunate people who found themselves here.

A new batch awaited our arrival. They stood clustered together as if for protection. Two women and six men. Their numbers seemed to rise every week. Crane wouldn't have any humans left if he kept going at this pace.

The smiley nurse joined us. She was one of the few in this city who seemed at ease with me, chatting and forever smiling, smiling, smiling. My face ached on her behalf.

Crane called her over for a quick exchange. Her head bobbed rapidly in agreement. He turned to me. 'You're to assist Nurse Rachel today. She'll need help with the recruits.' I glanced at the group. One of the women wept silently, the hands she held over her face failing to hide her tears. The man beside her slipped his arm around her and pulled her to his chest. She buried her face in his shirt. The others stood stoically, their silence emphasising the snorting fear of the sobbing woman.

'Nurse, you stay here. We need to go pick ourselves a candidate.' He motioned to me. 'Follow me, Commander.'

We wound our way through a maze of rooms, many of them empty. A long and narrow corridor led us down a flight of stairs. We reached a door guarded by two soldiers. Bradley and Caiden. I'd wondered why I hadn't seen them around, dreading, despite everything, that they'd overstepped a line and ended up as subjects here. Caiden swung the door open, avoiding eye contact. The light was so dim it took me a moment to realise what the room contained. Cells. Neatly lined up on both sides of the room. The closest was tiny, barely high enough for an adult to stand up straight in, and so narrow the bed took up its entire width. Something rose from the bed. It straightened as much as possible. Back hunched, it hobbled to the cell door, fingers closing around the bars. A human face followed the fingers. Gaunt and pale, he blinked slowly and deliberately, eyes moving between us again and again.

My gaze moved along the length of the room and, as my eyes adjusted, I found that every cell was occupied. The occupants shuffled to their cell doors, their eyes moving from Crane and locking on me. The only sound was the dragging of their feet along the floor, and once they'd crossed to their cell doors, fingers clinging to the bars, there was silence.

'Choose one.'

'What is this?'

'Where do you think all the superhumans come from?'

I recalled the sketches from Crane's office. The pages of notes. The word TERMINATE. I swallowed hard, trying to fight off the nausea.

I looked over at the closest one, the man who had come forward first. His expression hadn't changed. Although he'd initially seemed drawn to his cell door, he showed no further interest in us. His gaze briefly settled on Crane, then me, then moved off.

'Come now commander. We have work to do.'

'What are they to be used for?'

'Transfers, of course.' Crane's foot tapped against the pocked floor, setting off a chain of echoes along the corridor. I remembered what Syra has said about the success rate of conversions and felt a wash of pity.

'How do I pick one?'

'There's no method to it. Just choose the one that strikes your fancy and we can get on with things.'

I wanted nothing to do with this. Any of it. I wanted no part of this suffering and torment, this plan of Crane's that seemed to have no goal but to inflict pain on others, human and Superhuman alike.

'Stalling will not get you out of this. Choose. Now.'

I pointed at random, keeping my eyes to the floor. Crane called out to the soldiers. A pair of feet strode to a cell door. The key screamed in the lock and the door opened. A long, low shriek filled the room. I couldn't place its source. I looked up. The sound was coming from the chosen Superhuman. His mouth moved, but the rest of his face remained frozen. He stood beside the soldier, unmoving.

The soldiers didn't touch him, or reach out to lead him. He stood quivering, his whole body vibrating with nerves, but made no attempt to escape.

'Come,' Crane said. The man moved obediently, his mouth verbalising his fear, his face still immobile.

He followed us back out to the laboratory. Crane halted him in front of the group of humans. In the harsh light of the room, the Superhuman looked haunted. His eyes were full of his suffering, his mouth forming that undulating sound that had moved from a whisper to a low moan. The humans drew back, colliding into one another in their haste to get away from the apparition that stood in front of them.

'You.' Crane pointed at the woman who'd shown such fear earlier. Her face still bore the marks of her tears – long clean lines that had cut through the dirt. 'Come forward. You're first.'

The woman shook her head vehemently, pushing back into the arms of the man who'd comforted her, trying to disappear into his embrace.

Crane smiled condescendingly. Caiden and Bradley had remained at their post. No other soldiers or guards seemed to occupy positions within the laboratory. I wondered how Crane would force the woman from the safety of her companions.

'Give her over to me, or you will be first.' He directed his words to the man holding her. The man stared back defiantly, his chin tilting up in a silent challenge. Crane turned his head and addressed the others. 'This transition can be very painful. But I can make it less so for those who cooperate. Hand her over, and I'll make sure you're injected with a sedative.'

A look passed between the other woman present and the man beside her. They moved together, working as a team until they had pried the terrified woman from her protector's arms. They pushed her forward. She stumbled and crumpled in a heap at Crane's feet, her sobs loud and grating. Smiley nurse helped the woman up and led her away, motioning for the Superhuman to follow her. Crane glanced at me, his expression as gleeful as that of a child's who has received an unexpected gift.

'Now you get to see something few others ever will.'

The room they'd dragged the woman to was tiny and oppressively warm, the closed door containing our body heat and raising the temperature even more. The only item in the room was a stretcher, identical to the one I'd seen in the sketches I'd found in Crane's office. That moment felt as if it had happened years ago, to someone I'd known distantly. So much had happened in between that, even though that had been my turning point, I felt removed from it. Indifference was my only ally now.

The nurse was strapping the woman down, tightening the bands around her wrists until her veins rose, their violent blue stark against her skin. The superhuman moved over to the stretcher, standing over the woman. Her screams were muffled by the rag the nurse had gagged her with. Her eyes bulged, fixing on me in a plea for help. I wanted to look away, but I couldn't. Crane was watching me, his gaze intent on my face, waiting for my reaction. It took every ounce of control to keep my face neutral, to push down on the emotions hard enough to bury them.

The superhuman raised his hands. A throbbing light appeared between his closely spaced palms. It grew brighter, lighting the room with such intensity that I had to shield my eyes. It dimmed again and separated from the superhuman, moving towards the woman. It spread along the length of her body until it covered her like a blanket. The superhuman shuffled forward and placed his hands on her shoulders, his meaty palms spanning her collarbone and his thumbs meeting at the hollow of her throat. Her body was convulsing. She strained against the bands, her back arching off the stretcher. Staring at his thumbs against her vulnerable pulse, I feared she would choke. She collapsed against the stretcher, her face contorting and then relaxing. A gush of blood poured from her nose, colouring the rag in her mouth and filling the room with its metallic stench.

Finally, the superhuman stepped back and the light drained away like water through a drain. The woman lay still and silent, her eyes closed, the blood congealing in small pools above and below her mouth.

'Go on. Take a closer look.' Crane nudged me forward, directing me to her head. I forced my feet to obey. I looked down at her. If it weren't for the blood and bindings, it would be easy to mistake her pose for that of sleep. Her chest rose and fell. Her face had lost its mask of pain and fear. Her eyes snapped open. They were scarlet, brimming with bloody tears.

Dominico

Turns out it was easier than I thought to lift the keys from his belt. I thought he'd hear them jangle, but the perfect opportunity just came along. I didn't plan it. A fellow guard yelled down to him from the tower and one minute he was walking ahead, the next he had stopped, his head cocked to hear the guard's voice. My fingers moved on their own, and before I could second-guess myself, I had the keys in my hand. For a minute I panicked, not knowing where to hide them. There were many of them caught together on a clunky ring, heavier than they looked. Luckily my pants, the same ones I'd worn for days on end, had deep pockets, and their bagginess hid the bulge.

When he took off ahead of me again, taking a minute to check where I was, I was sure he'd notice they were missing. He mistook my hesitation for biding my time, and barked at me to hurry up. I quickly caught up and fell in behind him again. The black rings under his eyes had deepened over the past few days. He watched me day and night. No one arrived to take over his watch. I couldn't believe Crane's confidence. One guard, at all hours of the day and night, to watch over a commodity as precious as me? Although, it had to be mentioned that I was probably no longer as valuable as I used to be. The drugs they had pumped into me, plus the endless vials of blood I was supplying, had left me weak and unable to focus. I was human again. How ironic.

The guard led me through the winding passages of Crane's mansion. There were several doors along the way, all of them closed. So many rooms, and no one to live in them. The whole place smelled of dust and neglect. I was sure that if I touched the walls, I'd leave finger-sized tracks behind. When we reached my room, I realised how stupid I'd been. Now was when he'd reach for his keys. Even as the thought came, his fingers began to fumble for them.

'Where are they?' he muttered, more to himself than me. He looked up, his face tight with suspicion. He stepped closer, his hands shooting out to search me.

What would Crane do to them if he found out? I pictured their faces – tight and painfully thin. Adrenaline pumped through me. His hands groped at my pockets, thrusting them downward. His fingers closed around the keys, and he yanked them out, dangling them in front of me as if challenging me to deny taking them. I didn't. I dug deeper than I ever had. I stared at him, willing him to see nothing at all in his hand, urging his mind to twist in on itself and confuse events until he had no idea what had just happened. It was too much. My exhaustion ran too deep. My mind was full of holes, and trying to focus my energy inward was like trying to collect water in a bucket full of holes.

He drew his hand back. It came at me, aiming for my cheek. I pushed harder, willing myself to find the core, to dig my fingers in and hold onto it. I felt the tiniest of responses. A nugget of heat that flared for a moment, but then died. *Come on come on come on.* His hand found my cheek, and maybe the sting of the blow helped me latch on. His hand dropped. His face creased. He blinked, his mouth open. He shuffled back a few steps, then turned and slumped against the wall. His eyes closed. Seconds later, he was snoring.

I ran shaky fingers through my hair. Reaching into my pocket, I pulled out the ring of keys. The key to my room, and five others. Now that I had them, what was I going to do with them? I hadn't really thought further than getting my hands on them. One of these could unlock the front door of this mansion, but what would be the point? There were guards at the gate and soldiers patrolling around the clock.

I fingered one key that stood out from the rest. It was bigger than the others. Instead of a round head, it had been shaped into three intersecting circles. Which of the dozens of rooms in this place would it unlock?

I knew I should be playing it safe, not taking risks. But since the day I'd arrived here Crane had kept me under lock and key. I hadn't seen Mom and Dad since my first day. I was being used as an experimental pincushion, poked for hours every day, and then locked away as soon as they were done with me. I had no idea what they'd been injecting me with, but it had left me weak and shaky. I often vomited when I got back to my room and, since there was nowhere else to do it, I would find myself kneeling over the bucket that was half-filled with my waste. The room stank even after it had been emptied.

I felt stronger today than I had in a while. I wanted to do something to change my situation, even if it was something as pointless as wandering the empty rooms of Crane's home.

I glanced down at the snoring guard. It was a big risk. I knew that everything I did would come down on Mom and Dad's heads, but was this really all we could hope for, for the rest of our lives?

I walked around the guard and took a few hesitant steps. It was still daytime outside but, with its closed doors, the passage was heavy with shadows. I turned in the opposite direction from where we'd come from. I fitted each key into the locks I passed, but none of them would turn. I felt edgy, my ears tuned for the sound of someone coming. The semi-darkness made me jump at every movement, real or imagined.

Ahead of me, I could see nothing. There were no lights. I put my hands out, feeling blindly in the dark. A few steps later, my hands brushed something solid. I slid my fingers down, and realised it was a door. Instinctively I reached for the keys, feeling for the one with the weird pattern. I found the keyhole with my other hand and slowly slotted the key in, terrified that if I did it any faster I'd drop the keys.

The key turned in the lock. I pushed the handle down and the door swung inwards. The room beyond was dimly lit, but at least there was some light to guide me through. A king-sized bed took up most of the room. I touched the bedding. It was so soft, its deep blue colour soothing and inviting. The carpet was so thick my feet sank into it. A lamp sat on a bedside table. I wanted to flick its switch, just to see if it would work, but its brightness would be a dead giveaway in all the murky half-light.

I turned, and for the first time, noticed another door. I tried the round knob but it turned uselessly in my hand. I fished out the keys again, wondering if one of the other three would fit the lock. Just as I was about to try, a whisper came from the other side of the door. I jumped back as if I'd been burned, my heart in my throat. It came again, but I couldn't make out any words. I put my ear against the wood. 'Hello?'

'Hello.' I wasn't hearing things. There was someone on the other side, and it sounded like a girl.

'Who are you?'

Footsteps. Coming from the direction I had just taken. Shit! I looked frantically for a place to hide. Two choices – the freestanding cupboard, or under the bed. Closer. Whoever it was would be at the door in seconds, and it was standing wide open. No time. I dived under the bed.

A pair of booted feet paused in the doorway. I could imagine their owner standing there, trying to figure out why the door was unlocked, never mind open.

'Layla?'

Oh god, oh no. I crawled a little closer, trying to see who it was without giving myself away.

'Layla?' The voice was becoming panicked. The feet rushed towards the other door. The jangle of keys, and then the scrape of metal on metal. I could see more now – calves and thighs, clad in a pair of spotless pants. Not jeans, but pants. No holes, no dirt, no patches. I swallowed. Crane.

He pushed the door open and, as I'd suspected, a little girl stood in the room beyond. She was tiny, and couldn't be older than seven or eight. Crane dropped to his knees and pulled her into his arms. Her face was half visible over his shoulder, and I felt her gaze on me. She stiffened in his arms, allowing him to hug her but seeming reluctant to return it. He held onto her a moment longer, as if hoping she would reciprocate. When she didn't, he held her at arms' length, his hands on her shoulders. 'Layla, what happened here? Who opened this door?'

I stopped breathing. I waited for her to out me, to point a finger over his shoulder and give me away. 'I don't know, Daddy.' *Daddy?*

'It didn't open itself. Who opened it?'

'I couldn't see. My door was closed.'

Her logic was hard to argue with. Still, Crane sighed as if disappointed. He looked around the room, as if it had only just occurred to him that they might not be alone. His eyes moved to the bed, and I instinctively backed up a little, trying not to make a sound. If he came any closer, he would find me. Sweat dripped down my back. It soaked into my t-shirt, and I wondered if the smell of my fear would reach Crane's nose.

'Daddy, did you bring me anything?'

Crane's attention moved from the bed and back to his daughter. 'Of course, dear one.' He handed her something that looked like a package of food, and something else that, judging from the sloshing sound, was a bottle of water. The smell of something sweet drifted my way, and my mouth watered. I hadn't had anything to eat since my tasteless breakfast. The same hard, dark bread I'd eaten at home with Mom and Dad, in what now felt like another lifetime.

He motioned her towards a chair and table directly across from the bed. The chair faced the wall. As she sat in the seat and Crane turned his back to me, I breathed easier. He waited in silence for her to finish eating. My mind was racing. Over the years I'd heard my share of stories and rumours about Crane. People loved to talk about him. They would compete with each other to see who could come up with the best background story – the more outrageous the better. But never had anyone said anything about a child. Why was she locked away here, like a dirty secret? Who was her mother? Why was Crane hiding her?

My eyes moved back to the girl. She was really tiny. Her size made her seem younger than I'd guessed, although she spoke in a way that made me think she could be older. She sat, keeping more than an arm's length between Crane and her. Once or twice he shifted closer, and she would shift further back, careful to stay just out of his reach.

As soon as she'd eaten her meal, Crane got up to leave. The girl left her chair and stood beside it, her doll-like hands folded in front of her. Crane bent for another hug but she remained where she was, her eyes fixed on him, ever watchful. I got the feeling it wasn't because she didn't want him to leave. He waited, but when she refused to move into his arms, he sighed and shooed her back. I tried to see beyond them, but it was too dark to see much of anything. I felt sorry for her, having to go back into that space. With the door closed, it was probably too dark for her to see her hand in front of her face. Surely he didn't leave her there, for hours on end, with nothing to do but stare into the blackness until his next visit?

Crane closed the door and locked it with a decisive click. He crossed the room and left, locking the door to what I now assumed was his bedroom. I let out my breath in a sigh of relief. I waited a few minutes, giving him time to move down the passage. I crawled out from beneath the bed, brushing at my clothes. I looked at the door between the girl and me, and felt a powerful pull to stay here and talk to her, to find out everything I could about her. But I'd been out of my room for too long already. I'd taken a huge risk, but I knew I would do it again. I felt that this girl held the key to getting out of here. To getting Mom and Dad out of here too, alive.

I hurried back down the passage, arriving at the door to my prison in less time than I'd taken to leave it. The guard was still slumped in the position I'd left him in. I felt a brief flare of worry that he still hadn't woken, but pushed it aside. There was no way I'd done any permanent damage in the state I was in. I should just count myself lucky that he hadn't woken up already. I pulled his keys out of my pocket, and clipped them back onto his belt, keeping the key to my bedroom. He stirred a little. I froze, sucking in my breath and holding it. He snorted and then relaxed again. I knew the missing key would draw suspicion, but I couldn't part with it now. I'd have to keep it hidden somewhere they'd never look.

Chapter Twenty-Six

Syra

The training hall was overflowing. The warmth of all those bodies was stifling. In another hour or so, the morning heat would be too oppressive for all of us to be sandwiched in here. That was fine by me. The sooner I made this announcement, the sooner I could make my way across The Waste to Drake. I was keenly aware of the passing of time, of how much we had already wasted. If we were going to strike first, we had to do it within the next few weeks. Crane wouldn't wait much longer, and the worst thing that could happen would be for us to be caught unaware. Ray and Raven stood on the fringes of the crowd, their heads close together. I never seemed to see one without the other lately. Their alliance made me feel like an outsider, like a child who had been pushed out of their circle of friendship. I felt abandoned.

With effort I tore my gaze from them and raised my hands for silence, hoping fervently that I wouldn't need to summon Ray to get them to quiet down. The hall fell silent. Grateful, I stepped to the front of the training ring, my throat closing with anxiety. I cleared it several times, knowing that I still had a minute to stop this, to step off this platform and not say the things I'd planned to. I shook my head vigorously, trying to rid myself of the doubts Ray had so ably put there.

'I've called you all here to make two announcements.' I glanced again at Ray. I could read his expression perfectly, but even if I hadn't been able to, his crossed arms spoke more succinctly than anything he could've said.

'First, to tell you that the five children who are currently finishing up their schooling will be fast-tracked into training.'

I couldn't have gone on even if the word children hadn't stuck in my throat like a piece of food refusing to go down. The crowd roared in protest. The five children in question, who stood together as they always did at gatherings like these, were the only ones who looked pleased. Connor slapped Jasper on the back. Even with the angry shouting of what I feared might soon become a mob, I could hear his crow of excitement. Only Abbie had the sense to be afraid, and for a moment I felt my doubts creep up again.

Ever pushed through the crowd, ignoring the howls of protest as she stood on someone's foot and elbowed someone else in her haste to get to the front.

'How can you do this?' Her voice carried even over the enraged yelling of the others. I stared at her. Elliot wasn't one of the children who would be affected. He was one year shy of his sixteenth birthday.

'This isn't our way. We don't force parents to hand over their children to a war they might never come back from!'

Those around her quietened. The silence spread rapidly, like a river breaking its banks. 'Elliot won't be one of them, Ever.'

'What does that matter? The children you're sending into war belong to someone, and hasn't it always been the Elders' teaching that our children are precious and to be protected at all costs?'

A roar of approval from the crowd. I wanted to look at Ray. I so badly needed him to look back at me with encouragement, with faith. But he was no longer my ally.

'The Elders are dead. They've left us a great legacy to follow, but right now we have a war coming, and it'll happen, whether we are prepared for it or not. I know it seems as if I'm putting them in harm's way, but that's not my intention. I'm giving them the tools and knowledge to protect themselves, to help protect their home and loved ones. The Elders taught us always to be in service of others. That's what this is.'

I expected more protest and outrage, but the training hall was silent. A breeze blew in from the open door, a fan of nature that I hoped would not only cool the tightly packed bodies, but their tempers too. The smell of sweat drifted with it, curling around me in an invisible cloud.

Ever was shoving her way back to her family, shoulders hunched. I was sure that, if I could see her face, it would be lined with fury.

'What about our vote?' Violet called.

For the first time I was starting to see Draiken's point. I had never understood his frustration, until now. The constant questions, the utter lack of faith. He'd always argued against democracy. People need a leader, he'd said. Someone who would show them the way, and take the burden of decision from them.

'There will be no vote.' Voices crowded together, each trying to outdo the other in their desperation to be heard. It was too much. The din wrapped around me like a vice, one that would keep squeezing until I burst. 'Silence!' For once, my voice carried. The noise dropped away like a stone thrown from a cliff.

'I'm your leader. I have decided that this is our best chance of survival. With Dominico gone, we've lost our advantage. We need to be united. We need all those who are capable, to fight.' Before anyone could interrupt me again, I rushed ahead. 'Secondly, I will be recruiting Draiken and the others, for the same reason I'm rushing the training. They will not be returning to Jozenburg permanently, but they will be here for the time we have left to prepare for the war.'

I waited for mayhem to break out, but no one moved or spoke. Even Violet, who was known never to miss an opportunity to state her opinion. She stood motionless, her gaze fixed on me in a way that made me feel she was looking through me. I looked over the crowd, searching for an ally, for just one person who saw it my way and stood by my decision. There was no one. I turned and exited at the opposite end of the training ring without another word. The flood of their thoughts which I normally kept at bay, came rushing in. A tidal wave of criticism.

***

The training of the youngest recruits in our history started the following day. Despite the atmosphere between Raven and me, and Ray's frosty attitude, I arrived to supervise. Initially I had wanted to do the training myself, but even I could see how invasive that would be, like usurping Raven from her post. Instead I remained in the background, making suggestions only when I felt Raven was straying from what I needed done. She was polite, but said little in return. I suppose there was nothing left to say. I'd taken over and made myself a dictator. But I could see no other way.

A few hours later, I decided to go past Ray's place. He'd made it clear he had nothing to say to me, yet I still hoped there was something in him I could appeal to. I'd always been a loner, but this isolation was like being forced behind a fence, where I could see everyone I knew, but could neither make myself seen nor heard.

I was over a hundred metres from the door when I picked up the sound of voices, hushed and strained. I stopped. I couldn't just stand in the middle of nowhere, but I also didn't want to get close enough to be heard. I glanced around. It was late afternoon, the sinking sun creating shadows. No one else was around. It was just before everyone finished up for the day and headed home. I only had a few minutes before the streets would fill up with potential onlookers. I sidled closer, focusing intently on the conversation going on behind Ray's closed door.

'...a possibility.' Raven. Of course. Ray's new bosom buddy. He muttered something in reply, but his words were muffled, as if he'd moved further into the house. I shuffled slightly left, then stopped, afraid they would hear the dragging of my feet. '...she's untrustworthy. There could be an uprising.'

I leaned my entire body towards the house. 'They won't accept Draiken...' Ray's voice, suddenly clear, as if he were standing just on the other side of the wall I was now pressed against. 'She's lost her way. We have to pull her back. Judging her, and trying to take her position away, isn't right.'

I pushed away from the wall. I couldn't hear anymore. The hope I'd had of patching things between Ray and me had disappeared.

***

The sun was setting, casting its final rays as it sank towards the horizon. The Elders' quarters should've been empty. It had become my place of solace, the only place where I felt safe from people coming to look for me, where I wouldn't have to stare into eyes so accusing the heat of it burnt against my skin. But as I approached I could hear voices, the low and constant hum of too many conversations going on at once. Before I could get close enough to hear a word, I knew. I crept closer anyway, hoping I was wrong, but knowing from the roar of blood in my ears that my hope was in vain.

I couldn't see through the coloured glass of the windows, so I moved towards the door. It was closed, but I could hear everything from the other side as clearly as if I were standing in the room.

'We're afraid, Ray. She's making decisions without consulting us. You're her co-leader, surely there's something you can do to stop her?' Ever. I closed my eyes and leaned against the door for support, the roughness of the wood scratching at my skin. My legs felt rubbery.

'You mean demote her?'

Cries of assent. Their high-pitched calls reminded me of a flock of crows pecking at a carcass. Triumphant and bloodthirsty.

'I can't do that. Not just yet.'

'You're planning to talk some sense into her?' Raven. The derisive snort that followed her question made my skin tighten and prickle, as if my body was expanding with the heat of their betrayal.

'Yes. I believe it isn't too late to get her to change her mind. She's still mourning Draiken's absence, and the loss of the Elders. We need to give her one more chance. She deserves that.'

My heart swelled a little. Maybe all was not lost. Maybe we could still come out of this with some semblance of our friendship intact.

'She's gone crazy! How do you expect to reason with her?' That was Violet. I waited for Ray to say something else in my defence.

'I'll talk to her, alright?'

There were murmurs of dissent, but no one else argued. The sound of rising and shuffling towards the door was what finally made my feet move.

I would leave as soon as I could pack the supplies. I wasn't going to give Ray the chance to talk anything over with me. I would be gone with nothing but a note as explanation.

Rogan

I couldn't get the smell of blood off my hands, no matter how many times, or how vigorously, I scrubbed. My skin became scarlet and raw, but I couldn't stop. I imagined the smell was still there, seeping through my skin and into my bloodstream where no amount of water or soap would reach. I'd had to kill her. She'd rushed at me in a state of unhinged madness, screaming, her hands a pair of claws. She'd thrown herself at me, arms clutching at my neck and teeth snapping at my face. It had only been the unexpected weight of her, making me rock back on my heels, that had saved my cheek from being gouged and my nose from being bitten in two.

It had taken Nurse Smiley, Crane, and the doctor to pry her off me. She'd then shifted her focus to Crane, her hands wrapping around his throat before any of us could step between them and stop her. It had crossed my mind, however briefly, that letting her throttle him to death would be sweet irony, but one look at the nurse and doctor's faces and I knew I was alone in this.

We couldn't break her grip. No amount of pulling or shoving lessened her hold. His skin went from scarlet to a deep purple, his eyes bulging out of his skull. I could hear his hopeless gargling above the cacophony of the nurse's screams and the doctor's shouted commands.

'Kill her! Kill her!' It took me a moment to realise the doctor's instructions were directed at me. Of course. I was the ex-commander, the one who had dealt in deliberate blood and death. At least in theory. I had a minute or less before Crane took his final breath. I watched him flail like an animal in a trap, his fingers worrying at the hands wrapped around him, too weak to move one finger from his throat. My callous observation shocked me. I was the only one who could save him, and yet here I stood, watching impassively, weighing up my options as if Crane's life were something to be measured. The doctor threw himself at me, his hands seizing the front of my shirt in a show of aggression. 'Do something now. Or I will make sure that you become the next test subject!'

My paralysis broke. It had less to do with his threat, and more to do with the thought that had occurred to me as I watched Crane struggle for breath. He could die now, on this offensively white tiled floor, at the hands of one of his experiments, or he could pay for the things that he'd done. He could be punished.

I reached for the woman through a fog of denial, not wanting to kill her but seeing no alternative. My blow landed exactly where I'd intended it – over the cheek and into the side of her nose. The bone shattered beneath my fist, and blood streamed over her mouth and chin. She seemed momentarily stunned, her fingers closing on a spasm, and then opening. She touched the blood on her face, staring at her hands with a dumb wonder, as if amazed she could bleed. Without warning she flew at me, but this time I was prepared. I raised my fist and she raced straight into it. I had neither heard nor felt her skull caving in, but that's what must've happened. She collapsed to the floor, her eyes wide with surprise, her nose still leaking blood. Crane lay next to her, his body heaving as he fought to breathe. His skin gradually lost its purple tinge. He reached a shaking hand towards me. I stared at it, then at the woman. I left then, without helping him to his feet, and without acknowledging his gratitude.

***

I knew Dominico was in the lab. I needed to talk to her, needed to intercept her somehow. I wanted to know what they were doing to her, and if she had any hope at all that we could escape this place once more.

Since the incident with the woman, I had hated every moment I was forced to spend in the lab. The air of hopelessness and fear. The screams as humans and superhumans alike were strapped down and had needles inserted into their arms, their protests growing weak as the drugs took hold. And that smiling nurse. I had never struck a woman, but something about her permanently creased face made my hand twitch.

So I waited. Waited for an opportunity, or for a gap in which I could create one. It came some time after the incident.

***

The doctor forgot to sedate the superhuman. He and Crane seemed to have miscommunicated, as no needle was produced. I wondered if they had done it before we arrived, although he'd always done it in our presence before.

This could be it. Crane was standing too close to the cell. The superhuman shuffled to the front, movements slow and lumbering, as if acting the part of being sedated. His hand shot through the bars and he grabbed Crane's arm. In one fluid movement he jerked Crane forward. Crane's forehead met the bars with a crack. He dropped to the floor without a sound.

The doctor chose that moment to step into the room. He caught sight of Crane's prostrate figure and ran to him. 'What the hell happened?' The superhuman grinned gleefully and pointed to his own chest, his mouth rounding on the low victorious syllables escaping him. The doctor rounded on me. 'Go get the nurse. Now!'

I found the nurse almost immediately, and without pausing to see if I was following her, she hurried around the corner to assist Crane. I didn't have long before they noticed my absence. I knew the room where I'd last seen Dominico. But finding it, in these endless twisting corridors, would be another matter altogether.

I turned left and found myself in the middle of a large, empty room, from which several corridors led. I chose the middle one, looking behind me constantly, waiting for that inevitable moment when someone would appear and chase me down. I walked, even though every cell in my body screamed at me to sprint. The corridor stretched ahead, with only one door at the end of it. I strode the length of it, my ears filling with the sound of my blood beating through my body. I reached for the door handle, pushing it down before I could change my mind. It swung open, revealing a figure strapped to a stretcher. Dominico. My breath left my body on an exhalation of relief.

I reached for her hand. Her skin was freezing. Her eyes were closed. I squeezed her palm gently, and her eyelids twitched, gradually opening. Her gaze focused on the ceiling, then glided over to my face. I waited for the moment of recognition, but her expression remained neutral, her eyes a green void. Her inner elbow was patterned with bruises. Her face was emaciated, her cheeks so hollow she looked skeletal. Her red hair, once so vibrant, was dull and matted. Loose strands covered the pillow in clumps, which explained the bald patches along her forehead.

'Dominico. Hey. I'm here. Remember me?' I kept my voice low, my gaze swooping from her face to the door, acutely aware of every passing second. She blinked, slowly at first, and then rapidly, as if something had lodged in her eye. I felt the slightest pressure of her fingers against my hand, but the blank expression remained, making me wonder if I'd imagined it.

'Dominico. You need to fight this. Whatever they've done to you, you need to fight back. I need your help.' No response. Her pulse was slow and steady, the only proof, apart from her manic blinking, that she wasn't a corpse. Her skin felt papery and delicate, like that of a much older woman.

'Rogan.' She breathed my name instead of speaking it, the effort of enunciating it too much for her. I bent over, leaning close. Her gaze was focused. Her mouth twitched, the corners turning up ever so slightly, more of a grimace than a smile.

'No...time. The girl. Crane...has a girl. She's the...' I couldn't catch the final word of her sentence. It was lost in the cacophony as Crane and the doctor rushed into the room, followed so closely by the nurse I didn't see her until all three were crowded around Dominico's stretcher. The doctor yanked my hand from Dominico's arm, breaking the contact with such force that I stumbled back, crashing into Crane and the nurse. She yelped as my full weight came down on her foot. I felt no shame at the pleasure it brought me to hear her scream.

'Get him out of here,' Crane shouted, struggling to regain his authority despite his loss of dignity. The doctor seized my arm. Dominico's eyes were on me, her mouth still trying to form that final word. I smiled at her, trying to communicate everything I hadn't had the time to say. She reached a hand out to me in response, her arm trembling with the effort.

Seeing her like that, strapped like an animal to that stretcher, treated like a science experiment, I was rapidly reaching my limit. I allowed the doctor to pull me from the room and into the corridor. His face was the same shade as the bruises on Dominico's arm. His fingers dug into my forearm in a show of domination that I found laughable. There would be consequences for this, but it didn't matter. If Dominico's words meant what I thought they did, I finally had what I needed.

***

I returned home after a tongue-lashing from Crane. I doubted that would be the end of it, but I was too wrung out to speculate on what might follow. I found Aunt Carrie sprawled at the kitchen table, arms flung out across the battered wood, her forehead resting against its surface. Alarm coursed through me. Normally when I got home, she would be bustling around preparing dinner, pausing long enough only to throw some snide comment over her shoulder.

'Aunt Carrie?' Her head shot up. In the faint light of the bare lightbulb, she looked vulnerable. Every inch her sixty-five-year-old self. She blinked blearily, her eyes bloodshot. I edged closer, meaning to help her up and to her bed. Her breath on my face was foul enough to make me rear back. My foot connected with something, sending it skittering across the room. I walked over to retrieve it. No label, just a nondescript bottle with a black screw cap. I opened it and warily sniffed the contents. Sure enough, the smell of alcohol filled my nose, sharp and stinging.

'Where did you get this?'

I expected her to rail at me for questioning her, but instead she waved her hand in my general direction, a strange grin plastered across her face. 'It was a gift. Would've been a shame –' She let loose a belch. The sound seemed to delight her. Her grin grew wider and a girlish giggle escaped. I shook my head. Alcohol was almost impossible to come by, unless you got it from the black market. Those who did, generally kept their purchase and their furtive swigs hidden from sight. I held the bottle up to the light. 'Was this full?'

'Obviously.'

'It's nearly empty.'

'Again, an astute observation.'

I stood there with the bottle in my hand, torn between going to my room and leaving her to it, or helping her to bed so she wouldn't pass out on the table or the floor. My instinct to help was always stronger than my urge to exact whatever petty revenge I could on her. Her predictions of what I would become had ironically moulded me into just the opposite.

'Why don't you sit down, eh? And bring that bottle with you.' She waited until I did as I was told, then rose unsteadily. She made her way across the kitchen to the opposite counter, which I'd only noticed now held a plate of covered food. 'At least I got drunk after I already cooked your meal. Can't say I don't look after you, now can you?'

I said nothing, but nodded my thanks, even though food was the last thing on my mind. Still, I took the plate from her.

She sat down again and made herself comfortable. Taking a long, greedy swig, she swayed gently in her chair, her face serene. 'You look so much like her.'

I stiffened. Any talk of my mother always whipped Aunt Carrie into a frenzy of anger and self-righteousness.

'She was a beauty. All that honey hair, those green eyes. Bewitched any man who came across her path. Never met a man who could resist her.'

I kept my eyes on my plate, feigning a riveted interest in its contents. I couldn't risk pushing her over the edge. It took very little – a misinterpreted look, a carelessly placed word.

'I never thought your father would be the kind of man to fall for it, but in that respect he was like all the others. Fell for the hair tossing and eyelash batting.'

I stared at her. In all the years I'd lived with her, she'd never breathed a word about my father. Whenever I asked, she insisted she knew nothing about his whereabouts, or his identity.

'I thought you never knew my father.'

She snorted. 'Now where would you get an idea like that?'

'You always said you didn't know who he was.'

She smiled, giving me a sly sideways glance. 'It was never in your best interests to know.'

'And now it is?' I tried not to sound incredulous, or give away the vicious anger that was rising in me. 'Tell me who it is.'

She glared at me, her chin tilting until her nose pointed to the ceiling. She turned back to her bottle, stifling a belch with the back of her hand. 'Why should I? Besides, I was tasked with making sure you never knew, and never found out.'

Her gaze was unfocused, but she pronounced every syllable with extreme care. From her expression of intense concentration, I could tell her thoughts were slow to reach her mouth.

'He would've wanted me, if it wasn't for your mother. I would've had a very different life. One that didn't involve you.'

I'd heard a variation of those words my whole life. They no longer stung the way they used to. Instead, they worried at an old wound, one that had never quite closed. Hearing that she and my mother had once had a common interest in the same man, was, however, news to me.

'Who was he?' I kept my voice low, my tone neutral. An abandoned child never quite lets go of the belief that his parents had left only because they'd had no other choice. That in the near future they would return, restoring the family circle.

She either didn't hear me, or pretended not to. 'He was so taken by what she called her "unseeing eye". She used to be able to predict things – silly things like if we would be getting rain or what sex an unborn child would be.'

'What? My mother was a superhuman?'

She laughed, the sound high and grating. 'No no, nothing like that. She just had what she called "premonitions". Utter nonsense of course. She was just talented at guessing.

'I was sure they would announce their intention to marry, and she would have everything I'd wanted, everything I...' She trailed off, as if she'd lost her train of thought. She fidgeted with the bottle. There was but a mouthful left. She stared at the contents, fixating on it so she wouldn't have to look at me. 'One day your mother rushed in here, babbling about some laboratory and human experiments. She always did have an overactive imagination.'

My mind was so filled with colliding thoughts that I couldn't get a coherent one to leave my mouth. How had she found out? How did she gain access to the lab? Was she a part of Crane's experiments? Finally, I grasped at the question I had to ask. 'She left? You told me she disappeared!'

Aunt Carrie flapped a hand impatiently. 'Yes. That's what I told you. But that's not what happened.' Her cheeks were so filled with colour she looked grotesque in the low light, like a doll come to life. She smiled again, beaming so widely I was sure it must've hurt. 'You still haven't worked out who he is, have you?

I stood abruptly, knocking my chair over. 'I've had enough of this. Tell me the truth, or we're done talking.'

'Tut tut. Mind the furniture. We won't be getting a replacement if you break it.' She broke into a round of high cackles, riding a wave of alcohol-induced euphoria.

I'd had enough. There was no point in waiting around for her to get to the point. How did I even know she was being truthful? She was drunk. I bent to retrieve the chair, setting it upright.

'Good night.' I strode across the kitchen, reaching the passage that led to my bedroom in three strides.

'You would do well to mind him. The only reason you haven't been executed is because you're his son.'

I stopped. The room felt dark and close, as if the walls had shifted inward. 'You're lying.'

She rose unsteadily, almost falling over in her haste to get to her feet. She pointed a shaking finger at me. 'Your mother seduced him. When she came home that night, going on about this fictional laboratory, she was eight months pregnant. The following day she went into labour. Two weeks later she was gone. She left you with me. Abandoned you, so she could pursue some ridiculous fantasy about getting help from the other human cities. She didn't even know if she would find anyone alive.

'You were two weeks old and already unwanted. Count yourself lucky at least one of your parents has seen to your well-being. I wouldn't count on his patience and generosity much longer.'

She reached for the cane that was propped up against the wall behind her. She hobbled from the room, weaving in a gentle undulated rhythm. 'You turned out exactly as I warned him you would – a duplicate of your mother.'

Chapter Twenty-Seven

Dominico

They thought I was too weak to move. Why else would they have allowed the guard to leave his post at my door? I acted the part, pretending to need help to get up, leaning heavily on my escorts and struggling to put a coherent sentence together.

I still hadn't been allowed to see Mom and Dad. I knew Crane was keeping them from me, the only hand he had to play. Little did he realise he'd already lost that control. Somewhere along the way I'd stopped being afraid that he'd kill them, or me. Before, I was sure that being obedient was the key to keeping us safe. Now I thought that same inaction could cost us everything. Seeing Rogan, and how he had risked so much to find me in the lab, made me realise that we all had something, or someone, to lose. Even if it was only ourselves.

They'd started giving me pills instead of injections. They couldn't get a needle into me anymore without my veins collapsing. They had punished me for it, as if I had any control over my own body anymore. After a while though, they had realised that trying to force a needle into my vein would no longer give them the result they wanted. So now they stuffed little white pills into my mouth, holding my nose closed so that I either choked on them, or I swallowed. But after lots of practice, I'd figured out how to tuck them into my cheek. They were getting sloppy with me, comfortable in their belief that I was the model of obedience. When they left, I spat the pills into my hand and hid them in my clothes.

I had to go to Layla again. Seeing Rogan through the fog of drugs, not knowing if he had understood me or not, made me realise that I had to explore every opportunity to expose Crane for who he really was. I had never thought about it before, but as much as I'd always viewed this city as a kind of prison, I had never considered our keeper to be the threat.

I crept out of my room, using my stolen key to unlock the door. No one had mentioned it, although its absence must've been noticed. Instead, they had simply replaced it, another oversight I took as a sign that they no longer considered me a threat.

I wound through the corridors, finding my way more easily now that I had done it once before. I moved quickly, knowing that my guard would be back any time now.

I found the room within minutes. The door to Crane's room was locked, as I'd thought it would be. I called to Layla, unsure if she'd hear me through the two doors separating us. At first, there was nothing but silence. I called out again, a bit louder. I glanced over my shoulder. I should've kept the key to Crane's room. But I doubted its disappearance would've been taken as casually, and I couldn't afford to make them suspicious. 'Layla. Can you hear me?'

A few seconds of nothing, and then a soft click. The door swung open by itself. I backed up a step, my hands going to my mouth to muffle the squeal of fear that had left my throat. The room was dark, except for the light of the bedside lamp, and the slit of sunlight peeking from under the heavy curtains. There was a second click, and the door to Layla's room drifted open. She walked into Crane's room, eyes huge in her small face, a wary smile on her lips.

Stunned by her appearance, and the mysterious opening of the doors, I could do nothing but stare, my mouth working uselessly around a word, any word.

'Hello,' she whispered.

'How did you do that?' I blurted.

'I can manipulate physical things, like doors and chairs and lamps.' Crane's bedroom door swung closed, pushed by an invisible hand. I only realised she'd done it after hearing the gentle click. She smiled again. I stared at her. She looked no older than four or five years, and yet her speech was that of an adult.

She pointed at me. 'Who are you?'

'I'm Dominico.' I didn't know how much to tell her. She was

Crane's daughter after all.

'Why are you here?'

'Are you Cra – I mean, President Crane's daughter?'

'Yes,' she said simply. 'Why are you here?'

Her directness was a bit weird. Like she only had so many responses in her, like she'd been pre-programmed with a limited number of specific phrases.

'I wanted to talk to you.'

She strode back into her room, and for a minute I was afraid she was going to slam the door in my face. Instead, she came back with something in her arms. She held it out to me. A doll, its face painted. Two clear blue eyes, two spots of bright pink on its cheeks. Blonde ringlets fell to its waist. I took it from her. The softness of its body was a sharp contrast to the hardness of its face.

'Isn't she pretty?' I was more confused than ever. She seemed to swing between adult and child, as if she had a bit of both within her.

'Yes.' I ran my fingers over the softness of its hair. I handed it back to her. 'Who gave it to you?'

'I saw you. The other day, when Daddy visited me, I saw you under the bed.'

'Why didn't you tell him I was there?'

'Because it didn't seem like you wanted him to know.'

I gaped.

'It's nice that you came to visit me again. I get so lonely here by myself all the time. Daddy only comes once a day, for a little while, and then he goes away again.'

I decided just to ask her the questions I wanted answering. It made no difference if she told Crane what we'd spoken about – it would be enough for him to know that I'd been here at all. The room was tilting a little. I put a hand out, steadying myself against the back of the chair Layla had sat in only days before. I put a hand to my forehead, my fingers coming away damp from the sweat at my hairline. The room was too dark. I felt enclosed by it, like I was walking into a trap that would close around me if I stayed too long. I wished I could pull back the curtains and let in some air. I forced my focus back to Layla.

'Why does he keep you locked away here?'

She frowned. 'I'm not locked away. I can open doors.'

'No one knows about you.'

'Daddy says it's not safe. That people would try to hurt me.' Her face fell, and I sensed the abrupt swell of fear rushing through her. 'You won't hurt me, will you?' She shook her head. Before I could reply, she answered herself. 'No, no you wouldn't. You're nice.'

'You're superhuman. How's that possible?'

'Daddy's not superhuman. But Mommy was. Mommy was until she died.' She said this with a smile plastered into place, as if she didn't quite grasp the meaning of her own words. My mind went into overdrive. Her mother a superhuman? Did that mean... I could barely contain my excitement. Not only was there a locked-away daughter, but the mother was a superhuman. I had to stop myself from grabbing Layla and hugging her.

I sensed that saying anything negative about Crane wouldn't get me anywhere. She'd seemed afraid of him, but assuming anything about their relationship seemed like a bad idea. I needed to wheedle more details out of her. I was sure that if I came across as pushy, she would withdraw.

'Layla. Does your father ever talk to you about his plans?'

She was focused on the doll, her hands quickly transforming the doll's curls into a complicated plait.

'Layla?' She looked up, blinking as if she'd forgotten I was still there.

'Plans? No. No plans. He doesn't really talk to me. Just to ask if I'm ok and if I'm hungry or need anything.' Her hands went back to the doll, smoothing its clothes. 'Maybe I should ask him for another doll.' She smiled at the thought, and started humming to herself.

I knew I didn't have much time left. They wouldn't leave me alone in my room for long, despite their more relaxed attitude.

'We need your help, Layla.'

'Help?'

'Yes. Your father...' I changed tack at the last minute, hoping for one last chance at taking the safer route. 'Did he ever tell you there are others like you?'

She laughed, the sound high and girlish. 'Yes. He told me he was making others like me, so that we could all live in peace and never have to worry about anyone hurting me, or anyone else, again.'

Wow. He'd dressed it up beautifully, making it sound as if he were doing something heroic, a plan that would keep us all safe. My last shred of patience snapped.

'He's lying. He's making more like you, so he can fight the other superhumans in another city, so he can take their city, and when he's done doing that, he'll kill all of them.' The words rushed out of me, careless and panicked.

Her head shot up, and she fixed me with eyes that were huge with alarm and anger. She dropped the doll. It rolled off her lap and onto the carpet, face first. I wasn't sure if her reaction was to what I'd said, or the way I'd said it.

I was seconds away from losing her. 'Please Layla, you have to help us. You can help us stop this –'

She jumped to her feet, hands flying up as if to ward me off. 'No, no no! Can't help you, will be in trouble, big trouble...' And with that she ran for her bedroom, leaving her doll where it had fallen. The slam of her door vibrated through the room.

Syra

In my hurry to leave, I'd taken very little with me. Food that would last me two days, if I was lucky. One bottle of water. Not much to keep me going, but I intended to find Drake as soon as I could. I'd left the note for Ray pinned to his pillow, where he couldn't miss it. I hoped that when he found it he would know that I'd overheard not only his discussion with Raven, but with the others too. I hoped he would feel the guilt as keenly as I'd felt his betrayal.

The guards at the gate were confused by my sudden departure, but didn't dare question me. I stepped out into The Waste, refusing to look back even as the gates screamed closed behind me. I didn't know how far I'd need to go before I could start calling for Drake. We'd never had to test our connection, and how far it could stretch.

The sun was at its most intense. I judged it to be around midday, a suicidal time of day to start a journey through The Waste. I just couldn't wait any longer to leave Jozenburg. I had no allies, and no more friends. I needed the reassurance and safety my brother would provide. *Now that you're agreeable to his terms.* I shoved the voice away, burying it beneath the many defensive layers I'd built up since the start of this whole mess.

I tramped along the main roads, following the old N1 highway, stopping occasionally to read the faded signs. The highway split at a juncture more or less halfway between Jozenburg and Toria. To miss the split would mean several more hours on the road, backtracking to return to the right path. I kept my ears tuned to any unusual sounds, refusing to be caught unawares again like the last time I'd made this trip.

I looked out at the winding stretch of highway. The tar was cracked in some places, completely missing in others. Abandoned cars stretched as far as the eye could see, metal carcasses fading in the sun. Weeds were growing around some of them, winding through broken windows and around steering wheels, until the car was so entangled it almost looked like an extension of the plant itself.

There were no trees. I'd seen photographs of this area before the human war. In them, there'd not only been trees, but also stretches of open fields, the grass green and lush in the summer, tall and golden in the winter. Looking out now, there was nothing but kilometres of barren land, dotted with disintegrating buildings.

After walking for several hours I reached out to Drake. I kept a constant line of communication open between us, hoping that if I was not yet reaching him, I would within the next kilometre or two. A few minutes later, I heard him answer, faint and unclear. I called again, breaking into a jog, wanting nothing more than to see him, to feel the reassurance that his presence had always brought me before. He'd gone silent again. I stopped in midstride, afraid that I was moving away from him instead of towards him, even though I was still heading in the direction of Toria.

'Drake!' Silly to call his name out loud – his hearing wasn't anywhere near as attuned as mine.

A figure appeared ahead of me, running down the slope of the road to meet me. I sprinted forward, and we met in a collision of limbs, laughing and embracing. He lifted me off the ground and twirled me around, something he hadn't done since we were kids.

'Sy. Sy I'm so happy to see you. I knew you would come around, I knew it.'

I disentangled myself from his embrace. 'What do you mean?'

'I've been reaching out to you. Trying to feel out how you were doing, what kind of head-space you were in. I couldn't hear your thoughts exactly, but I could feel that there was a chance you'd come to me again, this time with a different mind-set.' His boyish grin lit up his face. His hair had grown longer. It flopped over his forehead, falling into his eyes.

'It works over that distance?'

'Sort of.'

He slipped an arm around my shoulders. 'Come on. Stay with us tonight and in the morning we can head back to Jozenburg.'

Everything that I'd kept pent up and locked away flooded out of me. I finally had someone to talk to, someone who could help me sift through my thoughts and work through the things I couldn't figure out on my own.

'Ray and I aren't on speaking terms.'

Drake nodded, saying nothing. 'He thinks I'm incompetent, that the decisions I'm making are the wrong ones.' I looked at him. His gaze was steady, his expression sympathetic. He reached for my hand, giving it an emphatic squeeze. 'Go on.'

I talked until I ran dry. Until I had nothing more stored up, and I was blissfully drained of every word and emotion I'd kept inside. Drake listened without comment, sensing that I needed to get it all out. When I finally fell silent, we had arrived at Drake's new home. I looked up at the building, remembering the last time I was here. The sight of Mohina looking down at us sharpened the memory, and I felt a sharp stab of discomfort. Could I really do this, despite what Drake had done? I thought of the many weeks that had passed since he'd left. I'd never felt more alone. Or so overwhelmed. And it had all started with Drake's decision. He'd left me no choice, and despite what he'd said, I doubted he'd spent much time thinking of me at all.

***

Drake had allowed me time to greet the others. Their response had varied, from wary (Mohina and Trey had both stared at me in shock, their returned greeting strained) to pleasantly surprised.

Drake led me to a room on the far side of the building that was mostly intact. Inside were a desk and two chairs, in surprisingly good shape. The door closed, although not completely. It got stuck three quarters of the way, a result of the missing bottom hinges. He motioned for me to take the chair closest to the door and I sank into it gratefully, my feet aching from all the walking.

'I thought we'd talk alone to start off with,' he said.

'We need your help, Drake. You and the others. Crane won't wait much longer before declaring war. We need as many to help us as possible.' I found it difficult to look him in the eye. I'd refused to go with him when he'd needed me. Refused to back him when he'd asked. And now here I was, asking for his help. He had every right to refuse me.

'Of course, Sy.'

He sensed my gratitude and smiled a little, his expression somewhat condescending. 'We need to get rid of Crane once and for all. And we need to show the humans that taking us on means certain death. Once we have control of them, we'll never have to worry about increasing our numbers again.'

My stomach coiled. Even now, with the coming war and the threat to our survival, I wanted no part of Drake's plan to enslave the humans. An image of Rogan slipped past my defences, filling my mind with his face. I'd been mostly successful in keeping thoughts of him at bay, but now I could see him so clearly, I could make out the tiniest details of his features. The lines that appeared with his infrequent smiles. The arresting blue of his eyes. The blonde stubble that was only visible to other people up close, but which I could see even when standing several metres from him. I'd made no effort to shield my thoughts from Draiken, mostly because I was unused to being with someone who could read them. Too late, I caught the expression on his face. Dismay. Horror.

'Commander Rogan?' There was a warning edge to his tone. Nothing good could come of this discussion, but there was no way to avoid it.

It was inevitable, really. He would've found out, one way or another, whether from me, or someone else. Maybe it was best to get it all out into the open, although I didn't even know how to explain it myself.

'You let him stay in the city?' He looked floored. 'How did you pull that off?' Relief flooded me. He hadn't picked up on the specific details of my thoughts. He'd only seen bits and pieces, nothing that would reveal my confusion regarding Rogan.

'Drake. It's a long story. One that doesn't matter. I'm here to discuss the war, and how we're going to convince the others that a union is the best thing for everyone. We've got our work cut out for us, considering how everyone else feels about you and the others.'

The barb worked as I'd hoped it would. It distracted him from asking anything more about Rogan, and threw him on the defensive. 'I did   what –'

I held up a hand. 'No arguing, ok? Let's work this out.'

'What happened?'

For a moment I was sure he was back to the subject of Rogan. 'What?'

'Something must've happened for you to come here. Besides the imminent war, of course.' He smiled teasingly.

I'd hoped to skip over this. 'Ray and I haven't been able to...agree on certain things.'

Drake rose from his chair and moved to sit on the edge of the desk, closer to me. It creaked in protest beneath his weight. 'You mentioned that earlier.' He paused, studying me.

'So he finally told you.'

'Told me what?'

'How he feels about you.'

I threw up my hands and half rose, almost knocking Drake off his perch. He eased me back into my chair, his hands on my shoulders a much-needed comfort. 'How is it that everyone except me knew about this?'

'Don't exaggerate. Not everyone knew. Just me, him, and Raven.'

Her name slipped like a blade between my ribs, the tip teasing at my heart.

'Why didn't you tell me?'

'Come on Sy. It wasn't for me to tell. Ray and I were friends. Telling you would've meant a breach of confidence. Besides, he didn't technically tell me. I guessed.' He gave me a look, half amused, half exasperated. 'For someone who has finely-tuned senses, you did a really crappy job of reading him.'

I looked down at my hands. My fingers were twisting together with painful intensity. I forced them to stop. 'He never treated me that way. He treated me like a sister, a friend. I was one of you.'

'You were both to him, Sy, for a long time. But sometimes a lifetime of close proximity breeds something more.'

'It wasn't the only thing that drove us apart. You leaving...' He started to say something but I rushed on before he could get a word in '...it left me drifting. You were always my anchor. Without you, I had nothing to keep me centred. I made decisions without consulting Ray, and the ones I did consult him on, I went against his judgement.'

I looked up at Drake, pleading with him to understand. 'I went with my gut. I did what I thought was best. But Ray, and many of the others, started questioning my leadership. My sanity too, in some ways.' I gave a short laugh. It teetered dangerously on the edge of a sob.

'What about the girl?'

I started at the sudden change in subject, at his deliberate snub of my grief.

'What about her?'

He swung himself off the desk and crossed the room to the cracked, but miraculously intact, window. The sun was starting to creep through it, its rays reaching like fingers across the windowsill, trying to heave itself into the room. I doubted he could see much through the filth and collection of cracks, but he gazed out of it intently. His shoulders were rising, a sure sign of agitation. What had tipped him off so abruptly?

'You shouldn't have let her go. She was the key.'

'Drake, I had no choice...' His shoulders were now just below his earlobes. 'Wait. How did you know about her?'

He kept his back to me. His hands crept behind him to link together, his fingers worrying at each other in a nervous habit we'd both had since we were children.

'Drake?'

He turned to face me, his expression relaxed, his shoulders sinking back to their usual place. 'It's obvious, Sy. You wouldn't be this strung out if you still had the girl.'

His reply did nothing to explain how he'd known about her in the first place. An image flashed through my mind, brief but blindingly detailed. Two hands joined in a handshake. Drake smiling in triumph, the other man faceless and yet familiar. It was gone as quickly as it had come. It left me feeling disorientated and strange, as if it was a thought that belonged to someone else, one that I'd picked randomly out of a maze of others.

Drake pulled me out of my chair by the hand, closing his arms around me. I relaxed against him. 'You're tired. You need to rest. Tomorrow we'll go to Jozenburg, and work out our strategy for the war.'

I nodded against his chest, the cotton of his shirt soothing against my cheek. My mind felt cloudy, like that last moment of consciousness before sleep.

***

We left before the sun had topped the horizon. Both of us could see clearly, despite the murk of the coming dawn. We decided it would be best to get to Jozenburg as early as possible. Drake would have to make the journey home alone, and travelling in The Waste after dark, even with excellent vision, was something even he wouldn't attempt.

As soon as the sun rose above the horizon, the heat of the day set in. It hung over us and The Waste, a haze of brilliance. Dust swirled in a hot breeze, and just minutes after leaving Drake's home, we were covered in it.

The trip was uneventful, and too soon, the gates of Jozenburg came into view. I swiped a hand across my forehead. My fingers came away damp, and my hairline was immediately bathed in a new layer of sweat. I turned to Drake. Sensing my nervousness, he reached for my hand and gave it a quick squeeze. 'You're doing the right thing Sy. They may not see it now, but sometime in the future they'll thank you for seeing what they couldn't.' I nodded, my throat clogged with words that threatened to choke me.

A greeting sounded across The Waste. One of the guards was waving madly. They'd spotted us. I forced a slow breath in, and released it on a controlled exhale. Some of the tension in my shoulders and back eased, and with more confidence than I felt, I pushed onwards towards the city. Drake shifted closer, our shoulders brushing with each step.

The moment we stepped through the gates, I felt the chill of the atmosphere. No one had been able to identify Drake from a distance, but now that they realised who my companion was, silence fell with the weight of a dropped corpse. The guards above us froze in the middle of their greeting. Hands that had been in the act of waving stopped, then fell to their sides. Ahead of us, a group of soldiers paused on their way somewhere, then headed towards us. I tensed, sure that a confrontation would follow. The last thing we needed now was for Drake to lose his temper and fan an already blazing fire.

They stopped a few strides short of standing toe to toe with us.

Jasper, Malcolm and Carson. The last three individuals I would've chosen to run into had I had any say in it.

'Gentlemen,' Drake said smoothly. 'Nice to see you all again.' Not a hint of aggression or provocation in his stance or tone, but his words were enough to make Malcolm step forward until he was inches from Drake.

'You're not welcome here.'

He turned to me, his stance shifting slightly, the edge of his aggression softening.

'What is he doing here?'

'Good morning. You will all be called for a meeting shortly. I'll explain everything then. Would you round up everyone and get them to meet me in the training hall?' He blinked stupidly at my request, as if I'd asked him to produce water out of thin air.

'Malcolm?'

He took a step back, nodding rapidly. 'Yes. Um... will do.' He did a ridiculous little bow and then stumbled off with the others, their furious whispers making me smile.

Drake grinned. 'Wow. Way to use your authority, Sy.'

I barely heard him. A figure was striding towards us, and even with the distance between us, I could make out the rage on his face. A smaller figure followed, and I felt the now familiar pinch of resentment.

Drake had spotted them too. 'Ray! Hey buddy!'

Ray's expression deepened into one of black fury. Ignoring Drake, he turned on me. 'I got your note. Nice of you to let me know in person.' Raven twitched at Ray's side, her will to say something contained only by Ray's restraining hand.

I'd promised myself I wouldn't mention having overheard him and Raven, nor their meeting with the others. But something about his proprietary attitude, his assumption that he still had the right to question my movements, loosened my tongue.

'Oh I'm sorry. You're right. Except that, when I did try to tell you in person, you were too busy with your closed meeting. I didn't want to disturb you all, especially since the topic of discussion was my teetering sanity.'

He blanched. 'Sy...' He reached for my arm like a blind man groping for balance. I reared away from him, narrowly missing Drake.

'Don't call me that. You no longer have the right. And don't... don't you touch me.'

Drake locked a hand on my elbow, steadying me. 'Syra's called a meeting. Everyone's to meet us in the training hall. We could use some help gathering the crowds.'

His use of the plural had not escaped Ray. He looked at me, a silent plea twisting his features. For a moment, something in me gave way. My hand left my side of its own accord and reached for him.

'Syra.' Raven's voice jarred me, breaking the moment. I dropped my hand and nodded, resolute in my determination not to look directly at her. I felt the childishness of my behaviour, but, for the first time, I no longer cared what either of them thought of me. I had Drake. I was no longer alone.

Rogan

Despite my misgivings, I confronted Aunt Carrie the following morning. I'd been up most of the night, going over our conversation again and again. I wondered if anything she'd said was true, or if she'd simply been playing one of the mind games she was so fond of engaging me in.

Finally, when the first light of day crept from beneath my bedroom curtains, I threw off my blankets and went to the kitchen. She lay slumped where I'd left her hours before, sprawled across the table. A dark patch had formed around the cheek she lay on. A trail of saliva glinted in the low light, meeting the patch on the table.

I briefly contemplated leaving her a while longer, letting her catch a few more minutes of sleep. Instead, I yanked out the chair next to her, and the scrape of the wood against tile roused her.

She glared at me even through the fug of sleep. 'You did that on purpose.'

'Is any of it true?'

She closed her eyes again, perhaps hopeful that when she reopened them I would be gone. I nudged her chair, and her eyes sprang open. 'Leave me be. I'll take the cane to you.'

She hadn't taken the cane to me since I was fifteen years old and big enough to take it from her. I don't think she ever got over that, the fact that she could no longer wield her instrument of fear. Sensing my gaze on her, she opened one eye.

'What?'

'Everything you told me last night. Did any of it really happen?' Or were you just trying to hurt me?

Her face closed in on itself, a sign I knew well. There would be no more discussion on the topic. It would be shelved, along with everything else she'd ever told me about my life, never to be spoken of again. Still, I couldn't let it go without attempting to pry it out of her.

'What you told me about my mother, and Crane.'

She squinted at me as if I'd presented her with a riddle. 'Boy, what are you banging on about now? We had no such discussion.'

In all the years she'd hurt me, she'd taught me how fear could imprison a boy who never felt safe. No one entered, and I could never leave its borders. In all that time, I'd never struck her, even when I was old enough and large enough to do it. I refused to follow the principles she'd taught me, however unconsciously she'd passed them on. But now, in this moment, when the heat of my fury pulsed behind my eyes and my body burned with years of emotions, I could picture my palm against her cheek, hear the shocked snap of her neck as her head rocked back from the blow.

'Go ahead.' Her voice was just above a whisper. 'I know you've wanted to do it all these years.' I hated that she could read me so well.

I shoved my hands into my armpits. 'So you're going to pretend now that you don't remember a word of our conversation?'

She smiled. 'Who says I'm pretending?'

***

Crane arrived late that morning to collect me. That's how I'd started thinking of it – *collection*, as if I were an errant child who couldn't be left alone. His tardiness was out of character. I'd never known him to be late for anything. He motioned for me to follow without calling his usual greeting to Aunt Carrie. I stared at him as if I'd never seen him before. I searched his face for some similarity between us, but dreaded finding it. I could ask him right out, but there was no guarantee he would tell me the truth.

'Come Commander. We have a visitor, and he can't be kept waiting. I want him out of Toria before anyone discovers he's here.'

I nodded distractedly, hardly taking in a word. If I had, I wouldn't have been so shocked when I found myself staring at a face I'd hoped never to see again.

'Hello, Commander,' said Draiken.

I halted in the doorway. Crane was already pulling out his chair and waving for us to join him around the desk. My mouth worked to form a greeting, or just a syllable, but nothing came out.

Draiken smiled. I found it so repugnant that my first impulse was to cross the room and slam my fist into his face. 'Speechless, I see?'

'What are you doing here?'

'A well thought-out question, commander.' He waved magnanimously at the more comfortable chair facing Crane's desk, the one I'd always occupied when my title had meant something, and hadn't served as a cause for mockery.

I sank into the soft leather of the seat, unable to think of anything else to do. The shock had left me reeling, my normally responsive tongue immobile.

Draiken sat in the chair beside me, his focus returning to Crane. 'I'm pressed for time, as you know. Syra is expecting me to return to Jozenburg in two days, and I need to prepare before we make the trip.'

Her name on his tongue was like a lash against my skin. I turned on him, my mind finally breaking free from its paralysis. 'How dare you? How can you do this to her? Your own sister! Your twin! Have you no shame?'

He watched me with lazy amusement, as if my antics were nothing less than he'd expected of me. 'I understand your outrage, Commander, truly I do. But I need to do what is best for all of us.' The way he said the word 'us' made me want to launch myself at him and have the satisfaction of wrapping my hands around his neck. Crane waved for us to be quiet, the movement jerky and agitated. He must've known this would not go well. He must've realised what my reaction would be.

'Let's get down to business, shall we?' Crane turned to Drake. 'What was the conclusion of your discussion with Syra?'

I gripped the armrests of my chair with the urgency of a drowning man reaching for a life raft. I was sure that if I let go, my hands would do things that would land me in the stocks.

Draiken leaned back into his seat, getting comfortable. 'I talked her into bringing the war here. We'll come through the old structure beneath the barracks. I know that trap door has been locked down, but those with physical abilities will find it simple enough to crack through the wood and break the lock.'

Crane smiled, pressing the tips of his fingers together in a gesture I remember all too well from my years of serving him. 'Excellent.'

'Make sure it isn't too easy to get in, or she'll become suspicious.'

'Of course. You'll be diligent about keeping your thoughts to yourself, yes?'

'Of course,' Draiken mimicked Crane.

I couldn't be silent any longer. 'Why am I here?'

Crane turned to me, looking puzzled. 'You're the commander. You must be informed of all plans for the war.'

I half rose out of my chair. 'I'm not going along with this. You think I want to lead this war?'

Crane frowned. 'Why wouldn't you? You've been trained for this. You trained others for this. It was always our plan for you.' There was an odd gleam in his eyes, as if he knew things had changed for me. I'd given myself away.

I stood up, needing to leave this room, needing air and space and a moment to think about how I could warn Syra and the others.

'Sit down, commander.'

I was about to refuse, but his next words made my knees give out from underneath me. I sank back into the chair.

'You think you have nothing left to lose. But we both know that isn't really the case, don't we?'

Was he referring to Dominico? Syra? Dread gathered in the pit of my stomach, forming a ball of acid so repugnant I was sure I would be sick. The thought gave me a nugget of pleasure – my vomit ruining the plush softness of his ridiculous carpet.

'You will lead the men into this war because that is your job.'

'You really think, after everything that's happened, they'll want to follow me? Are you out of your mind?'

He leaned forward, his face tightening into an expression of deep displeasure. 'They will do as they're told. Just as you will.' His fingers tapped the table in a frenzy of agitation. 'Haven't you wondered why you're still alive?'

The words were out before I could stop them. 'Yes. Aunt Carrie very kindly informed me that I'm not an orphan, despite many years of being led to believe the opposite.'

I waited for the outburst I was sure would follow. Another smile crawled across his face instead, his gaze steady. 'I've groomed you for many years for this moment. It's only fitting that my son will lead my army into this war.' I caught Draiken's expression of shock out of the corner of my eye. Finally, something he hadn't known before me. He wisely kept his mouth shut, looking intensely uncomfortable to be caught in this crossfire of family secrets.

'Why didn't you tell me?'

Crane laughed. 'Whatever for?'

'I thought my parents were dead. You left me with that woman –'

'That woman housed, clothed and fed you. That was our deal.'

'You made a woman who was in love with you look after the child you fathered with another woman? Her own sister? No wonder she treated me the way she did.'

Crane's mouth flattened until it all but disappeared. 'She was instructed to keep you in line.'

I stumbled from the office, black spots crowding my vision. I didn't know who I was angrier at – Crane, or myself.

Chapter Twenty-Eight

Dominico

The days had crawled by. With nothing to occupy me, not even the torturous visits to the lab, the hours blended into each other, the changing light beneath the curtains my only clock. My guard had been replaced. I had no idea what had happened to the first, but this one rarely left the door for longer than five minutes at a time, and sometimes, watching him through the keyhole, I wondered if he ever slept. Every now and then, I heard voices through the door, low and rapid, and the shuffling of footsteps moving away. Sometime later, I would hear feet along the corridor again, another whispered conversation, and then silence. My door was no longer left unguarded.

I wondered if they'd finally figured out I'd been leaving my room. That I still had the key. If that were the case, why hadn't they changed the lock? Or made me give up my key? I had the feeling I didn't want to know the answer to either of those questions. What use was I now, powerless and weak, just another human mouth to feed? Maybe if I tried to leave the room again they would simply shoot me – a permanent solution to their problem of keeping me contained.

Had Layla told them about my visits? I pictured her in that locked room of hers. She had the means to leave, but seemed content to stay in her cage. Like an animal that had never known freedom, she seemed afraid of what lay beyond her four walls. Was that Crane's true power? His ability to instil such fear in others? I felt sick at the thought. Not even his own daughter had escaped his net.

When I heard the shuffle of footsteps outside my door I barely stirred. Another guard change, apparently. It was only when the door swung open that I looked up. Layla stood in the doorway. Her gaze met mine. She looked puzzled, as if she wasn't sure why she was here. Behind her, I could see the limp figure of my guard, sprawled on the ground.

She followed my gaze, then looked back at me. One of her tiny hands went to her mouth, as if trying to hide her sudden smile. 'Don't worry. I didn't hurt him.' A giggle escaped her, so out of place that I jumped a little. 'I made his shirt come out of his pants and around his face. He ran straight into the wall and knocked himself out.'

Despite myself, I smiled too, the image hanging between us for a moment. 'That must've hurt at least a little.'

She glanced back at him, her eyes wide.

'I'm sure he's okay though.'

She nodded, reassured.

'Layla. What are you doing here?'

Her smile faded, and her hands moved to her jeans, worrying at the fabric until I was sure she was going to tear a hole in it.

'I don't really know. I thought about what you said. About the others like me.' She looked up. Her eyes were wide and blinking. I knew she was fighting back tears. 'I don't want him to hurt the others. Not like he's hurt me.' As she spoke, she pulled at the sleeve of her shirt, hiking it up around her elbow. A jagged scar ran along the length of her forearm, ending at her wrist. I stared at it, somehow unsurprised by this violence, even towards his own child.

'He tried to change it. Change me. He tried to take it away. My superhumanness. But he couldn't. And that made him angry.'

Something moved me across the room, until I was standing so close I could breathe her in. She smelled surprisingly childlike – warm and sweet. I raised my hand slowly, watching her face as I did. She stilled. She stood so rigidly I was afraid she might shatter if I startled her. I ran my fingers along the scar. It was twisted and raised, an ugly mark against her otherwise perfect skin. Something wet fell onto my hand, and I realised she was crying. Huge silent tears traced along her cheeks and dripped onto me, her, the floor.

She looked at me, her face open and vulnerable. She allowed me to keep stroking the scar, leaning into me as only someone who had been deprived of touch would.

'He said he wanted me to be like him. Not like *her*. But then he seemed to change his mind, and he started to bring his doctor along to our visits. The doctor used needles...' She trailed off, shuddering. 'He kept taking blood from me, trying to figure out if they could somehow use what I had. One day I think they got what they wanted, because soon after that, the others arrived. The others like me.'

Outside the door, the guard stirred. A low moan escaped him, his fingers twitching with life as he regained consciousness. Layla caught my eye, her face tightening with tension. She turned away, leaping across the room with surprising grace, and did something out of sight that must've knocked the guard out cold again.

She returned, this time keeping a distance between us. 'I'll help you, but only if you can promise no one will hurt him.'

I stared at her, wondering why his well-being was so important to her, when hers was so clearly not a priority for him. It would be easy to lie. I could promise her, get the help I needed, and then go back on my word. There was too much to lose if I risked honesty. And yet, looking at her face, and into the endless blue of her eyes, which so resembled her doll's, I couldn't. She had been lied to enough. I was sure she wouldn't tell anyone, including Crane, of our visits. If she refused to help us, I would have to find another way. But I hoped, with a fierceness I hadn't thought I still had in me, that she would be moved by our need.

'I can't promise that.'

She bit her lip, her teeth sinking so far into the tender flesh that I winced, convinced she would draw blood.

'I don't want anyone to hurt him.'

I crossed the space between us and reached out my hands, not wanting to assume I could touch her again simply because she had let me do just that a moment ago. She hesitated, then put her hands in mine. I closed my fingers around hers. 'I will do my best to make sure no one hurts him. But if that's not what happens, I promise you won't be alone. I'll look after you. You can come with me to the Superhuman city. No one will lock you away there. You'll be free.'

From the look of fear on her face I realised too late that I'd said too much. That as much as Crane had hurt her, he was still all she had. She pulled her hands from mine.

'What do you want me to do?' She asked this with her head down, her chin tucked defensively close to her chest.

I hadn't wanted her to feel cornered, or afraid, the way she obviously felt right now. I'd hoped to find a way for her to help me without feeling like she was doing something wrong. But it was too late for that. I had to take what I could get.

'I need you to take a message to a friend of mine.' Even as I asked her this, I wondered if she would leave her prison, and if she'd find her way unseen.

She nodded. 'I have paper and a pen in my room. I'll bring them to you.'

I started. Paper and a pen? When was the last time I'd seen either of those? At school, we had no means to take notes. So we had to memorise everything. Tests were verbal.

'How will you find your way?'

She smiled. 'I've lived here for years. I didn't always live in my room.'

I blinked. 'For years? But...how old are you?'

'Sixteen. Like you, right?'

Before I could ask for an explanation, she slipped away, disappearing into the dimness of the passage.

Syra

The meeting was a disaster. I could feel the vibrations of their anger, the seethe of their resentment. I'd taken their future out of their hands. I'd become a dictator. And beside me, my twin, who, despite the heat of the crowd's dislike, didn't falter once. I didn't know whether to admire him, or resent his unwavering confidence. I kept my own anger close at hand, knowing that if I let it go, I would be defenceless in the face of how wrong this all was.

Drake and I sat in our old home. His presence only accentuated Rogan and Dominico's absence. I never thought I'd miss the girl in particular, but I found myself wanting to see her skulk through the front door. I wanted to hear her monosyllabic answers, because then everything would be as it was before, when I was sure of who I was.

Drake broke the silence. 'Come on Sy. All isn't lost. They agreed to let me stay, didn't they?'

I toyed with the glass in my hand. Drake had brought a full bottle of vodka, the likes of which I hadn't seen since I was allowed to drink at all. The clear liquid had done nothing to clear my mind of its clutter. Instead, the alcohol had filled me with a morbid sense of doom, as if everything that had happened up until this point was only the prelude to what was to come. Something bigger than any of us.

'They didn't have a choice, Drake.'

He waved his glass merrily, the liquid sloshing dangerously close to the lip. 'Of course they did. They could've said no and sent me on my way.'

I shook my head and rose, abruptly furious at the sight of his carelessness. I paced to the window. Dusk was falling, the world disappearing beneath a sheet of darkness.

'Do you think they want to risk more instability within these walls? Don't you think, thanks to you, they've had enough of that?' Finally, I saw it clearly. I turned back to him, feeling as if I was turning on an orbit that might never end.

'That was your plan all along, wasn't it?' It was so clear to me in that moment that I couldn't believe I hadn't seen it before. 'You were counting on the instability, on everyone needing leadership so badly they'd follow anyone. And you knew I'd cave and come back to you.'

He said nothing. He leaned back in his seat and tipped his head to the ceiling, his eyes closing as if preparing for sleep.

'Didn't you?' My voice rebounded off the walls and came back at me, an accusation thrown at my brother, when in fact, I was the one to blame.

***

Preparations were underway. We would march to Toria tomorrow. Raven was frantic with a last-minute training session, trying to cram in every last instruction she could think of. Her quiet panic ignited the younger trainees, and for the first time since my announcement, the boys seemed afraid. I shared Raven's unease. The trainees were far from prepared. They had never seen a war, had never fought against anyone other than each other.

The seasoned soldiers had gathered together in the centre of town, taking shelter from the sun in the shade of the nearby houses. They strategised and talked, their voices a low hum of activity. I watched them from a short distance away. I wanted to hear their conversation without intruding. They seemed relaxed and prepared, but even that had done little to reassure me.

The plan had been laid out for them in careful detail. The problem with a plan, of course, was that it relied on a set of favourable circumstances. From the coil of dread in the pit of my stomach, I knew favour was not on our side. I racked my brain to think of a way to stop this. I felt we were sending our entire species into a war we could not win. We had no idea what abilities Crane's army had. We didn't know how many of them there were. For all we knew, Crane could've bred an army aimed specifically at targeting our weaknesses.

Drake and I had not spoken since our confrontation the night before. My expectation of safety had turned out to be nothing more than a colossal error in judgement. I longed to be able to turn to Ray, but his avoidance of me meant I hadn't seen him at all since I'd arrived home with Drake in tow.

Drake's followers were to arrive this morning. I had tried to convince him to give it more time, to push back the start of the war by a day, but he'd been immovable. I feared their arrival would only feed the already volatile atmosphere, but he'd insisted they needed to be briefed without further delay.

I was startled out of my thoughts by the heavy hand that landed on my shoulder. 'Sy.' I turned to Drake, tense beneath his touch and fighting the urge to shrug it off.

'They're here.' I nodded and stepped away from him, forcing him to drop his hand. 'I know you're still angry. But honestly Sy, there's no time for that now. The others are here and need to be briefed. Tomorrow is a fresh start. We'll be free.'

'Don't you ever think of them?'

'Who?'

'The Elders. Don't you ever feel guilty for what you did?'

He looked at me steadily, his thoughts open and clear. There was no shame in him. Nothing at all that spoke of any comprehension of what he'd done. 'I cleared the way for us all. The Elders and their antiquated ways would've meant the end of our species. I'll do anything to ensure our survival and growth.'

I turned away, clutching at my thoughts in a desperate bid to keep them hidden. I had never feared him. I had never considered that perhaps our paths were diverging for good. But looking at him now, at his clear gaze and raised chin, the face I'd known and loved the most throughout our lives, I knew with complete certainty that one way or another, I would have to put a stop to his growing madness.

***

Mohina and Trey were at the head of the group. They came through the open gates swiftly, relaxed and smiling, as if they'd known all along this moment would come. They walked in as if they'd never left the city. The sight of them, and the others following behind, made Jozenburg seem somehow smaller, as if their very presence made even this open space feel claustrophobic. No one other than Drake and I had known the time of their arrival. We had avoided announcing it, reasoning it was better for everyone to go about their day as they normally would. There was no sense in forcing them to welcome those they felt had no place here.

Drake stepped forward and welcomed them with open arms, that infernal smile pasted into place. I felt the heightened tension within me, building like a heavy cloud formation before the release of rain.

I remained where I was, watching Drake embrace Mohina, and clap Trey on the back. I felt sick at the display of affection and camaraderie, knowing it was a deliberate show of unity for our benefit.

Mohina stepped out of Drake's arms and moved towards me. If she opened her arms there was no chance I would allow them to enfold me. She seemed to sense this and held out her hand instead, her smile cool and fixed. I took it briefly, wanting to break the contact as soon as my skin grazed hers. Her gaze was steely, the gleam of triumph unmistakable. I dropped her hand and stared resolutely over her shoulder, waiting as the others lined up to greet me, forcing Mohina to step aside.

Trey was next in line. His initial cockiness had solidified into something more concrete and fixed. His overconfidence made me think of Levin, and my feeling of dread intensified. One arrogant Superhuman on the battlefield already presented a danger. Add a second to the mix, and I was afraid not only for them, but for all of us.

Before I had to greet any more of those who had landed us in this precarious position, I motioned for them all to follow me to the training hall. Despite what Drake had initially wanted, I planned to do this without the rest of Jozenburg as an audience. He'd had his way too many times already. In this, even if it was something small, I could spare the others the spectacle. There was enough fear already.

Rogan

I didn't see her at first because only the light of a single bulb illuminated the kitchen. Even when the daylight had crept in, I still would've missed her if I hadn't sat in the chair facing the window. I finally spotted her as the sun's rays found the windowpane. She was wedged beneath the gap of the kitchen sink and the floor, where a cupboard used to be.

Knowing I'd spotted her, she crawled out of the tiny space, making no further effort to hide. She stared at me openly, her gaze assessing in that unnerving way only children had. She held out a scrap of paper wordlessly. When I didn't take it, she sighed impatiently and shoved it at me, forcing it into my hand.

'What's this? Who are you?'

She gestured for me to read it, her eyes never leaving the crumpled paper.

I smoothed it out against the kitchen table. *Crane's daughter. She's like me. He has hurt her. She could be an ally. D.*

I looked up at her. If she was Crane's and so was I... I had a sister. I'd never had any family to call my own except Aunt Carrie, whom I'd never considered family anyway.

'She wants you to write back. She said I must come back with your reply.' Her voice startled me. It was light and musical, and childlike, as I would have expected from a girl her size, yet her vocabulary was distinctly adult.

'What's your name?'

She twisted the long blonde braid that fell over her shoulder, looking at me from beneath lowered lids. 'Layla.'

She said it so quietly I had to strain to hear her. 'Layla. Pretty.'

She flushed, colour blooming in her cheeks. I glanced at the long sleeves of her dress and wondered if her skin was once marked with bruises that told of frequent needles, as Dominico's was. Her vulnerability, and her delicacy, would make her the perfect candidate to showcase Crane's crimes. She was helping us now, but that didn't mean she would continue to do so. Not if it meant standing up in front of him and the others and laying his sins out for all to see.

'We appreciate your help Layla. More than you know.'

She nodded stiffly, her eyes on her feet. Her fingers continued to work at her braid so that it resembled now a fraying knot of rope, instead of the sleek mass of gold it had been when she'd arrived.

'Why are you helping us?' Even as I said it, I wondered if such a direct question were a mistake. She looked ready to flee as it was.

The end of her braid hovered at her mouth, as if she were contemplating eating it. She dropped it abruptly, and finally met my gaze. 'Will my daddy be hurt?' *Daddy*. Such a childlike word for one whose vocabulary was anything but.

I knelt so I could look her in the eye without forcing her to crane her neck. 'I don't know. Because he's the president, his soldiers and guards will do everything they can to protect him.' It was true, but only as things stood now. There was no telling how they would react should the truth of Crane's experiments, and his cruelty to his own child, become public knowledge. Assuming, of course, that she'd help. Right now, I was being very presumptuous, unable to consider the alternative.

'I'm helping because I can. Daddy always said we should help others, if we can.'

I stared at her, finding it impossible to believe that Crane had ever uttered those words.

'You're not scared you'll get into trouble?'

Her large blue eyes were almost too big for her face. Now, when they were filled with tears, she made such a pitiful figure that I had to stop myself reaching for her. The kitchen was flooded with light, and I knew we had only minutes more before Aunt Carrie rose.

'I need a pen. And paper.'

I rooted around fruitlessly for a pen, opening one drawer after another. She held one out a moment later, turning the paper with Dominico's message over in her hand and holding that out for me too.

Feeling a touch foolish, I scribbled my reply. I handed it back to Layla. She snatched it from my fingers, as if afraid to touch me. She turned to leave, and an unbearable weight settled on me.

'Layla. Wait.' She paused but remained with her back to me. 'I know you might be afraid of being alone, if something happens to your father.' She stilled. 'But you won't be. I promise you that.'

She shook her head. 'She said that too.'

'Who?'

'Your friend. She said I could go live with her and the others, who are like me.'

She turned back to me. The look on her face was unbearable. A cross between devastating hope and doubt, her need to believe in us so strong it filled the air like a physical being. She raised a hand in farewell, and then disappeared through the front door, moving out into the daylight as if she had every right to do so.

Chapter Twenty-Nine

Syra

The morning dawned in a glory of scarlet. Blood on the horizon. I watched the sun rise with mounting dread. I had barely slept. I'd spent the night in the company of the horrors of my imagination, scenarios playing through my mind on repeat, each bloodier and more horrifying than the one before. I'd listened to Drake's snores coming from the next room, and wondered how he could sleep so soundly, knowing what was coming. In the early hours I'd finally slipped from my bed, pulling a worn hoodie over my head. I'd stepped out of the house and into the cool night air, welcoming the feel of it on my skin, wanting nothing more than to put some space between my brother and me.

I'd stood there for only a few minutes when I heard footsteps. Ray appeared in the dim morning light, wearing nothing but a pair of sleeping shorts and a white vest. His feet were bare. I watched his approach with a mingled sense of dread and anticipation. He hadn't willingly spoken to me in weeks. Whatever dialogue we'd exchanged had been stilted and forced, the conversation of two people who had too much to say and no way to say it.

He stood beside me silently, close enough for me to feel the warmth of his body, to smell the woolly scent of sleep on his skin.

In the quiet of the night, I could hear the slow and content breathing of those who'd found sleep. Someone muttered something, the bed creaking as they rolled over. For me, the night was never silent.

I motioned for Ray to follow me. If we were going to talk, I didn't want to take the chance that Drake would overhear us. We walked a short distance on a path that took us away from the other houses. The path sloped downwards, into a small gully. It insulated us, as though we were tucked away from the rest of the city, wrapped in a bubble of isolation.

'Couldn't sleep?' His voice was low, the acid tone of the past few weeks gone.

'No. I couldn't lie there any longer. Tossing and turning. Mind wouldn't shut down.'

He looked down at his hands, as if unsure of what to do with them. 'I wanted to apologise. For having those meetings. For not standing up for you.'

I stared intently into the darkness, riding the wave of emotion that hit me with breathtaking force. When I felt composed again, I turned to him. 'Why now, Ray? I would've thought with Drake's arrival you'd be even more furious with me.' I couldn't help the sharp blade of my tone.

'I know this isn't what you want.'

I started. Had I really been that transparent?

As if plucking the thought from my mind, he shook his head. 'You've hidden it well enough. But I could feel it coming off you.' I felt his gaze on me briefly, and I was warmed by the contact. 'I think Drake knows it too.'

'I've made it quite clear to him that I'm in two minds about this.'

'Is there no way to stop it?'

'The war? No. If we don't go to Crane, he'll come to us. It's gone too far now. There's no preventing it.'

'I didn't want to go into this war without having spoken to you.'

I nodded, feeling the cursed knot of tears in my throat. I had wanted his apology for so long, but it changed nothing. We could never go back now. Our friendship had been based on our mutual, but sibling-like, affection for each other. Now that was tainted with his changed feelings for me. The scale had tipped.

'I'm sorry too.'

'For what?'

'For...' I scrabbled desperately, trying to find a way to articulate the impossible. 'For what you're feeling –' He held up a hand and I trailed off, relieved at not having to go on, disappointed that I didn't have the courage to.

'There's no need to get into that.'

I nodded, and brushed his hand with mine, wanting somehow to communicate my regret through my fingertips.

Now, as I rose and dressed, feeling exhausted and unfocused, I tried to push away the constant nagging doubt that I'd overlooked something vital. Something I couldn't name or identify.

Drake strolled into the kitchen a few minutes later, looking well-rested and buoyant. I sat hunched at the table, a precious cup of coffee in front of me. Our rationed stock was nearly up. After that, there would be no more coffee for any of us.

Drake glanced at me, a brief shadow crossing his face. 'Rough night?'

I nodded, keeping my gaze fixed on the black liquid in my cup.

Drake rummaged through a drawer. The clatter of cutlery made my head ache. He sat across from me. I sensed his eyes on me, but I couldn't make myself meet them.

When he spoke, I knew it wasn't what he'd initially wanted to say. 'We only have a few minutes before we need to gather everyone. The trip across The Waste will take —'

I rose. 'I know. We've discussed this already. I'm done.' I dumped my untouched coffee down the drain.

***

We reached the parking lot beneath Toria in good time. I'd walked the entire distance in silence, ignoring Drake's attempts at engaging me in conversation. I could tell he was both annoyed and worried at my reticence, but I had no room in my mind for that.

The mood of the group was dangerously divided. Drake's followers moved closely behind him, while the others remained behind Ray and me, a visible gap between the two. I found it fitting. The chasm between Drake and me had never been wider.

I'd gone over our plan again and again in my head, looking for holes and problems we may not have considered before. The layout of the parking lot slowed our approach considerably, and by the time we reached the trapdoor in the ceiling, I was sweating with nerves. This was the part of our plan I'd questioned, knowing that we could only climb the steps one at a time, temporarily separating individuals from the group. All it would take was one soldier walking into the barracks at the wrong moment. Those who had already climbed the stairs would be trapped. For this reason, Drake, Ray and I would be the first ones to go.

Drake had pointed out, impatiently, that it was the only point of entry into the city. Even if it had been sealed shut, which surely was the case after the debacle with Dominico, her parents, and Rogan, it would be no problem to break through.

Mohina separated from the rest to do the honours. Neither Drake nor I had called her forward, and I found myself thinking how typical it was of her to make herself indispensable. A quality that had often, irrationally, irritated me. She held out a hand and turned her attention to the door. A glow emanated from her palm. Seconds later, we heard the crunch of wood breaking and a soft clunk. The wood had split down the centre, forming two separate planks. She carefully removed one of them, opening a gap wide enough to slip a hand through. She nodded to us and stepped back. Drake took up the first position, with Ray following behind. I took up the rear, concentrating on the steps ahead of me, and nothing else. Whatever happened now, it was too late to change direction.

Rogan

The men had gathered at first light. The insults and comments I'd endured when I'd first arrived back in Toria were conspicuously absent. They kept their silence, and if there was any resentment towards me for resuming my position, no one dared express it. I looked down at my armour, a term I used lightly, seeing as it was made up of an old bulletproof vest, jeans and heavy combat boots. Someone had cleaned the shoes until they gleamed. The vest and boots had been in storage in the depths of Crane's mansion, along with the numerous guns that had been collected during the human war. I'd had no need of them, until now.

Ammunition had been stockpiled for years, scavenged from The Waste, and choosing my gun from all that weaponry had made me feel ill. Many lives would be lost to them. Lives that might've been spared, if we'd had a different leader.

While the men talked among themselves, some preparing and others cracking weak jokes in an effort to distract themselves, I waited. Every time someone walked towards me, or even looked in my direction, adrenaline would shoot through me, like a needle to my veins. I was aware of time passing, every second a bell tolling in my head, a countdown to the inevitable. Syra was drawing closer with each toll, and still Layla hadn't arrived. I'd been sure she would come. I hadn't considered the alternative. I was here only because my belief had propelled me to be. Now, my choices were narrowing, and there would be no avoiding the war.

I wondered if Dominico would be permitted to fight, but recalling her appearance when I'd last seen her, I doubted she would see anything of this day at all. When Crane had first taken her, I'd assumed he would use her like the rest of the superhumans. She was, after all, one of the most powerful, and presumed to be the key to winning the war. But the more I thought about it, the more it made sense for Crane to keep her out of it completely. If she weren't drugged the way she had been, and was at her peak, Crane would never be able to control her the way he did the others. She would be a wild card in a war Crane couldn't afford to lose.

My gaze wandered over the men as I tried to distract myself. Riley was among them, his back taut with animosity, his gaze carefully averted. I didn't mistake his avoidance for submission – if anything, it was a quiet form of insolence, a refusal to accept me as his commander again. Caiden and Bradley had done everything they could to avoid speaking to me directly. They'd seen me back into this city under a shroud of shame, and they'd enjoyed their role as my persecutors. Now they were under my command again, subject to my instructions. It was just like Crane to muddy the waters this way. I hated it. I wanted nothing more than to be away from here. I wanted no part of this, but hope stayed my feet, even as time grew dangerously short.

Crane would arrive any minute now. I gazed over the heads of the men, trying to convince myself that there was still time. Perhaps at this very moment, Layla was moving through the crowd, searching for me. Even as the thought came, I knew I didn't believe it. She wasn't coming. I couldn't blame her. She was a mere child. One that had been kept away from society like a dirty secret. One that had been punished for being born something her father had created.

I considered my options. I could leave now. I could duck through the crowd. No one would stop me. By the time they realised I was gone, it would be too late.

Crane appeared, pulling me from my thoughts. Behind him shuffled his superhuman army. In the past few days he'd turned out more than a dozen new recruits. I hadn't bothered questioning the wisdom of putting inexperienced fighters in a battle as momentous as this. I was too overwhelmed by my disgust at his casual disregard for the lives he'd turned. It would've been lost on him anyway. Human life only meant something when it served him.

I focused on the superhuman directly behind Crane. He was massive, a hulk of a figure. He dwarfed the men in both height and width. I estimated that even I would only be level with his chest. His arms were about the size of my thighs, his head a boulder on the platform of his shoulders. I imagined his eyes to be flat and empty, the eyes of a predator with no mercy. There was no remnant of the human he used to be. None of the human soldiers would recognise their comrades, or their townspeople, because there was nothing left of them. Whatever they had been before falling prey to Crane's experiments was gone.

Crane raised his hands for quiet, but there was no need. The sight of the superhumans had already seen to it. There was only the sound of shuffling feet, and the atmosphere of betrayal that hung so heavily it fell on the group like a cloak. Only a select few soldiers had known about Crane's on-going experiments. Discussing them with anyone outside of the laboratory was to risk their lives.

'The day has finally come. As we speak, the superhumans are entering our city. This is a direct violation of the treaty. Those standing behind me' – here he motioned to the superhuman army - 'will assist us in stamping them out, once and for all.'

A roar rose up from the soldiers. My gaze fell on a cluster that had moved closer together – Connor, Jasper and Abbie had grouped themselves with Caiden and Bradley. They were among the youngest to fight today. They remained silent as the others shouted their approval and support. Caiden and Bradley stood stiffly, their faces strained with the effort to remain neutral.

'When this is done, we'll no longer have to suffer under the threat of superhumans. We'll take their city, and we'll be free to roam The Waste without fear of them.'

Crane made no attempt to explain the presence of the superhumans. Where they'd come from, or why they were fighting with us. None of the soldiers asked. It was to be as it always had been under Crane's rule – unquestioning obedience.

Dominico

They'd herded me out with the rest of the women and children. I expected open hostility, and although I got a few shocked and wary glances, it was no more than that. I watched a woman kneel in front of her child. He was frantic, his screams carrying over the crowd, igniting panic in the other children. She held his hands in hers, waiting it out, murmuring to him until his screams finally died down to whimpers. She took him in her arms, rubbing his back in circles of reassurance. He melted into her embrace without hesitation, his face pressed into the curve of her neck. I envied how easy it was for the little boy to find solace. If I only I could be so easily reassured.

I passed a young couple, unable to tear my eyes away from them. The woman clung to him, weeping openly. He was dressed in a soldier's uniform. It looked brand new, marred only by the dark spots on his chest from her tears. He looked both exasperated and tender, kissing her and whispering into her ear. He caught me staring at them and I turned away, embarrassed. I increased my pace as much as I could, given that I was caught in the middle of the slow-moving crowd.

I craned my neck, looking for my mother. She had to be somewhere in this group. I scanned over the sea of heads, trying to spot her blonde crown among the predominantly brunette women. Just as I was about to give up, I felt a hand on my arm.

'Domo.' She pulled me to her, ignoring the protests of those who were forced to move around us. She breathed me in, her hands pressing against my back with a force that left me breathless.

She stepped back to look at me, smoothing the hair from my face. Even though she was smiling, there were tears in her eyes.

'What are you doing here?'

'What do you mean?'

'I thought...' she shook her head. 'I thought you'd be fighting with the others.'

I'd thought the same thing. When I'd heard the public announcement this morning, I'd waited for someone to fetch me. Only when my guard had ordered me towards the growing crowd of women and children did I realise that Crane had deemed me useless as a fighter.

'No. I'm too weak. They've been giving me these drugs...' I trailed off when I saw the look of shock on her face. I flapped a hand, as if it were no big deal. 'I'm fine. Just not the secret weapon he thought I was.' I didn't tell her what I suspected. The days in Crane's laboratory were mostly one big blur of pain and fear. What I did remember clearly, was the many vials of blood they'd taken. I'd assumed they were testing it, trying to pinpoint what made me different. And maybe that's exactly what they'd been doing. But it had occurred to me that they could've gone a step further. Maybe they were trying to capture the essence of what set me apart, in an effort to duplicate it. Duplicate it, and use it.

Mom swiped at her eyes and gave me another quick hug. Then she took my hand and we moved with the crowd again.

'Have you seen Dad?'

Her smiled slipped. 'This morning. When soldiers arrived to fit him for a uniform.'

'A...what?'

'Crane's ordered every able man to fight.'

I felt all the blood leave my face. I swayed a little, bumping into someone walking beside me. He grunted something and shifted, but I barely heard him over the rush of fear that washed over me.

Mom patted my shoulder briskly. 'It'll be okay honey. He used to be a commander, remember?'

'That was years ago, Mom. He hasn't fired a gun since.' I shook my head, my nails digging into my palms. 'Has Crane lost his mind?'

Mom shot me a sharp look, glancing meaningfully around us. But she didn't bawl me out, the way she used to.

'Apparently they need every man who can reasonably aim and shoot.'

My feet suddenly felt too heavy for me to move them. I felt glued to the ground. The crowd parted around us again, like water around a boulder. Mom's hands went to my shoulders. She propelled me forward. 'I know, love. I'm worried too. But there's nothing we can do for him now.' She looked at me. Her eyes were huge with strain, and there was no hope in them. 'What are these superhumans like?'

I started at the oddness of her question, the abrupt change of subject. Then I realised what she was really asking me. I wanted to give her a gift, give her something to hold on to. But I couldn't do that without lying. 'They're like humans, Mom. Some of them value all life. And some of them only value their own.'

She nodded tightly, as if she hadn't expected me to answer any differently. I took her hand and squeezed it. 'We have each other. At least we're together, right?' She smiled weakly. I knew she heard the empty optimism in my voice. It wasn't enough. We were supposed to be three.

Chapter Thirty

Syra

My chest closed as I watched Drake, and then Ray, climb the steps and disappear into the barracks above. My breath was caught in my throat, fluttering there like a trapped insect, humming its discontent against my vocal cords. I forced my right foot onto the first step, leaning my torso forward in order to hoist myself further up the ladder. It was too low for me to stand upright, so I climbed using my hands and feet, pushing back the dark thoughts that warred in my mind for acknowledgement. A hand appeared through the opening and I took it. I was yanked upwards into the barracks, skipping past the last two steps.

The helping hand belonged to Ray. Surprised, I thanked him and hastily stepped back, breaking the contact. We shuffled further in to make room for the others. Although it must've been only minutes before we were all crowded into the barracks, it felt much longer. Time stretched out like a rubber band until the wait became unbearable.

'Let's go,' Drake said. My gaze darted around the space, moving over the long line of double bunks. I glanced towards the only window. There was no movement behind the clear glass. All the same, I couldn't shake the feeling we were being watched. Something was wrong. There were none of the noises you'd expect of an inhabited city – no conversations, no movement of feet, no sound at all to indicate activity. I paused, reaching out a hand for Drake.

'It's too quiet.' He didn't reply. I glanced at his profile. His jaw was clenched and a small tic was showing in his cheek. His whole body language had changed. A few minutes ago, he'd been alert and relaxed. Now his body pulsed with a tension so intense it felt like a wall had come up between us. I tightened my grip on his shoulder, hoping to elicit a response. 'Drake?'

He shook me off with a violence that shocked me. 'Move out!' I flinched. His voice was too loud. Taking the city by surprise was key. The feeling grew that something was off. I started to say something else but at Drake's order, everyone moved forward, forcing me along.

We stepped out into the brightness of the day. Temporarily blinded by the light, it took me a few moments to digest what was in front of me. Crane. And an army. He stood elevated above his soldiers on a gentle hill, his smile of triumph wide and unmistakable.

'Syra. We've been expecting you.'

Our plan to use the element of surprise had failed. I expected Drake to order our army forward, but instead he did nothing. He simply remained where he was, his face devoid of the horror and shock that I felt on my own. He looked expectant. The thought that had been scratching at the surface of my mind forced its way through. For the first time since my dream, I could see the features of the man whose hand was joined with Drake's in a picture of solidarity. I stumbled back a step, shock vibrating through me like a current. Several pairs of hands caught and steadied me. Before any of them could ask anything, Drake stepped forward, meeting Crane between our two armies as he descended the hill, like a king meeting his loyal subject.

Their hands met in an identical handshake to the one I'd just seen in my mind's eye. Exclamations of shock rose from both armies, which quickly spiralled into a storm of shouting and screaming, human and superhuman voices united in our mutual disgust.

Only my shame outweighed my panic. It flooded me, a hot flush that crawled along my skin and raged through me like an inferno. I should've known. How could I have let it get this far? How could he do this to me, a second betrayal so soon after the first?

My gaze moved frantically over the human soldiers, searching for one wrong move, one act of aggression that could tip this moment into full-scale war. My eyes ran over him without registering whom I was seeing. A moment later I felt as if I'd been punched in the chest. I searched for him, and sure enough, there he stood, in a tatty vest and jeans, a gun strapped low on his hips. I was sure I was seeing things. He couldn't be standing there. He was dead. And yet, even as I watched, he raised a hand in greeting, such a casual gesture that it made my throat swell and close. Rogan. How he came to be standing at the head of Crane's army, I had no idea, and I didn't care. He was alive. I started to raise my hand in return, when I saw the others. My hand stopped in mid-air, a feeble half-wave.

I stared. It had been years since I'd last seen them, but there was no mistaking them. The superhumans from the lab: Esther, Rose, Annie. Behind them, Kellen, Abe and Toby. I'd thought they were dead. Looking at their faces from where I stood, they might as well be. There was no spark of recognition. They looked drugged. Judging from their blank gazes and frozen figures, Crane had pumped them full of something to keep them docile. I didn't know how he thought they were going to fight in their state, but there they were, as real as the hand I was now waving at them in desperation, despite knowing they wouldn't wave back.

There were other superhumans too, but none that I recognised. They were grotesquely huge, with bulging arms, and thighs wider and longer than any I'd ever seen on a superhuman. I focused on the one closest to me. His gaze was flat, yet alert, and his body vibrated with the need to move. I shivered at the images I plucked from his mind.

I didn't know how much time had passed since I'd noticed Rogan and the superhumans, but when I looked back to where Draiken and Crane stood, their hands were still locked in a handshake. The noise around me had grown in volume, a dense invisible cloud, and no shouts or gestures from either Draiken or Crane could quiet them. In the ensuing chaos, I got a glimpse of Draiken releasing Crane's hand. Someone was moving rapidly through the crowd, slipping through the tight gaps left by the human army. Something about his body language, what I could see of it, felt wrong. I tried to reach his thoughts, but I could hear nothing but the garbled static of too many voices.

I shifted against the press of bodies, straining to see over the heads of those in front of me. I pushed my way through the crowd, muttering apologies to those I stood on or elbowed. I'd somehow lost the man in the crowd. I scanned the crush of people, trying to find the mop of dark hair I'd glimpsed. I couldn't understand why I couldn't find him. Tracking a moving figure should've been a simple task in a sea of immobile bodies.

I found him when he was only metres from the backs of Drake and Crane. I shoved harder against those blocking my path, unapologetic in my rising panic. As I got to the front of the crowd, the man pulled something from his hip. The gun caught the light of the morning sun as he raised it to the back of Drake's head.

A scream tore from my throat, leaving it raw and aching. My panic drew a wave of noise from the crowd both behind and in front of me, but I felt strangely disconnected from it, hearing only my own scream reverberate in my head like a ball bouncing between two closely spaced walls. Drake's eyes found mine. He smiled. My heart wrenched, wondering if that were the last I was to see of him. I broke into a sprint, knowing even as my legs obeyed that I had run out of time, that any second now a bullet would enter my brother's brain.

Drake turned towards his assailant, although his movement was so quick most of the crowd would not have seen it. He snatched the gun, flipping it around until the muzzle was pressed against the man's temple. The atmosphere was charged with tension, the same muffled feeling that grew before the break of a thunderstorm.

I felt giddy with relief, until I realised that Drake was intending to act on his threat. I could see the precipice – it was this moment, this action, which would topple us over the edge. I tried to find my voice to call out, to stop him before he pulled the trigger, but even as I opened my mouth, the sound of a shot filled the air. The man's lifeless legs gave way beneath him. He dropped to the ground in a soundless fall. I pressed a hand to my mouth, my eyes fixed on Drake. He found me in the crowd and smiled, as if this had been the plan all along.

Rogan

My eyes weren't on Riley as he fell. Instead, I watched Syra, her face closing in on itself as she watched the corpse fall. There was a moment of pure shock among the crowd, everyone frozen to the spot in a split second of indecision. I stepped towards my men, wanting to halt the storm before it could erupt. I held up my hands as if to ward off the inevitable, hoping they wouldn't react to Riley's death with the churning emotion that was already stirring the crowd. He'd taken his life into his hands. I had no pity for his loss. He may as well have pulled the trigger himself.

It was too late. My men surged forward, first the front line, then the rest followed on their heels. I was swamped by bodies, almost losing my footing several times. I turned towards the superhuman army. They were surging towards us. There was no stopping it now. Gunfire filled the air as I fought my way to the front. I'd wanted no part of this, but the time for choice was over now, and as the commander, I had to head the army.

I finally broke free of my men, bursting to the front of the line. There was pandemonium. I turned to my right, where the fighting was dense and frenetic. I raced towards Caiden and Bradley, who were fighting off Raven. Dread curled my stomach. I knew her. I'd lived in her city, helped build houses for her people. I'd pulled one of her people's treasured children out of the reservoir. But I'd known Caiden and Bradley all my life. They'd trained under me, and I'd favoured them as two of my best men. I stopped dead. I was of no use in this war. I couldn't kill on either side. Protection of one meant murder of another. I needed to stop this. I'd hoped I could do just that before the fighting started, before anyone died. I'd relied on Layla's arrival, on her ability to influence. I'd had it all wrong. It was up to me to finish this. And only one person could help me do it.

I turned to run in the opposite direction. Caiden called out to me, his voice almost drowned by the screams and shouts polluting the air. I looked over at him. Raven had him in an invisible grip, arms locked behind his back. She was strangling him, her Minder ability like a hand of vaporous steel around his throat. His mouth formed words I could no longer hear. He stared at me mutely, eyes pleading for help.

I rushed at Raven. I felt something come up between us, an invisible barrier that I slammed into with such force I stumbled backward, my vision blackening around the edges.

I pounded on it, then tried to sprint around it, but it seemed to grow in length, matching each of my strides with its development.

'Raven!' I had no idea if she could hear me, but I had to try. My gaze moved to Caiden. Bradley was trying to break the force that was strangling the life out of his comrade, but there was no weakening her grip.

'Raven!' She turned, her face impassive, eyes unblinking. She seemed to be caught in a trance, wrapped in the exertion of her power.

'Let him go. It doesn't have to be this way. We can solve this. Just... just let him go.' She smiled, a slow parting of her lips. She snapped his neck. The sound shouldn't have been audible over the chaos, but I heard it all the same. He fell, his lifeless face turned towards me as he met the dust.

Dominico

We were herded towards the houses right at the edge of the city, as far away from the scene of the war as we could get without actually leaving the city. We huddled together in messy lines against the city wall. The sun was already beating down on us, but the guards seemed reluctant to allow us to break into smaller groups and find relief in the houses. I guessed they were worried about the logistics of being able to protect us if we split off, although I felt it was less about that than making sure no one slipped away. Already, several of the younger boys, those deemed too young to carry a gun, had tried to give the guards the slip. I don't know what they intended to do – it wasn't as if they could arm themselves, but I understood their need to do something. Something besides sitting in the baking heat, waiting for an outcome.

I shifted position, glancing at Mom. She sat completely still, mouth slightly open. She hadn't said one word since our exchange about Dad. She held my hand loosely, her fingers limp and sweaty against my palm. I squeezed hers gently, but she merely blinked in response. Her eyes were fixed straight ahead, unseeing. I wondered if she were picturing Dad in the uniform they'd fitted for him. If she was guarding against imagining that uniform spattered with blood, both that of others, and his own.

The only reason I hadn't already tried to make a break for it was Mom. I hated sitting here, not knowing if Layla had done anything. But I guessed from the sounds that carried over to us that it was too late and the battle was already raging. I hated knowing that I could be out there. I didn't want bloodshed. I was stuck between two worlds. I'd lived with both, and I'd got to know those who made up each side. But maybe just by being out there, I could prevent more deaths. Mom reached out and stilled my foot. I realised it had been tapping out a frenzied rhythm. For the first time since we'd sat down, she looked at me directly.

'Go.'

I blinked at her. 'I can't Mom. I can't leave you here alone, worrying about us.'

'I know you need to. And you could be the key to stop this thing. Go. Before too many die.'

I didn't need to be told again. I hugged her, breathing in her sweat and her familiarity, imprinting it on my brain. I ran a hand over her golden hair, and instead of feeling the matted dirt that had ruined her best feature, I felt the silk of its former glory.

'See you soon.'

She kissed my cheek. 'Go, I'll distract them.'

She began to wail, her voice carrying over the crowd to the nearest guard. She stood and stumbled towards him, hands outstretched. He paused, frowning, then strode towards her, his face puckered with annoyance. I glanced at the other guards standing nearby. Their attention was focused on Mom, but it still wouldn't be easy slipping away when everyone was seated. I shuffled along the crowd, moving towards the back, keeping low. When I'd got as far as I could without calling attention to myself, I shot to my feet and ran. It only took seconds before shouts rang out behind me, but I dug in harder, willing my feet to fly. I didn't turn, even when a gunshot sounded behind me.

Syra

My only thought when the pandemonium broke out was to find Draiken. I had to stop him. The crowd had swallowed him, a multi-limbed, multi-headed creature. The noise was overwhelming. I pushed through the crowd using my torso, hands clamped over my ears in a futile attempt to muffle the sound. People's thoughts threaded through the general noise, until it was a din of indiscernible syllables. The sound of fear. All thought of what we'd planned evaporated like water in The Waste. All the organisation we'd put into how we would fight, the Physicals in front to absorb the first onslaught, the Minders disabling the front line of soldiers, disappeared. I had no help as a small knot of soldiers rushed at me, their weapons raised. I was fast, but dodging a volley of bullets from multiple guns was beyond even my abilities.

I was shoved from behind. It was so forceful I stumbled to my knees, my outstretched hands halting my fall. Gunshots rang out. I was sure I could feel the air move around me as they flew past, inches from my head. I turned. Several soldiers lay in the dirt, mere metres from me. They'd shot their own kind in their attempt to kill me. The earth around them was darkening with their blood. The mix filled my nose, heavy and moist, the scent of a grave. I scrambled to my feet and ran. It was only when the battle thinned around me that I paused.

I scanned the crowd. I could barely bring myself to believe what I'd witnessed. Drake's hand in Crane's. The smile he'd cast my way. His callousness, and just how calculated this move had been. The betrayal of his kind, but also of me. It burned in me, a fire that needed no further stoking. My anger was a physical thing, a weapon I hoped to sharpen and use to keep him at a distance. I'd had enough of his excuses and explanations. There was no going back from this.

I kept shoving my way through the mass, aware that I wasn't paying enough attention to the fighting around me. If I wasn't careful, I could end up dead before I found Draiken. I slowed, forcing myself to focus on my immediate surroundings. Much of the battle around me had been reduced to hand to hand combat. Having no physical weapons, we were at a disadvantage at a distance. The superhumans made sure to disarm those who came at them. For now, I was safe from stray bullets.

I knew that if the others saw me pushing through the crowd, instead of standing my ground and doing my bit, they would consider me a failed leader. But I wanted to avoid bloodshed, even though my efforts so far had failed. Killing either side felt wrong, a sin I couldn't bring myself to commit. Somewhere in this writhing mass of bodies was Ray. He would be in the thick of things, right where his people needed him. I, on the other hand, was doing what I'd always done – fighting my way to Draiken's side.

Just when I was about to give up on finding him, I felt a hand on my shoulder. I whipped around, preparing myself for an assault. Rogan stood in front of me, his eyes searching my face. He seemed to be drinking me in, committing every detail to memory. Before I could say a word he pulled me to him. I buried my face in the crook of his neck. The noise and activity fell away, insulating us from the judgement of possible onlookers. For a moment, we were alone, untouched and separated from the fighting going on around us.

He pulled back, and the moment was broken. He tried to say

something over the noise, but I could only watch the movement of his mouth, the shape of his syllables. I cupped a hand around my ear, shaking my head. He leaned closer, trying to shout over the din. His hand closed around my arm. He pulled me close enough to feel his breath against my ear. His hand tightened with such sudden force I cried out. He shoved me behind him, his bulk blocking my view. I caught a rush of movement, and only just managed to jump out of the way before Rogan hit the dirt, right in the place I'd been standing. Draiken stood over him, his chest heaving with an anger that pulsed from him in waves of heat.

'What are you doing?' I screamed. The noise of the battle swallowed my words, but it wouldn't have mattered if there'd been a vacuum of silence around us. Draiken was beyond hearing me, beyond reason.

He threw himself at Rogan, straddling his chest and dealing out a volley of punches so rapid I could barely follow the movement of his fists. I jumped on Draiken's back and tried to haul him off Rogan, but he held fast, knees clamped around the width of Rogan's chest. I dug my nails into the dip below his collarbone. It was enough of a distraction for Rogan to aim a punch at Draiken's chin. His head snapped back from the blow, and an arc of blood flew from his nose.

He grabbed my arms and flipped me over his back with such force I met the dirt face first. Grit caught between my teeth. I scrambled to my feet, swiping at my mouth and nose. They felt stopped up with earth. My lungs felt as if they'd collapsed – I felt as if I was being buried alive.

Rogan had temporarily gained the upper hand. He'd somehow flipped Drake over onto his front, arms pinned behind him. Rogan looked up at me. I could sense his smile before it came, a smile that was meant to reassure me. But he knew nothing of Drake's abilities. Mine were more attuned, and I had more control. But when he was pushed to the end of his endurance, his abilities far surpassed my own. It would be brief, but overwhelming. Rogan removed one hand from Drake's wrists, reaching for his gun.

I started to shout out a warning, but before I could think to form the words, Drake had made his move. He pushed back against Rogan's weight, flipping him onto his back as if he were no heavier than an infant. Rogan's grunt of surprise was audible. His gun, which he'd managed to pull from its holster, flew from his hand. Drake drew his head back and brought it down against Rogan's nose in one short and sharp movement. The crunch of bone was unmistakable.

'Drake! Drake! Stop it, please stop it!' I threw myself on top of him, my hands slipping on Rogan's blood. I knelt in front of Drake and, placing a hand on either side of his face, forced his gaze forward. He refused to focus on me, his eyes trained over my shoulder. 'Drake, please. Look at me.' I pressed my palms against his cheeks. Sometimes, when we were just kids, I'd sit on his chest, my hands on his face. We'd stare at each other until one of us finally gave in to fits of laughter. It felt like a different kind of game now. It seemed that as long as he didn't look at me, he could pretend we were still those same kids. He could pretend nothing had changed.

I squeezed harder, trying not to watch the steady flow of blood weeping from Rogan's nose, trying not to see the glaze in his expression.

Finally, Drake's gaze shifted. He focused on me with such intensity I wondered if he was really seeing me. 'Don't do this. Let him go.'

A smile started at the corner of his mouth, spreading until it turned into a grin – wide and empty. He looked me straight in the eye. 'A human. A human over me. You can never lead. Your priorities are all wrong. I love you Sy, but you're such a disappointment.'

He rolled over, taking me with him. He forced me onto my back. His hands looped around my throat. The gesture was so casual, it was like he was draping an arm around my shoulders. It was only when his hands tightened that I realised what he planned to do.

My gaze locked on Rogan. He dived out of my line of sight, presumably on the hunt for this gun.

I bucked beneath Drake, trying to dislodge his grip, but his hands only tightened. His eyes were dim, his focus on something beyond me. I gurgled, trying to speak. He couldn't be strangling me. My blood. My only family. I stared at him through increasingly blurred vision, my head filling with incomplete thoughts, unable to latch onto anything long enough to finish it. The world was shrinking. I could feel nothing beyond Drake's hands. There was nothing but the growing tunnel of blackness that beckoned me, and no sound beyond Drake's manic grunts, as he fought to squeeze every last drop of life out of me.

Just as I was sure my lungs would collapse, Drake's weight lifted from me, his hands making a last grab for my throat. I rolled onto my side, dry heaving and gasping, the world flooding back into focus. The noise of the war filled my ears, the screams, the shouts, the rush of feet along the dirt. I forced breath into my lungs, trying to ignore the searing pain of every inhalation. I looked up from my position on the ground, finally able to focus on what was happening around me. Rogan and Drake were struggling again, rolling in the dirt like two schoolboys. Rogan had his gun in hand, but couldn't bring it up between them. Drake was straddling Rogan, his hands locked around his neck and head. I knew that pose. Early on in training, those of us with physical gifts were taught a manoeuvre called a headlock. Once in the right position, and with a tight enough grip, the neck was snapped in one quick, fluid motion. I shot to my feet and started towards them, my stomach roiling with fear, my mouth filled with its metallic taste.

Before I could take one step further, Ray appeared out of nowhere, launching himself at Drake. Caught on the defensive, Drake was taken with the momentum of Ray's flight, his hands ripped from their position. I stopped, my hand at my mouth, feeling the bile rise in my throat. Whether Ray's actions were driven by empathy for Rogan, or his recent hatred of Drake, was unclear. I didn't care either way. I was just grateful. I ran to Rogan, conscious of how vulnerable we all were, fighting among ourselves in the eye of the war, all of us too preoccupied to watch our own, or each other's backs. I knelt beside him, my hand on his shoulder. He reached out, his fingers grazing my throat. The skin already felt tender and chafed. I fought the urge to lean into his touch, and offered him a hand up instead. We both turned to the battle between Ray and Drake, wanting to return the favour. Rogan pointed his gun at them, but he couldn't get a clear enough shot without endangering Ray. Watching his finger curl around the trigger, preparing to fire, I fought the urge to close my hand around the weapon, and pry it away from him. Could I stand here, witness to my brother's death, and do nothing?

I was momentarily distracted by a figure. Strolling through the push and shove of bodies, she moved towards us, oblivious of the mayhem. Even from where I stood I could see the halo of scarlet, catching like a small blaze in the morning heat.

Dominico

I walked through the heaving crowd, the sounds of the battle far away and somehow faded, as if I were walking encased in my own private bubble. I kept my eyes focused ahead. I could see the bob and weave of movement out of the corner of my eye. Every time I licked my lips I tasted grit. The smell of blood filled my nose. I refused to look. I was sure that if I kept walking straight on, I would find them. As if sensing my remoteness, no one tried to lay a hand on me. I was completely inside my own head, searching for the key to unlock my old strength, and bring my abilities to the surface. I had to find my reserves. It would be enough to finish this.

I spotted them together, and only when I saw two figures on the ground, did I start to run. At first my chest heaved. My throat filled with a knot of trapped breath that refused to budge, seeming to grow until I was sure I would choke on it. My calves burned, unused to working so hard. I pushed harder, trying to force myself through that barrier within me, the one that kept telling me I was too weak, that my abilities were too far under the blanket of drugs Crane had smothered them with. Then I felt it. Something gave within me, opening a gap, just wide enough for everything to come rushing through. That nugget of heat inside me caught fire, and everything became easier. My feet felt lighter. I released the breath in my throat. My lungs opened. The weakness drained out of me. The feeling was so physical I was convinced that if I looked behind me I'd see a trail of glistening liquid.

A wall of bodies reared up in front of me, thrashing across my path. I had no time to see who they were. I leaped over them, barely making it as they crashed to the ground in a heap of swinging limbs.

I was nearly there. Syra and Rogan's attention were on the fighting figures. It took me a minute to figure out who was pounding his fists into Ray's body. This, then, must be Draiken. Syra and Rogan were trying to help but, despite their respective strengths, neither could pry him off Ray. He was like a man possessed, arms moving at high speed, fists flying in a blur of fury. Rogan's gun hung from his hand, useless. I knew he wouldn't take the shot and risk killing Ray. *Quickly.* I closed my eyes. I would need to use my abilities in tandem. I had no idea if I could do it. I'd had no occasion to practise them together, and Raven had never asked me to do it in training. It had never occurred to me to mention it.

My body warmed rapidly, the heat building until I felt like I was burning from the inside, the flame becoming an inferno. I opened my eyes. Ray was on his back in the dirt, Draiken's hands moving to his throat in a grip that set off a wave of panic within me. The scene I was imagining wouldn't come. *Push harder.* Ray's hands rose. They moved between him and Draiken. He shoved Draiken off him, the movement sending Draiken stumbling back just far enough for Ray to get to his feet.

Draiken heaved himself in the opposite direction, landing on his belly, hands reaching for something. They closed around air. Despite this, Draiken's face filled with triumph. He moved them rapidly upward, as if he were gripping something and using it for leverage. It was a smoke screen. A scene layered over reality, a scene that only Draiken could see. I had to hold it as long as I could, but already the strain of keeping the scene intact weighed on me. Sweat prickled at my hairline. I wanted to give Syra and the others time to regroup, to figure out how to deal with Draiken. And I wanted to give Draiken a moment to expend some of his violent energy, for the zealous edge of his anger to cool. And for the others to act on his temporary distraction.

My legs began to wobble. I gritted my teeth hard enough to make them ache. Just a little longer. The façade was showing cracks. Details of the real world were starting to edge in, breaking through the imagined scene. I let it go. I sank to the ground, knowing that after that feat I would have nothing more to give. I was spent – despite my earlier energy I'd used very last drop of strength I had in reserve.

I opened my eyes. The others were crowded around Draiken. I couldn't see what they were doing. Their bodies formed a huddle, their backs turned. I looked around us, worried that others would notice our vulnerability and take advantage of it. But funnily enough, even though we were in the middle of the fighting, no one seemed to be paying any attention to us. I got shakily to my feet. The others were still standing around Draiken, silent and motionless. Something was wrong. I started to shuffle towards them, but before I could put one foot in front of the other, Draiken leaped from the circle of people around him. He managed to clear their heads with space to spare. I'd never seen anyone, human or superhuman, manage a jump like that.

He landed centimetres from me, his feet meeting the dirt lightly, as if he were no heavier than a drift of sand. It was the first time I'd seen him up close. He had Syra's nose, her cheekbones and hair. But his eyes were nothing like hers. They seemed endless, twin pools of black water. I took a step back, fighting against the urge to run. If he reached for me now, I would never be able to fight him off. He stood staring back at me, twitching with indecision. The others were close at his back, their hands reaching out to grab him. Sensing their nearness, he gave me a quick smile, then bounded off like a canine on the hunt. He was gone before the others could even change direction.

Chapter Thirty-One

Rogan

We stood together in our odd little circle, an uneasy mix of human and superhuman. Ray refused to look at me, even when I offered my hand in thanks. He nodded stiffly, refusing to return the gesture. The girl looked haggard. Her skin was so pale her freckles stood out in stark contrast, glowing fiercely in the late morning heat. Her red hair was damp, sticking in clumps to her cheeks and neck. She looked ready to collapse.

I moved over and put an arm around her. She leaned into me without protest, the incredible strength I'd seen pouring out of her minutes before gone. I glanced around at the others. The battle seemed to have shifted further away from us. I felt uneasy about the distance. I'd felt more comfortable when the fighting had flanked us, both containing and, oddly, keeping us safe from attacks. The obvious gap made us much easier targets.

Syra came around Dominico's other side, propping her up between us. Even through her weakness, Dominico smiled at each of us in turn. Ray stood aside, his head swivelling in one direction and then another. He looked as nervous as I felt at our exposure.

'We need to move. We can't stay out in the open like this.' His words were directed at us in general. For the first time I felt the discomfiture between him and Syra. There was an odd tension between them, alive and electric. Thankful that, for the moment, there was no time to ponder the reason, I nodded and Syra and I began to shuffle back towards the mayhem of the battle. Ray trailed behind us. I knew without having to look that he was forming a one-man shield, trying to keep an eye out for any possible attacks.

The going was slow, but eventually we were close enough to blend into the chaos. Syra glanced at me over Dominico's head and, without her saying a word, I knew what she was thinking. She looked doubtful about our plan to place ourselves so close to the battle, to risk an attack when we were so vulnerable. Ray pressed closer, closing ranks around Dominico. We kept going, shuffling around the perimeter of the battle, close enough not to be too separate, but with just enough distance to allow us an escape route should we need one.

It came just as I'd lulled myself into a sense of security. I felt a blow at my back, the pain shooting up from my kidneys and carving a path up my spine. I tried to hold onto Dominico but she slipped from my grip, leaving Syra to bear her full weight. I looked up at her as I fell, the pain searing. Syra caught Dominico with ease, but had her arms full when two more men flanked her and flew at her simultaneously. I glimpsed her moment of agonising indecision: whether to drop Dominico and defend herself, or turn away with her precious cargo and flee. Seconds later, brawny arms wrapped around my throat, squeezing the air from my lungs. The world swam, details bleeding into each other and forming a milky haze that rapidly began to darken. I willed my hands from their ineffective clawing, driving both elbows into the torso pressed against me. The body absorbed the blow without flinching, the hold on my throat intensifying. I could no longer make out Syra or the others. I could only see movement, their figures blurring with the landscape.

Panic gripped me. Dominico couldn't defend herself. Syra had been caught by surprise. Gathering every last shred of consciousness, I slipped my arms around my captor, gripping him in a macabre embrace. I bucked as violently as I could. As I'd hoped, the pressure on my windpipe eased. I bucked again, buoyed by my small success. On my third try, I managed to bring my opponent over my head, landing him at my feet. My gun, my gun, where was my gun? It was no longer at my hip. I must've dropped it at some point, although I didn't remember doing it. Now the only weapon I had was my fists.

I forced myself up, only getting as far as my hands and knees. The world swam back into focus, hurtling from shades of grey, to black and white, to the full glory of colour. I retched onto the ground, gasping around the band of fire in my throat. The feeling of oxygen filling my lungs was both euphoric and painful.

I pushed up off my knees, staggering to my feet. I glanced around for my attacker, but he was nowhere to be seen. Apparently he'd found me an unsatisfactory target and gone off in search of more cooperative prey. Syra stood over three men, their bodies dusted with dirt. Taking a look at their faces, I felt a jolt of recognition. They'd trained under me some years back. They'd had promise.

My stomach did a slow, sick roll as I took in their unnatural stillness. I'd been a fool to think we could get to the other side of this pointless war without casualties. Both sides would suffer losses, and no matter what the outcome, none of those sacrifices could ever be justified by those who loved them.

I wanted to kneel beside them, say something in their honour. Acknowledge them as men, and not merely three more casualties among the growing pile of corpses. There was no time.

I crouched beside Syra and Dominico, and lifted the girl into my arms. 'I'll take care of her. I'll make sure she's safe.'

I had to bellow over the raging battle, but paused long enough to be sure Syra had heard me. I stood with Dominico's delicate frame against my chest, her breathing shallow and rapid. But I took that moment to truly look at Syra, to take her in with as much detail as I could commit to memory. And in that final glance, it was clear that she would do only what she needed to in this war. She would contribute the only way she knew how – she would cut down the source of it. She gave me a tiny nod, an acknowledgment, a gesture of farewell. I watched as she turned towards the mayhem, and allowed it to swallow her. Ray glanced at me, meeting my gaze straight on for the first time today. He raised a tentative hand in farewell, and then followed Syra into the heart of the mob.

I tucked Dominico as close to my chest as I could without suffocating her, and ran. I didn't dare look up. I feared that if I made eye contact with anyone, they would be encouraged either to challenge me, or try to bring my headlong flight to a halt. I could afford neither scenario. I knew these grounds and the layout of this city so well that I could bring up a map in my mind. I knocked aside several bodies without looking up to see whom they belonged to. None of the impacts slowed me down. I moved as if I were in a field alone, with nothing but the wind in my ears and the slap of my feet for company. I plummeted down the gentle slope that would lead me to Crane's mansion. Left, and then right. A corpse in my path caught my gaze. A human soldier sprawled on his back. His arms were spread wide, as if he were trying to embrace the very heavens. A hole in his chest, the size of a fist, leaked his lifeblood. I had no desire to pause, but did so anyway. Where the heart of the corpse should have been, there was nothing but a gaping cavity.

I stumbled backwards. In all my years as commander, I'd done nothing but train and prepare. I'd never seen the reality of war, the brutal bloodshed. Something gave way under my foot, soft and yielding. The missing heart compressed beneath my weight. Its presence outside of a body, covered in dirt, was obscene. I stepped back, unable to force my gaze away. I imagined a fist driving into the soldier's torso, the hand opening in a deadly grasp, closing around the heart. I saw it all in the exquisite detail of slow motion, but the soldier would not have seen it coming. I'd seen the superhumans train. I knew the Physicals were stronger and faster than any human could ever hope to be. But I'd only seen their abilities in practice. This gory violence seemed removed from the grace and beauty I'd witnessed in the training ring. It was like the desecration of a holy place – the ruin of something so otherworldly.

Dominico moaned in my arms. I'd forgotten I was carrying her. I'd temporarily abandoned my mission, to stare at the work of the beings my kind were fighting. I needed to get back. I needed to find a way to stop this, before this soldier's corpse was joined by hundreds of others. Shifting the girl carefully to my right side, I knelt beside the soldier, avoiding looking at his face. Inevitably, I would know him, and I couldn't cope with that familiarity right now. The faces of the men Syra had killed were already imprinted on my brain. I didn't need to add another. I reached out and closed the lids on his staring gaze. His skin was already cooling, the life trickling out of him in a tacky pool of blood.

I stood, gathering Dominico against my chest. I looked up for the first time, and realised I was only about two hundred metres from the gates of the mansion. I'd left the battle behind, with only the scattering of corpses in my wake to tell its story.

I looked up at the imposing walls of Crane's home. They kept the mansion from view, the elaborate pattern of the gate offering only a glimpse of its immense and mockingly intact walls. I wasn't sure why I'd brought her back to the site of her imprisonment. Crane would be within its four walls, waiting out the bloodshed he'd ordered until he could leave his sanctuary and lead what was left of his people. I glanced down at the girl. Her eyes opened slightly, her lids fluttering weakly. She nodded an answer to my silent question. Her lips moved, straining to get the words out. I leaned closer. Even with my ear right against her mouth, I couldn't catch a syllable of what she was saying. I felt a hot flash of alarm. Could I really leave her alone in the mansion, unguarded and vulnerable? Was she just weak from exerting herself too far, or was it something more?

'Leave...me...at the...mansion. Will...be...fine'. She tipped her head against my arm, exhausted from her effort. I stood in place, paralysed by indecision. I couldn't have her life on my hands, but I couldn't stand here dithering any longer either. I looked up at the gates again. They stood cold and silent, the gates that would've bordered my childhood had Crane owned up to my parentage. I could hide her somewhere safe until I could make it back. There were plenty of unused rooms and dark corners to hide such a tiny girl. Making up my mind, I forced my feet forward, pushing away the doubts that threatened to root me to the ground once again.

The guards at the gate glared at me with suspicion. 'Open the gates.' I raised Dominico up for inspection, knowing their perch in the watchtower was too high up for them to recognise her.

'We were instructed to keep the gates closed. No one is allowed in.'

I'd expected this. I no longer had the luxury of making my way anywhere I liked without being questioned. If anything, my movements were closely watched, not only by Crane, but by every guard and soldier in this city. They resented my presence, puzzled by the leniency Crane had shown me.

'This girl ran from the civilians and tried to join the battle. She was unauthorised to do so. President Crane instructed me to bring in all those who disobeyed.'

I couldn't see his face clearly enough to read his expression, but I felt his indecision as surely as if we were standing face to face. For a moment I almost pitied him. If he refused me entry, and Crane had indeed issued these instructions, he would be severely punished. But if he allowed me in, and only later learnt of my dishonesty, the consequences would be dire.

The sun had shifted. I could feel its heat beating down on us. Time was passing. I'd been away dangerously long. 'Come on man! I don't have all day.'

The guard couldn't resist the note of authority in my voice. He was like a well-trained dog, one that couldn't disobey his master. As he disappeared from the opening of the watchtower, I smiled grimly. We were impeccably trained, all of us. Crane had done a tremendous job of creating an army of men who no longer thought for themselves, but followed the chain of command like obedient children.

The gate cranked open slowly, its scream of protest working on my already jangled nerves. I nodded my thanks to the guard, careful to keep Dominico's face turned into my chest. Forcing myself to walk calmly but purposefully, I strode towards the massive front doors. The guards on either side tried to block my passage, but no longer caring for pretence, I shoved past them, muttering that Crane was expecting me. I strode through the entrance hall and took the stairs two at a time, wondering as I went if the guards would report my arrival. It no longer mattered. Once Dominico was safely tucked away, I could return to the battle, and find a way to make the men listen.

Syra

The air was thick with dust. We were right in the eye of the battle, and when I wasn't fending off would-be attacks, I was stepping over fallen men, both human and superhuman. I tried not to look at their faces, but the smell of their blood filled my nostrils, thick and overpowering, and my head swivelled of its own accord to follow the scent. A soldier lay curled on his side, his head turned so his blank gaze met the unforgiving white-blue of the sky. I recognised him. He was one of the soldiers who had come to Jozenburg to force Rogan and Dominico to return to Toria. I stared at his lifeless face, trying to recall his name.

Where his abdomen should've been, there was a crater. A quick glance revealed that his innards had been ripped out so cleanly it looked as if they'd been cut away with slow and deliberate care. I shuddered and looked away.

A second soldier lay close by. Because he lay face-down, and I couldn't locate any blood that appeared to be his, I couldn't make out the cause of his death. Not understanding my need to do this, I nudged him over with my foot. With difficulty, I managed to roll him over until he lay on his back. His own hands were clamped around his throat, his grip tight and merciless. He was the victim of a Minder. Only one other superhuman besides Dominico had this ability. I felt a surge of sympathy, knowing that the last thing this soldier had seen was Trey's face.

Ray touched my shoulder. I sensed his urgency and rose. I took one last look at the soldier, a tightness in my chest. I was filled with a sense of my own ineptness. No matter what I did, or how many I avoided killing, this battle had taken on a life of its own. And it would continue, relentless and without mercy, until there was nothing left to fight for.

Ray followed closely at my side. When I had paused beside the fallen bodies, he had paused too, but instead of taking in the lifeless soldiers, he had concentrated on the fighting around us. He knew I was paying less attention to my surroundings than I should.

'Syra. We should keep moving.' He spoke close to my ear, the better to be heard over the pandemonium, but it unsettled me anyway. Although I was glad we were finally communicating and working together again, I felt the sudden change unnerving. I nodded, tearing my eyes away from the dead soldiers. Before I could move away, Ray took hold of my arm and spoke again. 'I know you want to find Draiken. But we're not being of much help here. They're dying, and we're doing nothing to stop it.'

'I can find him alone Ray. You're right – they need at least one of us to be of some help. And we both know the only thing I can do is look for my brother.'

I didn't add that, as much as I needed to find Drake, I also needed to do something that didn't involve my killing anyone. I felt the blood of the three soldiers on my hands, although I'd made sure their deaths were quick and painless. I didn't want any more deaths on my conscience.

Ray paused a moment, then nodded. 'Be careful.' Before I could pull away, he kissed my cheek, lingering so close his features became a blur.

I stepped back, nodding in acknowledgement, unable to force my tongue to form a single word. He plunged back into the fray, his voice carrying over the grunts and screams of battle, calling out instructions to a group of superhumans nearby. His calm and efficiency pulled them together, moulding them into a perfectly aligned team. I turned away, knowing that Ray's impeccable leadership would mean many more deaths. My limbs felt heavy and lethargic and, at that moment, I would've given anything to be anywhere but here. It hadn't escaped me that, of the few corpses I'd examined, none had been superhuman. This fact should've brought me relief, but I felt only dread at what it could mean.

Forcing my limbs out of their stupor, I broke into a run. I ran until I was far enough away from the fighting to reconnect to my inner voice. I started searching for Draiken. I reached out, tentatively probing, pushing aside voices that tried to disrupt my concentration, wading through the general babble. I couldn't tell if he were blocking my attempts, or if I simply couldn't locate him in the chaotic medley of voices. I narrowed my concentration, forcing out all outside noises, zeroing in on voices that sounded similar to Drake's. There. I caught a snippet of something, but as I reached for it the voice cut off.

There was a glimpse of something. A wall, painted a stark white. A steel table, cold to the touch. Then long, seemingly endless passages, gloomy and lit only by occasional, inexplicable patches of light. He was searching for something. Or someone. He called out a word, one that took me a moment to take in. Crane.

I sprinted in the direction of the mansion, my lethargy forgotten, my feet closing the distance so rapidly I barely felt the earth beneath them. I'd seen a glimpse of his plan. The details were murky and undefined, but I felt his keen excitement, and I'd caught a glimpse of a young girl. We had only one young girl in common.

***

There were no guards at the gate of the mansion. I could only presume they were dead. So were the two at the front door, their heads caved in on opposite sides, as if Drake had banged them together in a crude show of his abilities. He could've made their deaths more grotesque, a showcase for what he was capable of, but I could tell that he'd been in a hurry. As I neared the front door, I heard the shuffle of footsteps. I turned towards the sound, tensing for a fight. The guard stalled, startled at my presence. His gaze darted to the corpses of his comrades. He paled, his mouth forming words he couldn't get out. He raised his weapon in a threatening gesture. I raised an eyebrow and gestured towards his fallen colleagues, happy for the moment to take credit for their deaths. I motioned for him to move away while I took a step closer. He turned and ran. I watched him go, grateful for his common sense. I stepped into the mansion cautiously. No sense in alerting Drake, if in fact he was still unaware of my presence.

I moved silently. Having only been within these walls once, I was faced with a maze of long and shadow-laden passages, none of which gave any indication of where they would lead. Quietly, I let out a long breath, collecting myself. The air was fastidiously clean and fresh, much like its owner. None of the dust that permeated Jozenburg had seeped into this house. There was no crunch of grit beneath my shoes, blown in on the frequent dust storms from The Waste. It was clinical and sterile, just the way I imagined the torture chamber he called his laboratory, hulking somewhere above me.

If Rogan had made it here, Dominico would be in one of these many rooms. I looked up at the grandeur of the staircase. It led to the second floor. From what I could tell, there were rooms on this floor as well, although in the gloom I could only make out more shadowy passages. Hesitating, I took a step towards the stairs, straining to hear any sound that would help pinpoint either Drake's or Dominico's location.

I crept up the stairs, my feet light and soundless, a hand trailing the spotless banister. Arriving at the landing, I paused again, not daring to reach out to Draiken in case the contact alerted him to my presence, but growing increasingly panicked and frustrated as the house remained stubbornly silent.

I moved up the second flight, my steps muffled by the ridiculously lush carpet that covered the stairs. I stopped at the top, straining for the slightest sound. I was starting to wonder what I'd been thinking coming here. I needed to stop Draiken, but Rogan had brought Dominico here, and he knew all its dark corners and hiding places. If he hadn't wanted Dominico found, then she would be safe. Draiken had no more knowledge of the design of this place than I did. Maybe the better course of action would be to wait until he came out in the open. Just as I was about to turn back the way I'd come, I heard a thump from the passage to my left.

I crept towards its source, not wanting to rush into an unknown situation. The sound came again, this time accompanied by a scream. Forgetting my own advice, I rushed through a doorway straight ahead. The room was as shadowy as the others, the only source of light a strip of sunlight from beneath the curtains. The room was empty. I stood, puzzled, sure that this was the room the noise had come from. But aside from a bed and a three-legged bedside table, there was nothing filling the space but me. The noise came again but, because I was standing in the room, I realised it was coming from the other side of the wall. A second scream. I raced to the wall, feeling along its smooth surface, pushing against it as if I could somehow force it out of my way.

My fingers found what felt like a latch embedded in the wall. It stuck out only about a centimetre. No one with large hands or thick fingers would ever be able to work it. After several attempts, I managed to flick it up. The wall I was leaning heavily against moved inwards, dropping me unceremoniously into the space beyond. The darkness was even more intense here, but even so I could make out two figures, and knew without doubt that the one standing was Drake. His stance, towering over the figure on the floor, was unmistakable. His head snapped in my direction.

'Drake.' I spoke into the darkness, hoping my voice would stay him for at least a few seconds. I was shaking and unsteady. I needed those few precious moments to compose myself. I was starting to understand there would be no other way out of this. That only two of us would leave this room, and I couldn't allow him to take what was not his. Only now did I truly understand the lengths to which he would go. His mind was wide open and, instead of answering me out loud, he let me in, showing me his thoughts in the kind of detail I didn't want to see.

'It was the girl all along, you see.' He spoke as if we were in the middle of a conversation, uninterrupted by his attempt to strangle me, undivided by his unforgivable choices. 'She's been the key to everything.' He seemed to be working his way around the room, close to the wall. I watched him warily. The room flooded with abrupt light. He stood on the other side of the room, his hand on a light switch. He smiled triumphantly. 'Ah. There you are. Crane can always be counted on to have electricity.'

My gaze moved to the small, crumpled figure on the floor. Instead of the wild tangle of red hair I'd been expecting, I was met with long blonde curls. Her face was hidden in her arms, tucked away from sight. Her tiny shoulders heaved with silent sobs. I took an inadvertent step forward, my feet carrying me of their own volition.

Drake crossed the room in three strides to stand in front of the girl, blocking my view. 'Who is she?' My heart felt enlarged, its beat frantic and alarmingly quick.

He smiled. 'She's the game-changer.' He reached down to stroke her blonde crown. She gave a little shriek and shuffled away from his touch, half emerging from behind his legs.

'Can you believe he's kept her hidden all these years? Like an exotic bird in a cage.'

I could feel the onset of a headache. It was subtle but already uncomfortable, like a pebble caught between my toes. It warned of the slicing pain to come. The discomfort set my nerves on edge, warring for my attention.

'What the hell are you talking about?' I stepped forward, intending on shoving him out of my way. His smile slipped a notch, stopping me in my tracks. His eyes honed in on me, intent and fathomless, and for the second time in one day, I feared him.

The girl had lifted her head, eyes darting between us with a panic so raw its scent filled my nose and mouth with metal. Her eyes were two huge blue orbs in her head. They were threaded with red, the result, I guessed, of her crying.

Lifting my eyes to my brother, I clamped down on my thoughts, closing off the path to my mind.

'What is she the key to?' The question seemed to take him aback, as if he'd expected me to confront him and try to force him to give her up. His shoulders relaxed. There was the almost imperceptible release of tension in his body, evident only in the quiet exhale of his breath. I forced myself to mimic him, not wanting to alert him to my intentions.

'Everything Sy. I thought Dominico was it, and she would've been, if Crane hadn't used his serum on her. By the time I could've used her, he'd made sure she was too weak to be of any use to anyone. I think that's why he did it – to make sure she wouldn't turn on him and back us instead. But to keep your own daughter locked up like an animal, well, I think even the most loyal of Crane's soldiers would question that.'

'Daughter?' I blinked. In all the time Crane had ruled this city, no one had ever mentioned a wife or partner, much less a daughter. 'But...how?'

He shook his head, looking down at the terrified girl, as if marvelling at her existence. 'I don't know, but I'm planning to find out.'

He hunched down next to her and touched her shoulder. She let out a loud sob and scrambled to her feet, bolting for the door. Her pitiful attempt to escape tore at my heart. Drake was on her like a cat on its prey, his movements so fluid and fast his form became a blur. 'So eager! Yes little one, let us go to your father. Do you know where he is?'

His hand was on her shoulder, his grip tight enough to halt her and keep her in place, but not quite firm enough to snap her shoulder. He was dangerously close, and sensing it, the girl broke down completely, her wails filling the tiny room until I felt surrounded and accosted by the noise. Drake stood there, careful to keep her from bolting again, but in no hurry to silence her, his face filling with child-like glee.

A deep instinct told me to make a grab for the girl and run. It filled my blood with its intent, my limbs tensing to spring at him and take him down. It screamed that if I didn't do it now, it would be too late, and the consequences would be irreparable. Before I could make my move, a figure appeared in the doorway. His usually immaculate pants were stained and wrinkled, and his iron composure shattered when he took in the scene.

'Crane. How nice of you to join us,' Drake said.

Chapter Thirty-Two

Dominico

I felt fragile enough to break. I lay on the unmade bed, the dirt of the mattress filling my nose. The room was dark and musty, the only window covered by the same hideous curtains I'd seen throughout the mansion. It gave me the tiniest twinge of satisfaction to see that with this one detail, at least, Crane didn't have it all.

I was exhausted, but I couldn't sleep. Closing my eyes only made me more aware of the grit in them, like tiny grains of sand beneath my lids. I wanted to sleep so badly, to drift away from here and not have to worry that, at any moment, someone would open the door to this abandoned room and find me here.

The fear was the worst. It hunkered down in my mind, whispering poisonous thoughts, forcing me to look death in the eye. It felt like dying, although I couldn't say for sure. My breath came with extreme effort, each exhalation riding on a wheeze. My body felt heavy and leaden, but at the same time I was sure that, if I rolled off this bed, I would break a bone. I couldn't even lift a hand to my face. Small droplets of sweat ran down my cheeks like tears.

I wondered if my absence meant something. Could I have made a difference if I'd been my old self? Could I have killed, knowing that in some way, I belonged to both, opposing, sides? I hated not knowing. I hated that I'd left Mom's side, only to be stuck here and of no help to anyone.

I stared into the darkness, the quiet maddening. How did Crane live here alone, with his daughter locked away in the middle of this wasteful mansion, and not go crazy from the silence? How could he stand the solitude?

I wanted to shift off my right side. It was the position Rogan had laid me down in, but now I couldn't find the strength to roll over. My arm had gone numb. It felt as if I were lying on a phantom limb, one that had been cut off years ago. I tried anyway, wanting to get more comfortable, unsure how long I would lie here before someone came to get me. If they came to get me. The thought made my stomach curl in on itself, wondering if I would lie here and starve to death or die of thirst, a corpse that would slowly rot away until it was nothing more than a husk. I shoved the thought away, and summoned all the willpower I had to roll off my right side. I managed it on the first try, and my dead arm came to life with the prickling of pins and needles.

A soft thud sounded below me. At first I was sure I'd imagined it, just so I could end the silence. But then it came again, a hard thud and then a series of smaller ones, as if someone had fallen and then taken off running. A muffled scream followed the footsteps, and then another thump, as if they'd fallen again. I lifted my head with difficulty, straining to hear. Another small shriek, high-pitched and filled with fear, the scream of a child. Layla. I forced myself up, my arms shaking with the effort. I shoved myself off the bed, convinced that the snap of a bone would follow, but I landed in a graceless heap, unhurt.

I struggled to my feet, forcing my legs to lock into place and keep me standing. I could feel my knees curving inwards, but I forced my feet forward, each trembling step a small triumph. I wobbled to the door, cracking it open carefully and using it as a crutch. I looked down the passage. The room I was in was at the far end, with two doors on each side of the passage stretching ahead of me. It curved left and right, disappearing from view. I hoped that on the other side of one of those curves I would find the staircase.

Another small shriek, high and desperate. Then another voice, a woman, yelling. I froze with my hand on the doorway. I was sure the voice belonged to Syra. What was she doing here? I willed myself out of the room, using the walls for support as I tottered along the passage. The point where it opened on to other rooms seemed to shrink away, instead of drawing closer. I shook with the effort of each step, sweat pouring down my face in rivulets of salty tears. I couldn't risk taking my hand away from the wall to brush them away, so they flooded into my eyes, blurring the length of the passage into a wavering hallway.

I finally reached the end of it. A wide staircase was on my left. Tears of relief filled my eyes. Taking in the number of stairs I would need to walk down, and the narrowness of each step, my relief was short-lived, drying up like a small puddle in the heat of the sun. How was I going to get down them without risking breaking my neck? And more to the point, how was I going to be of any use to Syra when I got there?

I stopped for a second, leaning my back against the wall, closing my eyes against the wave of dizziness that rushed over me. I pushed away a nagging awareness of the passing of time. I drew a deep breath, in, out, until the dizziness passed. I pictured Mom in the only home I'd ever know in this city. I took in the beautiful drop of blonde hair, the clear skin, the sparkling eyes. I went back further, thinking about the one and only time she had ever said anything positive about my abilities. She'd come into my bedroom just before bedtime, looking worried. She'd sat on the edge of my bed and reached over to smooth my curls off my forehead. I'd pulled back from her touch, irritated by an argument we'd had earlier. She had looked at me sadly, her hand dropping to the faded blue duvet cover.

'Domo. I know you think I hate that you're different.' I'd started to interrupt her, but she held up a hand, her expression pleading for understanding. 'You are more than your abilities. Besides your image-projection, and your mind control, you'll find you have great inner strength. You've practised your abilities in   secret –' I opened my mouth to protest but she kept going, ignoring my attempt to get a word in. 'And you've had to keep them hidden. I think all of that has shaped you in ways you have yet to discover. I think one day, when you are unable to take one step further, you'll find just how deep those reserves go.' She had patted my hand and closed the door behind her, leaving me staring after her.

**

I hoped to heaven my mother would prove to be right. I pushed myself away from the wall, willing myself to cross the space to get to the head of the stairs. My legs shook beneath me, but I took one step at a time anyway, counting them in my head, telling myself I was nearly there, just one more stair. By the time I reached the ground floor my body was slick with sweat. I felt like a new-born calf just finding its feet. Turning to my left, I strained to hear anything more, but the house was once again draped in silence.

Syra

Crane stood in the doorway, his eyes glazed with fury. 'Give her to me. Now.' He spoke deliberately, enunciating each syllable. I could tell he was fighting for control, his usual composure gone.

Drake smiled at him, the gesture friendly and open, as if he were conversing with an old friend. 'So you admit she's yours?'

The colour drained from his face, leaving him with a sickly pallor. Watching the emotions flit across his face, I realised that he hadn't considered the extent of Draiken's knowledge. He'd thought that Draiken had found her accidentally, and had no idea of her worth.

'Please.' His voice shook with barely concealed panic, his shaking hands reaching out in supplication.

Drake frowned. 'Wait a minute. I'm a little confused. Why would you want her now, when you've kept her like a prisoner in this place? Like a dirty secret?' He tipped the girl's chin upward with his index finger. Tears streamed down her cheeks, silent and rapid. 'Why does he hide you away? Hmm?'

Crane took two steps into the room, his body vibrating with anger and fear. 'I have numerous enemies. A child could serve as a perfect bargaining tool. She would become a target. I've kept her locked away for her own protection.'

Drake had tasted the lie as surely as I had, yet his expression remained impassive. He nodded, as if accepting Crane's explanation. He turned back to the girl, wiping at her tears with his thumb. Another observer might have interpreted the gesture as one of compassion, but I felt Drake's pent-up glee, his delight in taunting Crane. Crane took another step. The room was small enough that if he took another two, he'd be toe to toe with Drake.

Drake held up a hand in warning. 'Not an inch closer, understand?' He looked at Crane, tipping his head to the side, considering him. 'Do you think I can't tell when you're lying?' His tone was pleasant, mellow and coaxing. It threw Crane off, giving him a moment of false security. His tension eased, but only until he grasped the meaning of Drake's words.

He grew so still he looked as if he'd been carved out of rock. I could hear his thoughts as surely as if he'd spoken them aloud. He was scrabbling to lock them down and store them away from Drake's reach. He turned to me, his eyes pleading. 'Syra. She's the only child I've -' He trailed off, drawing a shuddering breath. 'Give her to me.'

If I'd been human, I imagine I would've been taken in by Crane's words and expression. But because I could dig beyond the boundaries of dialogue and the intricacies of body language, I knew he was lying. I felt the prickle of it on my skin, its deep copper edge heavy on my tongue.

I glanced at Drake. When we'd first arrived at the Creator's laboratory, he'd often told us that being one of a pair of twins was like having a copy of yourself out in the world. He explained that our connection would always be stronger than those of mere siblings. Even as children, we'd been able to gauge each other's moods, and hold entire conversations in silence. But not until our conversion were we capable of reading each other's thoughts like words on a page. And at this moment, I could read his thoughts as easily as if they were my own.

I looked back at Crane, my ongoing silence making him uneasy. He'd considered me the reasonable one, the one to bargain with. But Drake and I shared an intuition that Crane was hiding something, that his desperation to get his child away from us was not just a protective paternal instinct. His eyes were wild with frustration, his fists clenched into knuckles of fury.

The room was becoming desperately close. The window was shut tight, allowing no air circulation. The accumulated warmth of four bodies heated the room as effectively as if the curtains were wide open. Sweat was gathering under my arms, the droplets sliding down my sides. The discomfort was both maddening and lulling, the heat forming a cocoon that invited sleep.

I circled the room carefully, keeping an eye on both Draiken and Crane. Drake showed no sign of being uneasy at my approach, so I kept moving until I was standing next to him, the two of us forming a superhuman barrier between Crane and his daughter.

'Tell us the truth, Crane. There's something more to this than a father-child relationship. I get the feeling you've kept her hidden away more to protect yourself than her. So what's the big secret?'

Crane shook his head. I could feel him battling against his panic, trying to overlay it with a veneer of calm. I watched as he took a deep breath. On the exhale he launched himself across the room. It was so unexpected that he succeeded in knocking us aside, creating a gap just large enough to reach through and grab hold of his girl. His cry of triumph was short-lived. No sooner had he laid his hands on her than Drake had locked a hand around his throat, lifting him from his crouched position until his feet left the floor, his strangled breath echoing in the room.

The little girl shot to her feet. 'Let him go! Let him go!'

I felt a curious heat that had nothing to do with the stuffiness of the room. It was as if a small globe of invisible fire had formed around the girl, whipping itself into a circle of heat so intense the room felt robbed of oxygen. I felt the push just as she aimed it at Drake. Before I could close the distance between us, his feet gave out beneath him. He crumbled, taking Crane with him. I stared at the girl, the pieces falling into place and forming a picture of perfect clarity.

Free of Drake's grip, Crane stumbled to his feet, his hands clutching at his throat as if he could somehow open the airway wider. Drake remained on the floor, his laughter filling the room with a manic trill. He got to his feet, still laughing. His mood remained unchanged even when the little girl flew into her father's arms, sobbing. Crane looked ready to bolt now that he had his prize, but I couldn't get myself to move.

Finally Drake fell silent, still grinning like a fool. 'She's one of us.'

'She belongs to me,' Crane snarled. 'She has nothing to do with your kind.'

Drake motioned to the girl. 'Did you make her like this? Was she one of your first experiments?'

Crane clutched her to him, her face pressed to his chest. She was too close to him. I heard the catch of her breath as she struggled against Crane's stranglehold. I called out a warning, but the force of it died on my lips when another figure rushed into the room, gun aloft and ready for action. It was the young guard I'd encountered outside the mansion. I stifled the urge to groan. He'd escaped what he'd considered certain death and now here he was again, rushing into its arms for the second time.

'President Crane.' He lowered his gun and pointed it at us,

motioning for Crane to move behind him. His gaze flitted to his leader, then lingered as he took in the girl's presence.

Drake sighed heavily. 'Why don't you just go back to wherever it is you came from? We have business to attend to here.'

The snap of the gun being cocked was Drake's answer. I reached for the man's thoughts, gently probing into his mind with the care a parent would use to tend to their wounded child. He was deeply afraid, although he was hiding it well. His confusion over the girl's presence was breaking his concentration, but he desired, above all, to be a hero. To be lifted out of the ranks of his fellow colleagues, to be a celebrated man. He was merely a guard, but he longed for the esteemed title of soldier.

The girl, meanwhile, had managed to pull away from the folds of Crane's shirt. Her large blue eyes moved around the room from the protection of her father's embrace. She watched us with fear and curiosity, alert for any attempt to harm her father again.

Crane edged towards the guard, shuffling the girl along with him. Drake watched him with vague amusement. There was nowhere for him to hide now. Drake crossed the room in two graceful bounds, his movements that of an unparalleled predator, one who knows he has nothing to fear from another living creature. He arrived in front of the guard before the man could even register Drake's move. Placing his hands on each of the guard's shoulders, he pushed him aside with a surprising gentleness, like a man asking a friend to step aside. The guard obeyed, his entire being quivering with fear.

Drake reached for the girl, expecting a fight. Instead, Crane shoved the girl from his embrace to the guard's. 'Take her! Now!' He then threw himself at Drake, latching onto him like a ravenous insect. He held a syringe aloft, one that contained a strange-looking liquid.

The guard scooped up the little girl and disappeared from the room. I was too distracted by what the syringe might contain to attempt to stop them. Crane brandished it like a weapon, and a coldness crept over me. I knew what was in it.

'Drake! Don't struggle.' Crane eyed me, a smile creeping across his face.

'Unless you want to be human again, I suggest you follow her advice.'

Drake's eyes met mine. He could snap Crane's arm in one move, but the needle was hovering too close to Drake's skin. All it would take was a moment of contact, and Crane would press that plunger home.

I knew he was simply buying time. He couldn't hope to contain us both for long. My timing had to be perfect. I waited a beat, then another. Crane's gaze moved over my shoulder to the doorway, and I sprang.

Rogan

I'd achieved little since leaving Dominico. I'd tried talking to several of the men, but they'd all looked at me like I was insane, wanting a little chat while the battle heaved around us. The more I considered my plan, the more I could see it had more holes than a house in the poor section of Toria. I'd done nothing more than dodge attacks and talk pointlessly into the ears of reluctant and fearful men. I was paralysed not by fear, but by being unable to kill on either side. What use was a commander who wouldn't draw his weapon?

As I stood there, I realised the crowd around me was starting to move as one, a vast wave of bodies all rushing in the same direction. The reaction of the mob puzzled me at first – what would they be collectively running from? I tried to see over their heads. One of the youngest soldiers, Amos, was running towards me. Before he could pass, I grabbed his arm and yanked him to a stop.

'What's going on?'

He clawed frantically at my hand, trying to free himself. I shook him hard enough to rattle his teeth, forcing him to focus on me.

'Why is everyone running?'

He lifted a shaking finger, pointing behind me. Five of the massive, misshapen superhumans Crane had created were tearing towards us. Despite their bulk, they moved with the grace of creatures built for speed. Still gripping Amos's arm, I ran with him, joining the mass retreat.

The earth vibrated beneath my feet. Glancing briefly behind me, I realised they were moving faster than seemed possible, closing the distance between them and us with ease. A soldier flew over us, a wingless bird. His blood spattered us like a grisly rain. He landed a metre or two ahead, forcing me to veer around him.

They reached the fringes of the crowd in one bound and began tearing through the mass of people. Grown men were lifted as easily as infants, and tossed aside. I watched a superhuman grab a nearby soldier with both meaty fists. The soldier's head was swallowed by a mass of fingers and knuckles. The Superhuman lifted the soldier off his feet, dangling him like a tasty morsel. He slammed the soldier against the ground, his hands still clamped around his victim's head. It took only one blow. The soldier lay in the dirt, forgotten and trampled by the panicked feet of his comrades.

Now was my time. I felt no pity for these creatures, only for the beings they used to be. Their humanity had been lost within the violent bulk of these monsters. They had lost their claim on their bodies and minds. They had become soulless weapons, uncontrollable and unstoppable. I didn't doubt that when they had nothing left to kill, they would turn on each other. Crane had unleashed them with no thought for how he would rein them in when they had completed what he'd created them for.

The city wall was ahead of us. The soldiers who reached it first cowered against it. The mutations had backed us against the thing that was intended to keep us safe. We were trapped like rats, our backs to the wall. I yelled over the cacophony of sound, motioning to the closest group of soldiers.

'Form a line!' The men stared at me with blank eyes, bodies unable to obey through their fear. 'Do it now! Form a line!'

One soldier took a tentative step forward, as if testing the stability of his legs. That was all it took for the others to fall into line, their resolve strengthening with the habit of years of training.

'Raise your weapons. Aim for their heads.'

The beasts were almost on us, towering over us like creatures from a child's nightmare. I raised my own gun, my mind clear of everything except the orb of the creature's head.

'Fire!'

Ten guns fired simultaneously. Some had shot at the same target in pairs, others in trios. The gunshots seemed to do little more than enrage them. Not one fell back a step.

'Keep firing!'

Out of the corner of my eye I saw one of the soldiers drop his gun. It fell from his trembling hands and he scrabbled in the dirt to retrieve it. He dropped it a second time. Those around him watched, diverted by his display of fear. Their hesitation brought the beasts too close to get a clear head shot.

'Run between them. Quickly.'

Although they were uncannily fast for their size, they still couldn't change direction quickly enough. I made a dash for it, just managing to dodge their massive hands. I glanced about. The men were still with me. We ran until we had enough distance then, turning as one, the men reloaded and fired. This time, one of the beasts raised his hands to his head, touching a small wound. A red stream trickled down across his face. It seemed the men had all fired at the same Superhuman. While it would've been a sensible plan had there been only one, it meant the other four were still advancing, untouched.

The men no longer needed my encouragement or instruction. They worked together, dodging, reloading, firing. Instinctively, the injured superhuman had fallen back a few steps. He kept touching the wound, seemingly bewildered and newly enraged each time his fingers came away marked with blood.

The men fired together at the beast nearest to us. I realised with a growing horror that it had once been a woman, if its shape and longer hair were anything to go by. Her movements were the same as the others – driven by a bloodthirsty and unforgiving need to kill. The bullets tore into her, one going slightly astray and hitting her in the throat instead of the head. The wound spurted blood in waves. She wavered for a moment, as if unsure of what had happened. Her hands wandered to her throat, swiping at the wound. There was no time for panic. She simply dropped like a fallen boulder, scattering men as they scrambled to avoid being crushed by her corpse.

The four remaining beasts stared at their fallen comrade. Their temporary hesitation gave us the narrow gap we needed.

'Their throats. Go for their throats.'

Guns were loaded and snapped into place with a precision inspired by our small victory. The spray of bullets that followed miraculously hit their mark, cutting down two more of the superhumans in quick succession. The remaining two panicked. They ran straight into the final volley fire, their simultaneous collapse sending a massive vibration through the earth.

There was a long silence. It felt as if the entire battle had paused to observe the fall of these grotesque giants. The men stood around in disbelief, unable to absorb the enormity of their victory. There was an odd smatter of applause from the other soldiers, as if we'd just performed some amazing feat for their entertainment. My gun drooped from my hand, my body limp as the adrenaline rushed out of me. I was vaguely aware of the battle raging on. A shot rang through the air. A superhuman and a soldier crashed into each other as the former launched himself at the latter. I felt weary to the marrow of my bones. It felt as if there would be no end to this.

Dominico

I stumbled over the final stair. The warning buzz in my ears and the gathering blackness meant I was close to passing out. I leaned against the rail, breathing through the wave of dizziness, forcing myself to stay on my feet. I straightened slowly, shoving away the feeling that I was already too late, that all of this stumbling and clawing would be pointless when I got there. I finally rounded the corner, heading towards the room I was sure they were in. When I reached it, I found it empty. I leaned heavily against the doorway, fighting back tears of frustration and pain.

A hand grabbed at mine. I turned so quickly the room swooped. I stumbled, desperately trying to make out who was behind me. The hand let go. I squinted through my fatigue and dizziness. A tiny girl came into focus.

'Layla.' She took a hasty step back, eyes wide. I wanted to grab her and squeeze her until I made myself believe she was really standing right here in front of me. But judging from the alarm on her face, I knew sudden physical contact might make her run.

'What are you doing out of your room?'

'I want to help.' She said it so quietly I was sure I'd misheard her.

'You what?'

She raised her chin, her eyes meeting mine. 'I'm going to help.'

I took her hand. I moved slowly and deliberately, watching her carefully. The last thing I needed was to scare her off.

'You're doing the right thing. Thank you.'

We stepped out into the passage again, but before we could go one step further, two figures ran at us, crowding us back into the cramped room.

'Not so fast. Back up, now.'

Draiken herded us into the room, blocking the doorway. Syra followed him in, her eyes meeting mine in a silent reassurance. I didn't know what to make of finding them together like this, but I knew I had to trust Syra. Without that, we were all on our own.

Layla cowered behind me, her small hands clutching at mine, her skin so cold it sent a shiver through me.

'There you are.' Draiken addressed Layla, which made my alarm levels spike. The way he was staring at her, with such open fascination, made me think he knew who she was.

'Step aside.' He motioned to me. Layla clung even harder, her fingers wrapping around mine so tightly I felt them go numb.

I glanced over his shoulder at Syra for help. She was watching him carefully. She looked like she was biding her time, waiting for the right opportunity. As much as I trusted her, I didn't trust his proximity to Layla.

I took a step back, forcing Layla to back up.

'No.'

Draiken's expression switched to one of amusement. 'It's sweet you want to protect her, but really, you must know you can't fight me. Move.'

'I have to take her out of the mansion. She can help us end this.' I spoke to Syra over Draiken's shoulder, pretending he wasn't there. She crossed the room, moving in front of Draiken and cutting him off from Layla and me. She placed a hand on my shoulder, pushing us towards the door.

'What are you doing?' Draiken's voice boomed behind us. I ignored him and kept going. One foot in front of the other.

'You heard her,' Syra replied. 'We need to expose Crane for what he really is. It's a chance to stop the fighting.'

I felt rather than saw Draiken move across the room. He was in front of me before I could draw my next breath, before my left foot could take another step. He loomed over me, his silent threat clear. 'You're not taking her anywhere. Let them kill each other. Crane will call a stop to it soon enough.'

I looked up at him, knowing that if he forced me aside I would have no choice but to let him take Layla. I was no match for him, not while I was in this state.

'Drake,' Syra said. He glanced at her, his expression stony. 'This is our chance. We can work something out with the humans now, while there are still some of them left. They're suffering huge losses. You know we can't survive without them.'

Syra's eyes met mine briefly, before darting back to Draiken.

He shook his head. 'Crane and I had a deal. He'll call off the fighting when he sees fit. When the humans have lost just enough to warrant making a deal with us.'

'Crane isn't in his right mind. He won't be giving orders, Drake. Anyone can see that.'

'He's doing what needs to be done. He's a leader. He has to lead.'

'Listen to you, Drake. Why are you defending him? He's our enemy. He's the reason we're here in the first place. Your dealings with him have put us all in danger. You betrayed us.'

I could tell from Syra's clenched fists that this conversation was getting away from her. I imagined she'd wanted to avoid this particular confrontation for the moment, and had only wanted to talk him into allowing me to pass.

He didn't seem to have heard her. He planted himself in front of me, immovable. Although his face remained impassive, I wasn't fooled into thinking he'd remain that way if I tried to get past him. He glanced briefly at Syra before his gaze darted back to me, as though afraid that if he took his eyes off me for too long, I'd disappear like smoke.

'You said yourself we needed humans. With our birth rate, we'll die out in a couple of decades. That's something you told me. Without the humans, we'll have no one to turn. Our future numbers are dropping with every human life that's spilled out there.'

I watched as Draiken's expression shifted. Something moved across his face, and for a minute I thought he'd be swayed by Syra's logic, and step aside.

'So now you agree with me? After all the times you fought me on exactly this?' His arm shot out and he grabbed me, his fingers digging into my arms. His grip was brutal. He shoved me aside, advancing on Layla with such menace etched into his face I felt my stomach curl with fear.

'Drake. Stop. Leave her alone. You need to let Dominico take the girl.'

Draiken shook his head vehemently. 'If I break my part of the deal, then he has no reason to honour his. He promised me numbers when this was all over. The only way to make them agree to being turned is to threaten their numbers so much that they fear extinction. Until enough of them have died, none of us are leaving this room.'

I looked at Syra. I watched her face, knowing she must be going through agony trying to decide what to do. I sensed the moment she made up her mind. Her expression set. The air in the room seemed to shift, as if in preparation.

Chapter Thirty-Three

Syra

I'd tried to avoid thinking about it, although it had come up again and again, each time in a different guise. Each time I'd brushed it aside, burying it deep so I wouldn't have to acknowledge it. But it remained there, stubborn and irrefutable, surfacing more frequently as the gap grew between Draiken and me. There was no avoiding it now. He stood between me and the door, between Dominico and the rapidly narrowing chance we had to stop the battle raging on beyond these walls. I wished I'd been able to prevent all this. That I'd been able to talk Draiken round to my way of thinking. I should've tried harder. I should've pushed further. If I had, maybe we wouldn't be here, facing off, leaving me with the choice I'd dreaded all along.

'Drake, please. I'm asking you one last time. Step aside. Let us do this.'

He laughed, the sound high and strangled. For the first time since this confrontation had started, I sensed the fear he'd buried beneath his bravado. 'Don't you understand? If I break this deal with Crane, I'll be hunted until I'm dead. There will be no future for me. I have no more alliances. I've been living like a rat since leaving Jozenburg, scratching for scraps and stuck in that hole while trying to secure a future for us.'

'For us? Please. You were thinking only of your survival. You sold us out to make a deal with our direct enemy.' I took one step closer, testing his reaction. He neither warned me off, nor backed away. I lowered my voice, softening my tone, careful to keep my thoughts hidden. 'We're family Drake. If you do this for us, I'll make sure everyone knows. I'll make you the hero. I'll convince them to let you and the others come home.'

I hated myself then. Hated that my priority was no longer him. Hated that the bond between us had become fragile. Most of all I hated that he'd given me no choice.

I glanced at Dominico. Drake's attention was on me. I gave her a nod, quick and decisive, hoping she would know what I meant. Without hesitation, she grabbed Layla's arm and ran.

Too late, Drake tried to snatch at Layla's departing back. His hand groped at air. I had only seconds before he kicked into gear, and then it would be a race between us, one I knew I could win only by the smallest margin. I flew across the room and locked my arms around him in a violent embrace. As children, when we'd been newly turned by the Creator, we'd often wrestled, each trying to overpower the other, amazed by our new abilities. I'd been stronger every time, but Drake never gave up trying to outdo me. We hadn't wrestled for a long time. Drake had kept his talents finely-tuned, while I had taken mine for granted, until war had seemed inevitable. My talents were more advanced, but I was less practised than he was.

He struggled, almost succeeding in breaking my hold. Through the doorway, there was no sign of the girls. I hoped that meant that they were out of the house and running towards the battle, and that Dominico hadn't collapsed only metres from here.

I pulled him in tighter, squeezing him against me, careful not to do it so hard that he'd be unable to breathe. I couldn't remember the last time we'd stood together this close, his breath becoming mine, our bodies melding together in a tie of blood and tissue and bone.

'Let me go!' He yelled straight into my ear. I tilted my head away from him, my ear ringing. 'Drake, stop struggling. Dominico has to do this. It'll be okay, I promise Drake. I'll find a way.' A sob filled my throat, huge and choking. I forced it back. If I let it escape now I would break.

He bolted from my arms. He made for the door in a blur of movement. I blinked, and he was gone.

Instinct took over. My feet broke into a sprint and I raced after him, but he had already disappeared from view. I could only hear the slap of his feet against the earth, the sharp inhale and exhale of his breath.

A door was ripped from its hinges and flew at me. I ducked and skidded as it sailed over my head, crashing into the staircase behind me. The front doorway was a gaping hole, like a tooth missing from an open mouth.

I broke out of Crane's mansion and into the daylight. Stunned by the brightness of the afternoon, I ran blindly after Drake, following the sound of his footsteps. I blinked rapidly, willing my vision to clear. I stumbled several times, nearly falling to my knees. Fleetingly, and through the haze of the day's heat, I glimpsed the corpses I was dodging and tripping over.

My eyes were adjusting, and my surroundings came into sharp focus. I was on the fringe of the battle, about to plunge into the violent push and pull of the fight. The small crumb of hope I'd clung to vanished. It would take me too long to find him now. I'd wanted to catch him before he melded in with the heave of the mob. The girls were nowhere in sight either. I didn't know whether to be relieved or terrified.

Dominico

I'd lost her. Of all the moments to lose focus. One minute she'd been just in front of me, darting like a deranged butterfly, the next, she was gone. I couldn't keep pushing through the crowd, not knowing which way she'd gone. I stopped, panting. I'd lost her because I couldn't keep up. For every moment of weakness, my anger towards Crane trebled. It wasn't supposed to be like this. I was supposed to have been the key to all this, the one everyone believed would save them. And here I was, unable to carry out even this simple task while Syra held Draiken off.

What the hell were we going to do, anyway? Stand in the middle of the brawl and scream our heads off, in the hope that someone would look up and hear us out? So stupid. Someone hit me from behind, a clumsy offhand blow I knew hadn't been meant for me. All the same, I needed to get out of range. Considering my current state, arming myself seemed like a good idea. I glanced around, trying to see if any guns had been dropped nearby, while still keeping an eye on my surroundings. A human soldier, straightening from his crouch over a fallen comrade, raised a hand to his forehead. He was close enough for me to see the blood he left behind. He seemed to be marking himself deliberately with the blood of his fellow fighter, like those warriors we'd read about in school. Before battle, they would draw symbols on their faces. Symbols they believed would protect and strengthen them. The soldier looked up, and his gaze locked on mine.

He raised his gun. He was close enough for it to be an easy shot, and all I could think about was that, if I died now, my entire existence would've amounted to nothing. Kat's death would mean nothing. Mom and Dad's suffering would be in vain. Not knowing what else to do, I ran. I ducked and dived through the bodies, hoping that once his chance at a clear shot was gone, he wouldn't risk killing someone from his side.

I caught sight of Rogan. He was fighting off a superhuman, a Physical who was trying to lock his arms around Rogan's neck. Rogan was rapidly tiring, and it wouldn't be long before the superhuman succeeded in breaking his neck. I gathered myself, focusing inward. It wouldn't take that much out of me to push off one superhuman, but it would be another thing to keep fighting him off. I gave a hard shove, and the superhuman's grip weakened. Rogan twisted around to face his opponent. He raised his gun. For a long, sickening moment, I thought Rogan was going to shoot him. Instead, he used his height advantage and clubbed him in the face instead. The superhuman fell, unconscious.

I watched his mouth form my name. He grabbed me in a hug. It felt like his arms were long enough to go around me twice. The thought brought me a strange comfort.

I wanted to tell him about Layla, but now wasn't the time. I pulled on his arm and we shoved through the mob, Rogan's gun trained ahead of us. A moment later, we'd managed to break free from the worst of the fighting. Just ahead of us, a group of soldiers were clumped together. Their backs were turned to the battle. Rogan and I exchanged a glance. They were so focused on the centre of their circle that we could probably incapacitate all of them before they could even make a move. We drew closer. I touched Rogan's arm, wanting to get my thought across. But Rogan's attention was now being drawn by whatever the soldiers were looking at. I couldn't see a thing over their heads, but we were getting too close for comfort, and I tightened my grip in warning.

Instead of stopping, or even pausing, he pushed ahead, dragging me along behind him. What the hell was wrong with him? He shoved the soldiers out of his way, heedless of their protests. Their guns followed our progress, cocked and ready. Rogan came to a stop. He slipped out of my grasp, reaching into the centre of the circle. I caught a glimpse of a blonde crown. Layla cried out our names, the sweetest sound I'd ever heard.

I glanced around at the circle of soldiers. They watched us warily, their guns at the ready. Layla grabbed my hands, and I turned my focus to her, all too aware of the threat we faced.

'I tried to come. But there were three soldiers at my door. Daddy was worried after those superhumans tried to take me.' I shook my head, confused. She wrung her hands, her eyes filled with worry. 'I wanted to get here before it started, but first the superhumans found me, and then the soldiers put me back in my room.' Now wasn't the time for questions. I squeezed her hands. They were ice-cold.

'It's okay.' I rubbed her hands, trying to warm them. 'You're here now.' I glanced at Rogan. None of us stated the obvious. There didn't seem to be much she could do now. The war seemed too far gone. Still, the group surrounding us could be told. If they believed us, they could spread the word. We had to try.

I opened my mouth to speak. The soldier closest to me snapped a salute. Confused, I looked to my left. Crane was moving through the group, parting them in a silent wave. He looked at the soldier who'd acknowledged him. He spoke quietly, but I still caught his words.

'What is she doing here? I put you in charge of keeping her in the mansion. That was your only job.'

His voice had risen, and several of the other soldiers looked up. I could tell from their expressions that they had no idea who Layla was, or what her connection to Crane was.

'Sir, I –'

Crane cut him short with a look. He reached out a hand to Layla. 'Come. You must go back to your room until this is all over.'

I started to say something, but my attention was drawn to the mass movement I caught out of the corner of my eye. A group of superhumans were coming our way. None of Draiken's group, fortunately, but it still meant trouble. They'd obviously been watching us, and were taking their opportunity to attack while our attention was diverted. I touched Rogan's arm, not wanting to alarm the soldiers.

He followed my gaze. They knew we'd seen them, which only accelerated their approach. I turned back to Layla. She was refusing to take Crane's hand. His face flushed. His temper felt close, on the verge of breaking through the thin layer of control which remained, like a bird pecking at the inside of its shell.

'Layla. Come now.' His words were loud, unnecessarily so. Layla shied away from him. She shifted until she was closer to us. Her movement made the soldiers shift too, the circle closing even more. The group of superhumans had paused. The soldiers had still not seen them. We were balanced in this moment, thin as the blade of a knife. I stood there, the heat of many bodies making me sweat, wanting something to happen just to break the tension, but dreading it all the same.

The soldier who had been in charge of watching Layla stepped forward. 'Sir...' But Crane was beyond listening. He grabbed Layla's arm, his fingers closing around her flesh with such force she cried out. He yanked her towards him. 'Daddy, Daddy, no!' In her panic, she pushed back at him, but without laying a finger on him. He flew back a metre or two, bumping into the soldiers behind him.

The realisation dawned on one soldier's face, and then the next, like lights flicking on in a house, one room at a time. Crane, having lost all control, stepped forward again and lashed out, his hand connecting with her delicate cheek. 'I kept you away from all of this for your own protection! Don't you see that? Now it's done – you'll never be safe again.'

Rogan stepped forward, forcing Crane to step away from Layla. He pushed her gently towards me, and I moved her behind me. The silence that followed was broken only by Layla's quiet sobs. The soldiers stood where they were, their eyes moving between Crane and Layla, our presence all but forgotten. Their faces were heavy with shock, and I waited, knowing that soon a sense of betrayal would set in. I glanced over my shoulders. The superhumans had heard every word. They looked as shocked and outraged as the soldiers, but they too had not moved a muscle, waiting out their enemies.

Unable to bear the tension one second longer, I stepped into the circle, refocusing the group's attention on me.

'We don't know how Layla came to be. But as I'm sure you've

figured out for yourselves, she was either born, or made. Either way, this man, the one who has taught us to hate and fear the superhumans, the one who has spouted family values above all else, has a daughter with abilities, one whom he's kept hidden away from us. Look at her arms.'

I pushed Layla gently forward, motioning for her to push up her sleeves. She stared at me with wide eyes, mutely shaking her head. 'Please Layla?' She hesitated, then did as I asked. The scars along her arms stood out against her pale skin, almost seeming to pulse, as if insects ran beneath. A murmur ran through the crowd. Crane remained where he was, rigid as he struggled to regain his composure.

A minute went by, then two. The soldiers remained where they were, keeping their silence and, as it stretched, I realised we'd played this all wrong. Layla's connection to Crane didn't seem to be enough. Their thirst for blood, for conquering, wouldn't be quenched with the realisation that their leader was nothing he'd claimed to be. And even though he'd turned out to be a complete hypocrite, punishing those for transgressions he himself had committed, the men stood by, too indoctrinated to react. The superhumans were coming closer. One soldier spotted them, then another. Their guns, forgotten at their sides, rose, and I knew it would take only one wrong move for these groups to annihilate each other. I glanced at Rogan. His face mirrored the emotions I felt – disbelief, disappointment, rage and exhaustion. I'd expected more of the superhumans. I'd thought their fear of loss of numbers would keep them cautious, but apparently their success so far had given them more confidence. With their renewed commitment to the cause, any hope we'd had of stopping this peacefully was gone.

There was only one thing left for me to do. I took one more glance around, drawing breath into my lungs, taking it all in one last time.

Rogan

Something drew my gaze to her. A visceral pull at my gut, an instinct too strong to question. She smiled, her eyes alight with life, an inappropriate reaction to the situation. She studied me for a moment, her gaze flitting over my face. Then she tipped her chin to the sky, her eyes closing. I lunged for her, propelled by a need I didn't understand to stall her.

The sudden movement set off a chain reaction. The superhumans surged forward, surrounding us. The soldiers reacted in turn, swinging as one to face the onslaught. I raised my own weapon, knowing even as I did I wouldn't be firing it, unless I had no choice. My finger moved to the trigger, my line of sight filling with the mass of superhumans as they ran at us.

A calm settled over me. I couldn't place the source. I tried to grab hold of my thoughts, but they slipped from my grasp, drifting away like a balloon from a child's hand. I couldn't remember what I'd been doing just a second before. I couldn't identify the object I held in my hand, so I let it fall. I looked around. I was surrounded by men in uniforms. They too held similar objects, and as each dropped his into a growing pile, I caught sight of another group standing nearby. Their hands were empty, and the confusion I felt was mirrored by their own. Where was I? Who were all these people? Something called to me from the deepest recesses of my mind, trying to bring me back to myself. A girl. That was all I got before every thought was swallowed up by a blankness that was impossible to fight.

It was only when my gaze fell on her – *the girl* – that I was brought back to myself. Everything flooded me at once, the noise of the crowd rising as they struggled to work out where they were, and what they were there for, the colour and heat of the day, the feeling that I once again belonged to myself. Dominico. Her eyes were still closed, her face tipped to the skies. A trickle of blood ran from her nose. I stared at it, watching it trace its way down to her chin, dripping from her face like red rain. I glanced around frantically, unable to believe what my mind was trying to tell me. From where I stood, I could see across the expanse of the battlefield. The fighting had stopped. Those I could see milled around pointlessly, much the same as the soldiers and superhumans around me. She was controlling them all.

I ran to her, trying to shake her out of it. The trickle from her nose had turned into a steady stream, but no amount of shaking or shouting brought her out of it. I tapped her cheeks, then slapped them. Her eyelids snapped open. Her gaze was white and blank. Her eyes had rolled to the back of her head. Her legs buckled, and she sank into my arms. Even before I cocked an ear to her mouth, I knew she was gone.

Chapter Thirty-Four

Syra

He stared at me through the bars of his cell, his expression the same as a minute ago, unchanged since the day before. He still didn't recognise me. He greeted me the same way as everyone else, hustling to the door of his cell with upturned palms, like a child waiting for a treat.

I sat on the small stool outside his cell. I hated seeing him like this – a caged animal, completely unaware of being imprisoned. He'd become a simpleton. Robbed of all his memories of himself, his life, and everything that encompassed, he was reduced to this. Every morning that I visited him, I both hoped and dreaded seeing a change in him, a sign that he was returning to himself.

'Hi Drake. How you doing today?'

He smiled a wide and guileless grin. 'Fine, fine. And how are you?'

He asked this only because he'd learned it was the standard response. Although he'd retained the ability to speak, to string sentences together, to listen and respond, he'd lost all sense of other forms of communication. He knew nothing of tone, or body language, or any other basic social cues. With the loss of these skills, he'd lost his abilities too. We kept him in this cell in preparation for the day he regained his memory, but none of us knew for sure if that day would come.

'I'm fine, thank you.' I folded my hands in my lap. 'Some of the others are coming back, remembering.' I wished I could forget. How I'd felt in that moment, a fleeting trickle of time in which I couldn't recall a single detail of my life, who I was, or why I was standing in the middle of a city I didn't recognise, surrounded by corpses. How that moment of horror had passed, only to be replaced by an image I was too far away to actually see – Dominico, face tipped to the sky, eyes leaking rivulets of bloody tears. I had run, but nowhere near fast enough. It wouldn't have mattered anyway. I was already too late.

Drake nodded, although I knew he had no real understanding of what I was saying. His grip on reality was tenuous. After all, his reality was now, in this cell, with no knowledge that he was a prisoner.

'They can't remember everything, but things are coming back to them. Pieces of their lives... before all this.' The air in these cells felt sparse, as if there wasn't enough of it to go around. Almost as if the purpose of the place, to imprison, applied to the air as well. I reached for Drake's hand through the bars. He took mine amiably enough, but in the same way he would've accepted a stranger's hand. Polite. Detached.

'Drake.' His gaze latched onto mine, and for just a second, I saw something spark in the dark depths of his eyes. It blazed, and his fingers tightened around mine with a memory of his previous strength. Then it was gone. His hand turned limp, withdrawing from my touch.

I turned away. My stomach churned with the possibility that one day, Drake would return. And what it would mean if he did.

**

I made my way along the line of cells. I hated this part of my day, but there was no avoiding it. I couldn't shirk my duty, not when so many were choosing to end up here.

Raven stood at my approach. She usually ignored me completely, not because she didn't know who I was, but because it was one of the few choices she had left. I watched her warily. Her abilities were not what they'd once been, but they seemed to strengthen as she did and, on the days she tried to fight me, the difference was obvious. She, and many of the others who were here, had recovered their memories only days after the incident.

'Come to fulfil your morning duty, have you?'

I said nothing. The truth of it stung. Seeing her behind those bars, like so many of the others, was a painful reminder that the war had done nothing but set us back. Instead of gaining freedom, we were imprisoning our own, for the sake of maintaining a precarious peace that I knew would not last.

Several others came to the front of their cells, most staring at me with open animosity. There was no segregation here. Humans and superhumans alike filled these cells, united in their determination to rebel against the new laws of unity. The accusation in their eyes pricked at me like dozens of fingers pinching at my skin. I stood silently against their scrutiny, refusing to break.

I met Raven's gaze.

'This was your choice.' I raised my voice, so I'd be heard further along the line.

'You decided you'd rather be here than accept. How long you stay here is up to you. We need everyone to help us rebuild. We need a common attitude of peace and acceptance.'

I wanted to believe my own words. And I did – to a certain degree. I wanted peace. I wanted unity. But I also knew, looking into the faces behind those bars, that this could never be achieved with force. We needed time, and for those who instigated violence, there was no other place but here.

Raven snorted. Her face was lined with dirt. Buckets of water were brought in daily, for drinking and washing. In a kind of resolute protest, Raven used her ration only for drinking. She looked every inch the prisoner she was, and I sometimes wondered if she did this purely to play on my tremendous sense of guilt. I would never admit it, but it achieved exactly those results.

'Please. It's not a choice if choosing one option means imprisonment.' A murmur of agreement hummed along the length of cells. Even some of the humans were nodding, and the irony of their unity in this made me want to scream until my voice was gone.

'We're trying to achieve something here. Surely you can see that? Something that will benefit us all. Keep us safe.'

Raven looked me over with a lingering glare of disgust. 'If you really think that, then there's no getting out for me.'

Rogan

Crane had been separated from the rest. He was alone in a set of cells on the opposite side of the city. Syra and I had thought it best to keep him isolated for now. Dominico had left him untouched. Him, along with Layla, Syra and myself. The fact that she'd been able to do that, to control her ability to such an extent that it passed over certain people, was a testament to just how powerful she'd been. To achieve that, in her weakened state, was beyond anything even the superhumans had ever seen.

I sat across from him, as I'd done for the past several weeks since Dominico's death. The bench was cold and unyielding beneath me, but I liked to be at the same height as Crane, to treat him like an equal. As much as was possible under the circumstances, in any case.

He met my gaze, amusement flitting beneath his cool exterior. I'd thought prison would humble him. I'd hoped it would level things and force him to descend from his self-built pedestal. But he regarded me the same way. With a tolerance he seemed to consider generous.

'Rogan.' He'd stopped referring to me by my rank the moment the war had been lost. As if it meant nothing now he was no longer president. Which, I suppose, was the truth.

'Crane.' His amusement slipped for a moment. Without his position, he was one of us. And with his crimes now out in the open, he was ranked lower than the lowliest field hand. He was considered a dangerous criminal, and as such, there would be no release for him.

'Have you given any more thought to my questions, since our last discussion?'

He pressed the pads of his fingers together, forming a steeple. His habitual thinking pose.

'I don't know how you think I can help with this. I've tried for many years to duplicate the serum we found in that laboratory all those years ago. You know we had no success doing so.'

I leant forward, resting my elbows on my knees. This close, I could pick out the finer details of his face. For a startling moment, I saw something of myself in his features. I blinked, and the moment was gone.

'You mean to tell me, in all the years of your experiments, with your fancy lab equipment and all those genius scientists, you still weren't able to even pinpoint the reactive ingredient?'

'That's precisely what I'm saying.' He searched my face. 'How many of them are still lost?'

I sat back. 'Too many. Some have returned with fragments of memories, but they are no more themselves now than they were the day it happened.'

'I can't help you, Rogan. I don't know how this happened, and even with all the work that's been done over the years, I was no closer to understanding what made them different. I built an army of them through conversion, using the original superhumans we captured from the laboratory. Every transformation happened that way.'

I waved a hand impatiently. 'I know all this. You've got nothing else for me? Nothing?'

The familiar frustration that had plagued me since that day returned. I stared at Crane, searching his face, wishing I could see past the skin, blood and bone and into his mind. Syra had done just that many times, to no avail. She believed he was being truthful, but that meant we were no closer to bringing the others back to themselves, to their lives, to their loved ones. Knowing that meant we could do nothing more. And I couldn't accept that.

'Have you considered that perhaps the girl meant for it to happen this way?'

'What?'

'She wanted peace. She belonged to both species, in some way or another. Maybe she saw no other way to solve it. Maybe they're not meant to remember, or recall anything at all of their previous lives or selves.'

'But some have. Raven, and a handful of others.'

'Yes. But none of them have regained their abilities fully. I doubt they ever will.'

I rose and paced. The only air that reached this place came through the cracks in the wall. There were no windows, and no natural light. Despite that, it was cool, even at the height of the day. It ran underground, discovered only months after Toria was first walled in and declared. The coolness did nothing to curb the sweat that had sprung to my forehead and which lined my upper lip. I couldn't believe how blind I'd been. How I hadn't worked out what seemed so obvious now that Crane had pointed it out. It seemed too brutal for Dominico. Too final. She had never considered herself a leader, so why would she force this tremendous burden on us, like a totalitarian? Why would she leave a handful of us intact, while around us hundreds of others were left as blank as an empty space?

As if plucking the thought from my mind, Crane smiled. 'Maybe she wanted us to start again. A clean slate.' He clucked. 'Pity she didn't take into account that human nature doesn't rely on memories. It can never change. Human or superhuman, we all harbour a sense of violence within us. And that is impossible to forget.'

I left Crane to the dank isolation of his cells. I ran without purpose or direction, knowing I needed to speak to Syra, but too caught up in the tide of my thoughts to pick a clear route.

Rage was blackening the edges of my vision, and with no one else to pinpoint, I laid it all on Dominico. The fact that she wasn't around to hear it only fed my frustration, and after several minutes of running like a maddened bull, I slowed and forced myself to breathe. I pressed my palms against my thighs, my head hanging low, concentrating only on the air filling and leaving my lungs. Finally I straightened, my pulse slowing.

How could she play god like this and leave us with so few choices? The fact that key figures like myself and Syra had been left untouched couldn't be a coincidence. She must've planned it, although when or how, I couldn't begin to speculate.

I was at the very edge of the city now, facing the wall. Behind me, I could hear the hum of activity as people went about their day. Despite the calamity that had befallen so many of them, life continued.

'Rogan?'

I turned. Syra stood with the morning sun behind her, framing her in a halo of light. She stepped closer. Her face was pale, her eyes bracketed by lines of fatigue.

'Syra, I –'

She took my hand. 'I know.'

'What?'

She smiled. It was sad and small, a smile devoid of hope. 'I heard your thoughts. They were loud, even over the distance.'

'You keeping tabs on me?'

She smiled again. This time it reached her eyes. 'Only a little.'

She pulled on my hand. 'Come, I want to show you something.'

I followed her to the centre of town. Several pairs of eyes latched onto us as we passed. Those who remembered, watched with disapproval. It passed over us like a wave of heat. It would be some time before we could walk through our own city without judgement following at our backs. Or perhaps even the passing of time wouldn't be enough to dissolve their attitudes. It was regrettable, but understandable.

Syra motioned to a group of children. In the centre of them stood Layla. They were laughing and pointing. I jerked out of Syra's grasp, angry at her for allowing the children to tease her.

She caught my hand again, squeezing it hard enough to make my eyes water. 'Look at her face.'

'I can see –'.

'They're not laughing *at* her. They're laughing *with* her.'

She was right. Layla was in their centre, clapping and singing. The children sang the same words back at her, and I realised she was teaching them a song.

My throat locked. I couldn't speak. Watching her stand there, surrounded by a group of human children, singing and laughing with the uncomplicated happiness of someone caught in a moment, I felt a spark of hope.

I turned to face Syra. 'There could be more of them,' she said. 'A mix.' She motioned to a group of adults standing nearby, watching the children as we were. Some were human, others were not. Some wore expressions of befuddlement, as if they sensed they should be disapproving but unable to recall why. A select few watched with wonder and amusement.

'Layla is a perfect mix of our two worlds. There could be more like her.'

I stared at her. 'Procreation. Between humans and superhumans?'

She nodded, a smile growing on her face. 'Layla was conceived that way. Why not others?'

I looked back at the children, then the adults. It was an outrageous concept.

'It'll take time, I'll admit. But maybe humans will come to see the benefits. If we can pass on our abilities, why not our health, and longevity? Their children will live longer. They'll have a greater chance at survival.'

'What if all the memories return?'

She brushed my cheek with her fingers, her touch long and lingering.

'What if they don't?'

ABOUT THE AUTHOR

Jennifer Withers has been writing since she was seven years old, banging out stories about dragons and damsels in distress on an ancient typewriter. She went on to earn a BA in English Studies at the University of Pretoria. Since then, she has taken writing courses through Writer's Write, and Allaboutwriting. Jennifer lives in Pretoria, with her husband, two dogs, and her ageing cat. *The War Between* is her first novel.